JAN 24

RADIANT HEAT

As Alison unlocked the door to Sal's car she looked back into the beer garden, saw a middle-aged man she'd never met before slide into the seat she'd just vacated. He held out a hand to Bob Arnold and shook hard, clapping the spare one on the older man's back. Journalist, probably, Alison thought, as she slung her legs into the car and twisted the key in the ignition. He reminded her of her father, the way he held himself.

"OK, we have vodka, and we have half a bottle of Chardy, and I know there's a slab of warm VB in the garage." Meg whirled around, holding the Chardonnay in her left hand, waggling it. "This is three days old. It's probably off." She screwed up her nose and walked with purpose toward the sink, unscrewing the wine's cap.

Alison rushed to grab the bottle from her before she could dump it out. "Whoa. What are you wasting good wine for?"

"It's three days old. Mum says if you don't drink it in the first twenty-four hours, it goes bad."

Alison laughed. "Your mum is having you on. It's a screw top. It's been in the fridge. It's fine!" She opened the bottle and sniffed. Notes of straw and sugar, nothing sour—crisp apples and new oak furniture. She swigged it back, straight from the neck. It was fine. Nothing more, nothing less. She pulled two glasses from Meg's cupboard. Filled them up.

Meg picked hers up, examined it. "High tide, huh?"

Alison laughed. "I thought we were getting wasted."

"Oh, we are." Meg gulped back the wine as though it were water.

"Well, as enticing as warm VB sounds, I think I'll chance the Chardy." She raised her glass and clinked it against Meg's and they both drank deeply.

"Let's play a game, Alison King."

"Like Annie said, even if he didn't physically do it, he's the reason she was here in the first place." He pulled a battered photograph out of his pocket. A Polaroid. Slipped it over the uneven wood of the table, his fingers obscuring the faces until he pulled them away and Alison could see them properly. Blue eyes flecked gold, shimmering in the flash's light, that unmistakable jawline, the sweep of his hair, the smirk-smile.

Gil. Alison blinked. Checked again, to be sure. It was him all right. Her Gil.

Simone beside him, his arm around her as though he possessed her. She felt the pinch of his fingers on her waist like a reflex she couldn't contain. The piece of paper with her address. The overwhelming sense of unease she'd been feeling. It was him. Alison felt her chest constrict and she tried to keep her breathing steady, tried to keep her expression neutral. She didn't want them to know. She couldn't explain it. She needed *a minute*. To think about what all this meant before anyone else found out.

"I'm so sorry I can't be more help. If I think of anything, I promise I'll let you know." She didn't tell them about the sounds in the bush, the penetrating feeling like someone was staring in those moments before she found Simone. She didn't tell them her ex-boyfriend was their daughter's ex-boyfriend. Gil. He must have been there. Where was he now?

Alison wanted to get out. She felt clammy and cold despite the heat of the day and the warmth from the vodka, which churned in her stomach. She downed the rest of it, shivered a little, and smiled in the Arnolds' direction. "I've got to go, sorry. Please stay in touch, let me know anything, anything at all." Alison hastily scrawled her number on the back of a coaster, handed it to Bob. He shook her hand, weakly. Anne nodded good-bye, wiped a tear from the apple of her cheek. Alison thought she could see suspicion in the woman's eyes. A lingering accusation.

RADIANT
HEAT

SARAH-JANE COLLINS

BERKLEY
New York

BERKLEY
An imprint of Penguin Random House LLC
penguinrandomhouse.com

Library of Congress Cataloging-in-Publication Data

Names: Collins, Sarah-Jane, author.
Title: Radiant heat / Sarah-Jane Collins.
Description: New York : Berkley, 2024.
Identifiers: LCCN 2023016615 (print) | LCCN 2023016616 (ebook) |
ISBN 9780593550342 (hardcover) | ISBN 9780593550359 (ebook)
Subjects: LCGFT: Thrillers (Fiction) |
Novels. Classification: LCC PR9619.4.C654 R33 2024 (print) |
LCC PR9619.4.C654 (ebook) | DDC 823/.92—dc23/eng/20230606
LC record available at https://lccn.loc.gov/2023016615
LC ebook record available at https://lccn.loc.gov/2023016616

Printed in the United States of America
1st Printing

Book design by Ashley Tucker
Interior art by My Photo Buddy / Shutterstock.com

For Buster

RADIANT HEAT

1.

Alison was still alive. It felt like hours, but looking at her watch as she emerged from her blanket cocoon, she couldn't quite believe it had been only thirty minutes or so. She crawled, dripping sweat and soggy clothing, to the nearest window, stopping to drink a little from the bathtub and extinguish the few stray embers smoldering on the tile. She peered through the space where the windowpane had been. Outside, the stillness seemed to be a trick, concealing what had gone before. But the sky was red-orange, and there was smoke on the air, clinging to the trees, the eaves, the roof, the veranda, and the gutters. The ground was covered in ashen debris. Ghost-white-chalky-black-dusty-mingled-gray soot covered everything.

The day was a little cooler now. No more than ninety-five as the sun crept low, a long way from its midday peak. Alison was alone, which didn't normally jar, but lying under the sill, staring up at the sky, the acrid smell of death and ash surrounding her, for once she allowed herself to be lonely. It was just a few seconds. And then she forgot to continue wallowing. The house was shrouded in smoke and had a few broken windows, but otherwise it was, somehow, all right. She moved slowly through the rooms, checking for damage. There was no power, no water in the taps, and where the fire had torn through the bush the trees were stripped and blackened. No viable limbs remained. Outside, she knew there would be work to do. Fences and trees down, the driveway surely blocked, impassable.

The screen door was hot to the touch, and an arm's length from the veranda the closest blackened trunk stood, barely upright. It would have to come down. Alison followed the sweep of the hill with her eyes. There was uncountable debris. Licking at the edge of the house, the fire front had suddenly moved around to the side and stormed off down the drive, lighting up one side of the unsealed road and leaving nothing but ash and black-brittle splinters in its wake. On the other side, the trees were the same mottled green-brown of hot high summer, as though nothing had happened.

She would have to wait for the State Emergency Service to come through and clear the drive before she'd be able to get the car out. That could take days, maybe longer, depending on the scale of the fire. The road was a kilometer away. She grabbed a bag and shoved a few things in it, checked her phone. No service. Time to go.

On the dirt path Alison sifted her way through the wreckage back to bitumen. It was quiet now, the usual sounds of the bush dampened by death. What little wildlife had been able to flee would not return in a hurry. She thought of the family of tawny frogmouths that had lived in that now-blackened tree by the front door, their delicate feathers and round amber brown eyes, the curve of their sharp-edged beaks, and the sound of their calls, dragged up from their throats and percolated in the backs of their mouths.

As she walked, Alison tried to reorder her mind. *You're fine.* But it was hard not to get stuck dwelling on how likely it was that some of her neighbors were not. Alison hadn't seen it coming—how would anyone have seen it coming? She tried to arrange the past twenty-four hours in her head, tried to remember the normal course of her day, the things that happened before this happened. Pull apart the edges and put them back together so what had happened made some sort of sense, closed her eyes and in the sandy soot-covered space of the drive sunk down onto her knees and let the memories roll over her—the hours before everything changed, again.

By midmorning the heat was up there, pushing 104 degrees before the clock hit eleven, a hot wind racing up to a hundred kilometers an hour, air forced around the state like a giant dryer, not a drop of moisture about—humidity as low as two percent—and even in bayside Melbourne, where Alison had spent the night at a friend's, it felt as though her eyeballs might cook in her skull.

She'd tossed her backpack into the boot of her car, slid into the driver's seat, and turned the key in the ignition, the radio stuttering to life . . . *a high like that forecast, it's going to be a scorcher, and a total fire ban is in place, with the premier urging people in high-risk areas to stay close to their radios for updates* . . . Alison knew the warnings about fires you can't escape, moments you can't change, houses you can't save, lives you can't get back; she'd heard it from her grandfather every summer since she was small.

The sound of a gum tree falling, one with a hundred years or more on its ledger, is the loudest, most sustained crack of thunder you'll ever hear, as limbs fold and crumple and crash and tumble all that long way down to the ground; timber splits and splinters with a wrenching that slices through time and tears at the tranquility of the day. You're in the eye of a storm when the thunder and lightning are simultaneous. Sound travels slower than light. When you can hear something loud enough to shake your eardrums and clatter about in the space between your ribs, it's right on top of you.

When Alison heard the first scream of the fire, she thought it was a gum blown down in the breeze. But at the window in her bedroom, she looked out across the bush and saw the smoke, heard more crashes—and then she saw it, coming fast, glimpses of red-hot movement among the trunks. Embers pushed the fire forward, rushing and crackling and spreading their blazing fury wide; there didn't seem to be time to even consider leaving—the car was on the other side of the house, but Alison had no way to know whether the fire was farther down the drive, making escape an impossibility. Instead, she had grabbed a blanket from the linen cupboard in the hall and rushed into the bathroom, dunking it in the bathtub.

Outside, the fire grabbed at trees and closed around them, two, three, four at a time, obliterating them with its gaping jaws, spitting still-smoldering remnants forward, leaving smoked skeletons in its wake; the bathroom was on the northeastern side of the house and Alison cowered there, her entire body swaddled in the thick, wet woolen blanket, the tile floor damp and cool as her cheek pressed hard against it. The noise was unbearable—a roaring, whooshing, crackling din; she closed her eyes and waited, uncertain what to do when you don't believe in prayer, and the sticky camphor smell of the blanket distracted her, made her hold the air in her lungs. With a start, she remembered to breathe, not sure how long it had been between gasps—it was so hot. She was sweating and the air felt empty, like the oxygen was all gone. A shower of glass rained down on the blanket, and Alison could feel the pressure in the room change; she lifted a corner of the blanket, saw a smoky, hazy, wide-open rectangle where the window had been, and flames just barely a meter away, spewing embers and thick smoke in her direction, and then, with one fickle twist, the firestorm receded—like a giant had drawn a deep breath in—the front changing tack as a southerly blew through.

Sitting now with the bitter char of burned eucalypt in the back of her nostrils, Alison felt as though she had been split in two. Slumped in the dirty ash, she traced the lines of her name with her fingers, rubbed them out, pushed the black dust back into place, and used her little finger to trace a quiet curve like the bend of the tawny frogmouth's neck, where the fine, sharp feathers curved from the base of its head to the tops of its wings. The way the brown dirt mingled with the whitest parts of the ashy ends of sticks and leaves and whatever else evoked the mottle of their coats. The sun sunk lower still in the sky of wild red.

Get up. Keep moving.

She didn't listen to the unsettled voice inside her, just kept thinking about her morning, knees dug deep into the soot, rocks pressing into the soft hardness of her patellas. Still on her knees, she felt uneasy with the recollection, uneasy with the way it swished about in her brain. The pieces weren't quite whole, the moments not quite matching. Like the night the cops had knocked on her door and told her about the accident. Taken her parents away with a sentence. Stopped up the one remaining valve in her calcifying heart. She heard the whoosh of the cooling southerly breeze as it tickled the strands of hair at the nape of her neck, on her temples, and over her ears. From the silent bush she felt an intensity, as if it were staring at her. *I'm losing it.* She peered through the gaps in the thick low brush, tried to locate the feeling's source. A sharp jump in her bones as a twig snapped somewhere in that direction. The crisp, easy break of small wood under a big foot. *There's some-one there.*

"Who's there?" Her voice carried into the trees, where it was absorbed and flattened. Deadened and muted by too much clutter. Nothing came back out.

Alison stood up and tried to shake the shuddering shiver from her frame. Could be anything. Could be nothing. Could be the snap and pop of wood returning to rest from heat-swelled discomfort. *No one's going to be out here in the middle of this.* Alison knew she shouldn't be either; it was time to get moving again.

There was a cocoon-like quality to this stretch, dense trees one way, the view of the house receding atop the hill, a hump in the road obscuring the lower part of the drive, and the black-white wall of stripped trees on the other side, making the familiar feel like the unknown. Goose bumps rose up on the flesh of her forearms as Alison fumbled over the hump and down toward the highway. An old-growth trunk had fallen as it burned, obstructing the path. Still smoking at the base, it was as wide as Alison was tall and stretched from the moon-scape of the burned-out bush to the thick pale green bouquet on the other side. Alison raised her hands out in front of her, touched the unburned wood of the trunk near the top of what she could reach. The bark was slippery and sloughed off easily. Getting a foothold to clamber over the trunk would be dangerous. She cursed under her breath and looked around for another way through.

To the right, there was a narrow passage near the root base. Alison skirted the tree and emerged on the other side, soot smeared down her jeans. She blinked and saw something she couldn't process. Something that shouldn't be there.

She tried to blink it away. Tried to piece it together. Gather it up in a way that made sense. The hard outline of metal and glass, rubber and bright paint, against the soft chaos of the bush and the long dirt drive.

The car didn't seem real. Like the noise in the bush or the bird she'd sketched out in the ash, could it be a product of her uncooperative mind? No. It was covered in soot, but bright cherry red peeked through where Alison smeared her hand along the car. Felt the heat of the steel that had absorbed the fire. The windows were blown out and the bonnet was wedged, crumpled, under the heavy tree trunk. Apprehensive, she crept toward the door, not sure that she wanted to confirm what she saw the outline of inside, but unable to stop herself.

Fuck. There was a woman in the driver's seat, seemingly untouched by the chaos around her. Alison closed her eyes for a full minute before she willed herself to move around the car to the driver's side and lean in to check for any signs the woman might still be alive, but as she reached out to feel for a pulse, she knew there would not be one. The woman's eyes were open wide; the blue-gray of the pupils seemed washed-out, faded. Did they always look like that? When the last breath is drawn does the light really leave you?

She tried to remember her parents, at the funeral home. In the caskets. Their eyes were glassy like the marbles she had shot with her grandpa as a kid. These eyes weren't any kind of glass. Stone maybe. The kind you find in the sand, washed down smooth from the waves, dried out in the sun. The woman's skin was clammy but hot, and Alison shuddered at the sensation. Panic rose in her chest, making it hard to take deep breaths, or any breaths at all. The fog of it seeped into her brain and rang bells in her ears. She needed to know something, anything, that she could use as an anchor. Stop the whole world from spinning.

In the center console lay a purse and a mobile phone. She reached in and grabbed the purse. It was gray calfskin leather, worn smooth in patches where its owner's long fingers had gripped it tightly. There were lots of cards, the plastic corners peeling on some, others shiny and new. The woman was thirty-three. Alison's age. Her driver's license showed they were born weeks apart. They were the same height. They both needed to wear glasses when they drove. The card was old, Alison noticed as she scrutinized the Queensland crest super-imposed over the details, the five years of validity almost up. The address was somewhere in the suburbs of Cairns, which surprised Alison, since she'd lived in Cairns too, a couple of years ago. She looked at the body again. Her face wasn't famil-iar, and neither was her name.

What was Simone Arnold doing there? In the middle of a bushfire, on the driveway to Alison's house? From the license a face full of life stared back at Alison. Here they were, her real eyes, dancing with light, and her cheeks, close to curving for a smile, light laugh lines visible at her temples. Simone Arnold looked like fun, Alison thought. Her dirty-blond hair sat in a long, neat braid that fell down the right side of her chest. She wore jeans and a pale pink camisole. Alison saw a blanket on the back seat, and she reached through the broken window for it. She threw it gently over Simone, not wanting to leave her exposed. She softly dragged her fingertips over her eyelids, concealing the dulled stare. She wasn't able to parse it. To hold this dead woman's story in her head. It was too much al-ready.

She gripped the purse tightly in her own hand. It calmed her to squeeze it. The foggy din in her head receded enough to remember where she was and what she was supposed to be doing. It was time to keep going.

Alison reluctantly continued to walk down the drive, toward the black tar, now visible ahead, pockmarked and blistered from the inferno. Evening was settling in, in pink and orange hues. Overhead a confused clutch of wrens flitted around in search of a suitable home. A few strides from the highway Alison stopped and turned back, again trying to take it all in. The car was still there. *Of course it is.* The tires were flat, causing it to sag into the drive, the exhaust pipe almost touching the ground.

It isn't going to go away.

For a second Alison panicked. She wanted to turn around and seek out the familiarity of home. She wanted to go back and drag Simone Arnold from the car, try to force the air back into her lungs, shake the life back into her arms, pump the blood back into her heart. She wanted to scream. She wanted to swap places. She wanted to die on the bathroom floor, covered in wet wool, breathing in smoke and cinders. Dissolving into the dirt.

The low-level buzz of a headache started up in her skull. She looked down and realized she was still holding on to Simone Arnold's purse. She didn't want to go back up to the car, so she forced herself to head toward the gravel shoulder, the leather gripped tight against her palm. From her house to the road was roughly a full click, and she reached the highway as the light began to truly drain away for the day. She'd only been walking toward town for a few minutes when a ute pulled up beside her.

"Alison?" It was her neighbor Jim Allenby.

"My drive is blocked." She knew she looked a mess, her hair still wild from hiding under the blanket, her arms and legs streaked with white ash from the car, a smear of it over her left eye.

"Come on, then, I'll take you in." Jim reached across the cab of the ute and pushed the door open.

Alison swung up onto the seat.

"There's a car in it," Alison said quietly.

"Your driveway? Did you try to get out in that little Co-rolla? Well, no wonder you didn't make it. I'll bet you've got trees down all over the place."

"Yes, everywhere." They pulled away from the shoulder, leaving thick treads in the charcoal and ash.

"You can stay in town tonight. I'm sure Sal will have you." Jim was driving as fast as he safely could, the ute jostling over the broken road, crunching the twigs and branches that had fallen in the firestorm.

"There's a woman in the car." Alison's voice barely registered any emotion. As she spoke, she felt a rushing in her ears, like too much blood was trying to get to her brain.

"What car? Your car?" Jim kept driving, one hand on the gear stick, the elbow of the other arm propped up on the window. Alison noticed the hairs on the back of his leathery left arm seemed to have almost disappeared, and the skin looked redder than usual.

"No. The car in my driveway. What happened to your arm?" She knew she wasn't making sense.

"Whose car is in the drive?" Jim turned and looked at her, finally figuring out that she was saying something important.

"Simone's." Saying her name to someone else, even Jim, seemed strange. Saying the name at all made it realer than Alison wanted it to be.

"Friend of yours? Did she stay with the car?" He slowed a little; the blackened trunks out the window became distinct pillars, a thousand individual husks where there once was bush.

"She's not my friend. She's dead."

He stopped the ute a little too quickly and Alison's chest jerked forward.

"There's a dead woman in a car in your driveway?" Jim asked slowly.

"Yes. I think it must have been the smoke."

Neither of them said anything, and Alison began to feel, sitting in the ute, surrounded by the ghosts of trees and the incinerated bodies of birds, lizards, bugs, snakes, and marsupials, like they were the last two people on earth. A siren's wail carried on the breeze from high up on the hill and broke the silence.

"Radiant heat, more likely," Jim said, turning the key in the ignition. They needed to get to town. "You know her?"

"No."

He accelerated slowly, his weathered face strained.

"We better tell the coppers." Alison began to cry. "Alison?" Jim paused, thinking. "How do you know her name?"

"She's the same age as me. She's thirty-three." He didn't respond. "We're the same height. Her hair is blond. I always thought I would like to be blond."

"Alison, I think you're in shock. Just try not to think about it. We'll get there soon."

"I looked in her purse, to see who she was. I thought maybe if I could call her name, it might make her wake up." She remembered, as she said this, that she hadn't said anything to Simone, hadn't tried at all to break her from the grip of death with words. The purse, which she'd pulled out of her bag to wave in Jim's direction, felt heavy in her hands.

"Come on, now, stop it. You'll work yourself into a state."

Jim was speeding. Alison's breathing was ragged. Her voice was high and tight. The words were hard to distinguish from the sobs.

"Maybe if I'd got there sooner."

"No, Alison. Fire like the one today, the only way you'd have seen her alive would've been if you'd died right alongside her."

There was silence. Alison was too upset now to cry, too

exhausted to speak. The old Ford barreled along the two-lane highway, high beams on. To the south, in the rearview, a ridge of flame snaked across the plain. Ahead, the lights of the town were beginning to emerge. Alison was surprised there was power still, but grateful for the sense of normalcy it imposed.

"There's nothing you could do."

She wrapped her arms around herself. Tucked her chin into her chest. After a few minutes, she opened Simone's purse again, having kept it clutched in her sweaty hand. They were the same age. She thumbed through the cards, counted the cash—a lot of it, Alison realized now, almost seven hundred dollars in notes, another eight in change. Tucked among the fifties, a piece of paper.

Alison King, 5872 Cook Creek Road, Lake Bend, Victoria

The words, scrawled across a torn corner of a yellow pad lined red, jolted Alison. She stared, her back straight against the seat, hairs on her arms rising. She glanced over at Jim, wondering, had he seen her reaction? He was focused on the road, cluttered as it was with the windblown remains of the bush. Alison had no idea what it meant. Was she the reason this woman had died? Who was she? What was she doing there? Alison's head throbbed as the ute navigated the early dusk. The handwriting was not unlike Alison's, all uppercase, no respect for the imposed guidelines of the notepaper. Flourish on the *R*, the *B*, the *K*. *Fuck*. Alison tried to contain the energy she felt coiled inside her, the howl that wanted to escape through her smoke-singed throat. She took three deep breaths, in through the nose, out through the mouth. Felt a little better. Felt a little worse. Jim still wasn't talking. They rocked along the road at a steady pace as Alison tried to settle. She couldn't.

2.

Jim pulled up outside Sal Marsh's place as proper dark descended. He shook Alison to rouse her and they walked up the short path to the front door. Sal's home was a weatherboard, with a wide veranda that wrapped around the front, and a sprawling deck off the back. The road-facing front of the house was flush to the ground, but it dropped off quickly at the back, with the decking high off the slope of the mountain. The boards were painted a faded cream, and the iron lacework on the railings was Sal's pride and joy.

Alison had known Sal her whole life. Sal had babysat her as a child, overseen endless games of Marco Polo in the pool on a stinkin'-hot day, patched up her rollerblading scrapes, her bike mishaps. When Alison had returned home after her parents' death, Sal had helped her with the funeral, the will, the obligations. If she didn't have any family around, Alison at least had Sal. The heavy front door absorbed the thud of Jim's fist until he pounded hard enough to rattle the mottled bottle-green glass. A figure, distorted in the pane, hurried down the hall. Sal cracked the door and beamed, relieved.

"Jim, Alison, so good to see you both all right. It's a mess out there—I heard it ripped through right down to the bend on Cook Creek Road." As she spoke, Sal ushered them into the hall, linking her arm through Alison's and pulling her in from the doormat. The bend was beyond Alison's house, just before Jim's. It was the marker that vaguely separated their property, and if the fire had gotten all the way there, Alison wouldn't have survived.

"Not quite, Sal," Jim replied. "But Alison had a real close call, from what I can gather. Power's out at her place and she needs somewhere to bunk tonight. I didn't think you'd mind." They walked down the hall toward the kitchen, Alison aware of just how tightly she was gripping Sal's arm.

"Not at all, come on, I'll make some tea." Sal pulled a chair out at the Formica-topped table and deposited Alison in it, gently prying her arm from Alison's hand.

"Is your landline working?" Jim asked.

"Should be, had a tone about half an hour ago; it's on the stand in the hall."

Jim nodded and headed back the way they'd come. Sal was filling the kettle at the sink and got caught up looking at Alison, so distracted by her blank, dirty face, she didn't notice it bubble over. "Shit, all right, that's full, then," she said as cheerily as she could. Alison didn't respond. "Are you all right, love?" Sal opened her mouth to say something else and then closed it again.

Alison nodded at her. "Sorry to be a pain, Sal, but have you got anything to eat? I'm starving." She attempted to smile.

"Of course. I've got some bread and there's a roast chook in the fridge. I can make you a sandwich?"

"Nah, I'll get it—do you mind?" She stood up, wanting all of a sudden to be busy.

"What's mine is yours." Sal reached under the counter and pulled out a chopping board. Jim came back into the kitchen as Alison was slicing the bread.

"Make me one while you're at it, would you?" he asked, pulling out a chair and sitting down. "Coppers on their way, although they're running around like chooks with no heads by the sounds of it; might take a while." Alison hoped it would be Billy Meaker who turned up, if he was still alive. It felt weird even to throw the word around in her head—bounce it around like whether someone was alive was the sort of thing a normal person, in normal circumstances, would have to consider. Where were the people who mattered to her now?

"What do you need the police for?"

Jim ran his hand through his hair and locked eyes with Sal. "Alison's got a strange car in the drive. There's a dead girl in it; she got caught in the fire."

"Oh dear. Oh, Ally, love, I'm sorry."

"I didn't know her. I don't know why she was there. A tree fell on her car; she got trapped, I think." Alison carefully sliced into the breast of the bird, slim sheets of meat falling onto the board as she spoke.

"How do you know you don't know her if she's . . ." Sal paused, and Alison could tell she didn't know how to finish the sentence.

"Not burned, not a mark on her. Her name's Simone; I saw her driver's license."

"It'll be the radiant heat. When the fireys came through for that back burn a few months back, I was chatting with one who said it's the radiant heat nine times out of ten. You just cook—it's so damn hot." As he talked Jim was scratching at the red skin on his arm, inspecting the casualties, one hair by one.

"Awful. It wasn't Simone McDonald, was it? She's been coming up here some weekends 'cause she's seeing Ted Alton's boy." Sal's house, on the fringe of the town, on the main road in and out, was the perfect place to sit on the veranda all afternoon and collect the secrets of the people coming and going. Sal attempted to collect them all.

"Nope, I went to school with Simmy. Not her." Alison slathered mayonnaise on the thick slabs of bread she'd cut, and piled chicken on top. She tore some lettuce from its perfectly round shell and topped the meat off with slices of sharp cheddar.

"No salt on mine, thanks," Jim interjected, tapping his palm to his heart as she held the grinder over the sandwiches.

Alison capped each sandwich off with a second slice of bread and brought the board over to the table. They sat eating in silence. Halfway through her sandwich Alison began to feel exhaustion wash over her uncontrollably. Every bone in her body ached, every muscle slowly unfurling the tension it had been holding. She winced as she shifted in her chair and suddenly felt like even eating was painful. Like her jaw was too damn tired to chew. She pushed the sandwich away.

"I need to go to sleep." She stood up, aware she was a little unsteady on her feet, and waited for Sal to show her which room she could use. Sal gave her a worried look but quickly led Alison down the hall to the front room that was once June's, Sal's mother's, before she'd gone into the home, and before Sal's daughter, Suze, had made it her own. Sal fussed about in the wardrobe locating sheets, and while Alison stood leaning on the doorframe, she made the bed. Alison felt bad that she wasn't helping, but she was using every ounce of energy she had just to stand. When Sal was done, she kicked off her shoes, wiggled out of her jeans, unhooked her bra, and slipped it out from under her shirt through an armhole.

"Do you want a nightie, or maybe a shower?" Sal watched her closely.

"No, it's OK, but if I could borrow a shirt tomorrow, that'd be good," Alison replied, forgetting the things she'd packed. She slid into the bed and felt at once the relief of the cold, crisp sheets on her legs, the pillow soft against her cheek. Sal picked up her jeans and bra from the floor and, standing in the doorway, switched off the light.

"I'm going to wash these, Ally, get the soot off. They'll be good to go in the morning."

"Thanks, Sal, night."

"Good night."

The door shut, and Sal's footsteps faintly echoed in the room as she retreated up the hall. Alone, Alison checked her phone to see if she had any signal. None.

The last thing Alison heard as she settled in was whispered speculation about Simone, or as she heard Jim tell it, "The woman in her driveway." *She has a name.* But Alison wasn't sure why it mattered so much that she knew what it was.

3.

Alison slept uneasily, but by the time she uncurled herself, the day was half-over. She'd expected to be woken at some point by the police with their questions. But no one disturbed her. She shuffled into the kitchen, where Sal was standing over the sink, her hands in rubber gloves.

"There's coffee in the pot, love, just zap it for a few seconds."

Sal nodded toward the microwave.

The cup was pale blue, with the feathered stains of too many coffees drunk over the years.

Alison's hands shook as she took up the pot.

"Quite a shock yesterday," Sal said, watching Alison closely.

Alison got the milk from the fridge door and tipped it in, more than she intended. She shoved the cup into the microwave and watched the seconds count down.

"Billy was by earlier. They've finished up at your place. They've cleared the car." Billy Meaker, who'd dared her to jump off the shed when they were ten, and she'd badly broken her wrist doing it. Billy, who was never interesting enough to make things complicated.

The coffee was too hot.

"I can drive you down a bit later if you want."

Sal balanced a saucepan on top of the drying rack and pulled out the plug from the drain. Wiping down the sink, she turned, focused on Alison.

The coffee was still too hot.

"It's not your fault, love. You couldn't have known she was there. You're lucky enough as it is."

"Did he say what she was doing there?"

"No, he said you should stop by the station later and he'll tell you what they know."

"Right."

She let the coffee sit a little until she could swill great mouthfuls of it. Cup finished, she stared at the dregs.

"All right. Guess I'll have a shower."

In the middle of the firestorm Alison had lain under the heavy damp blanket on the floor and considered the situation. If this was it, she had reasoned, then *that's OK, I don't really mind if I'm done.* Now, as the water beat down on her back as she sat on the shower tiles, she wanted to know if Simone had been OK with it. Or had it happened too fast for her to even think? Alison closed her eyes, saw the blackness, felt the steam well up in the space around her, the hot clarity of the white vapor, pure and smooth, safe to draw in, to suck down her throat without fear. It was still too much like the day before.

Sal banged on the door.

"Alison, love, you've been in there forty minutes."

The room too was full of steam. Her fingertips were shriveled.

"Yep, getting out, Sal," she yelled back.

The floor was cool underfoot and she wiped a circle in the mirror, cutting through the condensation in three strokes. Her face and neck were red. Her hair—shoulder dusting, brown—was plastered down on her forehead. Her green eyes mostly pupil in the dim light.

"Get it together," she told her reflection.

Alison biked over to the cop shop on Sal's old gray three-speed. She left it leaning on the fence and pushed through the heavy doors to the front desk. Billy Meaker, Alison saw, relieved, was on duty. Still a friend after that arm-breaking dare as a kid, and all the teenage shit that came after, Billy was one of the people Alison trusted most in town. As a rule, she didn't like cops—pigs, her grandfather had called them, his nose upturned in contempt, whenever the subject came up—but for Billy she made an exception. And living in a small town like Lake Bend, she'd gotten to know them all, in spite of her efforts to ignore them.

"Alison, glad you're all right." He smiled at her with tired eyes, his shirt rumpled, his shoes, Alison noticed, scuffed with soot.

"Thanks, Billy, pretty lucky."

"You here about the girl in your drive?"

"Sal said you told her I could come down, get some information."

"Yeah, of course, come on through—we're still waiting on her parents, but I can tell you her name is—"

"Simone Arnold."

"Yeah."

"I saw her driver's license. I was trying to figure out who she was." Alison slid the purse over the counter. It no longer contained the piece of paper with her address on it. When she'd gone to tug on her freshly washed jeans, she'd felt a crumpled lump in the pocket. Pulled out a wad of water-damaged notepaper, remembered slipping it in there on the drive with Jim. Now she was ashamed that she'd snooped, but uneasy about the note, she decided to keep it to herself. She wasn't sure why she didn't want Billy to know, but she didn't. Billy picked up the purse and frowned at her.

"I don't know why I took this, sorry."

"So they'll be your fingerprints we found all over the car, then? The blanket your handiwork? Gotta ask you to give us your prints, so we can see if there are any that shouldn't have been there."

"She was killed in a massive bushfire, Billy, it's hardly premeditated."

"Yeah, almost certainly, but her parents say she was running away from something."

"Running from what?"

"Old boyfriend."

"Aren't we all?"

"Well, that's not funny." He gave her the same hard-done-by face he used to give Mrs. Elliot when she caught him smoking in the woodworking sheds at lunchtime.

"Sorry. Bad time to make a joke."

"Sure is, Ally, but you never did have much sense of timing. Come through. We'll do the fingerprints and I'll take a statement about finding her and what you saw and all that. You sure you didn't know her?"

"Never heard of her." Now was definitely the time to come clean about the address. She didn't, and she didn't know why she didn't.

In the station, low-hanging ceiling fans pushed the thick summer air around in circles. They did little to cool the room or dislodge the band of flies that swarmed around the kitchen. Through the back, past the desks and filing cabinets, there was a small interrogation room and, a little farther on, one cell. It was usually empty and today was no different. What

21

was different, though, was the total absence of other coppers. Usually the whole lot of them would be here, cooling their heels on their desks.

"Your place OK, Billy?"

"Yeah, it missed town almost completely—just a couple of places down the Ridge Road and the industrial strip on Orchard didn't make it, but everything else was untouched. Yarra Ridge's not so lucky; the SES boys through a bit earlier said they couldn't even begin to say how bad it was yet."

"Shit."

"No words strong enough for this fire, Ally. That's damn sure."

The walls of the station were pale green, the casement windows filled with that mottled glass, same as Sal's front door. The whole place was small; only about six coppers worked out of here, covering a large regional area. The door to the interrogation room was closed, and Billy steered her to the far side of the main room instead, where the kitchen met the office and a small table sat tucked in a corner for meals.

"Where're your sidekicks?"

"We've been taking turns back here. Everyone else is out, dealing with calls. No one's slept more than a couple of hours. I'm on station duty until the relief gets here from Melbourne, and then we've all got twenty-four off, since we've basically just done thirty-six on."

He got the fingerprint kit and asked her questions while he worked. When did she first see the car? Why did she look for the purse? Was Simone definitely dead when she found her? How did Alison know for sure? When they were done Billy leaned back in his seat a bit, shed the outer layer.

"You look like hell." He smiled at her, the dimples in his cheeks attempting to make up for the insult.

"Gee, thanks, you really know how to perk me up." She smiled back anyway.

"Come to the Imperial tonight—they're opening up. I'll be there, could murder a beer after this shift; most of town'll be there too probably."

"Are her parents coming here?"

"On their way now, coming down from Cairns." He articulated it wrong, forgot to drop the *ir*, like a local would. Alison knew the trick, though, on account of her years up there after art school, working a shit-kicking job, painting in her spare time, before she'd gotten established enough to live off her art.

"Ever been there, Billy?"

"Me? Never been anywhere, really. Melbourne's as far as I get."

"It's 'Cans.' Like a can."

"What? Why'd they spell it differently, then?"

"Probably to weed out the foreigners."

He didn't get it. "Coming for a drink tonight, then?"

"Maybe. Can you let me know when her parents get here? I'd like to talk to them."

"Why?"

"She was on her way to my house; maybe they know why."

"You don't know her, so why do you think she was coming to you? Maybe she panicked in the fire; with the visibility so low, maybe she didn't even know where she was."

"Maybe, maybe not. We don't know. I'd just—I'd like to meet them, is all." She thought of the note again, bit her lip, held her tongue.

"All right, I'll let them know when they get here."

"Thanks, Billy." Alison, wanting to convey more levity than she felt, winked at him as she waved good-bye, and strolled back out into the muggy afternoon.

————

In the street she got back on Sal's three-speed and pedaled down the main drag. The town was small, a few streets jutting off it, no more than fifty houses inside the boundaries. Everyone else lived on bush blocks a short drive out. It was hard to imagine anyone untouched by a fire of this scale. If they survived at all, most people had lost property, livestock, or crops in the blaze. Some had lost loved ones. The paper on Sal's table that morning put the death toll at fifty-five and rising. Sal had wanted to talk to her about it, but Alison was trying not to think about it. Trying to silence the voice that kept asking why she had escaped what had seemed like certain death. There wouldn't be a fuller picture until they'd been able to go through all the damaged areas, count the missing. Today, fires were still burning, the heat and smoke and destruction not done with this community yet.

That was the thing about bushfires. They didn't eat just the bush; they swallowed homes, shops, and cars. Whole streets. Whole populations. Fifty-five people dead. She rolled it around in her brain, trying not to think about how that meant everyone knew someone. Everyone lost someone. There was no avoiding a death toll like this one. Alison didn't know where to start thinking about it. She had friends she couldn't reach, whom she hadn't been able to bring herself even to try to raise. It would be a long time before Lake Bend would be back to some version of "normal," and even longer before the gaps were somehow plugged. The missing mechanic or teacher, or accountant or ranger. There was no way to map the long way back or speed up the process of turning the grief into something softer but, somehow, stronger.

The road curved around the mountains; on one side the land was char and ash. Twisted metal slumped on concrete slab—these were houses, but now they made a graveyard of sorts. Ashes caught on the wind, and when she breathed, Alison didn't know what she was inhaling. Was it the remains of trees, homes, pictures, furniture—or was it human? She held her breath as long as she could.

4.

In Sal's pool, Alison floated, arms buoyant, legs sinking, immersed in salty ribbons of smooth coolness. The air was thick with smoky warnings, but close to the water, all that she caught was briny sweetness, like the smooth curl of an abalone shell freshly shucked from the sea. The water was filthy, sticks and leaves and charcoal and ash collected in the pool's corners, untroubled by the filter. She didn't care.

In Cairns, the apartment block where she'd lived had a pool—chlorine, not salt, and the old man who looked after the block didn't much worry about safe limits. Some days, Alison would go down for a dip and see accumulated piles of chemical, like tiny pearls heaped in mounds on the stairs and in the shallow curves of the kidney bean. It stung her eyes and turned them red, gave her headaches if she stayed in too long, but that pool was a place to be alone when it wasn't possible anywhere else. It was a place to gather her strength and restore her sore muscles on bad days. Out there in the blazing sun, a wall of units on three sides. Public enough to never feel alone, private enough to never have to talk to anyone. That pool, Alison truly believed, had saved her many times.

Sal's pool was secluded. No nearby neighbors. No passing cars. Alison wasn't able to fully relax here. Every sound made her jump; every rustling branch or far-off rumble of tires made her flinch, tense her arms, find the concrete underfoot, ready herself to run. She kept thinking about what Billy had told her about Simone. A bad boyfriend. It made her skin crawl. She didn't want to think about it, but the more she tried to push it out, the more it wormed its way back in. She sucked the salty air into her nostrils deeply. Tried to think about ways to record the color in these clouds, the specific grays, the blushing red, the murky blue. Simone's blue eyes stared back at her from the sky, suspended in the hazy afternoon light, searching. Not playful like in the license or stone-cold like in real life, but somewhere in between, alive and sad, Alison thought. She blinked a few times, tried to make them go away. She needed something else for that. Salt water wasn't going to do it. As she heaved herself out of the pool, she heard branches rustling in the bush. But there was no wind. She shivered and hurried inside, heart skipping.

Billy was right: the Imperial was heaving. Alison pushed through the doors and inched her way through the crowd up to the bar, wiggling between Cath, who ran the local bakery, and Pete, the town mechanic. She nodded at them both and leaned over onto the wet blond timber, waving her arm to get Molly's attention. She looked up from the jug she was filling and nodded in Alison's direction.

"I'll get a Coopers Green, thanks, Mol." She raised her voice above the din, and Molly nodded again, this time in confirmation.

"Glad to see you, love," Pete said, leaning over to Alison.

"You too, Pete. Heard Orchard Street is a bit of a shit show?"

"Lost the shop, but we're still alive, so counting my blessings," he said, raising his pint. The beer slopped over the side of his glass and dribbled down his hand. A little sloshed already, Pete licked it up, seemingly not wanting to leave a drop.

"How about you, Cath?"

"My Jean lost her house all the way over near Kangaroo Ground, but we're all right up there on Main Street; fire turned before it could get to us."

"Jean and the kids OK?" Alison asked, the flash of a few giggling blond heads in her mind's eye. Three maybe?

"Yeah, they're all right. Bit shaken up. Had a close call, sheltered under the water tank—it was touch and go for a bit." There were tears in Cath's eyes and Alison was sorry she'd brought it up. She wanted to get out of there. This was the last thing she needed right now. She took a large swig of her beer, feeling ashamed that she didn't have the strength to listen, and shocked at how badly all this hurt. As she set down the glass and searched for a way out of the conversation, Alison could smell Billy behind her. Too much sandalwood.

"You on the hunt tonight?" she asked him, turning around. He looked cartoonishly wounded and grinned at her with those stupid dimples again.

"Always pays to be prepared, Alison."

"What are you, a Boy Scout? Freshly showered, doused in whatever that bloody cologne is, and no doubt a franger in your back pocket. The number one most eligible bachelor in a ten-K radius."

"It's nice when your publicist does their job," he shot back.

Alison returned to her pint glass, banged it down empty, and tapped the counter. Two sharp raps of her flat palm on the wood in quick succession.

"We'll get another of these, and two shots of your most terrible whiskey, please, Molly."

"Hang on, there, you might want to take it slow. It's not

even seven." Billy looked at her, taking in the fatigue behind her eyes.

"Nah, not every day you survive a bushfire. I'm well ready to get hammered. Don't ruin it for me."

Molly was back again, with the beer and shots, and Alison thrust one toward Billy, raising the other in the air, waiting for his cheers. He reluctantly obliged, and they tipped their heads back in unison, before slamming the glasses down on the bar. Alison chased hers down with her beer and gestured for another.

"And two waters, thanks," Billy shouted as Molly nodded in their direction.

Toward the back of the beer garden they found a table wedged in between folks on the right side of the wind, who, Alison imagined, were like her. Wanting to celebrate their good fortune and mourn those who hadn't been so lucky, but also maybe not think about any of it too much in case it got the better of them.

The air was heavy with death dodged, and grief for friends and neighbors lost. No one here was untouched. Everyone was drinking; some people were crying. Silent tears, full pints. There was an uneasiness in the room, a kind of melancholy that was hard to describe. Usually, the Imperial was loud, rowdy, sweaty. Tonight, it was more like the lounge room of her home in the hours after her parents' funeral. Sad eyes, full glasses, soft voices.

In the corner, Jason and Mick, arguing over the dartboard; by the French doors, the woman who ran a little pottery boutique on Main Street, Casey something, three empty pints on the table in front of her. Everyone Alison clocked wore on their face a weariness she recognized from her own in the mirror. She gulped bitter beer silently, until she couldn't anymore.

Alison wanted to talk, she realized about halfway through her third beer. She thought about Simone, about how her address was in the dead woman's purse. It felt secret, like something between just them. Not something that should be shared, and definitely not with the police. Billy sat there, not prompting her, not pushing her, waiting for Alison to say what she wanted to. He'd always been good at that. But now it annoyed Alison, made her want to provoke him.

"Is humoring sad idiots like me part of your training?"

"Don't be daft," he interjected. "You're not part of the job."

Alison tried to ignore the meaning she heard in his tone and told Billy a story she was willing to share.

"When the radio said it was too late to evacuate, I didn't think it'd be a problem. Last time I'd checked, the fire wasn't close enough to reach me, and so I didn't understand why they were saying it was too late to leave. That was the kind of warning they gave when you were too close to escape, when it was better to try and stay put, hope the wind went your way. I thought about trying to get out anyway, but then I heard a crash and I looked out the back, and I could see, over toward the ridge, the smoke. Everything happened so bloody fast. One minute I was fucking around in my studio; the next I was eating the floor, wet wool up my nose. Thinking about my obituary."

She paused for more beer, but Billy pulled it away and pushed the water into her hand.

"Killjoy. Anyway, I was thinking, if I am dead—I mean, this is what I was thinking then, not now—but if I was dead, what would they say?" Alison raised her glass above her head and began her own obituary.

"'A promising artist, Alison King, and all of her unfinished works were burned to a crisp.'" She took a swig of her beer and even though she knew she shouldn't, she kept going.

"Bloody likely that's all they'll remember me for. A pile of ashes and unfulfilled promises. The granddaughter of the town's proudest cricketing export, who lived his own existence in Don Bradman's shadow. Pathetic. I don't even have a husband to perish alongside me and make everyone feel bad about the babies that won't be born." The room was spinning a little, or her head was having trouble with the beer; maybe both, she thought.

She drained the water glass, reached again for the beer, and took a large swig before Billy could stop her.

"Ally, keep your voice down. I know you're upset, but there are people here that have lost people." Billy grabbed her hands. Stopped her picking up her beer again.

"I lost a person. I lost a person. A person was lost in my fucking driveway. Have you forgotten?" She raised her voice, and people at the tables nearby began to turn to look.

"And what about Meg? Has anyone heard from her?" Meg Russell was Alison's oldest friend, they met on the first day of kindergarten; Alison swapped her a green crayon for a yellow. *You can make green with yellow, so I don't need it.* They had grown apart over the years, but when Alison moved back to town, Meg had made a big effort to reconnect with her. She wondered, where was her friend now? Or was she one of them? The erased.

"Meg's place wasn't in the way, but no one's heard from her yet." He paused, waiting as she took another gulp of beer. "Hey, I've got an idea. Let's get out of here. We'll pick up a slab of beer and drink it at my place; that way you can be as maudlin and offensive as you like, and no one will clock you for it."

It was a solution of sorts.

"If I agree, do you promise to actually cut loose with me?"

"Yes. I promise to drink as much as I possibly can in pursuit of your dream of total incapacitation." He put his hand on his heart as he spoke.

"All right. Let's get blind and watch horror movies. Why the fuck not?" She got up from the table and pulled Billy by the hand toward the car park. They stopped off at the bottle shop and picked up beer, whiskey, and two packets of cigarettes. Alison could feel the alcohol already in her system doing its work. She felt loose, free. In control in an out-of-control way. She headed for Sal's car, rifling through her bag for the key. The hair on the back of her neck pricked up when Billy grabbed her by the arm and pulled her toward him.

"Where are you going?" he asked her, slightly amused.

"To the car. I gotta get Sal's car back to her." Alison felt the swim of drink in her head again. A flash of tires slipping on a bend, the crunch of a tree trunk, unmoved. She shook it away. She didn't want to think about the accident. She didn't care right now how reckless she was being. But Billy did.

"There's no way in hell you're driving; you can come pick it up in the morning," he told her, forcing her into the passenger seat of his own car, his hands rough on her arms, a loose curl of his dark brown hair falling into his eyes as he corralled her. Alison's stomach flipped, turned; the hairs on her arms stood on end.

She settled in for the drive, and watched the buildings roll by her window as they headed to Billy's. It wasn't far, five minutes along the main street, and then off toward the highway a few turns. The house was Billy's grandmother's. She'd lived there until she died, and Billy had inherited it. He'd done nothing to fix it up; it still sagged and sighed like a grumpy old woman. Alison had been round a few times since she'd been back, for parties, or occasionally to shoot the shit and drink whiskey on the back deck. They weren't best friends, but Alison always felt safe around him.

As she followed Billy up the drive, Alison knew something was different tonight. She knew she was making a choice that couldn't be reversed, and she didn't care. While Billy unlocked the front door, Alison smoothed her hair and licked her lips. She reached into her top and rearranged her breasts, shoring them up against gravity, and then she picked her undies out of her arse and sucked in her stomach. Billy turned around as he pushed the door in and swept his arm up in a welcoming gesture.

"Come on in, plenty of carpet to puke on."

It occurred to Alison that Billy didn't know what she wanted, or even, by the look on his face, what he wanted. She smiled as she moved past him, brushing against his body, a seemingly unintentional encounter. She felt him tense up as her arm lingered on his. She wouldn't have to push too hard.

"Gee, Billy, you've really spruced this place up."

The carpet in the lounge room was worn thin where Billy and his brother, and Billy's mother and her brother, had wrestled for supremacy as children. The red roses were faded pink, their green leaves dulled to gray, the cream surrounds now the beige of a thousand feet. On the walls, the paper was yellowed and peeling in the corners, a mid-century dream turned to dust, one year at a time.

"Are you ever not a sarcastic bitch?" He looked as though he wanted it to hurt. They were both pushing boundaries.

"No, I guess not. Sorry." Alison sat on the floor, her back against the peeling paper, her arm resting on the plush fat side of an overstuffed chair.

They looked at each other for a while, and eventually it seemed to Alison that Billy made a decision. He sat down on the floor next to her and handed her a beer.

"I'm sorry about what happened to you, Al, I really am."

"Not your fault." Alison took a swig, the bubbles catching in her throat as she gulped down a large mouthful.

"Just so you know, though: he might be a legend, but I'm

more of a Steve Waugh fan, to be honest." Billy took a sip of his beer. He was pacing himself.

"What are you talking about?" She leaned her head on his shoulder. He still stank of sandalwood.

"Bradman. Great batsman, sure, one of the greatest, in test cricket, yes. But I'm saying I prefer Steve Waugh. In the end, he was a better captain."

"This is well off topic." Alison laughed, and meant it.

"I didn't know your great-granddad played cricket."

"Shut up, idiot, you did." Alison moved to push him, but Billy grabbed her wrist to stop her. He caught her eye and held it. "My nan's favorite was Steve Waugh too," she added, wanting to concede something.

"What are we doing, Al?" He didn't let go of her wrist, or drop her gaze, but his tone of voice had changed, less playful, more measured.

"We're drinking beer on the floor, and you are putting up with me because I almost died yesterday."

For the past twenty-four hours, Alison had avoided fully acknowledging it to herself. Instead she'd thought about how she'd survived. About how Simone hadn't. About what it felt like to be in her skin, walking around like any other person, as though the flames hadn't come that close. The memory of the wet wool on her face, the feeling that she was breathing in fibers, suffocating one breath at a time. Billy was still holding on to her arm and looking at her with those fucking sad eyes men get when they don't know what you want them to do.

"But you didn't die, you're still here." He spoke gently, and Alison couldn't keep his gaze any longer; she dropped her head, her hair falling over her face. Billy used his free hand to push it back and grabbed her, a little roughly, by the chin, forcing her eyes back up.

"It matters that you realize this, Al. You're OK. You're going to be fine. Your house is fine, the trees'll grow back. There's nothing here that's gone forever."

Alison wanted to scream at him; she wanted to dig her nails into the skin of his cheek, draw blood, force him to react, to be irrational, to lash out at her, hit her, hurt her, bruise her. Something visible, a way to wear the pain that people could see. His face was close to hers, and his hand still held her by the chin, the thumb resting below her lips.

Fuck it, she decided.

Alison lifted her free arm and pulled him close. He let it happen. She could feel him hesitate, and then he leaned into it, went with it, kissed her back. It was exactly how she'd expected. A little soft, a lot of stubble, and the kind of gentle pressure you wouldn't associate with a man who made his money as a copper. They broke apart.

"Long time coming," Billy said, smiling at her. The bloody dimples. Fuck, he was being sincere about it.

"Should have a license for those, Officer," Alison responded, trying to avoid being serious but possibly not sarcastically enough for it to register, while running her hand over his cheek. He rolled his eyes at her.

"If I had a dollar for every woman who'd said something that cheesy about my job, I'd have"—he paused, made a theatrical display of attempting to count—"at least fifty bucks by now."

Alison laughed, hard. "Fifty bucks. You're dreaming, Billy. There's not fifty single women in this whole damn town."

"All right, maybe five, then."

"I think what you're driving at is that I'm unoriginal." She began to unbutton his shirt. "I need to find some new material."

"You need to stop talking, would be my best suggestion," Billy replied.

He kissed her again. It felt good. Alison felt good. There was a fluttering in her stomach, which surprised her; she hadn't expected that. She pushed the feeling down and hooked her leg up and over, straddling him. Their mouths close, his arms firm on her back, her skirt bunched up around her waist, his shirt open, the button of his jeans undone, the checked green cotton of his boxer shorts revealed as she undid the zipper.

"Hope you've got that condom in your pocket."

He kissed her in that way boys do when they want to distract you. Alison felt the flutter again.

She pulled back. "Billy? Condom?"

"Er, well, no. But you're on the pill, right?" His hands were on the small of her back, applying just enough pressure to make her feel the urgency of the situation.

"Yes, of course, but Jesus fuck, Billy, I don't really have to have this fight with you, do I?" She looked straight into his eyes, and he didn't flinch.

"I'm sorry. I don't have any, but I'm clean. I promise. I don't have any because I see action so rarely the pack would expire before I got a chance to use it."

"Shit." Alison sat back on Billy's legs, putting a little distance between them. The spell was broken. She'd broken it. He looked away from her.

"Took us twenty years to get here; couldn't hurt to wait a little longer, could it?" It wasn't a question really, but it was infused with uncertainty. He looked hesitant. Alison was pissed off. With herself, with Billy. She tried to cool down, but she couldn't.

"OK, forget it. Forget it for good." She didn't know why she was so angry, the knot turning to heat in her stomach. She knew Billy could tell she meant it.

"Well, hang on, let's not be so hasty. Maybe we can come

to a compromise. Fool around a little, save the main event for later." He reached out to her, stroked her arm, his other palm still firm on the small of her back.

"Who says there'll be a later?"

"This isn't just a fuck and you know it." He looked pissed off now, and Alison knew she'd messed everything up. All she wanted was something uncomplicated. There was no denying that she wanted him right now. Not the way he wanted her, but enough to forget about the condom. *This isn't even the most dangerous thing that's happened to me this weekend.* She didn't care about the condom. She didn't care about anything.

"I guess we could fool around a little." Alison ran her hand through Billy's hair and let it rest on his cheek as she leaned in for a gentle kiss. It was too hot, and sweat pooled in the places where their bare skin met. She tossed her chin back, extending her neck, lengthening every muscle from the base of her spine to the crown of her head. She rocked backward a little, applying pressure to his legs, his hips, the straining fabric of his pants, the undone button digging into her inner thigh. Billy groaned a little bit, his face filled with longing and, Alison was pretty sure, disgust. She leaned in close and kissed his neck, the salty taste still on her lips when she kissed his, more tenderly than she meant, moments later.

He grabbed her by the wrists and pushed her back toward the carpet. They were still fully dressed, his shirt half-open, her skirt gathered in folds around her hips. Alison could feel the scratch of worn wool loops on her shoulder blades, increasing as she took the pressure of his body onto hers. The way her legs bent hurt a little. A lot. The right amount. The lights were on, the yellow glare of fluorescent tubing highlighting the curve of Billy's collarbone, the shadow of his nose long across the left side of his face. In all these years Alison had never seriously considered Billy before, and now she wasn't sure what had changed, or even if anything had. She pushed her pelvis up to meet him and unbuttoned his shirt the rest of the way. She hadn't seen his body since they were on the swim squad together, his teenage shape now all but erased. This man in his place was unfamiliar in all the right ways. She clocked the scar on his stomach, a hand span to the right of his navel; as big as her own closed fist. He saw her looking and leaned down to distract her with a kiss, his hands pulling her singlet straps down, exposing her bra. Slowly then, he kissed her all the way down her neck, lingered a while with her nipple in his mouth, tickled her stomach just enough to make her grin, and arrived at her cunt. The intimacy of it made her a little squeamish at first, but he knew what he was doing and as the endorphins began to flood in, Alison let go of the uncertainty.

She was on the edge when he stopped. "Well?" he asked her, having walked her all the way there. "Still insist on a condom?"

"That's not playing fair," Alison replied. But as she said it, she reached her hand down to guide him, so there could be no misunderstanding. He smiled a self-satisfied grin and pushed inside her. She felt the pressure and tightened her legs around him as he moved, slowly, into her. He brought his face close and watched intently for her response. When he tried to kiss her, she turned her face away. "I don't want to taste myself," she said, trying not to absorb the hurt in his eyes.

As they moved together Alison kept her eyes closed and tipped her head back. He put his hand behind her head and gently angled it toward him.

"Ally, open your eyes."

She met his gaze and he began to quicken his pace.

He was almost there.

She wasn't.

Alison closed her eyes again and tried to focus. She felt herself expanding and contracting, the pressure intensifying as she lost control over the muscles that mattered. Her body yielded to the feel of so many ripples inside her. But as the waves built, she built a resistance to them. She wanted to feel something, but the closer she got, the farther away she became.

When he was about to come, Alison felt him withdraw, quickly. He hovered over her. She looked away, felt that familiar warm viscosity on her stomach. Then he got up, left the room, and returned with a towel. He rubbed her stomach, her thighs, and lay back down beside her, on the floor, in their sweat and damp. She turned away. Billy kissed her shoulder and rolled over, flat on his back, his right shoulder wet with sweat against her back. She turned to look at him, wondering how badly she'd stuffed up.

"OK?" he asked her, pushing his hair out of his eyes.

"Yeah, OK." She found his hand with hers and laced their fingers together halfheartedly.

"Did you come?"

Alison laughed. She reached for her beer and took a swig, feeling at once that she both hated and longed for Billy more than she liked. "You know, Billy, if you have to ask . . ."

He looked a little too hurt but recovered his composure quickly. For a while they lay together on the floor, the carpet scratching their backs. Billy pulled her close, tucking her into his arm and making it hard for her to get away. Alison stayed there, not sure what to say.

"What happened to you?" she eventually asked.

"What do you mean?" Billy seemed surprised by the question.

"Your stomach, the scar." There was silence for a while. She could feel a distance developing.

"You weren't here. It doesn't matter. It's fine." Billy's tone was cold.

"You've got a fucking scar the size of my fist. What happened?" Alison leaned into him, her naked body on his.

"I got shot. I almost died. I didn't. I'm a cop, it happens."

"How have I never heard this before? Here, in Lake Bend?"

Billy sighed, took his time gathering the story.

"It wasn't long after I finally got my transfer back up here. I was the most junior person in the office. The bank alarm went and we thought it was a falsie. You know, we get falsies from various places about three times a week. But you still have to go out. We got there, they'd barricaded themselves, and realizing there was little in the way of options, they decided to shoot it out. Which is crazy. Who does that? No one. It's not the fucking Wild West."

Billy didn't say anything for a bit, his fingers tracing a pattern on the swell of her breast.

"What happened?" she prompted.

"I was shooting, and they were shooting, and suddenly I felt a burn like nothing else. I looked down, and I was bleeding. I just kept on shooting. I was useless, though. Utterly useless. Couldn't really even see straight. Eventually someone told me it was over and done. I don't remember who. I think I passed out."

He brought her hand up to his face and kissed the back of it.

Alison ran her other hand over the scar. His skin was smooth and hot, sweaty with the weather and the sex.

"Shit. I didn't know."

"It was in the news."

"I wasn't here."

"I know." He didn't sound like he thought this was enough of a reason.

They didn't talk for a while.

"For a few seconds time stopped moving, you know. I could hear everything like it was the loudest sound in the world, which really meant I could hear nothing. Pain sliced through me, and I felt the blood gushing down my legs— which, by the way, feels a lot like you've pissed yourself—and I really thought that was it. I knew gut wounds could be fatal. I thought that was the end. And you know what I realized? I didn't care. If that had been it, then that was OK. Which is pretty fucked up, right? I was OK with being done."

When she spoke, Alison lowered her voice to a whisper, not sure if she really wanted to be heard at all. "I felt like that yesterday."

Billy turned onto his side to face her and pulled his arm around her exposed waist. He leaned in close and took her in, unnerving her. She let him for a moment, and then she pulled away.

"Don't be sentimental," she told him. "None of this fucking means anything."

Alison turned away and tried to imagine what came next. She wanted to find a way to see it, but they were too opposite, too much of a clash for her to go down that road. When things shifted Billy didn't hesitate, always making a new way through. He was forceful in his decisions and never looked back on them with real regret. Although, Alison wasn't sure if he'd feel that way about tonight. She knew they would always be better friends than lovers. She was beginning to see just how radically their opinions on this diverged.

As she lay there seeing the full extent of Billy's desire for her clearly for the first time, in a way she couldn't deny, Alison thought about how whatever you imagine is the truth, you convince yourself it's real, and it usually never is. The world isn't going to lie to you until it does, and the safety you built, the measures you took to protect yourself, crumbles around you, and everything you think you know becomes immediately unknowable. All the adjustments, the small tightenings of the tap, the sequence of decisions that led you from where you've been to where you are. None of it necessarily connected, but it was possible—a few times in life, at least—to look back and plot your course, the twists and turns, from every little moment that seemed like nothing at the time. It was hands and feet, arms and body, all the momentum you could imagine. Building up, pressure mounting, the feeling of needing to escape pressing against your chest as you lie in your bed at night.

Without saying anything else, Alison got up from the floor and moved away from him. She picked up her bra and fastened it back in place, then pulled up her top.

"You're leaving?"

"Why would I stay?" Alison straightened her skirt as she wriggled back into it and smoothed down her hair, trying to avoid his eyes. Wanting to hurt him.

"Why wouldn't you?" He really did look good lying on the floor, propping his body up on his elbows, the flat curve of his stomach marred by the gunshot scar, his broad brown shoulders pronounced by the way he was lying. And then there were the dimples, which, if she was being honest, were a little too much.

"I think we both know this is a bad idea that is just going to end worse. I'm not trying to be mean, Billy, but there's a reason we haven't done this before."

He hesitated, like he knew telling the truth was the wrong call. Then he did it anyway. "When you came back to town and we went for drinks at the pub that first time you asked me how I was, and I wanted to tell you about it, but it seemed a bit . . . self-indulgent. I don't think that's the right word, but it seemed a bit like I was boasting to tell you. I figured you already knew from the papers."

"I stopped paying attention to the news down here." Alison knew she shouldn't interrupt him, but she couldn't help it.

"Well, anyway, I thought you must have known. It's a small town. People talk—cops don't get shot round here that often. Last one was twenty years before. So, when you didn't mention it, I guess I decided you knew me better than anyone. You knew I didn't want to talk about it, didn't want to be made to play the hero, didn't want to feel the pain again. I thought that you knew me the best. Turns out I was wrong. You didn't even know I'd been shot. How could you have known I didn't want to talk about something you never knew had happened?" He looked away from her, and Alison couldn't be sure, but she thought he was crying.

"I was terrified when I heard the fire went down your road. I guess I let my guard down because it felt like some kind of sign, that you were still here, that I was still here. I should have known better. I did know better. I knew what you were feeling wasn't real. I knew because after I got shot, I fucked the first woman who would let me. I didn't care that she was married. Or that I worked with her. Or that it was the worst idea I ever had. I wanted that feeling like nothing exists in the world except you and the person you're with, who you need, right then in that moment. Pure, uncomplicated euphoria, at least until it's over. The only feeling strong enough to take away the fear. And the shock." He turned his head now to look at Alison, and she found it hard to hold his gaze but knew she owed him that much.

"You're absolutely right," Alison said. "It isn't real."

She picked up her beer off the floor and took a long swig, still staring straight at him. Then she walked out of the room and down the hall, through the front door and onto the porch.

The gravel of the drive crunched beneath her as she plodded along. She didn't look back, or hesitate, worried if she did, he'd rush out to stop her.

The air was leaden with moisture, a thunderstorm threatening to burst through at any moment, but Alison decided to walk back to Sal's anyway. As Billy's house receded into the starlit, inky night, she began to relax a little for the first time in days. The feeling lasted a few minutes. Then the guilt of having used one of the only people she truly cared about rose in her throat. She gulped it back, felt the hot night air on her neck, the smoke still not fully receded, the uneasy smell of natural barbecue heavy on the wind. The itch of a mosquito at her shoulder blade as she stumbled a little from all the beer and the whiskey.

It was quiet in the deep night; the wildlife that usually filled the void with clicks and chirps was nowhere to be seen or heard. The stillness made her uneasy. She stopped and stared up at the stars that weren't obscured by cloud. There weren't many, and her head spun. A snap of a twig underfoot somewhere out there made her quicken her pace. It could have been nothing, but she wasn't sure.

The ash deadened the thud of her feet, making it impossible to hear if it was also masking someone else's. So she hurried faster, wishing she weren't alone, drunk, and embarrassed, each uneventful step convincing her she had imagined it.

When she arrived at Sal's, Alison was surprised to see the lights were still on. No prospect, then, of slipping in unnoticed.

5.

Smaller fires were still burning on the western side of
Cook Creek Road. In the unstable, fickle conditions,
the most direct route to Alison's house from town was
blocked. The back road twisted around the mountains with
sheer drops up to twenty meters on the eastern side. The
vertigo-inducing twister was usually masked by scrub and
saplings, but the sedimentary rock was exposed now, black
ash and trunks the only indication of what had been. Sal's car
hugged the inner shoulder, going carefully to avoid the odd log
that had fallen from above, blocking the way again, even after
the dozers went through.

On her way into town after the fire, in the growing dark,
her head filled with the outline of Simone's face, the curves of
her pale cheeks, the matte stare, the blond braid, the smooth
crisp of paper with Alison's address heating the space between
her fingers, the main road hadn't given Alison a true sense of
the extent of the damage. Now she was shocked all over again.
Where the flames had caught, running over huge tracts of
land, nothing was left. The papers had the death toll up at one
hundred fifty. More than four hundred people were injured,
and Alison had read in the *Age* as she ate her Weet-Bix that
morning that more than two thousand homes were estimated

destroyed. Lake Bend was luckier than some towns; the fire front headed right for it before it swerved at Alison's back door and went another way. But everyone knew someone who knew someone who hadn't been heard from since the fire. Alison still hadn't heard from Meg.

Alison had already left her a lot of messages, but they weren't returned, the acid in her stomach building with each unanswered attempt. Alison checked the morning papers for news again this morning, but there was nothing she hadn't already gleaned from the grapevine. The internet wasn't so reliable right now, and most people were getting their information the old-fashioned way, or directly from the journalists sent from Melbourne to cover the story. At the pub the night before she'd noticed a few unfamiliar faces, drinking in a corner.

Last night.

At first, Sal hadn't said anything when Alison had turned up drunk the night before, her hair a mess. When Billy called the house not five minutes after she walked in, Sal watched Alison shake her head in horror as she stretched the phone out toward her, and then pulled it back to her own ear, said Alison was home, and she was all right, but she didn't want to talk. After hanging up, she looked in Alison's eyes and read her face. Then she'd made them a cup of tea and ran Alison a bath. As Alison soaked in the lukewarm water, Sal had sat outside the bathroom door and talked through the wall.

"Billy sounded pretty upset, Al." She didn't respond. Sal tried again. "You two have been mates a long time. I'm sure if you talk to him, you'll be able to sort it out."

Alison sloshed the water around her, sinking as far down into the tub as she could, her knees sticking up in the air as she tried to immerse her whole torso. She didn't reply.

"I think you're going to regret ruining your friendship

when you've got a bit more distance. Right now, you're not really thinking straight."

"Why didn't you tell me about Billy getting shot?"

There was a long silence on the other side of the door. "I thought you knew, love; it was the talk of the town when it happened, but I guess you weren't here."

Alison clenched her fists tight, tried to calm herself down, stop reliving the stupidity of asking about the scar. Stop thinking about how selfish she must seem, how angry she was with Sal, with her parents, for never saying anything, with herself for never bothering to find out. As though the years she was gone from this place hadn't existed at all.

"Sal. I'm fine, really. I just want to be left alone. Please."

It was true, but it also wasn't. She heard Sal scuffling about in the hall, and then the soft retreat of her footsteps.

In the bath, Alison traced the lines of her body with her hands, her eyes closed, trying to get back the feeling of safety, the warmth and strength she'd felt as she'd walked back from Billy's, the moment of invincibility that came after the fact. It was long gone. All that was left was carpet rash and the deep burning shame of her ignorance blooming across her face.

She dunked her head under, holding her breath for as long as she could, and then emerged again. After all the warmth had leached from the bath, Alison pulled out the plug and turned on the shower. She rinsed off and, totally sober, toweled down and headed for bed. The sheets on her back were cool and light, and as she drifted in and out of sleep uneasily, her phone beeped. It glowed on the bedside table. It was Billy.

12:17 am

Night Al. Call me in the morning. x

Alison had turned the phone over so she couldn't see it glowing and flicked it to silent. There was no coming back from some choices; she knew that well enough by now. She hoped this wasn't one of them.

Alison closed her eyes and tried to think of something else, but as she pushed Billy to the back of her mind, the fire clawed its way to the front, more vividly than she thought possible. The deafening blasts that sounded like the ominous rat-tat-tat of firefight in a war movie as the gums caught and exploded. The screeches of birds—she imagined parakeets, and magpies and lorikeets, eagles and wrens—trying to flee, overtaken by the heat and the smoke.

"Ally, you sleeping?" Sal asked her softly.

"No, sorry, I just couldn't look at the trees anymore." She shifted in her seat, pulled out her phone to check if there was any service.

She had two bars, and five texts. Shit. Billy needed to give it a rest.

9:13 am

We need to talk. U at Sal's?

9:21 am

I've got the day off. Can I come see you?

9: 46 am

Al, please?

9:55 am

Are you really doing this?

10:12 am

I'm here, when you're ready to talk to me.

She started drafting a response. Deleted it, tried again, deleted it again. Finally settled on something that she hoped would get the message across.

10:17 am

I'm sorry Billy. There's nothing to talk about. It was what it was, but I don't want anything more than that. I think we'd be better off giving each other some space.

She saw the little bubble pop up. He was typing back, but no message came. Alison put the phone down and looked out the window. The damage stretched out across the ridges like scars across the land. She slouched down in her seat and closed her eyes again, waiting for the drive to be over. Sal fiddled with the radio, eventually found a fuzzy FM signal; "Bat Out of Hell" came through weakly. They hit the long, flat stretch of highway, just a couple of clicks from Alison's property, and she felt her shoulders tense up. Sal, not often quiet, was mercifully silent for most of the drive.

6.

S al turned into the driveway, the motion of the car catching Alison by surprise. She opened her eyes to orientate herself, and immediately regretted agreeing to come. Sinking down in her seat, she looked out the window at the decimated side of the drive. Over to the left, the bush untouched, dry and heavy but still all there, and then on the right, a blackened stripped-bare hellscape. She thought back to that moment on the day of the fire. The noise in the bush. The creeping feeling she'd had, the one of being surveilled. Not everything here was the same as that day. Ahead, the drive had been cleared. There was no sign of Simone's car, and the hulking trunk that had blocked the drive lay chopped and piled neatly to one side.

Sal drove straight past, not knowing, and pulled in at the top of the drive a minute later. The tires crunched on the loose gravel as Alison examined the outside of her house. The grass was burned away as close as a meter from the veranda, and the pale green paint had blistered and curled. Sooty dust blanketed the walls and windows on this side, covering the weatherboard in a thick film of gray. Alison wanted to trace her name in it with her fingers, but she suppressed the childish urge. She walked up the front steps and sat down on the old cane chair her grandfather had bought decades ago. Sal was wandering around the lawn, looking for the edges of the fire's path, the places the flame tongues had licked before the wind had forced the retreat.

"Are you going to go inside?" she called out.

"Not right now. I'm fine here."

Looking down the drive she could see a cop car kicking up dust in its wake. Alison didn't know why the police had wanted to meet her out here, but she'd agreed to the meeting reluctantly. As the car gained upon the house, it seemed to sag. It was filthy with ash and mud and dust, the windscreen caked in dirt, half-moons carved out by the wipers allowing the driver to see. As it got closer, Alison could see that the person driving was a woman. She didn't recognize her and couldn't see the usual baby blue of the uniform. A detective from the city, most likely. Alison had agreed to meet someone to go over what she knew about Simone, and she'd expected them to be a local. She didn't know who this was. Someone from the arson squad, maybe. Papers said some of the fires had been deliberately lit. That on a 115-degree day, without a lick of rain hanging in the clouds, and with a hot breeze surging through the trees, some idiots had decided to fiddle with matches.

The car rolled up next to Sal's, and Alison stood to greet it, raising a hand in a halfhearted wave. Sal walked over from somewhere near the water tank. The woman, in a light gray suit and immaculate white blouse that seemed ridiculous in this place, in this moment, swung out of the driver's seat and slammed the door before walking at a clip up the front steps.

"Alison King?" The woman cocked her head to one side as she spoke, her eyes locked on Alison.

"Yes, that's me." Alison gestured toward Sal. "This is my friend Sal Marsh. I'm staying at her place at the moment."

Sal nodded at the woman but didn't speak.

"I'm Detective Corrine Mitchell."

"Hi," Alison said, not sure what to do.

"Can we go inside?" Detective Mitchell asked, breaking the ten-bar silence.

"Of course, follow me." Alison realized she didn't have her keys. She put her hand on the doorknob and turned, holding her breath. It gave way easily, even though she thought she remembered locking it on her way out. *Had she?* Unnerved, she shoved the door inward with her shoulder, a little surprised by how far into the hall she propelled herself. She flicked the light switch but nothing happened. In the sooty half-light, Alison was intensely aware of the traffic jam forming behind her in the hall.

"Sorry, electricity's still out, it looks like."

Sal's voice carried through the gloom. "I'll check the box, love. Have you got any wire?"

"Should be some in the hall stand, thanks, Sal." Alison moved down the hall and into the dining room, where she swept her arm out, gesturing for Detective Mitchell to sit.

"I'll see if the water's on, fix us some tea."

But the detective followed Alison into the kitchen and watched as she turned the tap. Water sputtered a little in the pipe, but then came out thick and fast. Alison rummaged around in the cupboard, emerging quickly with the stovetop kettle; she didn't often make tea—made it only when Sal was visiting. Detective Mitchell watched, silent. The gas was, surprisingly, working too, so Alison lit the stove, momentarily hypnotized by the way the flame flickered and flared, and set the water on to boil. She went back to the cupboard for tea bags and busied herself collecting cups, sugar, and spoons. She found some long-life milk in the back, behind the cans of condensed milk her mother used to use to make caramel.

There was a packet of butternuts unopened on the top shelf and she pulled them out too.

"Can I help?" Detective Mitchell asked.

A crow of triumph from outside. Sal yelled, "Try the lights, Ally, reckon I've fixed it."

She walked over to the switch and flicked it. Nothing.

"Sorry, Sal, no go," she yelled back. "I'm right, Detective; if you could take the cups, I've got the rest."

Detective Mitchell disappeared down the hall with the tea-cups. Sal bustled into the room and began gathering up all the rest of the tea things. Alison stood there, watching the kettle, waiting for it to whistle. The longer it took, the more time she had to figure out what she wanted to know, what she wanted to say.

She turned around. Detective Mitchell was back, looking at her with what felt like suspicion. Alison tried to smile but the corners of her mouth didn't cooperate.

"I'd like to get a sense of your relationship with Simone," Detective Mitchell said abruptly.

"I didn't have one. Never met her." Alison watched the stream of steam increase in the spout, pushing out faster through the whistle.

"What would she be doing on your property if you didn't know her?"

"Well, you're the detective," Alison offered, shrugging.

Her expression hardened and Alison could tell she didn't appreciate the flippant response. The kettle began to hum.

"Alison Catherine King. Raised right here. Moved to Carlton to attend the Victorian College of the Arts, then ten years in Cairns after that, and the last couple of years here. Your Cairns address was unit 3B, 214 the Esplanade. That's you, isn't it?"

Alison spoke quietly when she answered. "Yes, that's me."

"Well, Simone Louise Arnold lived in that same block of flats for the last four years, up until about a month ago, when she disappeared off the face of the earth. Extraordinary coincidence she ends up here." Detective Mitchell didn't blink as she waited for a response. The kettle was whistling hard, the shrill note of an umpire's reprimand, unrelenting. The noise split the questions in Alison's head into a million fragments, none of them coherent. Alison thought about Simone's license; the address was different. She mustn't have updated it.

"It's a coincidence all right. I might have lived in her building, but I never met her. It's a big block, full of tourists and short-term rentals. I never paid much attention to who was coming and going." Alison racked her brain for anything. Any hint at all. Did she know her? Was that why Simone had been carrying her address? She couldn't remember. Shit.

The kettle's shrill call made her temples throb. Alison turned the gas off and picked it up by the handle. She grabbed a cork mat from the countertop and walked past Detective Mitchell and into the dining room. Put the kettle down on the mat and pulled out a chair.

Detective Mitchell came into the room. She sat down slowly, watching Alison the whole time. Alison busied herself with the tea. Detective Mitchell leaned forward in her chair and put her hand on Alison's arm.

"Can you tell me how you two knew each other?"

"We didn't. I just told you that. Why would I lie?" Alison's arm felt hot where the detective's hand clutched it, the sweat from her palm making the skin clammy with wet.

"Because you don't want to be blamed for Simone's death, maybe."

"She died in a fire. I nearly died in that fire. I had no idea she was there, no idea who she was."

"I'm just trying to figure this out. Simone, as I explained to you, went missing. Right now, it's not clear how she died. They're doing an autopsy, but she had extensive bruising that could be consistent with a struggle, and it appears some bleeding on the brain. Her parents are looking for answers, and if you can give them any, they'd be grateful."

"I thought they were going to be here too." Alison had agreed to the meeting only because she wanted to meet them.

"I thought it was best we talked first. OK, maybe you didn't know her. Maybe you knew her boyfriend"—she checked her notebook—"his name was Michael? Her parents say she was trying to get away from him."

Michael. No one came to mind.

"No, I didn't know her. I didn't know anything about her." Alison got up slowly from her chair and walked out of the room, down the hall, and into the bathroom. Simone was from the exact same apartment building in Cairns where everything had gone wrong in the first place. In the bathroom, the claustrophobia of the fire returned. And so did the sick feeling in her stomach, the fear of what might happen if she said the wrong thing, did the wrong thing. She felt trapped, not for the first time in this room, and not for the first time in her life.

Outside, through the broken window, a blur of movement in the blackened background, something out of place in the corner of her eye. What the fuck was going on? She stared hard into the landscape's gaping wound, the ghostly trunks and ashen stumps. Alison heard footsteps and turned to see Detective Mitchell standing behind her, arms folded across her chest. Something about the way she was looking at her made Alison furious.

"Do you see that blanket?" Alison pointed to the heavy woolen blanket on the tile floor. The bath was still full of water. The glass from the window still strewn over everything. Detective Mitchell nodded.

"That's where I was on Sunday. Underneath that fucking blanket, breathing through damp wool and increasingly convinced I would be dead before the day was out. I didn't know shit about Simone Arnold. I'd never met her; I'd no idea she was headed my way. I was cowering under a blanket while the trees outside popped and crackled."

Alison reached into the bath and pulled the plug out. The water began to drain, slowly at first, the whirlpool quietly gathering steam. She caught her finger on a sliver of glass that had nestled in the top of the plug. It sliced her cleanly, and she watched as the blood dripped into the water, clouding it rust. She didn't notice the pain.

"I filled that bath up to the brim on Sunday. I had no idea I'd actually need it. I had no idea this fire was going to happen, and I sure as shit didn't know about Simone Arnold on her way here or whatever she was doing. I lay here, terrified, for what felt like forever. After the fire turned, and I realized I was going to live, I drank some water straight from the tub. And then I got off the floor and walked out to the road. That's when I found her. I wish she'd made it up here. I wish I could have helped her. I didn't know her, but I would have let her share this blanket. I would have offered her this water." The drain gurgled as the last of the water drained out.

"OK, Alison, I'm getting the message loud and clear," Detective Mitchell said.

"Are you? Have you ever been in a fucking bushfire? You ever expected you were about to be cooked? You ever wished the heat or the smoke got you before the house burned down around you? You ever weighed the ways you could die and tried to maneuver it so you didn't end up facing the worst one?" Alison leaned in close and lowered her voice to a whisper. "I have." Her finger throbbed. Alison raised it high and squeezed it to try to stop the bleeding. Rummaged in the cabinet for a Band-Aid.

"I'm a police officer, Alison. I may not have been in a bushfire, but yes, I think I'm aware of how it feels to face a near-death experience."

Alison couldn't look at her, the mix of embarrassment and anger too much to bear. She busied herself patching the cut and waited for Detective Mitchell to leave the room.

Sal came into the bathroom, cleared her throat.

"I think I might pack up some of your things, Ally. You can stay with me a bit longer; you've got to get the electricity on and those windows fixed up."

"Thanks, Sal, that'd be good."

Alison walked back into the dining room. It was quiet. Detective Mitchell was staring out across the grass toward the ugly gash of darkness. She didn't turn around, didn't do anything to make it clear she knew Alison was there.

It seemed surreal, Alison thought, to have survived that fire—the papers were calling it once in a century—but to be here now, instead of Simone Arnold . . . a woman who, were it not for the wind, Alison could have been. Same age, same fucking apartment building. Her phone buzzed in her pocket. It was Billy. She watched it ring, once, twice, three times.

"Are you going to get that?" Detective Mitchell asked, still not turning around.

Alison pressed the reject button and slipped the phone back in her pocket. "Nah, not important."

After what felt like forever, Detective Mitchell got back into the car and drove away, the wheels kicking up ash and dirt in her wake. Alison watched her go until the car turned out of sight and back onto the sealed road. Sal came up behind her and placed a hand on her shoulder. "No point coming back here 'til you feel up to it."

"Thanks, Sal, I don't plan on staying at your place that long. I'll be right in a couple of days."

"You might not be, and that's OK." Sal walked down the front steps and headed to her car, a duffel bag stuffed with Alison's things slung over her shoulder. She chucked it in the back seat and walked around to the driver's side. "Ready?" she called out across the gravel, and Alison remembered she hadn't locked up. Not that it really mattered, given the windows, but she wanted to have one more look, on her own.

"Just a minute," she called and headed back inside. In the spare room, off the left of the hall at the front, her easel and paints were set up. She looked at the outlines on the canvas; she'd been halfway through blocking out a private commission. Working quickly, Alison wrapped her brushes in their roll and collected her small tubes of oils, enough reds and oranges to paint the fire back to life, some blacks and greens, white to mix for grays. She closed her eyes and saw a thousand shades of gray, hazy reds, and blacks.

In the low light of the white-walled gallery space, the brushstrokes that outlined the edges of her figure were accentuated by the downlights that allowed the eye to roam over the full curve of her hip, her thigh, her waist, her arm, and take it all in. She watched as he leaned in close, squinted a little to see where the oil rose up, the thickest parts of the paint, the heaviest proof of the brush, the places her hand had twitched and turned, where she had also leaned in close to scrutinize, to see that the pinks and whites and blacks and reds had melded like they should. That he should notice the work surprised her. He took care with it, raised his hand, rough and blistered from the kitchen, and traced the space a centimeter from the canvas, as if he were touching her. She felt the hairs on her arm prick up, the pull of him as if she were standing in the surf, trying to resist the undertow.

"Well?"

He stood up straight, rocked back on his heels. "You're beautiful." He had a playful glint in his eye as he spoke, making it difficult to tell what he meant. Sand shifted underfoot as the water swirled faster around her.

"But the painting?" The hard concrete of the gallery spun back into focus as she waited for him to deliver a verdict.

"I like the way the curves feel."

She drew in a breath and held it. Let it sit uncomfortably in her lungs and diaphragm. Tried to wait enough time for it to start to hurt before slowly letting it seep back out again. She didn't want him to notice she was on tiptoe, leaning in as far as she could to hear what he would say next.

"Like I'm touching you. My hand on your waist, in your hair, cupping your cheek, wiping that smear of mascara away from under your eye."

The scrutiny felt pointed in her true direction, and instinctively Alison lifted her hand to her face, tried to wipe away the slick black of mascara. She knew, as she did it, there wasn't anything there. She blushed, her cheeks rosy in the low light of the open space at dusk. He smiled. Leaned in close to her actual face.

"They're wonderful. You're wonderful."

She exhaled fully, not realizing she'd waited all this time to do it. He held her gaze. Gil's eyes were blue. Not International Klein Blue, or Matisse blue, or Starry Night blue. They were the flecked-gold blue of a pool of salt water in the rocks at the shore. Reflecting the light that dazzled in any room he entered. If they had a describable quality, it was the changeable fluidity of the sky after a storm, the flash of a wave on the sand; they seemed wet, always. As though he were constantly shifting internally, a little off keel. They fascinated her. She felt his hand on her waist and it pulled her out of herself. She panicked, shifted away from him.

"Well, I'm glad you like them."

His eyes clouded over, the grit deep in the bottom of the pools disturbed somehow. "Maybe I'll buy one." He tried to sound light, but there was an edge to the words.

The room was full of people scrutinizing Alison's work. Her friends from the hotel, the gallery's regular visitors, the tourists who'd sniffed out the free bubbles and cheese of an opening. She wanted to stand there with him, let him put his hands on her, let him scrutinize her real shape, compare it to the work, but something about the way she felt around him scared her. She needed more time to figure it out.

She left him there, with the most eye-catching canvases, and circulated the best she could. Some of the pieces were small, focused on a curve or two. A cheekbone, the line of a rib, the deep cleft of a shoulder blade. Others gave it all away. There were no whole depictions of her face among the works except for in the one painting he had studied. She'd had a point about the commodification of the female form; she thought she'd made it well enough, but as she watched a group of footballers who'd stumbled in half-cut, attracted by the light and the chatter, she saw them joke about the body parts, quantifying their qualities and composing out of them a woman that didn't exist.

"You can't control how it's interpreted, you know." It was Gil again.

"They don't get it." She gestured toward them, one crudely thrusting his hips at the oily slick of arse on the wall in front of him. The gallery attendant was there, on the scene, encouraging them to leave.

"I don't think I do either. I think they're melodic." Was he taking the piss?

"Melodic?"

"Like I'm looking at sheet music. You read this note, and then this one, and then this one." As he talked, he stood behind her, pointing her gaze in the direction of the different elements of her face. "Then this one, then this one, and then there's a whole face. Like you string the notes together to get the melody, banging them out one by one on the keys."

She saw he was being sincere. "That's not—I mean, yes, they are parts of a broader . . . I didn't intend for beauty to be the point."

"Not all music is beautiful." He leaned in and kissed her gently on her cheek, squeezed her hand, and waved good-bye.

"You're going?"

"It's your night, enjoy it." After he'd melted away into the humid street, she'd begun to circulate again, talking to strangers and friends, trying to seem cheered by their compliments. She kept looking around the room, connecting the works in her head, hearing his composition of them. When the gallery cleared out, the assistant began marking the canvases sold, placing red dots beside them. The big canvas, the whole of her, had sold before the show, to a frequent client of the gallery. Now, as the man went from square of canvas to square of canvas, she noticed that the bulk of the pieces that had sold accounted for her face.

"Who bought those?" she asked. He looked at the list.

"These five were purchased together, last name Watson."

A warmth spread inside her from the tips of her toes to the top of her scalp. She felt sick and scared and thrilled and disgusted and wanted him to have bought them all, or none of them. She knew she was getting into something more compli-cated than she'd expected.

Sal beeped the horn and Alison hustled out of the room and back out of the house, her hands full as she pulled the door shut.

Sal had turned around and was idling in the drive, tapping her fingers impatiently on the wheel, the stereo dimly tele-graphing "Lovefool" across the distance between them. Ali-son took one last look around her, at the blackened trees and scorched earth to the north, and the lush bush greenery to the south. Turning back to take in the house as she opened the car door, she was struck by the juxtaposition. It made for an eerie scene. Like the house had dropped there, one side in Kansas, the other in Oz. She swung into the passenger seat and buck-led her belt.

"Let's go." She tapped on the dashboard and smiled at Sal.

The car rolled forward and Alison felt her phone vibrate in her pocket, but she waited until they were far enough down the drive that she couldn't see the house anymore before turning around in her seat and pulling it out of her pocket. As they passed the spot where Simone's car had hit an obstacle, Alison unconsciously crossed herself and closed her eyes. Then she remembered the phone in her hand and looked at it.

11:31 am
Fuck you then.

Billy. Sometimes he still managed to surprise her.

Alison rolled down the window, and as Sal picked up speed on the highway she breathed in the singed air deeply, this time wanting to remember exactly how it tasted.

7.

They lay in the tangle of their own sweat and sheets. Gil's hand held her wrist, his leg wrapped across her torso. Alison watched him, his breath calming and coming back to a silent evenness. His eyes were closed. He often did that, she'd noticed. Like he was cataloging the moment that had just passed, wanted to remember it all just so. He opened them and saw her staring.

"Hi." He smiled wide.

"Hi." Moments were something Alison had never been good at. She was always thinking about how they would end while they were still happening. How she would preserve them and think of them later. What she would remember. She never remembered what it was to be in them. Just how they existed for her afterward.

"I love you."

"What?"

"I know it's early. I know it's risky for me to say it, but I love you, Alison."

She let out a long breath. "There are lots of different ways to love." She ran her hand across his damp, hairy chest.

"I know it seems fast, but I mean it and I don't want

to pretend that I don't. I'm serious about this. I'm serious about you."

She felt the vise clench in her, her lungs and heart too big for their cage. She couldn't give him what he wanted yet. She didn't know how to tell him that. And she didn't want to lose him. She spread her mouth into a smile. "Tell me something no one else knows about you."

He looked at her. For a moment she saw something cloudy in his expression, and then it was gone. "I don't like cheese."

Alison laughed. "What do you mean, you don't like cheese?"

"It's my deepest, darkest secret. People really look at you differently when they know, you know."

She wrapped herself around him more tightly somehow. "Really? How cruel of them."

"I never thought I'd meet someone who understood." He gently pushed her hair back from her forehead. They stared at each other.

"I don't like mushrooms."

Gil set his face in a look of mock shock. "Outrageous! How could I possibly love someone who doesn't like mushrooms?" He manipulated his voice so it matched the old ads. "Meat for vegetarians!" As he spoke, he flexed his arms, their strength fully on display. Alison pushed him playfully and he responded by wrestling her into his arms, flipping her so that he was suddenly on top of her. She couldn't have moved even if she'd wanted to.

She didn't want to. They kissed. He tasted like salt and weed. He pressed into her, hard, urgent. They broke apart.

"I never wanted to be a chef. I thought I would join the army. My family, that's what you do. But I . . . I have this weird heart thing. It's manageable, it's *fine*, but I'm not fit for military service."

"I never thought I'd end up in Cairns either. I wanted to live in Paris."

"Paris?"

"Yeah, god, it sounds so clichéd, but I was small-town. I guess I'm still small-town. I wanted to live in Paris and be an artist." She said it in an extravagant way, poking fun at herself. Wanting him to know she wasn't grandiose. Didn't have tickets on herself, wasn't going to fly too far. Alison had never understood why she'd wanted Paris so badly, but her whole life she'd never felt like she belonged in Lake Bend, and somehow Paris had seemed like the solution.

"You are an artist, though. Who needs Paris?"

"I do, maybe someday."

"I could be convinced." He ran his hands over her, gently caressing every curve of her body.

"I didn't say you were invited!" She said it playfully, and she knew she didn't mean it. She knew, in this moment, she couldn't imagine any life without him. It was a heavy realization. She would do anything he asked. She would turn herself inside out to please him. She knew that. It was terrifying to feel this much. Heady. Dangerous.

"I don't need an invitation." He said it without any adornment, just plain, honest insistence. She kissed him again. If this was a perfect moment, she was determined to stretch it out as long as she could.

In Sal's study the paints were spread out across newspapers hastily laid down as makeshift drops. Tubes half-expressed, pressed thin at the end, squeezed fast around the middle, rolled neatly to eke out the remainders, scattered across the space. The canvas was too big, or maybe it wasn't big enough; Alison couldn't decide.

She closed her eyes, tried to ground her visual memory in the moment she wanted to reconstruct. The air felt thick and cloying. It stuck in her throat and made it hard to breathe. The sky was black, but it was the middle of the day. Heat clawed at her from the inside out. She went over it again. The way the wind had felt, the depth of the darkness in the eye of it. She remembered it had felt so hot, she thought she couldn't bear it anymore; so baked, she wondered how she wasn't blistering.

And then it was gone.

Alison was frustrated. She couldn't express what it felt like, the way the moment had suspended her, twisted her up and hung her high above everything that was going on around her. As though she weren't really there at all. It passed over her like a shiver, and then, as quickly, it was gone again.

Alison lifted the brush and twitched at the corner of the canvas, thick white, spread fat and wide, kept dipping it in, spreading it in precise lines over the mess she'd already made. Ghosting the flames, then erasing them, one stripe at a time. She found it hard to breathe the air in this room without wheezing it out in spurts, as though there weren't enough of it. Her hands were shaking as she worked. They were small, her hands, a little fat around the fingers, meaty palms, nothing elegant or fine to behold.

A fortune-teller in Cairns had told her the heart line was broken in all the wrong places, asked to see her other hand, tucked her tongue in the side of her mouth and proclaimed Alison was destined to love until the day she died; it just wasn't clear whether she'd be loved in return. The woman had told her not to be concerned, because *your life line's not that robust either*. Alison had given her fifty dollars to be told she'd die early and possibly very alone. It seemed important now, because she hadn't died when maybe she should have. Had she cheated somehow?

The canvas's white expanse stretched before her, glistening with possibility, potential to be useful, good. But there was no meaning here. Hands are just hands. Paint is just slicks of color laid down how you decide. Life is just one moment after another, piled together into something that you can't properly understand or comprehend as you collect the breaths, the minutes, the conversations, the touches. Death won't uncomplicate it. It will simply unravel everything you've built.

Simone didn't plan to die; she didn't think of it, didn't ask for it. Alison thought about the bathroom floor, the tile, the exploded window. She closed her eyes and saw Simone's hands, a Band-Aid on a finger, slim wrists, no jewelry. She wished she knew what her palms looked like. How long was her life line? What did she do with her hands in those final moments? Did she try to get out of the car? No, Alison remembered the seat belt was still clicked in place. It must have been fast, too fast to know what it was. Did time stretch out for Simone, as it had for Alison? Her clammy skin, her warm throat, her pink singlet, her purse, with the paper. With Alison's address.

She dropped the paintbrush on the newsprint underfoot and drew her breath sharply, shallowly, erratically. That thing Billy had said, after he'd fucked her. About feeling like it was OK to die. Peace is not consolation; it's resignation. Now it nagged at her, the reprieve. Picked at her like she was a scab not ready to flake off on its own yet. *You pulled it off somehow. Got the skin back, a little less perfect than it was before. Every time you look at it now, you see the skin you can't have anymore. The life you can't have anymore.*

She burned with it, and she knew that choice of word was dangerous, disrespectful even, but it felt true, the feeling that every moment she wasted here painting and then repainting her memories of the fire, she was wasting the time she'd been handed. Wasting what she'd been allowed to keep. But she didn't know how to do anything differently. She didn't know how to be worthy of the reprieve.

There was a knock at the door, and then a familiar voice carried in on the wind. "Ma? You there?"

Alison wiped her hands on the rag tucked into her shorts and hurried down the hall to let Sal's youngest in.

Patrick Marsh looked a lot like his mother. Broad shoulders hunched permanently, freckled face, and sunny blond hair that flew in all directions, regardless of length or product applied. When Alison opened the door his hazel eyes squinted into the dark of the hallway, crinkling the skin about his temples, making him look older, more serious than he really was. Alison smiled at him, punched him softly on the shoulder, ushered him into the hall.

"Pat, Sal'll be pleased to see you."

"Yeah, got the day off to come up, wanted to see with my own two eyes that everything's all right up here."

"We're OK, somehow managed to avoid the very worst of it. How'd you get up here? Roadblocks all over, fires still going in some parts."

"Pulled a few strings, helps to know the right people."

"I bet."

They walked down the hall, toward the kitchen, and then through the back door to the deck. Sal was in the yard, fiddling with her roses. "Sal, got a visitor," Alison called, her voice carrying on the wind.

"Sure smells like fire." Patrick wrinkled his nose as he spoke, and Alison took a moment to take in the scent on the air, diminished, sure, but the unmistakable taint of wood smoke lingered. She'd gotten used to it.

"Yeah, you can see the damage down the ridge there." Alison swept her arm up and out over the fields that stretched behind Sal's. She saw her approaching slowly from the rose garden. The sun was in her eyes, and it wasn't until she got closer that Sal could properly see the outline of her son set against the house. She grinned and began walking faster, waving happily, letting out a whoop as she got close. When she reached them, Sal wrangled her much-bigger boy into her arms.

"Patty! You didn't tell me you were coming! Is Andrew here too?" She looked past him toward the house.

"Nah, Ma, he's in court today, got that drugs trial; it's closing arguments. He said to tell you he's thinking of you and he'll come with me next time."

"He better. I suppose you left the dogs at home too?"

"The dogs? Geez, it's not a social outing. I took the day off work. I was worried about you, all alone up here with these fires."

"Ah, I'm all right, mostly missed town. Poor Alison had quite the fright, but she's keeping me company for a bit, so I'm not alone." Sal linked her arm through her son's and led him back into the house. "Come on, then, I'll make us a cuppa."

"Bit hot for tea, Ma, don't you think?"

"Nonsense. Never too hot for tea."

Alison stayed a little longer in the wood-scented afternoon air. In the distance there was smoke on the horizon; far-off fires continued to smolder. The utter silence of the burned-out bush still shocked. In these quiet moments, there was nothing to pierce the silence but the few birds that had returned. No crack and tumble of bark stripped by lizards, or sticks crunched under kangaroo foot; no possums scurrying up and down in the night. The silence took some getting used to. Inside she imagined the clink of spoon against fine bone china, the hiss of the kettle, and then Sal's muffled shout floated out on the breeze, imploring her to come in and have some tea.

But she continued to stare out at the blackened ground. Alison hadn't seen Patrick since she'd crashed the Marsh family Christmas last year—Sal invited Alison both Christmases since she'd come back to town, but the first year she hadn't taken the offer up. Just stayed at home, drinking her father's favorite '57 Nebbiolo and eating Lean Cuisine lasagna. If she was honest, mostly just drinking her father's '57 Nebbiolo. That first Christmas, with his old Rolling Stones records on the turntable and a glass, a bottle, two bottles, three, of his wine in her hand, Alison had let herself go, finally, completely, and cried, and cried, and cried, and cried. Torn up some of the family photographs, gone through her father's desk and piled the papers in the grate, burning everything she could find, little wisps of his life catching the air and floating as embers onto the slate hearth. Smashed an empty bottle on the cold tile of the bathroom as she heaved up gluey béchamel and slimy beef product.

She had thought herself beyond it. Untouchable. Unshakably mad, unable to feel anything but white-hot righteous rage. She hadn't expected to miss him so physically. The way his arms felt around her when he pulled her in for a hug. The sweat that greased the folds of his neck and collected at the small of his back, and wet his shirts through on hot summer days, mixed with his spicy cologne and created a musky atmosphere that announced his presence in every room of the house, even when he wasn't there anymore.

The wine tasted woody and plummy and burned when she sucked it down too fast, didn't let it breathe and expand like he told her to. *Barolo needs to get complicated. Breathe,* he would tell her, when he'd uncorked one and decanted it, Alison immediately reaching for a glass. *Give it a minute. You're always in a rush.* She would roll her eyes, poke out her tongue, deliberately pour an overlarge glass and grin at him like she did when she was a child and she knew she was doing the wrong thing.

It was easy to mourn her mother. It wasn't laden with resentment and words unspoken. It was just grief. Her face in a photograph made Alison well with tears, made her ache in her stomach and short of breath in her chest, but it didn't make her skin crawl or her cheeks burn. Too many things she never got to say.

"Death's a bastard," Sal said to her at the funeral. "It traps us forever in the moment that it happened. You're never going to be able to right what was wrong or say what you wanted to but didn't." She'd squeezed Alison's hand and let her be, standing there in the portico of the church, as the hearses pulled away, her parents on their way to the incinerator.

8.

In Sal's backyard, Alison spent too long staring out at the ridge thinking too hard about too many people she would never get to talk to again. She heard Sal call to her again, and she turned and slowly covered the distance back to the house. On the top step she stopped again, feeling eyes at her back, and turned, scrutinizing the dense, dry, empty bush off to the left. Was someone in there? Watching her? Who would do that? And why? Alison tried to listen, as though she might hear them watching her. Be able to pinpoint their breath as it left their body. She tried to shake it off, but the feeling stuck. She turned her back on the bush, heart pumping hard, and went inside.

The floor was sticky with booze and Alison didn't want to think about all the spit accumulated on the microphone, all those women singing "I Will Survive" or the men bleating out "Livin' on a Prayer," or everyone screaming together to "Bohemian Rhapsody"; better to follow the music and forget about it. She was half-cut already, and there was a vodka soda in her left hand, the microphone gripped in her right. She could feel him watching her as she slowly articulated the words, found her groove in the melody.

Alison leaned into the song, forced all her energy out through the lyrics, and got caught up in it, as she always did. Forgot for a minute where she was, and then she caught his eye. The blue shimmering in the half-light of the club's back room. He smiled at her. Mouthed the words as she sang, raised a lighter in his hand over his head, lit it and waved it back and forth placidly as "Total Eclipse of the Heart" reached its crescendo.

She was blushing; despite the booze and the enthusiastic crowd and the confidence that she was good at this particular performance, she felt a little off-kilter. She finished the song, sculled the remainder of her drink, and pushed back into the crowd, soaking up the applause.

"Well, how am I supposed to follow that?" Gil asked, smiling, already moving toward the microphone. The MC was cuing up the next track.

"All right, all right, that was Alison with 'Total Eclipse of the Heart,' and next we have . . . Gil, singing 'Alison.'" She groaned, but the smile couldn't be contained; she wasn't cool enough to pretend she didn't like it. He started to croon like Elvis Costello, a straight and faithful impersonation. It surprised her. He threw his whole body into it, leaned into the microphone, tensed his thighs and his calves and his shoulders and every vein in his neck as he worked through the verses. It was almost comical in its faithfulness, and she tried to suppress the giggles she felt bubbling up. He was taking it seriously. She should take it seriously.

Tried to forget that her dad used to sing it to her when she wanted a song before bed, rewrote the cues in her heart and her mind from a familial appreciation and love to something more carnal. The lyrics, she'd never really paid attention to before. They were dark. Possessive. She watched the screen as they turned from white to yellow, watched Gil's face as he sang at her. There was violence in the premise, but it was the kind of violence that was expected of women and men and love and possession.

"My aim is true," Gil crooned, and she imagined the arrow, Cupid pulling back the bow and tightening the string and squaring his plump little cherubic shoulders and slinging a spike of metal and wood into the core of her body. Penetrating her. The imagery didn't escape her. When he was done, he raised his hands high above his head and basked in the applause that came from every corner of the dank and sticky lounge. He hopped off the stage and pulled her up into his arms, pressed her against him. He was sweaty and smiling and stank of booze. They laughed together and fell in a heap on the couch, watched as someone else stepped up to the mic.

"'Alison,' huh?"

"You like it?"

"Very impressive. You've got quite the Elvis Costello in your back pocket." He made her the kind of flirt she hated. So eager to please. But he was the same. He kissed her and she enjoyed it. Felt safe and happy and confident when he was around. She thought that maybe it would be nice to introduce him to her parents. To let him stay forever in her bed. To take his name or at least wear his ring. When she looked forward into the years that hadn't unfolded yet, Alison saw only Gil and the way he made her feel and the way he held her and spoke to her and kissed her and felt inside her. Saw no other future. She couldn't think past him or imagine a time when she ever would. It was still early days, but she wanted everything from him.

The MC came over to them on his way to take a smoke break. She felt Gil's arm tighten around her.

"Hey, you guys were great, you gonna sing another one?" He smiled at them, made eye contact with Alison.

"Yeah." She laughed. "Maybe a duet."

"You askin'?" the MC shot back, winking.

"Sure, I'm game." Alison laughed again.

"She's taken," Gil interjected, more seriously than the moment required.

"Uh, I decide that, thanks." Alison forced a laugh, trying to lighten the moment.

"No intentions, buddy, just being friendly," the MC said, hands up in surrender. He nodded at them and headed out for a smoke.

There was a hummingbird in her heart. She couldn't placate it.

On the deck Alison shook herself loose from the memory. Forced herself to go back into the house. She heard Sal and Patrick arguing as she approached.

"There's plenty of room, Ma, we've got a spare with an en suite now the reno's done, and you'd be a lot closer to Suzie and Chris and the kids, get in some proper grandmother time."

"It's not that simple, Patty." Sal looked up and saw Alison standing in the doorway. "Pat's saying he thinks I should sell up, move outta here."

"I think you should consider it. Or at least spend your summers with us."

"Away from these conditions, you mean?"

"Is that so terrible an idea? This area is thick with dry bush, houses up against eucalypt up against scrub up against more bloody trees, not a drop of water at the moment. Sun looks at it wrong, it starts smoking."

"So dramatic; it was a bad fire, but it didn't get me. If this one didn't get me, I'll probably be all right."

Patrick shook his head and looked at Alison, exasperated. "Come on, Ma, you know that's not how it works."

"I don't want to live in Melbourne. I don't want to leave. End of discussion. Drink your tea."

Alison thought it was more likely to be the start of a much longer one. "How's South Yarra anyway, Patty? That a Toorak tractor I saw parked out front?"

"Got the Range Rover last month. Andy's found a new campsite he's mad for in East Gippsland, four-wheel-drive access only. Plus it's better for driving around Sooty and Sweep." He bit a chunk out of a Monte Carlo, dragged the uneaten half through his tea, and sucked the creamy center out of it.

"Bloody hell those dogs are spoiled." Alison laughed as she said it.

"Want a cuppa, Ally?" Sal had the pot poised to pour.

"Nah, Sal, I'm gonna leave you to it, wanna get back to work. Come stick your head in before you go, Patty."

She walked down the hall and into the study Sal had allowed her to transform into a makeshift studio. The trunks of the trees she'd been working on that morning stared back at her, mottled grays mixing together, a wall of death and destruction. Now, thinking too much about the fire made her skin crawl. Alison picked up the large flat brush and painted over the ghostly hues, first with the palest gray, and then with pink tones, like filthy frangipani muddied up on the street after a storm. The flatness of it depressed her. She added some red, cherry red, and then blended more white, more ash-colored gray. When she looked at it she realized the red was the red of Simone's car.

Alison closed her eyes for a minute and thought about Simone's face, the contours of her cheek, the shade of her hair, the blue of her eyes. She traced the outline of the jaw in palest peach and then began with tiny strokes in deeper tones to articulate the curves and rises of her bones and flesh. The paint and the canvas and the light and the brush all seemed to be working together, calling her to paint Simone.

She didn't notice Patrick standing behind her, in the doorway, until she interrupted herself to reposition the canvas to make the most of the sinking sun. She couldn't tell how long she'd been working, or how long he'd been standing there. She felt like she'd been caught out doing something she shouldn't. Alison felt the flush creep up her cheeks and forced a smile.

"You painting a self-portrait?" Patrick pointed at the canvas and Alison looked at it with fresh eyes, saw the small resemblances, the way the nose curved up, the fullness of the cheeks, the shade of brown she'd painted the hair, intending to go back later and add in the dirty blond. But the eyes, the eyes were unmistakably the same iridescent blue as the ones Alison had stared into on her driveway. She'd spent time mixing it, getting the exact hue on the brush, the right level of blue, the right creep of gray on the rims of the irises. It mattered to her that the eyes were just right.

"I don't have blue eyes, Patty."

"Who's this, then?" He asked the question with the tone of someone who thought they already knew the answer. "Looks a hell of a lot like you, just a little bit . . . off."

"It's not." Alison left his question unanswered and they stared at each other. Patrick squirmed a little, shifted about on his feet, rubbed his neck until it left a red mark.

"Mum seems glad to have you here. It's good for her to have some company right now, I reckon."

"Happy to help."

"Not sure if you're helping her or she's helping you, but either way seems like it's working out for the minute."

"I appreciate her letting me stay here, that's for sure."

"Can you do me a favor, Al?"

"Sure, what do ya need?"

"Can you talk to her about selling this place, moving down to Melbourne? She's too old for this stuff. Bushfires and drought and all that." He lowered his voice to a whisper and stepped in close. "But she doesn't want to leave the bloody rose garden."

"Why not? Just roses, can't she take cuttings or something?"

"Dad gave 'em to her, every single one, and when he died she mixed his ashes in with the blood and bone and fertilized the whole damn garden with him."

"Christ."

"She's pretty lonely up here. Only person she really enjoys seeing these days is you. Your mum's death hit her real hard. She's isolated, and we've been trying to budge her for years. I thought this fire might finally change her mind, but all she could talk about today was you, and that woman who died in your driveway."

"Simone."

"Yeah, sure. Look, it's sad. I'm sorry that you had to go through that, Al, and it does sound like your place came pretty close, but I'm worried about her. Next fire turns the other way, both my parents gonna be ashes on the hill I grew up on."

"Jesus, Pat."

"This is the reality of living up here, and when they were younger it was OK, but Dad's gone and Mum's no spring chicken. Fires aren't going to get better; climate change is gonna make 'em worse."

Alison knew Pat was right. Every fire season was worse

than the last, unless the low-lying countryside was flooded. More and more "catastrophic" danger days every goddamn year.

"OK, OK, I get it. I'll talk to her. No point letting that reno go to waste, now, is there?"

"Thanks, mate." He paused, like he was trying to decide to push his luck. "Mum told me 'bout you and Billy."

"Shit."

"Always wondered what it'd be like. Those dimples." Patrick smiled slyly, leaned in as close as he could, whispered, "Used to sneak a peak in the change rooms after footy sometimes. A mighty fine arse on that one."

"No comment." Alison laughed in spite of herself.

"He's been into you since school, you know."

"What? Don't be daft."

"While I was staring at that fine backside, he was telling anyone who'd listen, he was gonna take you to formal."

"Ugh, I wish you hadn't told me that. Anyway, he never even asked me to formal."

"Nah, in the end Nicole Easterbrook asked him first and all the guys knew she was easy so he decided getting laid was better than facing possible rejection from you." Patrick spoke with a tone that dripped with conspiratorial sarcasm. He was having fun with it. Alison wanted to know more, in spite of her determination not to let Billy get to her.

"You telling me he ditched me for Nicole?"

"You can't ditch someone you're not seeing in the first place. Besides, you ever even notice Billy before this week? I know who you were crushing on in senior, and it wasn't him."

Patrick and Alison had stuck close at school. He was the only one who wanted to get the hell out like she did. And she was the only one who knew he lusted after the boys on his footy team, not the girls who threw themselves at him at backyard parties, sloshed on goon—too far gone to remember they'd never even made out when Pat said they did the day after. They kept each other's confidences then, but after they'd moved to Melbourne for uni, they'd grown apart. Monash was too far away, and the art crowd and the law crowd weren't so naturally aligned.

"Well, nothing's changed, then. Still not crushing on him."

"You've always been a stone-cold bitch. Hard not to admire that."

"I don't think that's fair, Patty."

"You don't give a shit how many hearts you stand on and that's admirable, in its own way."

"It's also not true."

"Come on, Al, you ever even had your heart broken? It's like you've got a wall up between your feelings and your cunt." They used to talk like this, but it had been too long.

"OK, that's enough. You don't know anything about my heart. About what I've been through, about what happened with me and Billy. Don't pretend you do."

"I used to. You're the one who stopped calling. You're the one who wouldn't even see me when I came to Cairns for that conference."

Alison knew he was right. She'd wanted to be cool at university, so she had ditched everything that she thought was uncool, including Patrick, whom her art school friends thought was uptight and boring. Years later, when he'd called her from the airport and said he was in town that week, she'd panicked for other reasons. She was learning how jealous Gil was. She didn't want to complicate things. Didn't want to upset him. Didn't want Patrick to see that her life wasn't as wonderful as she pretended it was in emails home to her mother—emails she knew were shared with Sal over gin and tonics on the back deck. Told him she was pulling doubles at the hotel and couldn't get the time for a drink. No way.

"I can't take back the past, but I can tell you that it's not that fucking simple. I don't like Billy like that. It seemed like a good idea when I was six beers deep. But it wasn't. It was a terrible, terrible mistake and I don't know how to fix it."

"Some things can't be fixed."

"Thanks for the moral support."

"Hey, I'm Team Billy. That man is fine, and sweet, and he's really into you. You can't walk away from that; that's stupid."

"I can, and I am. End of discussion."

Patrick raised his hands in surrender. "So, who's the woman?" He nodded toward the painting.

"No one. Just . . . a face I liked."

"She really does look like you." He paused a second. "Looks a bit like that picture of the dead woman that's been in the papers this week too, come to think about it." He stared at her long enough to make it clear he knew what she was really doing, and then Patrick cupped his hand and hit Alison on the shoulder affectionately. "I gotta get back; Andrew's making dinner." He nodded good-bye, raised his voice and yelled farewell to Sal, and then let himself out the front door.

Alison stared at Simone's face. The eyes stared back at her. She closed her own eyes. Tried to remember if Simone really did look like that, or if she was already replacing her with her own face, her own memories, her own experiences. However irrationally, she felt a connection between them, like a rope tightening around her arms, crushing her chest, pushing her lungs and heart and ribs and diaphragm into one another. She was having trouble breathing. She was having trouble not feeling the heat on her face.

She was having trouble leaving the fire behind.

9.

Her mother picked the yolk of the egg out of the white, dug it out with a spoon, and smeared it on a thick slab of toast using the curve of the metal to swipe it across the bread. Alison watched as she shook salt over the white, hollowed out, clean almost, and then picked up one half and chewed on it absentmindedly as she took hot strips of crisp brown bacon out of the fat and laid them over the yolks.

"Give that to your father." Every day, two boiled egg yolks, spread on dry toast, topped with bacon. *So crispy it's almost burned, don't forget, love!* He'd been eating the same breakfast for as long as Alison could remember, almost certainly longer than she'd been alive. She picked up the plate and turned, not needing to move her body that far—it was more of a swivel in the small space between the counter and her little dining table in the poky flat in Cairns.

"Thanks, love. You gonna sit?" He pulled the chair out next to him, stretched expansively as if it were his own table. "Where's the paper?"

"I don't get the paper delivered, but I can run over to the store and get it."

"You get the *Age* up here?"

"No, Dad, you know I don't."

He waved a hand dismissively. "Forget it, then, not inter-ested in that Murdoch crap."

"News is news, Mal." Alison's mother spoke with her mouth full of egg white as she pulled two more smooth brown eggs out of boiling water and rested them gently on a plate.

"Not true. What you leave out is just as important as what you include."

Alison rolled her eyes. She'd heard this before. In the kitchen her mother was rummaging around in the cupboards. Opening one after another, making little sighing noises when what she wanted wasn't there.

"Ma, what are you looking for?"

"Where are the egg cups?"

"I don't have egg cups. I barely have a saucepan." She'd been here for months, in this apartment—her first alone—but it hadn't felt urgent to buy any of that stuff. To fill the cup-boards and drawers and behave like she lived there. She felt the disapproval in her mother's movements, the way she slammed the knife down hard on the counter, pushed the drawer closed so it caught on the slide and she had to jam it in, had to use more force than patience would require.

"We'll take you shopping today, then, get you the things you need." She came out of the kitchen, plonked a small plate with a chip in the rim down in front of Alison. Two eggs still in their shells rolled across its surface, hitting each other and the lip of the plate over and over and over. In the middle of the table she placed more bacon, some toast, butter, a tomato, and an avocado. She sat across from Alison and smiled at her. Picked up the tomato and began slicing it, shearing slabs off and letting them pile up on her plate.

"Well, I thought maybe today we could go snorkeling. You can go shopping anywhere; not every day you're on the reef." Alison cracked the shells of the eggs on her plate with a knife.

Sawed through the membranes and into the whites. They'd sat a little too long and were no longer soft. "These are hard, Ma."

"Sorry, love, you don't have a timer, I was guessing."

"Dad's was perfect." She hadn't meant it to be loud enough to hear, and even as the words came out she didn't really know why she'd said it.

"Lord have mercy. I didn't travel three thousand kilometers to be assessed on my egg-making abilities, young lady."

"I didn't ask you to come. I didn't even know you were coming."

"We wanted to surprise you. Up here all alone for your birthday. It didn't seem right." Alison felt sick. She didn't know how to take it back or to make it better and it frustrated her that she couldn't help but be frustrated by her mother, even when she was trying to be kind. Alison looked at her watch: 10:17 a.m. Only thirty hours to go. They stretched in front of her as though they were the last thirty hours of her life. She pushed the eggs around on her plate. "Have some toast, love. There's plenty of bacon too." Even when she was an ungrateful bitch, her mother was always trying to placate her.

Alison took the offered plate; maybe appeasement would make it easier. She felt like a little bit of her washed away in every conversation with her mother. Like a tide going out on the beach. She bit the inside of her lip. Waited for her father to diffuse the tension like he always did. But he stayed silent, munching on his goddamned toast, fiddling with his mobile phone. A key turned in the front door. *Shit.* She'd forgotten to tell Gil to stay away. She'd found out only at the last minute her parents were coming, and she wasn't ready for them to meet him yet.

Gil cracked the door open, pushed his head and shoulders into the room, and was halfway through calling out to her when he saw them there, sitting at the table. Alison was surprised at how quickly he was able to rearrange his face into a beaming smile.

"Oh, hello, who have we got here?" He strode across the room, Alison trying to avoid looking him in the eye. It wasn't the right time; it was too much, too early, too stressful. "Alison, you didn't tell me your sister was coming to visit."

Alison's mother laughed, even though she knew it was base flattery. Alison hated Gil in that moment. So quick to move to insincere charm when he was annoyed, or defensive, or trying to impress someone. He never did it with her. But outside their little world he could be a walking cliché.

"You know I don't have a sister. These are my parents, Malcolm and Marie. Mum, Dad, this is my . . . friend Gil."

She couldn't be sure, but she thought she saw thunder in his eyes for a moment, and then he was beside her, wrapping an arm around her waist and extending the other over the tabletop to shake her father's hand. Broad smile, a kiss on the cheek for her mother. Where he held her waist it pinched a little, and then he pulled her in tight and kissed her with significant intent.

"Friend. Well, gosh, Alison, I hope you don't let all your friends sleep over." It was delivered like it was meant to be a joke. She'd told him her parents were progressive. She'd told him about how they'd given her condoms in grade eleven and said if she was going to have sex, she should do it at home because it was safer than some boy's car. She knew that he knew that her parents wouldn't be shocked by the news she was sleeping with him. But she couldn't help feeling as though he was enjoying her discomfort. After she'd told him her privacy mattered. After she'd told him to back off, told him that when she was ready, they'd know about him. She wasn't ready. She tried to laugh it off.

"Gil! So nice to put a face to the voice." Her mother was still grinning like an idiot. "Love, it was Gil's idea we come up and surprise you. He called me the other day, said he'd already booked the flights." She was so flushed with the excitement of this secret that it made Alison want to punch her mother in the face. She didn't know why, but it felt like something important had been taken from her, and she knew it was as much Gil's fault as her mother's—and as much her father's fault, but she was mad only at Marie.

"Oh gee, Marie, that was supposed to be our secret, remember?" Gil spoke with patience and levity, but Alison knew he was pissed off to be found out. She knew he'd wanted this to happen without her finding out he'd been involved. He'd been at her for weeks to tell her parents about him. Didn't understand why she hadn't. Couldn't drop it. She felt the bile rise, pushed it back down again, forced a smile.

"Well, here we all are. What a lovely birthday surprise. Thank you all, truly." She hoped it sounded sincere. She didn't want them ever to know how much she hated it. Gil caught her eye, held it. She smiled fiercely. He leaned in and kissed her on the forehead. Brushed his lips against her ear and whispered, "Happy birthday, baby. Now we're official."

10.

The back door of the rental car opened first, and a small, pale blond woman with a familiar nose and jawline got out. Oversize sunglasses obscured most of her face, but her lips were feathered at the edges the way they got after a solid crying jag. Her clothes were a little out of order, rumpled on one side, like she'd been lying down. She leaned on the doorframe, swaying a little. Was she drunk already? A man got out of the driver's seat. Squinting into the sun, he lifted his hand to shade his eyes and nodded in Alison's direction. She nodded back.

Simone Arnold's parents. Anne and Bob looked out of place in the car park of the Imperial in the late afternoon sun. There was something missing, something vacant about the way they covered the ground from the car to the beer garden where Alison was standing in the doorway, waiting for them.

They followed her to a table out of the sun and sat down. They still hadn't said a word.

"Can I get you a drink? Beer? They've got tea and coffee too, if you're off the stronger stuff."

Bob Arnold cleared his throat, looked toward his wife, who shook her head with the smallest motion possible, and said,

"I'll have a Fourex if they've got it, thanks. And two waters would be great while you're up."

Alison smiled, went into the bar and called Molly over, placed the order. Added a vodka soda for herself, extra lime. She carried the tray back to the table and tried not to slop the beer out of the pint glass as she set it down. Waited to see who would ask the first question.

Bob Arnold wouldn't look Alison in the eye. She wasn't sure exactly what Detective Mitchell had told them about the conversation they'd had at Alison's house two days before.

"Detective Mitchell told me Simone lived on the Esplanade, which is where I lived up there. It's a beautiful spot." Alison looked at Simone's parents. Did they too imagine Simone was her friend?

"Did you help her?" Anne Arnold asked, so softly Alison wasn't sure at first if she'd actually said anything or if she'd imagined it.

"I'm sorry, I don't understand. I didn't know your daughter—I told the detective that. When I found her in the driveway, she was already . . . gone." Alison took a large gulp of her drink.

"You really didn't know her?" Anne Arnold's face crumpled with the disappointment.

"No, I didn't. Why would I lie?" Her tone was agitated despite her attempt to stay cool. She really had wanted to meet the Arnolds, see what they were like, try to find out something, anything, about their daughter, but the conversation with Detective Mitchell had made her change her mind, and when the detective had called to say the meeting was set up, Alison tried to get out of it. But the city cop had talked her round, promised not to be there, said the Arnolds were hoping to speak with her and could she do them the courtesy, since their daughter was dead, and they were grieving? Alison hadn't expected they too would assume she knew more than she really did. Was the detective trying to trick her into admitting something?

"This is a mistake. Mr. and Mrs. Arnold, I'm so sorry for your loss, but I can't help you at all."

Anne Arnold was silently sobbing now, her head resting on her husband's chest.

"I'm sorry," Alison said again. "I don't know what the detective told you, but I honestly had never met your daughter. I'm very sorry she died. I want to help but I don't know how I can. Anything you want to know about the fire, or how Simone was when I found her, or anything I could tell you that might help you, I'll do my best to answer your questions. But I can't tell you why she was here, or what she was doing."

The Arnolds looked at each other, and Bob shook his head. Maybe she should tell them about the slip of paper with her address on it, but Alison couldn't form the words, and she didn't want to be more involved with these people and their grief. It was too much.

"We just want to know anything, anything at all." He looked down at his shoes and tightened his arm around his wife's shoulders.

"Did she look peaceful?" Anne Arnold asked through her tears.

Alison paused a minute before she spoke again, sanitized her memory to make it easier.

"She looked like she was asleep. There was nothing to show she was dead; when I reached out to her I thought maybe I could shake her and she'd wake up. Her face was kind of blank, and her eyes were closed."

But she hadn't shaken her, hadn't touched her, hadn't tried to revive her, she reminded herself, the hot shame of her own inadequacy flushing her cheeks pinkest rose.

She was curious now, curious again about the address and the coincidence of them both living in the same place in Cairns. The same age, the same place. According to Patrick—and her own, somewhat hazy memory—the same face.

"Do you know why she might have been in Victoria? What she was doing?" Alison asked, casting around for a place to begin.

"Her ex-boyfriend, fella named Michael, he was violent. When she broke up with him, he wouldn't leave her alone. One day she told us she had a plan to get rid of him, and then that was it. We never saw her again. For ages we thought he might have killed her." Simone's father talked with an even pace and understated volume. When he stopped it took Alison a moment to realize he was finished. He took a sip of his beer.

Alison closed her eyes, saw the headline in the article in the *Age* a couple of weeks ago. A woman killed by her partner every week last year. She knew—she really did know—how possible that was.

"He did kill her. She was running from him. If it weren't for him, she'd have been home and safe, not out here in a fire." When Anne Arnold spoke this time, she enunciated every word like she was spitting out venom.

"The police told me they're not sure if she died in the fire or from something else?"

"Yeah, *someone* else," Bob said. "The Queensland police were supposed to be watching him, but I guess they weren't really looking so hard."

"You really think he killed her in the middle of the fire and then escaped somehow?"

The Arnolds looked at each other. Alison remembered that feeling, in the minutes after the fire, on the driveway, that feeling like someone else was there, like she was being watched. She pushed it back down.

"Like Annie said, even if he didn't physically do it, he's the reason she was here in the first place." He pulled a battered photograph out of his pocket. A Polaroid. Slipped it over the uneven wood of the table, his fingers obscuring the faces until he pulled them away and Alison could see them properly. Blue eyes flecked gold, shimmering in the flash's light, that unmistakable jawline, the sweep of his hair, the smirk-smile.

Gil. Alison blinked. Checked again, to be sure. It was him all right. Her Gil.

Simone beside him, his arm around her as though he possessed her. She felt the pinch of his fingers on her waist like a reflex she couldn't contain. The piece of paper with her address. The overwhelming sense of unease she'd been feeling. It was him. Alison felt her chest constrict and she tried to keep her breathing steady, tried to keep her expression neutral. She didn't want them to know. She couldn't explain it. She needed *a minute*. To think about what all this meant before anyone else found out.

"I'm so sorry I can't be more help. If I think of anything, I promise I'll let you know." She didn't tell them about the sounds in the bush, the penetrating feeling like someone was staring in those moments before she found Simone. She didn't tell them her ex-boyfriend was their daughter's ex-boyfriend. Gil. He must have been there. Where was he now?

Alison wanted to get out. She felt clammy and cold despite the heat of the day and the warmth from the vodka, which churned in her stomach. She downed the rest of it, shivered a little, and smiled in the Arnolds' direction. "I've got to go, sorry. Please stay in touch, let me know anything, anything at all." Alison hastily scrawled her number on the back of a coaster, handed it to Bob. He shook her hand, weakly. Anne nodded good-bye, wiped a tear from the apple of her cheek. Alison thought she could see suspicion in the woman's eyes. A lingering accusation.

As Alison unlocked the door to Sal's car she looked back into the beer garden, saw a middle-aged man she'd never met before slide into the seat she'd just vacated. He held out a hand to Bob Arnold and shook hard, clapping the spare one on the older man's back. Journalist, probably, Alison thought, as she slung her legs into the car and twisted the key in the ignition. He reminded her of her father, the way he held himself.

"OK, we have vodka, and we have half a bottle of Chardy, and I know there's a slab of warm VB in the garage." Meg whirled around, holding the Chardonnay in her left hand, waggling it. "This is three days old. It's probably off." She screwed up her nose and walked with purpose toward the sink, unscrewing the wine's cap.

Alison rushed to grab the bottle from her before she could dump it out. "Whoa. What are you wasting good wine for?"

"It's three days old. Mum says if you don't drink it in the first twenty-four hours, it goes bad."

Alison laughed. "Your mum is having you on. It's a screw top. It's been in the fridge. It's fine!" She opened the bottle and sniffed. Notes of straw and sugar, nothing sour—crisp apples and new oak furniture. She swigged it back, straight from the neck. It was fine. Nothing more, nothing less. She pulled two glasses from Meg's cupboard. Filled them up.

Meg picked hers up, examined it. "High tide, huh?"

Alison laughed. "I thought we were getting wasted."

"Oh, we are." Meg gulped back the wine as though it were water.

"Well, as enticing as warm VB sounds, I think I'll chance the Chardy." She raised her glass and clinked it against Meg's and they both drank deeply.

"Let's play a game, Alison King."

All her life, people had called Alison by her full name. Like it was a joke. Some kind of royal taunt. "What kind of game?"

"Why did you move back to Lake Bend?" Meg was staring at her with an intensity that felt unsettling.

"That's not a game I'm familiar with," Alison replied.

Meg smiled. "I'll go first. After uni, I got a job in the Victorian Public Service. It was my dream job. I wanted more than anything in the world to advise the premier, to make a difference, and suddenly I was in briefings with his chief of staff. But it was so boring and, well, anticlimactic. The political advisers never listened to the public servants, and the politicians only listened to their advisers—if they listened to anyone at all. And then, I was home for a christening, and the mayor at the time—you remember Mayor Jackson? She saw me there, and she said she heard I was in the public service now, and she'd asked around. The council's chief of staff needed a new EA. Was I interested? She knew every right thing to say. And the money was somehow better. So I quit the public service and moved back to Lake Bend." She drained her wineglass and refilled it. "Now you."

Alison didn't know what to say. So she took a deep breath and decided it didn't matter anymore. "Well, my parents died. But you know that. So I came to bury them, and it coincided with some other shit in my life and I just . . . stayed."

Meg shook her head. "No. Not enough detail. What *really* happened?"

Alison emptied her glass. The wine bottle was empty now too. She went to the freezer and pulled out the vodka. Poured herself two generous fingers. Took a swig. "My boyfriend beat me. And then he cheated on me. And I could stand the beatings, but I couldn't stand the cheating."

It was quiet in Meg's kitchen. Alison thought, *What's that thing people say? You could hear a pin drop.* Alison thought that was too loud. You could hear cotton growing. You could hear silk moving. You could hear the sun shining. The moon glowing. Alison could hear the blood in her arteries, pumping around her body, and then, spent, back into her heart and lungs, to try all over again.

"I didn't know he hit you." It was odd, the way Meg said this. Like she had known he'd cheated but not that he'd been the total-demon-boyfriend package. Alison thought cheating wasn't really shocking; lots of people did it. But lots of people hit their partner too. *We shouldn't be shocked by it. It's utterly, devastatingly pedestrian.*

"He did. And then he cheated, and I guess that made it easier for me. He wasn't obsessed with me anymore, when I ended it. He was trying to control someone else. He was willing to let me go." It felt weird to say that out loud. She'd never told anyone the whole truth before. "That's why I'm here. It feels safe. It feels like a home that won't break me, no matter how sad I am about Mum and Dad. At least here, I can see them—or their ghosts, anyway—on every corner. It's nice to see friendly ghosts instead of scary ones."

Meg didn't say anything for a moment, seemingly gathering her placations and consolations into a delicate bouquet, and then, at the last second, throwing it in the bin. Instead, she raised her glass above her head. Alison lifted hers in reply. They drank, the vodka a flame in her chest. "Welcome home, then. I'm fucking glad you're here."

She drove without knowing where she would go. She needed to think it through. If Gil was Michael—if Gil was Simone's ex—Simone had to have had a real reason to be heading for Alison. What did she want from her? And why did it feel so important to Alison that no one know they were connected?

She should tell Billy. She should talk to Billy. She should give him everything. But she didn't have anything to give him. She didn't have the note. She didn't know what Simone wanted. All she knew was that she and Simone shared an ex. And Simone was dead.

Alison decided to keep it to herself for a little while. Maybe she could figure out what it was all about on her own. Maybe no one here ever needed to know the truth about who she was, and who she'd been. Meg knew, but Meg was gone. Gil was unpredictable. And he was terrifying. She didn't know if he knew she lived here. She didn't know what was going on, and she needed a lot more information before she told anyone about this connection. Gil could be capable of anything. He was a force all his own, and Alison didn't know what Simone had wanted from her, but she did know that she didn't want Gil to know she was here. She didn't want him anywhere near her. But she also needed answers.

If she told the police about their connection, it would all come out and she'd have no control. But maybe, if she could figure out what Simone had wanted from her, she could deal with it, whatever it was, without him ever knowing. It felt important to try. It felt important to know. It felt important to figure it out on her own.

After dinner that night Alison and Sal went down to the pool and cooled their feet in the water, sitting on the concrete edge and sipping whiskey while the silent bush absorbed the night. Alison wanted to tell Sal the truth. But instead she babbled.

"I can't get her out of my head. She's my age. She's from the same building as me in Cairns. It's creepy."

"It might be creepy, but maybe it's all a big coincidence. You never met her in Cairns?"

"No."

"You're sure?"

"Yes, I guess so. I don't know. I met a lot of people there, but I feel like I'd remember her—she sorta looks like me." Alison didn't say it: *She was the woman he beat after me.* She kept her mouth shut. Buried it down in the pit of her lungs, where it made it harder to take the deepest of breaths, the ones she really needed now.

"Does she? Or do you want her to?" Sal was gentle, but serious.

Alison looked away, didn't like the scrutiny. Even concrete things like faces were unknowable now. Nothing was solid. "I don't know her and I'm not sure what to do." Lying to Sal felt like dropping an egg on the floor and watching it seep into the cracks in the tile, little flecks of scarlet in the yolk, reminders of the bird it could have been, before now, before it wasn't even food anymore.

"Why do anything?" Sal asked, sounding like she wasn't quite convinced Alison didn't know more about Simone.

"Because what if she needed me, if I was supposed to help her somehow?"

"Oh, please, Alison. Figuring out what she was doing in your driveway won't bring her back from the dead."

"I can't stop thinking about her." It was a voice she didn't recognize, smaller than usual, less sure.

"I know." Sal reached out, squeezed her hand. "I think you should try, though."

"Easier said than done." Alison drained her glass. As she reached over to refill it from the bottle, she thought she saw movement in the bush down by the rose garden. She squinted toward the trees but couldn't see anything out of the ordinary. Nothing that shouldn't be there. Nothing that couldn't be explained by her imagination. The breeze rustled the leaves and Alison shivered where it touched her.

He rolled it slow, taking his time to make it tight, the paper fat to bursting with the leaf inside. The ceiling fan clicked around, blades blurred with speed, as it tried to push the heat away. High summer, so humid, it hurt to move; so hot, they never wanted to. Gil held the seam up to the light that snuck between the edge of the wooden blind and the window frame. The thick beam danced with dust and hit Alison across her bare stomach, where the sun raised beads of sweat without even trying. She shifted on the sheet, dug her elbows into the soft of the mattress, and sat up as high as she could.

"You gonna light it or just admire it?" she asked, a little teasing in her tone.

Gil flicked the lighter so the flame burst up and put the joint between his lips. He took his time lighting it. Sucked in the smoke, deep. Once. Twice. Three times. On the final exhale, he passed it over to her. He snapped the Zippo lid open and shut, the light glinting off the spade carved in the side. Alison drew in a deep breath, felt it stick in her lungs like always; it filled her up and made her feel like there wasn't any air left on earth to breathe. It caught in her throat coming back up and she coughed, tried to mask it, coughed again, forced herself to draw another plume of smoke down into her lungs, and held it there.

He was stroking the skin on the inside of her thigh, just above the bend of her knee. His fingers were even warmer than her skin, and where he touched her, she felt as if she were being scalded. *It's too soon to be stoned.* She drew in another puff and closed her eyes. She felt his hand find hers, take the joint gently from her, Gil not ever saying a word. Gil's other hand kept tracing the skin on her leg, wiping away the sweat that was accumulating. Alison opened her eyes. The fan still beat relentlessly. He was lying with his feet up near the head of the bed, his head hanging over the end, in the shade of the lowest part of the room. His free hand meandered higher on her leg. She focused on the fan, watched it spin, a perfect endless windmill, propelling the air inside the room who knows how far with every spin. The smoke from the joint mixed with the heavy air and circulated as if the bedroom were Alison's lungs.

"You feel it?" Gil's voice floated across the space between them, but even though it reached her ears, Alison thought it was too far away to understand it properly. She imagined it climbing down her ear canals, into the cavity of her mind, whispering to her synapses. There was electricity in there, a spark, like the one that lit the flame that lit the joint that she'd just inhaled.

"Do you think, if we put a lot of lighters together, connected them somehow, and then made them spark, you could make them think?"

Gil laughed. "Right, guess you're feeling it." How long had they been lying here? The sun still snaked across her skin. The fan still beat about as fast as her heart when he touched her. She understood the question he was asking too late to stop her reply.

"It feels like your fingers are flames."

He rolled off the bed, set the joint in the ashtray, shuffled out of the room. She heard him in the kitchen, opening the fridge, the seal sucking away from the frame; some rustling. No, he was in the freezer—*He's not in the freezer*. She visualized the plumes of fresh cold that would have rushed him when he opened it, the way they peeled off the walls, endlessly frigid. He came back, ran his cold hands over her shoulders, leaned in to kiss her, his mouth like the inside of the freezer, an ice cube stuffed into the side of his cheek. He passed it to her, and instinctively, Alison spat it out.

"Gross, Gil." She pushed him away gently, laughing. He picked up the ice from where it was melting on the sheet, cradled it in his palm, and ran it all over her stomach. She shivered. Felt the goose bumps rise where it touched her. She was hot and cold at once. "Pass me a puff, please." Eyes closed, she stretched her hand out. She felt him nestle the diminishing stick between her index and middle fingers. It was almost gone, and she sucked it hard to get what she could from it. The ice on her stomach had made a pool of lukewarm water. She felt Gil take the spliff from her lips and then she felt a quick flash of heat as it sizzled out in the pool. She bolted up, shocked. "Shit. What the fuck?"

"Sorry, I saw the water and I figured it wouldn't hurt you. I'm always putting out candles with wet fingers. What's the difference?"

It hadn't hurt, really, had just shocked her like static electricity. The water had splashed off her when she'd sat up, and there was no crescent moon marking the spot. Her head swam. He leaned in and kissed her where he'd done it. Let the rough wetness of his tongue attempt a physical apology. Alison lay back down. How many sparks did it take to create a thinking, living being? How many sparks did it take to burn one?

11.

Alison had found it easy to slip unnoticed into a sort of malaise.

Drink, sleep, paint. Repeat.

Her paintings had begun as landscapes, echoing the distress of her surrounds, but they had quickly become portraits of Simone. She painted her hair, her eyes, that same nose she'd seen wrinkle up on Anne Arnold's face just days after she'd seen it gray and lifeless on Simone's. Her lips were always a pale pink-blue, thin, a perfect rosebud. Sometimes she blocked out the lines of her own face with Simone's hair, her own green eyes in place of Simone's gray-blue ones. She saw those eyes staring at her from the driver's license every time she fell asleep.

She began to replay in her mind the years she'd spent in Cairns, wondering if she'd ever met Simone. Seen her in the car park, passed her at the shops, swum near her at the pool, drunk at the same bar. It seemed incredible she didn't know her. That she'd never met her before. That somehow, Simone was the woman who'd saved her from Gil, and she'd never met her.

No matter how much time she spent searching her memories, she came up with nothing. She'd read a long report on the mystery of the dead girl in the *Age*. Simone Arnold, Cairns native, missing for a few weeks, rumored violent ex-boyfriend, mysteriously pops up dead in the middle of a massive bushfire in Victoria. Thousands of kilometers from home, no explanations as to why immediately forthcoming. There weren't any more answers there than she'd been given by Detective Mitchell, and there was nothing about Gil connecting them. She was glad no one had put it together. But then, how would anyone? No one here had ever met Gil. No one here knew anything about him but his name. She wanted to help Simone, help herself, but right now, she didn't know how to without putting herself in danger.

It looked as though Simone Arnold's death would be the subject of a coronial inquiry. The autopsy hadn't been conclusive as to the cause. As it raced up the hill toward Alison's house the car had been struck by the falling log. The force of the impact was probably the cause of the bruising on Simone's chest and stomach, and the bump on her head that caused the bleeding that surprised Detective Mitchell and made her suspect something other than the bushfire was to blame.

But her neck was a problem, because the bruising could have been from the crash, or it could have been from the hands of a murderer closing around her windpipe, stealing what little air was left for her to inhale as the flames licked closer. While the idea of a murderer seemed incredible, sensational, ridiculous, the press had taken it up with gusto.

One theory had a strangler wringing the life out of Simone before being obliterated in the fire as he tried to escape. Another was that he'd gotten out as the wind changed, and was now probably halfway to Adelaide. Alison, still the only one who knew about the address Simone had carried with her, knew Simone was in her drive for a reason. She didn't know what the reason was, but she didn't believe a person fleeing that fire would turn up a driveway instead of continuing on the wide, flat highway as fast as they could for as long as they could. No. But the more she thought about it, the less sense it made for Simone to be on her way to Alison's house. She didn't like to think about the possibility that she'd been near a killer as she'd walked out after the fire that afternoon.

If Simone had been murdered, then the murderer had to have hidden nearby, or to have been nearby, retreating, when she came across the body. There was no way he hadn't been.

Knowing this, Alison was unable to hold a conversation, or complete a task, without Gil's face popping into her mind again. And again. She was sure it was him. She didn't know why she felt compelled to keep that to herself for now, but it felt too private to reveal until she knew for sure. She wanted the police to say the whole thing was an accident, to absolve Gil, which might then absolve Alison.

Alison woke up hot and sticky. The ceiling fan wasn't doing anything, and the bed felt damp from her sweat. She lay there, scrolling through her messages. Past Billy, past Jim telling her something about their fences, past Molly from the Imperial asking if she wanted to swing by later, to the last exchange she'd had with Meg.

Are we still on for Sunday?

Yeah, for sure

I'll come about 6?

Perf

Should I bring anything?

Booze? But otherwise I've got it covered

Cool

And then:

Are you ok?

Meg?

I know things are crazy but can you text me back and tell me you're ok?

Now Alison thought they might never talk again. It felt knotted somehow, this grief she carried from this "once in a century" fire. Once in a century on paper, but they came around more regularly these days. Her parents, that was just . . . pain. A hole that would never be filled. An ache that would never fully subside. Like the feeling in a bone you broke once when it rains. A healed deep cut on the finger, one that hits a nerve and tingles forever after.

Alison rolled out of bed and found something to shrug over her body. A T-shirt of her mother's she'd found when she'd finally cleaned out her parents' closets. It was one she'd worn to death when Alison was little. Soft cotton, with a large black swan and the words "Swan Lager" printed across it. From her parents' trip to Western Australia before she was born. It was almost threadbare in places, but somehow, even after all the times Alison had worn and washed it, it still smelled like her mother. Her denim shorts felt rigid and due for a wash, but she shimmied into them anyway. She heard Sal moving around down the other end of the house; the sound of the radio floated in disembodied snatches down the hall toward her.

In the kitchen, the kettle was starting to steam and toast popped up in the toaster. Sal turned as she stood in the doorway, watching her, and jumped at the sight of Alison.

"Goodness, girl, I didn't know you were up." The music for the news bulletin blared, and Sal reached for the dial, turning it down.

"You don't want to listen?" Alison saw the paper already in the recycling pile and went to fish it out.

"You don't want to read it, love, just a lot more names. No comforts there." Alison had clocked it before, but she hadn't been sure until now.

"Sal?"

Sal looked at her. "What?"

"I know it's awful, but we can't . . . we can't pretend it didn't happen."

She saw fury pass quickly across Sal's face. "Don't you try and handle me as well."

"I'm not trying to—"

"Chris called yesterday and he wouldn't back off about it. *How are you feeling, Ma, must be a shock, are you taking care of yourself?* Of course it's a bloody shock. Of course I feel awful, but learning all about it isn't going to make anything better. It isn't going to bring anyone back, is it?"

"But don't you think that at least acknowledging the people we've lost might help you . . ." Alison couldn't even finish the sentence because she knew exactly what Sal was trying to get at, and why. She couldn't even wrap her head around Meg's being gone; how would reading about all the other people she knew she'd never see again make it better? She also knew that after her parents died, she'd read everything she could get her hands on. The police report, the autopsies, medical journal articles about the specific injuries they'd had, the weather reports for the time of the crash, the history of the spot where they'd veered off the road. As though the knowledge of the little details, the mechanics of it, would somehow make it smaller, manageable, bearable.

Alison watched as her mother moved through the aisles at Target. She stopped and fingered a towel, the loops of cotton pressed under her palm. She frowned.

"Not very good quality, are they?" She moved on to the more expensive ones. "We should go to Adairs."

"Mum, I really don't need anything. I'm fine."

"Alison, your father dried himself off with your childhood beach towel this morning." Alison loved that towel. It was almost sheer in places, but it reminded her of long days on sweltering sand and the uncomplicated perfection of not having anyplace in the world she had to be.

"I'm just saying, Mum, you don't have to furnish my flat, OK? I am fine. I have what I need, and I don't want a lot of stuff." She gestured around herself at the shelves stacked high with towels and linen. A few aisles over, plates and cups, cutlery and glassware, and then the pots and pans. The trolley her mother had commandeered at the entrance was still empty, but Alison knew it could be very full, very quickly, if she didn't put a stop to this nonsense. Her phone vibrated, and she pulled it out of her pocket.

How's the homewares hunt?

Alison sighed. Mum wants to buy me the whole bloody store.

She watched as the three dots appeared. Gil was typing.

She's just trying to tell you she loves you Ally

105

Alison stared at the message for a full minute, not sure how to respond. He didn't get it. Even she didn't understand it. How much her mother aggravated her, just by trying to be nice to her. It felt forced. It felt like because they didn't have that easy rapport she shared with her father, somehow every gesture was futile even before it was attempted. It wasn't that she didn't love her mother; she did. A lot. She just didn't understand her, and she never had. Her mother had been a mystery to her since Alison had been old enough to understand her own body, her own mind, enough to see all the ways they weren't the same.

Other girls were carbon copies of their mothers. Sweet little mini-mes. Same hair, same body on the way one day, same eyes and smile. Same polite little giggle and preference for salad. They tried their mums' shoes on and coveted their dresses. Alison remembered how Suzie Marsh used to get in trouble smearing Sal's lipstick right across her face. Alison looked in the mirror and couldn't find her mother. She could see the slope of her father's brow, the tint of his irises. She could trace his shoulders, and his strength as she chopped wood in the winter, the axe making clean breaks in the trunks, heavily finding its mark. She hadn't gotten her mother's beautiful black curls, or her slender feet. She hadn't inherited her mother's beautiful singing voice or her sweetly trusting disposition. She was a ball of nerves and cynicism. Her mother liked to play the piano, to read long books about bare-chested stable boys and lonely housewives, and to collect fine porcelain from antique shops. Alison couldn't stand antique shops.

"What about this one, love—you like red?" She was holding up a thick, plush bath sheet, big enough to wrap two people luxuriously. "This'll go well with that wall you've painted in the bedroom."

"I don't keep bath towels in the bedroom, Mum."

"All right, I just meant, it's the same aesthetic. Come on, let me, would you?"

Alison forced herself to smile. "Yeah, OK, that one looks good." She saw a look of satisfaction briefly cross her mother's face, a tiny flickering of pride that she had gotten something right, picked something her contrary daughter liked. Alison hated it. She hated how mean she felt, just because she had different taste from her mother. She knew Marie was trying; she knew she was a shit of a kid for being so difficult. But she was also incapable of stopping herself. She went over to her mother and squeezed her hand.

"Thanks, Mum. I love you."

"I love you too, darling girl. I wish you would let me take care of you."

"How many people get killed by falling trees?" Alison asked Sal, suspecting the answer would be automatic.

"Fourteen across the country since 1960." Sal said it almost without thinking. And then the kettle began to wail and whistle. They didn't talk as Sal poured the hot water into the pot. Alison got mugs down from the cupboard, milk from the fridge, sugar from the table. Sal busied herself buttering her toast. Scraping a thin layer of Vegemite over the top. Alison fished the paper out of the bin and turned to the fire coverage. "It'll only make you sad, love." Sal said it almost too softly for Alison to hear.

"Fourteen. It must . . . Fourteen."

"Geoff was really unlucky. You know we used to joke about it. He'd get ten tickets in the meat raffle and the one right after his would win. He'd always get a run of red lights when he was trying to get somewhere fast in the city. He barely ever caught a fish unless someone else picked the spot. If he'd been at your house during the fire, the wind wouldn't have changed." Sal slapped a hand over her mouth, as though she'd shocked herself with her words. Alison began to laugh. It hiccupped out of her almost involuntarily, and she lost control of it. Sal laughed too.

Alison looked at the paper. Started reading the roll call. Halfway down, there it was. She knew now why Sal had tried to stop her.

"Meg."

"I'm sorry, love. Cam's mum said they identified her—"

"Don't tell me." She crumpled the paper up and threw it back in the bin. Sal turned the radio back up. The cricket was starting. Alison slowly poured herself some tea. Blood rushed to her head. She felt it pulsing in her ears, pressing on her temples.

"Alison?" Sal's voice sounded woolly. "Alison, your cup's full." Alison heard the words, but they didn't quite register. Then she felt the smack of the heat as the tea sloshed over the rim of the mug and over her fingers wrapped around the handle. Without thinking she dropped the mug and the teapot. They shattered all over the floor, tea spewing everywhere. She heard Sal curse, felt her arms on her own, pulling her out of the way. Alison looked at the mess she'd made. She grabbed the paper back out of the recycling and tossed it over the tannins seeping into the wood. She felt the tears on her cheeks, and sound returned to full volume in an overwhelming calamity of activity. Sal's cursing, the crowd's roar on the radio, the thwack of a ball on a bat, and over and over again, the replay of the splintering teapot, all clattering across her consciousness. She watched the newsprint blur and run as it mopped up the tea. Sal on her knees. Alison not knowing how to join her. Meg was gone. So many people were gone. Simone was gone. Alison wondered again why it was that she was not.

———

"At what point is sleeping supposed to get easier, do you think?" It was 2 a.m. and Alison and Sal were up on Sal's back deck, drinking whiskey and playing gin.

"Probably once you stop thinking about that girl so much, I'd imagine," Sal replied.

Sal didn't mind the late nights. It had been almost a decade since Geoff died when a huge gust of wind blew a rotting gum down on him while he was fishing with mates on the Yarra. Lonely but not willing to admit it, Sal had spent the week encouraging Alison to stay.

Alison had spent the days drinking late, sleeping late, and painting through the afternoon. Every day the papers carried more reports of deaths, people who'd initially survived, but their bodies couldn't cope and they died in the hospital, or a whole family identified from the DNA in a miraculously unburned toothbrush. The problem with a fire like this one was that so many people had simply disappeared, turned to ash on the ground, and been carried away on the wind. Each day there was news of a classmate or friend, or the family of someone close to her now gone forever. Small pictures and short paragraphs on their lives, buried in the middle of the paper, or tacked onto the end of a bigger story about the fires in the nightly news bulletin. There was still so much no one knew, so much no one could explain. None of what had happened really seemed to make a lot of sense.

"If she was murdered, it must have been that ex-boyfriend, don't you think?" Alison said, discarding an unwanted jack. Bringing him up was like twisting a pin into the flesh of her palm. It felt good and terrible all at once, and sometimes, it felt like the only thing to do.

"Alison, I think we have no idea what happened to that poor girl and the more you think about it, the less likely it is that you will ever be able to go to bed without a bottle of whiskey and a game of cards that never bloody ends."

Alison rearranged her hand and drained her glass. She laid her cards out faceup on the table. "Gin!"

"Christ, again? You've sold your soul for a good hand of cards."

"If only that were true, Sal, I'd make a killing at the casino."

Sal laughed and pulled the cards into a stack; she tucked them back into their case and pushed back her chair. "That's it for me. I'm done like a dinner," she said, and headed back into the house, busying herself in the bathroom.

Alison sat out in the darkness. Trees swayed in the early-morning breeze, the stillness of the night echoing the eerie darkness of the eye of the firestorm. She felt a shiver run down her spine and got up from her chair, reaching for the whiskey bottle to pour herself another measure. Standing on the back deck, Alison saw as far as the weak light of the moon would let her.

Sal's place, high up on the top of a hill that fell away to reveal, in daylight, acres of summer-gold fields stretching the one hundred and fifty kilometers to Melbourne, seemed both distant from—and very connected to—the wider world. The city's skyline sparkled now, its artificial glow like a distant lighthouse on the inky horizon. It was hot still, and the sweat stuck to Alison's chest, her forehead, and her arms, beads collecting on her neck and trickling down her spine. She heard Sal finish up in the bathroom. She picked up the bottle, the glass, and the cards and flicked off the light as she fastened the screen shut tight behind her.

Alison headed down the hall and put the bottle and glass on her bedside table, undressed in the half-light of the lamp, and wrapped herself in a towel. She padded back down the hall barefoot, back to the bathroom, where she took a long, cold shower. The water washed over her as she sat on the floor trying to absorb it, dissolve with it, a million individual droplets coursing down the drain. Wrinkled and shivering, she eventually turned off the tap and toweled herself down. Her fingers were numb, and her toes prickled with pins and needles. In her room, Alison threw off the towel and lay on the bed, overhead lights blazing now. She'd gotten into the habit of going to sleep with the light on, with nothing over her, not even a sheet. Sal said it was because she was traumatized from sheltering under the blanket in the dark of the fire. Alison said Sal should mind her business, it had been extraordinarily hot this week.

As she lay there, dozing and waking, she thought she heard a sound outside the window, maybe not right outside, but something out of place on the street. She got up from the bed and went over to the window, pulling apart the blinds to peek through a crack. With the lights on in the dead of night, she was at a disadvantage. If someone was out there, they'd know she'd heard something. She peered out into the front yard. The streetlights were out, but they'd been out since the fire, and there didn't appear to be anything out of place.

Alison turned and walked back to the bed, and as she lay down she heard the sound of a clutch catching, an engine revving to life. Wheels turning on loose gravel, spinning a little, the tread obviously worn down over time. She quickly moved back to the window, but all she could see was the red blur of taillights a ways up the road. It wasn't the first time she'd heard a car peel off in the middle of the night this week. Last time she'd done an inventory of the neighbors. Everyone's car was accounted for the next morning and no one had gone anywhere in the middle of the night. Sal said Alison was imagining it. But now it had happened again. Alison was convinced Gil was watching her.

She thought about the moment in the driveway, the crack of twigs underfoot in the thicket, the thing with Sal by the pool, all of it nothing but something. She lay back down and decided to try turning off the lights. She had forgotten how easy it was to see into a well-lit room at night, and she didn't want to make it easier for him to spy. She checked the windows were locked and, for the first time, turned the key in the bedroom door before lying back down.

12.

Alison didn't fall asleep again until she heard the first calls of the whipbirds that made their home in the tree outside her window. As the early light of day crept across the room, she allowed herself to relax, and she felt her eyelids, heavy with sleep lost, fall. When she woke up six hours later, the day was humid, and she could hear Sal vacuuming in the hallway.

"I'm up, Sal, promise," she called out.

"It's eleven a.m., Alison. You can't sleep all day, love."

"I could try," she responded, with a little too much grit in her tone.

Sal turned the vacuum cleaner off and retreated up the hall. Alison felt bad—she hadn't meant to snap—but she didn't feel like explaining herself.

Her phone buzzed on the bedside table and she looked at the number. Withheld. Which meant it was either Billy calling from the station or one of the many journalists who had tried to get interviews all week. She let it go to voicemail, and when the notification of a new message popped up, she played it.

"Alison, it's Chris Waters here from the *Age*, checking in to see if you'd be available for a chat today? I can come to you, no worries. Just want you to get your version out there, since right now we've only got the police reports and the parents' interview. Might be a good time to get on the record and say your piece, you know, before the inquiry. You'll have to give evidence then, so no point prolonging it, is there? Anyway, I'm up here with the premier today, I've got a snapper with me, and we're keen for some local stories, so if you've got halfa for a sit-down, that'd be ripper."

Bloody journalists. Maybe that was another name to add to the list of people who might be watching her at night.

Chris Waters.

Dickhead, most likely.

Malcolm King liked to wear his shirtsleeves rolled up, the cotton tails of the fabric untucked, his chinos rumpled, unironed, seeping bleed of ink spotting through on the pockets where he'd shoved a ballpoint in without securing the cap. He kept a little Spirax notebook in the front pocket of his button-up, and was always pulling it out to jot down something. At bedtime, he'd tuck his arm around Alison's shoulders and tell her about his day. About the story he'd written for the paper the next day, the way the councilman had tried to avoid his calls but he'd caught him anyway, handing out grants to his daughter's new shell company.

Alison didn't always understand the stories for the first few years—tax fraud and car accidents, a break-in at the Imperial, the thoroughbred horses stolen in the middle of the night, the kid from down the ridge who was going to be the first draft pick that year, and the one who hit his head diving into a waterhole and wouldn't ever walk again. Some of them upset her, but she liked the way he told them, the way he explained how the ink that rubbed gray on your fingers over breakfast got there in the first place. She liked how her dad knew everyone in town and everyone in town knew him. She liked how his name looked in the paper. She liked how what he wrote seemed to carry with it some kind of special power, to change the lives of the people around her.

When she was older, she liked knowing the next day's news before it came out, would ask him if there was anything she should know before she went to school. But he rarely had anything good, it seemed, when she was older. He'd say things like "Be nice to Mrs. Short today" or "Casey Scroggins is gonna need someone to watch out for him" and Alison would thumb through the paper at breakfast, looking for the reasons why.

Once, when she was little, he'd taken her to watch the presses. The way they rushed giant rolls of whitest paper around the room, zooming through the ink plates, cutting, folding, stacking, whirling, collecting in the gut of a rumbling truck, the thud-thump-thwack of the news a heartbeat, alive. Her dad would talk in lingo about his work. The photographers were *snappers*; the big story on page one was *the splash*. The people who chopped up his words were the *subs*; there were *sources*, *leads*, *yarns*, *ledes*, *slugs*, the *wheetie spit* (details too disgusting to read without spitting out your breakfast); one time an unflattering *dinkus* made him unhappy enough that he forced them to make him a new one. Malcolm King was shabby, a little overweight, but vain. He liked to be above the *fold*. He cursed if he was cut to a *short*. He wrote in *centimeters*, not words.

And then the internet came along and Malcolm King got made redundant. Small country papers, film cameras, hot metal presses, subeditors, Dictaphones, Malcolm King. All of them superfluous in this new digital age. He went back to his old job, his before job, teaching English at Middle Yarra High. Something changed in him. He spent less time at home. He obsessed over the papers, reading the *Age*, the *Herald Sun* (or the *Scum*, as he said everyone who didn't work there called it), and tutting over his breakfast about the grammar or the quotes or the way the stories ended. He wasn't bitter, but he was sad, and Alison missed her dad the storyteller who'd let her into his world and taught her all its secrets, before shutting her out completely.

Alison pulled on a T-shirt and a pair of shorts, slipped on some sandals, and gathered her hair up into a ponytail. She smoothed the sheets on the bed and unlocked the door, then stepped out into the hall and almost stood on Sal.

"Shit, Sal, what are you doing?"

"Sorry, I was trying to see if you were up yet. I was going to put the kettle on if you were."

"Too hot for bloody tea, don't you think?"

"Never too hot for tea." Sal hustled up the hallway into the kitchen and Alison could hear her pottering around. She picked up her bag off the hallstand and made the impulsive decision to leave the house for the first time since she'd discovered Gil and Michael were the same person. She needed to get out; it was beginning to feel like she was a prisoner in Sal's house. The problem was, with all the people she was avoiding—Billy, Detective Mitchell, Chris bloody Waters, that dickhead from the *Herald Sun*, and, of course, Gil—Alison had thought for the last little while that it was easier to just lie low. Now she wondered if maybe she should get out of town for a bit, go somewhere where no one knew who she was.

Alison King. Simone Arnold. Same age. Same face, kind of. Same scumbag boyfriend. Same bloody apartment block. Alison had felt Simone's clammy skin, seen her lifeless eyes. Seen them again in her sleep, again in the mirror, again on the canvas. Alison couldn't get other people to care the way she did. Couldn't make Sal follow her down the speculation spiral or the feedback loop of her ideas. Sometimes it seemed obvious that Simone had died in the fire, and then other times it was clear that the only explanation was that Gil had killed her. *Didn't he kill her either way?* She knew Simone's mother felt he did. But wasn't that the same as saying Alison was to blame because Simone had been coming to her, was carrying her address, when it happened? If Gil hadn't really done it, had just chased her south, then whatever Alison had done to pull Simone to her, well, wasn't that the same level of complicity? Alison didn't want the weight of a life on her. She felt the wet wool in her nostrils, the lack of pressure in the air; it was hard to breathe; it was easy to die. *It was easy to die.* It was easy to run away.

The difficulty was that running away would make it look like she had something to hide. A reason to hightail it out of there. She felt trapped. She'd done nothing wrong, and now she just wanted to get on with her life. But she wasn't sleeping; she wasn't able to work. Everyone thought she was part of some ridiculous conspiracy. Maybe if she could solve this, find the reason for Simone's trip, she could prove she'd never been involved.

She left the house without saying good-bye and jumped on Sal's bike. Rode up into the town center, stopped in at the bakery for a coffee and something to eat. It was going on midday and there were plenty of people about. She saw Jim sitting by himself in the courtyard, reading the paper.

"Morning, Jim, how's it going?" He peered over the top of the page reluctantly but broke into a smile when he saw her.

"Ally, how are you doing?" As he spoke, Jim tossed the *Herald Sun* on the table in front of him, open to a page with the headline NO ANSWERS IN AUTOPSY OF DEAD CAIRNS WOMAN. BLACK SUNDAY CASUALTIES TOP 160.

"It's been a bit rough. I'm all right, though. Can I sit down?"

She pulled out the chair opposite without waiting for a response and sat across from him. They stared at each other for a while, not saying anything. Alison cleared her throat and looked him straight in the eye, daring him to speak first.

"How's Sal?" he asked her, leaning back in his chair.

"Oh, she's fine, a real sweetheart actually, won't let me go two hours without a cuppa and a shortbread. I'll turn into a card-carrying member of the CWA at this rate."

Jim smiled, didn't offer any more conversation. It was quiet in the courtyard, but Alison saw the woman at the next table staring openly at her. She shifted in her seat, scratched the back of her neck, felt pressure in her shoulders.

"Hey, Jim, do you reckon you could drive me out to my place so I could pick up my car? I feel totally stranded at Sal's without it, and she's doing so much for me, I don't want to make her drive back out there again. I should have picked it up when we were there the other day, but I got . . . distracted."

"I can do that, sure. Is your drive good and clear now?"

"Yeah, it's fine; they had to clear it because they had to do all the crime scene stuff with Simone's car and the tree and all that. It's all good."

Jim nodded again and took a sip of his coffee. "When do you want to go?"

"If you're not up to anything after this, that'd work for me."

He checked his watch and looked at Alison again. "What's the rush? You've been without it for a week or so now. Why do you need it so suddenly?"

"It's not sudden. I'm just sick of being dependent on other people. I'm not used to it. I don't like it." She pushed the ball of her foot into the dirt as she talked.

"All right, meet me out the front of the bank in an hour. I'll be ready to go."

She smiled at him and they sat in silence again, eating

their pastries. After he finished his coffee Jim got up and dusted his shirt off, clapped Alison on the shoulder as he walked past.

"One hour. Don't be late. I've got plenty else to do today." Alison waved him off and gulped down her coffee. She'd put it off as long as she could, and now she needed to see Billy.

The texts had stopped before the calls, as though he thought a real conversation would force her to confront her bad behavior in a more satisfying way than a series of text messages ever could. He didn't want to let her get out of it easily. She felt bad, sure, but she also didn't think it was fair to expect a drunk wreck of a human being to always do the right thing. She swung back onto Sal's bike and rode over to the police station, the hot midday sun burning the back of her neck. When she got to the station, she saw Billy's ute parked out in the lot. Next to it was the car Detective Mitchell had driven to meet her the other day. Alison let out a deep sigh and started up the stairs into the station. She opened the door and pushed into the waiting room.

Three coppers looked up at her from their desks. Billy, that idiot Cameron McDougall, and the station's sergeant, Andrew Broad. Cameron let out a whistle under his breath and looked over at Billy, winking like an idiot.

"Shut up, Cam." Billy smacked him across the back of his head as he got up and loped over to the desk. "Ally, hi. Hang on a minute." He turned around. "Sarge, can I take lunch? I'm due." His boss nodded, and then nodded again in Alison's direction.

"Alison," he said.

"Sergeant, nice to see you, quite a week."

"Yep. Pretty awful."

"Your lot all good?"

"Got 'em out just in time, thanks, Al. Lost the shed, back of the house a little beaten up, but we could have done worse out of it."

"Well, I'm glad you're all right. Say hi to Laura for me."

"Will do." He nodded once more in Alison's direction.

Billy took off his belt and dumped it on his desk, then came out from behind the counter and pulled Alison out the door by her arm.

"Geez, Billy, calm down." She yanked his hand away as they stood on the steps to the station.

"I don't hear from you for a week and then you turn up at my work?"

"Ugh. This is exactly why you didn't hear from me."

His features rearranged, mouth and eyes downcast. "Well, I think it's pretty shitty that you don't seem to give a fuck about how I feel."

"OK, forget it. I can't have this conversation. I came here because I needed my friend Billy to help me with a problem. Not to get a fucking guilt trip." Alison started to walk away, but Billy caught her by the arm again to stop her.

"Wait, OK, fine. We can park that conversation, but I'm not going to forget about it. What do you need?"

Alison hesitated, but she wanted to know. "What do you know about the boyfriend? Michael whoever." *Did they know about her link to him?*

"What?"

"I know his first name is Michael, but I don't know anything else. I need more so I can figure out what Simone was doing here." She hoped she was convincingly clueless.

"This is not something for you to figure out. That guy is a potential murder suspect. You think I'm going to give you what we have on him?"

120

Alison rubbed her hand on his upper arm, tracing the lines of his muscles slowly, and cocked her head to one side and said, "Come on, Billy, please."

He pulled away from her and shook his head.

"You're fucked up, Al. You think that shit's going to work? Come see me when you're ready to talk for real." He turned. Then he stopped and looked at her. "Listen, Meg Russell's parents have asked if you can come help sort through her things. You should call Tina." Alison nodded, not sure what to say. She watched as he retreated into the station and left her standing there feeling ridiculous and miserable, but she was reassured that her secret was safe for now.

Alison got back on the bike and rode over to the bank. She sat outside, waiting for Jim to turn up. A little farther down Main Street, the state government had set up an emergency support check-in center. The idea was that people who had lost their homes, or worse, could check in there for government support and accommodation services. She watched as families lined up to speak with the caseworker; she was distracted by the blankness of their faces, the quiet patience with which they swatted flies away or shaded their eyes from the sunshine. A man she couldn't place but knew she'd seen before sat down next to her. Bald, soft in the middle, with a bushy beard, broad shoulders, and a tan like a Surfers Paradise lifer.

"Got a light?" he asked her.

"Nope, don't smoke, sorry." Alison pulled out her phone, tried to look busy.

"Are you Alison King?" He was looking at her intently. Alison became slightly concerned.

"Maybe. Who's asking?"

"Chris Waters, the *Age*, nice to meet you."

Alison swore under her breath. Went to get up.

"Wait," he said. "Hear me out. I just want to tell your side."

"I don't have a side. I don't know anything. I didn't know that woman. I don't know how she died. I don't know why she was on her way to my place. That's it, that's the whole story."

"You can't tell me anything about her boyfriend?"

"Like what?"

"Like why she'd have been heading to the home of her ex-boyfriend's ex?"

Oh shit. "What are you talking about?"

"Simone Arnold's ex-boyfriend is your ex-boyfriend. His full name is Michael Gilbert Watson. I believe you knew him as—"

"Gil." Alison kicked the dirt, hard. How did this guy know?

"So, you really didn't know, then?"

She lied as convincingly as she could. "No, I didn't. Shit. How do you know?"

"Sorry, can't tell you that."

"OK, right, whatever. Now you know, I didn't know shit. Write that story and leave me alone."

Alison checked the time on her phone and cursed Jim. He was running late. She saw him coming out of the bank and began walking toward him.

"I have to go, thanks for the info," she said to the journalist, not looking back. He followed her.

"Alison, would you consider a longer interview? You could go into more detail about him."

"No fucking way. If he is a killer, why would I want to provoke him?"

"Do you think he is?"

"No comment." Jim was next to her now. "Jim, let's get out of here."

"Who's this?" Jim, as usual, was in no hurry to move.

"He's a journo, wants a story, can we go?"

Chris Waters opened his mouth to speak, but Alison pulled Jim away forcefully.

"Hold your horses, I've got to pop over to the newsagent. You can wait in the ute if you want." He held up the key fob and the lights flashed on the ute. "Load your bike in and I'll be back in a jiff."

Alison hauled the bike into the tray of the ute and secured it with bungee cords. She slid up into the cab and waited for Jim to come back.

It was late on a Saturday night and she'd just come home from a double shift. There was a ship in town and the place had been packed from go to whoa. She'd served a table of moronic bucks, the groom so blind drunk, the hotel would have lost its license had the cops come calling. She hadn't noticed him slip into the bar, but he'd been there, meeting Johnny, his dealer, and he'd watched as she flirted for tips. Angled her head in the most flattering way as she set down the drinks, made sure she bent low enough for them to get a good look at her tits as she wiped up the spills from the round before. She'd come home that night with an extra one hundred fifty dollars in her purse. As far as drunk idiots went, these guys were a piece of cake. Didn't want anything other than to look, too scared of getting caught out to try anything more. As if she would have let them. But Gil didn't care about Alison's intentions.

She didn't see it coming.

She walked in the front door and he was waiting with the back of his hand, flat across her cheek before she'd even said hello. She felt the tears well in her eyes, but she blinked them back the best she could and told him to back off. It made him angrier. He pushed her up against the wall and held her wrists high above her head, using one hand to restrain her, as if to prove how much stronger he was. He used his other hand to press her throat into the wall as well. As she stared into his eyes, Alison took the deepest breath she could muster and waited as calmly as possible for him to stop. She felt the pressure of his hand against her windpipe and wondered how long she could go without more air. Her lungs began to ache the way they had when she stayed underwater in Sal's pool too long as a kid. She closed her eyes and pretended she was back there. Held her breath against the clock, not the man who was supposed to love her.

He let up on her throat and slapped her again, pulling her forward and then pushing her hard into the wall. He groped at her breasts with his free hand and snarled in her ear, "These belong to me, you fucking slut." Alison tried her best to stay calm and measured. She smiled through the pain and told him she loved only him. When he calmed down enough to let her wrists go, she let him lead her to the bedroom and fuck her. Unable to explain, even now, why she hadn't walked out the door and never looked back. The way it had ended had made her feel even stupider. His possession of her hadn't even been exclusive.

Probably he would get away with it. The media got tired of dead women quickly enough. The fire was enough to keep them occupied; no one was going to remember Simone Arnold in a few weeks. Already they had begun talking about the recovery and were looking toward the civil action against the company that owned the power lines that had fallen down in the wind, sparking the deadliest blaze, and the criminal case against the arsonists—kids with lighters who liked playing with fire on extreme-fire-danger days who the investigators said had set off a blaze over in a dried-up creek bed about fifty clicks northwest. There was plenty of fodder for the pulp mill; a B-side mystery about a woman who probably died from radiant heat would fade away in no time. Once the cops were over it, the papers would be too.

Alison felt a fresh flash of anger surge through her. She felt like Simone had died so that she could live. She wanted to make a difference, prove she was worth being the one who survived. Make sure Gil was held accountable. If it was all going to come out anyway, she thought maybe she had the upper hand. She knew him. She knew where he spent time, who his friends were. Alison might have survived only through chance, but she wasn't going to waste it.

Jim wrenched open the driver's-side door, surprising Alison.

"Ready to go?" he asked her cheerily.

"Yep, let's get out of here."

Jim put the ute in reverse and stretched his arm over the back of the seat and turned around to back out. Alison closed her eyes again and began to trace her steps in her head. She couldn't shake the feeling that if she didn't try to fix this, the best it could be fixed, she'd never really be able to go home again. Jim barreled down the main street in silence. The quiet suited Alison just fine.

With her eyes closed the afternoon sun hit her full in the face, her eyelids turning her field of vision a flaming orange as they raced toward the sun. She felt safe in the cab of the ute, the air-conditioning blasting onto her neck, the seat belt snug around her middle. If she spent too much time thinking about the fire, she might go crazy. It came in waves, sometimes when she was sleeping, or when she was showering, or playing cards with Sal, or painting. There was no way to predict when the next panic attack would hit her, the clammy feel of the skin on her face and chest her early warning sign. The only thing that leveled her out was thinking about Simone, about Gil, the quirk of fate that had allowed her to be here but extinguished someone else. She knew now that the next thing was to make it up to Simone. She didn't really even understand why that mattered to her, but it did. Sometimes she felt as if she were just flailing around, trying anything she could not to feel worse. A cloud obscured the sun and Alison opened her eyes.

"Where've you been?" Jim asked her.

"Nowhere yet."

The ute rocked along the twists and turns of the mountain highway. Out the window, to her surprise, Alison caught sight of budding green shoots on the shoulder. A little life upon the blackened ground.

13.

Jim dropped Alison off, mumbled something about needing to finish checking fences on his property, and reversed away. Alison was alone at the house for the first time since the fire. She felt a chill in the air, despite the midafternoon sunshine, and hustled inside to figure out what she needed.

Standing in front of her chest of drawers she saw the room with what felt like different eyes. The paint on the walls was dull the way old paint scrubbed too many times shines unevenly. It was palest green in here, her grandfather's favorite color. There were splits and cracks in the high-gloss white that sealed the window frames, and the floorboards were worn almost clean of polish. Alison's bed was a simple ensemble, no headboard, no space underneath to shove winter coats or love letters she'd never received. It felt impersonal, with white sheets that could be anybody's and the two sad overlslept-on pillows. There was nothing visible here to make the room hers.

She sat on the edge of the bed and pulled out the drawer of her grandmother's old-style dresser. It squeaked on its ungreased slide, the roughly sanded rosewood catching as it pulled against the grain. In here, Alison had unceremoniously dumped the evidence of her life. Cards, sketchbooks, little scraps of paper, or receipts she'd scrawled ideas on. Letters she'd written but never sent. In the pile, a card from her mother on her graduation day. Alison stared at it until the words swam. She hadn't looked at it since the accident. She pulled another one out. From the sulfur-crested cockatoo on the front she knew it was from Gil.

Ally,

The bird on this card is sweet like you. Happy birthday darlin, I love you.

Gil

She smiled at it still. Remembered how in those early days they'd shared so many good moments, lying in bed wrapped in the loud floral sheets that matched the personality of Cairns, the weather, the flora, the reptiles and birds that Alison would paint on her own time, when she wasn't thinking about making money. Wasn't hustling at all, was just enjoying the sensation of paint on paper, on canvas, on the wall even. Above their bed in the Cairns flat she'd painted a lush tropical scene, dripping ferns and crimson finches, palm cockatoos with their spiked black combs. He'd loved the wall when he first saw it and he was always encouraging Alison to add more.

"Saw a little gold bird on the way home, Ally—brilliant, like a coin fresh from the mint. Don't know what it is, but I couldn't stop thinking it'd look proper up here on that branch."

They'd pore over the book, find the right species (in that case, Alison remembered, it was a golden bowerbird), and Alison would sketch it out, carefully filling in the colors at night while she waited for Gil to get back from the pub, or the RSL, or the pier where he smoked up with his mates—or the bed where he fucked Simone, apparently. Alison felt a bitterness rise inside her; she pushed it down again.

"Don't get jealous of a dead woman," she told her reflection as it stared at her from the mirror. Shoved the cards back into the drawer a little too hard.

Alison had grown up feeling like she never really fit in and with an aching desire to get away, anywhere, but especially to Paris. When she'd left for art school in Melbourne, it hadn't felt far enough, so when she was done, she'd gotten into her absolute bomb of a car and driven as far north as it would take her, ending up in Cairns. She'd been happy there, building a profile through a series of art shows that had grabbed the attention of the local paper, mostly because they featured a set of nude self-portraits, something that almost guaranteed coverage. Alison was savvy enough to know she wasn't going to make it painting nudes in North Queensland, but after she met Gil, she was too in it, too distracted, and then too terrified to go anywhere or even dream of any other life.

Alison still remembered the day her mother called. It was late May, not so humid as it wound down to the dry season in the tropics. She'd been sketching something trivial, a flower maybe, or a shell; she couldn't see it on the page anymore when she closed her eyes. The phone buzzed, on vibrate, no sound; Alison hated the way phones sounded when they rang. Tinny, insistent, like a mosquito flying too close in the night. She ignored it. It rang out. It rang again, immediately. She rolled her eyes and picked it up.

"I'm working, Mum, what do you want?"

Her mother was crying through the words. Alison had never heard her cry like that before.

"Your father's seeing someone else."

Alison didn't believe it. "What? Mum, no. Don't be silly."

"I saw an email he wrote. He is."

"Aw, Mum, you're probably overreacting to something completely innocent. Dad loves you. He wouldn't."

"You always take his side."

Alison knew that was true.

"I don't, Mum, I don't believe he's cheating. He loves you."

"I'm going to send it to you. Do you have your computer?"

Alison got up from the table and roamed around the flat, looking for the laptop. It was on the floor on Gil's side of the bed. She grabbed it and perched on the mattress, opened it up, and went to her email account. There was one new email from her mother.

"Do you have it?" Alison heard her mother ask down the line. Her ear was hot from holding the phone so close. She focused on the words on the page. It was filth. Her father was definitely cheating on her mother. *I want to thrust inside your wet pussy right now.* Alison gagged a little. *Your tits are like the ripest mangoes. I want to suck their sweetness.* Alison didn't want to read it all, but she couldn't turn away. She looked at the email address of the person it was sent to. He'd begun the email with the charming nickname "Baby Girl." Alison's father was fifty-eight. Who the fuck was "Baby Girl"?

"Mum, I believe you. Look, I'm going to call you back, OK? I just need . . . I need a minute."

"What am I going to do, Ally?"

"Mum, I promise, I'll call you back."

She ended the call and stared at the email. Read it over and over again. It made her feel sick.

Alison stared next at the email address, but it looked like a throwaway Gmail address: bbygrrrrl88@gmail.com. She knew she wouldn't be able to trace who it was. She tried to feel less sick. It didn't go away. Alison lay on the bed, closed her eyes. Waited for everything to settle a bit. Felt the room spin as though she'd drunk too much wine. She called her mother back. Told her to kick her father out. Told her she'd support her, whatever she wanted to do next.

"Leave him, Mum. He doesn't deserve you," she'd told her over and over, both of them crying.

When he called she didn't pick up. She never picked up again. Her father's filthy words, the image of him rutting like a pig—*Your tits are like the ripest mangoes*—enough to rupture their life-long bond. Alison vowed to never be like her mother. To never allow a man to use her like that. How fucking naive.

The knock on the door came late enough to give Alison pause. She looked at her phone, glowing in the low light of her reading lamp: 11:43. Some people don't remember the small things. The color of the sky on the day they started a new job. The small tear in the shorts of the man who is walking away. The team logo on the cap of the driving instructor who just told them they passed their test. The height of the grass in those early spring days, when rain and warmth push it up faster. The time, the minute, everything changes forever.

Alison had always remembered the details. The smell of rain on the air, the sound of a plane somewhere distant overhead, the television blaring out the *Rage* theme on the morning she left for university, walked out the front door expecting never to come back, except for visits. And this time, the time: 11:43 p.m. Alison felt a knot in her stomach as she slipped out of bed to see. Her phone in her hand, ready to call the police if it was Gil. The knocks again, more insistent this time, and then a voice, female, clipped, succinct.

"Alison King? Alison King, if you're home please come to the door. It's the police." Alison's heart leaped, surprise over-taking her. The cops? She quickened her pace, got to the door, and was about to wrench it open when she stopped. Gil could still be there. He could just have a woman with him. She felt wildly out of control in her own head. She went to the window and peered out. There were two police officers out there, a man and a woman. No sign of Gil. She opened the door.

"Yes?"

"Are you Alison King?"

"Yes." She was confused.

"Your parents are Malcolm and Marie King, of Lake Bend, Victoria?"

She didn't understand why, but the question made her queasy. "Yes. What is this about?"

"Alison, may we come in?" The woman spoke gently now, the business in her voice giving way to tenderness. It was somehow more unsettling.

"OK, it's very late." She stepped aside, was aware of her light T-shirt and boxer shorts, and wondered, should she put on pants? She didn't know how to ask the question, so she didn't.

"Yes, we're very sorry. Say, do you think we could have a cup of tea maybe?"

What the fuck was going on? The police didn't just invite themselves over for tea at 11:43. "Um. I—I'd rather know what you are here for?" She tried to keep her voice calm.

"Of course, why don't you and me sit down here, and Constable Crow can put the kettle on?" The female officer nodded toward the kitchen, looking pointedly at the man.

"On it," he replied, and moved away from them. Alison let the cop guide her into a chair; unsure what this late-night kindness meant, but confident it was nothing good.

"Could you tell me what this is about?"

"Alison, my name is Senior Constable Sonia Andrianakis."

"OK."

"We're here tonight with some news about your parents." The click of the electric kettle seemed so much louder than she remembered it. Alison took a deep breath. Pushed the bile back down.

"OK."

"Alison, there was an accident tonight on the highway between Melbourne and Lake Bend. Your parents' car lost control and veered off the road. They unfortunately hit a tree at what appears to have been a very high speed."

There is a particular rush in your ears, a pressure change, or something; Alison has never understood the mechanics of it. But it's an immersion thing. You dunk your head under; there's a cushioning there, something confining and isolating. Senior Constable Sonia Andrianakis is still talking. Alison is thinking about words, phrases. She feels the absurdity of it. She pushes down a ridiculous laugh. She tries to listen.

"Your mother, it looks like it was very quick, she probably didn't feel anything. Your father sustained a very serious wound to his leg and it caused a significant loss of blood and he unfortunately wasn't—he didn't make it either."

Constable Crow set a weak, milky cup of tea down in front of her.

"I put two sugars in, it's good for you when you've had a bit of a shock."

A bit of a shock. A mosquito buzzed past her ear and landed on her arm. She whacked it, hard. The sound made the police officers jump. When she lifted up her hand a smear of blood and black remained. This blood, their blood. Their flesh. They had made her, and now she was all that was left.

She booked a seat on the first flight to Melbourne. Suzie Marsh met her at the airport, drove her out to Lake Bend. Past the curve in the road where safety glass and plastic light casing and twisted shards of tire scarred the spot, patched up with flowers left anonymously in great piles.

Coming back had been a shock, but as she spent the days and weeks clearing out her parents' things from the house, she found a sense of satisfaction and peace in her new, solitary life. Out in the bush, with no neighbors close by, and enough in the bank to see her through quite a few years of unemployment, Alison was able to focus on painting in ways she'd never thought she could.

A spring day, a list of errands too long to count them. Alison had been back in Lake Bend a few months, and they had blurred together mostly.

"Alison King!" The voice had been familiar, but Alison had still had to search her memory for the name that went with the face before her, and then she realized—this was her first friend. The green-crayon girl. It had been too long.

"Meg Russell." Alison smiled big and meant it. Meg cocked her head to one side, sizing Alison up warmly. Then she opened her arms and pulled Alison in for a hug. She smelled like oranges and cinnamon, Alison thought, and it reminded her of her mother.

"I thought you'd moved to Cairns." Meg kept a friendly hand on Alison's shoulder, her palm warm, but not uncomfortably so, where it squeezed her.

"I did, but I moved back when Mum and Dad . . ." She still had trouble saying it.

Meg's face scrunched up into a twisted flinching grimace, but she quickly maneuvered it to wide-eyed empathy. "Oh god, Alison, I'm sorry, I did hear that, but I guess I . . . forgot in the moment. I'm really sorry." She didn't meet Alison's eyes as she spoke, as though she were ashamed.

"No, it's OK, you know, it was actually nice to have someone greet me so damn cheerfully for once." Alison smiled, still meant it.

Meg made a straight line with her lips, slid her hand through the crook of Alison's elbow, and gently tugged her in the direction of the Imperial. "Come on, let me buy you an apology beer."

"Well, sure, won't say no." Meg and Alison were so close at school, until in year nine they'd had a fight about a boy. The bond hadn't recovered properly before Alison left for Melbourne. Meg had been married, she told Alison, but he'd gone to Afghanistan. Hadn't come back. Alison told her she'd left a man in Cairns, didn't tell her all the reasons why. One beer became two; two became four.

"So, you working now?" Meg had asked Alison three beers deep.

"I'm painting, a few private commissions. I sold one to a big-name restaurant in Melbourne. That got me some more attention, and I have a steady income from it. I'm not—I don't—I mean, I'm not strapped for cash right now. The house is all paid for, and both Mum and Dad had insurance and super and all that, so yeah, I'm OK."

Alison hadn't planned on staying put in Lake Bend long enough to draw breath, but somehow, she'd lasted almost three years. It was unexpected, and in spite of herself, she enjoyed it. Now here she was. She stared at her reflection in the mirror again. Pale, her cheeks hollower than usual, her hair greasy, unwashed. Meg gone, her car the wrong side of the hill, of the wind, of the moment. What would Meg say about Billy? About Simone? About any of this? She thought about Simone's parents. Anne Arnold had sounded like her own mother on the day she'd called about her world falling apart. Alison wished she could go back, not be so fucking stupid as to involve herself in this mess. But she was involved. It was her Simone had been looking for.

She got up from the bed, pulled her hair back with the tie on her wrist, and picked clothes from the drawers indiscriminately. She went into the kitchen and cleaned out the perishables from the fridge and the cupboards. She found an old canvas that fitted the blown-out bathroom window and wedged it into the gaping hole. She made quick work of shutting the house up enough to leave it indefinitely. She would come back. And she would stop by Meg's house and help her parents clear it out, but she couldn't do it right now. Right now, she had to do other things. She wouldn't be safe here until she had figured all of this out. It was a low-level hum, a feeling of constant vigilance. She could still feel his hands on her, his strength and rage, his menacing calm. She wanted to be far away. She wanted to never come across him again. She dragged Sal's bike onto her own back seat, packed into the boot what she'd collected from the house, and left again as quickly as she possibly could. Didn't stop to look back.

It was raining, hard, and Gil was out cold beside her. Alison was down to wearing her bathers as underpants, and even though her head throbbed with the reminder of last night's vodka, she forced herself out of the bed and pulled on her swimsuit and a pair of running shorts. The laundry basket in the corner was overflowing. She picked it up, moved through the flat, adding things as she went—a tea towel, a bath mat, the shirt Gil had peeled off her when they were drunk last night. She padded barefoot along the communal balcony, hugging close to the wall to avoid fat droplets that fell hard on the concrete and split open like eggs. She got to the laundry room and began separating the whites and colors. In the middle of the stack, a pale pink G-string. It wasn't hers. Alison didn't wear G-strings, ever.

It was quiet in the cool of the laundry room. No whirring drums on spin, no tumble of dryers today. Just Alison, the steady pops of the heavy rain, and the silent heat of her tears snaking down her cheeks. She piled the laundry into the machines, set them to cold, and pushed the start buttons. She wasn't wearing any shoes. Didn't have her phone. Her purse was on her bedside table. She'd have to go get it. She couldn't even just get away. She stuck her hands in the waist of her shorts, felt around for the little inside pocket. There was a crisp plastic note tucked in there. She pulled out a tenner. Not enough to get anywhere. She didn't know where she'd go anyway.

The washing machines were revving up. Alison decided to go for a walk. Under the cover of wet palms, she walked along the ocean path. Soaked to the bone; the water felt as if it had expanded her skin and shrunk it all at once. Her hair clung to her neck, her cheeks, her back, her ears, in thick ropes. The salt of her tears was lost in the sweet of the sky's. She tried to take long deep breaths, suck in the ocean's calmness. But it wasn't working. She kept seeing the mystery woman and her father. *I want to suck their sweetness.*

She had convinced herself Gil loved her. That he loved her too much. That he hurt her because he loved her so much, he couldn't bear the thought anyone else might even look at her. What they had was unique. Special. Except, it wasn't. *I want to thrust inside your wet pussy right now.* Alison felt like a fool. A fucking idiot. He was the same as her philandering father. He was worse. Every bruise. Every scar. Every excuse she'd made to cover for his violence sickened her. It was over.

———

On her way down the drive, Alison pulled over at the pile of wood that used to be the red gum. The dirt underfoot was crunchy with ash, and she could see a smattering of crushed orange plastic still on the ground where she assumed the lights of Simone's car had smashed under the weight of the tree. It surprised her there was still debris, proof of Simone, littering the ground. She'd watched enough crime procedurals to assume someone in a lab was supposed to be reassembling the light covers for fingerprints or blood spatter or some such shit. Guess not here.

In the still-breathing trees she felt a rustle of breeze. The snap of sticks startled her—was it still too early for lizards and birds? Too early for roos and the rest? Alison didn't know. She felt the fixed intensity of surveillance, like she had on the drive after the fire, before she'd known about Simone, about Gil, about any of it.

The hair on her neck stretched out toward the sun like spines. She whipped around once, twice, three times; there was nothing moving, nothing corporeal, that she could see. The breeze didn't even push the leaves anymore. The stillness was its own kind of unsettling. She closed her eyes and tried to quiet her brain. Tried to slow the pumping blood that beat in her ears and made it hard to hear or think or stand up straight. If she sliced her wrist open and let the blood drain out onto the dirt here, it would be warm and slick. A record of the damage. Proof of life and death and trauma. It would be honest and real; it would *mean something*. Unless it didn't.

Her back to the road, she heard the unmistakable sound of a car on the drive. It contrasted starkly with the silence of the burned bush. Alison turned around, waited for the source of the noise to emerge on the driveway, her lungs tightening.

14.

The beat-up white Ford station wagon didn't belong to anyone Alison knew. She would have hidden, but she was plainly visible standing there in the middle of the drive, with nowhere to go. The way allowed only one car at a time. She was trapped. There was nothing to do but wait and see. The car was ambling along, as if it were observing every detail of the trip up the drive. As it drew closer she felt her stomach flip, the sweat beading on her forehead drip down her temples. She tried to steady her breaths, the beats of her heart. The driver was close enough now that she could vaguely make out the shape of a man. Shorn of hair, with a beard, broad shoulders. Sunglasses too angular for a manufacturer to imagine them on a woman's face. He looked familiar. Alison gulped back the acid in her throat. Forced herself to stand strong. As the car pulled onto the shoulder, crunching plastic under the tires, Alison began to feel furious.

"What are you doing here?"

Chris Waters leaned an arm out the open window affably, seemingly unaffected by the hostility in Alison's voice. "G'day, Alison, must say I was hoping to find this spot unpopulated."

"Get off my property." She felt the burn on her cheeks as she spoke.

"Now, come on, you've no gate down the way, how can I be sure this isn't Crown land, property of His Majesty, and by extension, any of us poor subjects who might happen past?"

"I'm telling you, that's how. You a monarchist? King don't own shit around here. If it's not me, it's the Wurundjeri people you need to clear it with."

The journalist shrugged, tried to disguise the annoyance on his face with a forced smile.

"Did your grandparents ask or is that only required when it's convenient? I'm gonna need to keep going up so I can find a place to turn back around."

"You do that, Mr. the *Age*, but I'm going to use the time to call the police and tell 'em you're here, and you're not welcome." Alison felt stupid, but she pulled her phone out of her pocket and thumbed around looking for Billy's number.

"Hold up, hold up, no need to involve the local constabulary. I just wanted to get a sense of the place where it happened. I take it, from the way you're scratching around in the dirt over there, that that's where you found her." He looked a little too pleased with himself. But Alison really didn't want to ask Billy for help. She slid her phone back into her pocket.

"What do you want?"

"Why was she coming to visit you?"

"How should I know? I told you I didn't know who she was." Alison was irritated. "What are you doing focusing on this anyway? Plenty of other people died in this fire. Their lives are important too. Go write about someone else."

Chris Waters squinted at Alison in a way that felt to her like he was peeling the flesh off her bones. "No one else is a possible murder victim." He raised a calloused hand to his chin, scratched at a spot near his Adam's apple. "Word is, no one in Cairns has seen your mate Gil for over a fortnight."

"He's not my mate." Alison spat each word out slowly, poison in her tone. Chris Waters killed the engine of the Ford and cracked the door open. Alison heard the click of his seat belt uncoupling. He leaned into the door and a leg emerged below the chassis. One R.M. Williams–clad foot on the ground. *They're like cockroaches,* Alison thought. *You don't squash one quick enough, and they run as far as they can.*

"Do you think you might be able to point out where you found her, what it looked like, you know, while we're both here? I don't have to say you told me. It could be on background."

"What the fuck is background?" Her dad never taught her that one.

"You tell me, I write about it, except I don't say who told me or even that anyone told me, I just sort of let the information permeate the yarn, you know?" He winked at her.

"Don't bloody wink at me."

"Come on, Alison. You help me, I help you."

"And how exactly do you help me?"

"I get your side out there, before the inquest, before Steve St. John from the *Scum* gets into it and you become a villain. He's up here, you know, overheard him talking to some of the coppers on a smoko. One of them was telling a tale about you buttering up the police with your feminine wiles."

"The *Herald Sun* can say what it wants. I don't care. It's hardly going to look good for the police if the story they go with is that I've avoided scrutiny by banging the boys. I doubt they'd be keen to help Steve St. John with any more tips on their smoko if that's the angle he runs with. 'Specially since three-quarters of those blokes are married."

Chris Waters looked pissed. Alison knew he hadn't expected her to call his bluff. She was shocked the news about her and Billy had spread far enough to be flung back at her by a city journalist, but that was small-town life. It was one reason seventeen-year-old Alison, at her most awkward, most embarrassed by her parents, had longed so badly for the anonymity of Paris.

He held up his hands in a peace gesture. "All right, then, you help me, and maybe I owe you a favor." Alison opened her mouth to dismiss him again, but she stopped. Chris Waters was a major name. She'd read his reports in the papers for years. In the nineties he'd broken some huge stories about Melbourne gangland types and followed those up with rank political corruption in New South Wales. He'd written so many big stories, he was almost a story himself. Her dad used to single his reports out for his highest praise. *Knows how to work the shoe leather, that Chris Waters.* He knew police, lawyers, politicians, all over the country. Alison didn't know a thing about what she was getting into, what she wanted to do. But he might.

"What kind of favor?"

"Anything. You share information with me, maybe I can share information with you."

Alison thought about it for a minute. She was in over her head. She didn't know how to investigate something. She knew Gil and could maybe figure out where he was if she talked to the right people, but she didn't have access to the kinds of people and information someone like Chris Waters did. That was what Alison wanted. Someone with skills she needed who owed her something. She thought of Billy and immediately dismissed him. Someone who owed *her* something, not the other way around. Billy wouldn't help her now. Alison stuck out her hand and smiled at him.

"All right, Chris Waters of the *Age*, I reckon you've got a deal." He took her hand in his and they shook, both gripping tightly.

15.

Alison walked Chris Waters through the scene as she'd found it. Told him every detail she could remember, except the bit about the note with her name and address on it—she thought about the note all the time, and now she wasn't even sure it had been real; maybe she'd imagined Simone was looking for her. Her brain felt murky these days, turned upside down, and she was doubting what was real and what she'd imagined. She didn't trust her memory anymore. But he was satisfied she was telling the truth, and when they were finally done, he gave her a card and told her to call, *anytime, with any questions*. Alison double-checked the information she'd shared was "on background" and got in her car and on her way.

At the turn onto the freeway she pulled up again, waiting for Chris Waters's car to pass by. As she sat there, her eye caught the letterbox, knocked over to one side, like a car had run into it. She killed the engine and got out. Chris Waters honked twice as he barreled past and Alison raised an arm in good-bye. She walked over to the mailbox, pulled the top up. There hadn't been a proper mail service all week. Alison didn't expect the thick, creamy envelope in there at all. She tried to remember if she'd checked the mail on the way in on the day of the fire. She couldn't. The envelope wasn't postmarked anyway; it just said "Alison" on it. The *l* curved a little too much, like a *c*. She ripped the seal open and pulled out the letter, written on flimsy ruled paper, the kind ripped from a children's exercise book. He was here. He'd been here all along. She had been right to think someone had been watching her, to feel eyes on her in the shadows. Alison's breath caught in her throat; she felt the thump of her heart in her chest, the tightness of her diaphragm, the crawling itch across her skin. Shit. Was he watching her right now?

Alison

I know you've got the tapes.

Give them back and we can go our separate ways.

It wasn't signed. But the loops and slants were undeniably his. The sun was high in the sky and there was no breeze to speak of, but goose bumps rose high on her skin and sent a shiver down her spine. She hurried back to the car and skidded out into the road, felt the thump-thump-thump of the tires on the blistered road echoing the bump-bump-bump of her heart, the way it hummed against her ribs, quick as a hummingbird's in full flight. A blur of blood and bone and bitumen.

She had no idea what tapes he was talking about, but she did know she needed to get the hell out of town. As soon as the idea popped into her head, she couldn't stop thinking about it. Cairns. Cairns was far enough away that maybe Gil wouldn't think she'd go back there. And maybe she'd find something there. Something in Simone's flat? Something that would prove Gil was behind this, that he'd been there in the bush when Simone died. That he'd watched Alison find the car. That he was somehow watching her now. She knew it sounded crazy. If he'd been there, wouldn't he have come after her right then? Why would he wait? Why would he send her a note, or watch her in the late night, drinking herself to sleep?

She thought about it again. The tapes. If he thought she had something he wanted, it would make sense that he didn't attack her, that he waited and watched her instead. But she had no idea what these tapes could possibly be. Were they really even tapes? Who had videotapes anymore? Gil was a little old-school like that. He liked proper printed photographs, and he maintained his DVD collection, even now that streaming made it stupid. She remembered he called them all tapes. For all she knew, he could be talking about anything from an actual VHS tape to an audiocassette to a USB drive. She had no idea what he wanted from her. Nothing about this seemed right.

She pulled into Sal's drive, looked around, skittish. She was stopping only to drop off the bike and grab her toothbrush. She pulled the frame from the car in a hurry, overbalancing with the heft of it, landing on her arse on the grass. Sal popped her head out the front door.

"Alison, you all right?"

"Yep, fine, Sal, just wanted to drop your bike off." She dusted herself off and explained that she wanted to go north for a bit, get away from the fire, and the media, and the dead woman. But Sal wouldn't have it.

"Running away ain't going to fix it."

"You're right, but maybe I can figure out what happened to Simone."

"Oh, come on, Alison. I know you're hurting, but I talked to Cam's mother and she said the cops think she died in the fire. Said there's no evidence of anything else."

Sal and her *sources*. "They don't know. We don't know any-

145

thing." She thought of the destroyed address, the note with its distinctive lettering tucked into her pocket, the way Simone had looked in the car. Her eyes, stony, dulled. There was no point trying to convince Sal; no one was going to help her. She was on her own.

"I just want to get away for a bit." She didn't say anything else about Simone. It wasn't worth the argument. She didn't mention Gil either, or the way she felt sick when she breathed in the air too deeply or looked too hard along the ridgelines or thought about the cherry-red car sagging in her drive.

Instead, Alison retreated to her car, ignoring Sal's pleas to stay. Peeled out of town as if Gil were there on her tail—for all she knew, he was. The fear and the anger and the thump of her heart, the uneven, unsettled, erratic intake of her breath, the tightening in her gut—it cascaded over her and spun her into a sort of trance, pushed her onto the road and kept her foot on the pedal, kept her hands on the wheel, kept her straight up the Hume, even when the tank got low, even when fatigue crept in, on and on and on and on, until she began to feel as though she could relax a little more, feel a little warmer, rest a little easier. Distance; distance made it easier to breathe.

16.

I t was about four hours of driving on the highway before Alison began to feel exhaustion overwhelm her. She'd hit the New South Wales border about an hour back, and now, as she rolled into Holbrook, she searched for a place to sleep. The land-bound submarine in the center of town was opposite the first motel she spied with a flashing vacancy sign. She turned into the car park and sat for a minute in the car, her head resting on the steering wheel while she gathered her thoughts.

He couldn't know where she was. There was no way. He wouldn't expect her to go back to where they'd known each other, back to where they'd been together. Surely, if he expected her to flee it would be to Melbourne, not Cairns.

She had the advantage. She had the advantage. She had the advantage.

Alison was startled from her thoughts by a sharp rap on the window; she pulled up from the steering wheel and peered out into the darkness. A middle-aged woman with ratty brown hair and a cigarette in her hand was staring at her through the window, other hand on her hip.

"Not a bedroom, love; if you want one of those it'll be sixty dollars for the night."

Alison opened the car door. "Sorry, I've been driving for hours, I was just having a quick rest before I came in to see you."

"You want a room, then?"

"Yes, please."

"Well, come on, let's get you set up." The woman flicked the cigarette onto the ground and stepped on it as she lumbered into the office. The sprawling one-floor motel consisted of a row of redbrick rooms, a small fenced pool, and a dimly lit office off to the side of the driveway. Alison already knew the bed would be made with a cheap floral quilt and overstarched white sheets. She could see the brown glass sheeting of the shower cubicle and the dusky pink floor-to-ceiling accordion blinds on the floor-to-ceiling windows without even needing to check in. But she needed sleep, and this was as good a place as any. In the office the woman fussed about with Alison's ID and credit card for a good five minutes before handing over a key to room 14.

Alison threw her bag down on the bed and lay flat, stretching her arms above her head and arching her back up. She felt the dusty wallpaper with her fingertips before pulling her hands away from the wall and rolling onto her stomach. For a minute she closed her eyes and considered going straight to sleep. But her stomach grumbled loudly and she reluctantly pulled herself upright. At the very least she needed a drink after all that driving, and she sure as hell wasn't willing to pay minibar prices.

She'd walked for less than a minute down the brightly lit but eerily deserted main street before she saw the Holbrook Hotel. Inside Alison clocked the dining room. It was out the back and empty. She sat down and looked at the menu and settled on the steak and chips. A man came to take her order and brought her a glass of water and a shot of whiskey, as requested. While she waited for the food to come out she googled Gil. On the surface he seemed easy to find. His Facebook profile was unrestricted, and Alison could read his updates. They were inane, stupid comments about footy. Or the weather in Cairns. Or the last big fish he'd snagged. They stopped about two weeks ago. Alison looked at his personal information. There was an email address listed, the same one he had when they were together. She'd forgotten he was so open, so willing to let anyone in. Always looking for the way to leverage it best—get the most out of every interaction, every person who crossed his path.

She drafted him an email. If he was responsible for Simone's death, and he thought Alison had these tapes he wanted, then he might just be curious enough to say something useful. Alison thought maybe she could get information without giving away where she was.

Gil

I don't know what the fuck you're playing at. You don't get to ask me for anything. Maybe we should talk about the tapes. My number's in the signature.

Alison

Reaching out to him made her skin crawl. But she closed her eyes, saw Simone's face swimming in the dark before her, and sent the email anyway, then took a large swig of her whiskey and googled Chris Waters.

The last three articles he'd written popped up, all of them about the bushfire. She started to read, but every word, every quote from a friend or acquaintance about their lost loved ones, made the acid in her stomach rise. She was about to put her phone away when it buzzed.

Another message from Billy.

Sal says you've gone away. What the fuck are you doing?

Alison's face flushed. She felt the bile flip and twist in the pit of her belly. She didn't know how to tell him to back off. She didn't know if she wanted to tell him to back off. She drained the rest of the whiskey.

I'm looking for Michael Gilbert Watson. Don't worry about me Billy, I can handle this fine.

After she pressed send Alison spent longer than usual staring at the screen, waiting to see if he would send a response. She was interrupted when the waiter dumped her plate on the table. A small, fatty fillet, graying around the edges, sagged on a bed of soggy chips. This atrocity was cloaked in a green-brown pepper-flecked sauce and finished off with a side of wilted lettuce and thickly cut red onions. She called out and asked for hot English mustard. Anything to mask the overwhelming impression she was eating dinner either in a hospital or a nursing home.

Alison chewed on her overdone steak. The fibers turned from sinew to dust in her mouth. Another sip of whiskey would have washed it down well enough. She kept eating, hunched over her plate, trying not to catch anyone's eye. But the whiskey had disappeared faster than the food. The bartender called out to her from across the room.

"Want another, love?"

Alison nodded, raising her hand in thanks and smiling

weakly, her mouth full of food. He brought her a beer, not a whiskey, the head foamy, spilling over the top of the glass as he set it down. He smiled at her, seemed to be waiting for her to say something.

"Thanks, much appreciated." Alison tipped the glass in his direction before taking a sip.

"No worries. You passing through to Sydney?"

"Sure, passing through."

"Didn't think I knew you. I'm Matthew, this is my mum's pub."

He looked at least forty, the skin on his arms leathery from sun, permanently stained with a web of tattoos. His face was set with pure greed. Alison took another bite of the steak, the meat mushy in her mouth. She chewed slowly, thinking of a way to untangle herself from the conversation as painlessly as possible.

"Pass my compliments on to her, then. Nice place."

He nodded, seemingly satisfied with her response, took it as an invitation to sit.

"Not too busy. Don't mind if I take my break here, do ya?" Alison took another bite, didn't say anything. "Where're you staying tonight, then? The Main Street Inn, I imagine?"

"Not sure I'm staying, got a long way to go, so I might push on after dinner." Alison knew this lie would make it impossible for her to keep drinking.

"Shame, was going to give you your next one on the house, but can't be encouraging drink driving, can I?"

"You're too kind, but no, I am going to finish this one and be off." Their eyes locked across the table, long enough for Alison to see something in his. But maybe she was imagining it. He had a wedding band on his ring finger, and a soft, beer-padded belly.

Alison's phone rang. It was Billy. This time, she gladly answered.

"Hi." She forced her voice to sound lighthearted.

"What are you doing, Ally? Jesus."

"I'm in Holbrook. Making good time actually."

"What?"

"Well, I've still got a fair way to go, but it's a good start."

The bartender sat across from her, listening, staring as she spoke.

"I don't know what you think you're doing, but you need to come home. This is stupid. They did a second autopsy, and pending the inquest finding, they're pretty confident Simone died in the fire. Whatever you think you're looking for, it doesn't exist."

"I'll be back in a couple of days; you won't even miss me." She smiled at the bartender, trying to seem casual, keep her voice light. The woman at the motel had photocopied her license. She'd charged her card. If Billy needed to find her, he could. She thought about the open lot in front of the motel rooms. It was dark, with nowhere obvious to hide. The office would be closed now. The bartender was looking at her chest.

"Alison, you're not thinking straight. You need to come home. I know this is hard. I know you're probably in shock. I want to help you, but you won't fucking let me."

"Thanks, Billy, I gotta go."

He didn't say anything for a few beats. "Please don't do this, Al, it's not going to fix you."

Alison slipped her finger onto the phone screen, ending the call before she took it down from her ear.

She waited to be sure Billy wasn't there anymore and then said, "Love you too."

A shadow of annoyance passed over the bartender's face, and for the first time since he sat down, he looked away.

"Boyfriend?" he asked as she placed the phone back down on the table.

"Yeah, he's worried about me driving all this way alone."

"You're a big girl, what's he scared of?" He leaned forward enough for the whiff of onions and cigarettes, and something else, something long dead and rotted in his gullet, on his breath, to hit Alison full on. She tried not to physically react, kept the smile in place.

"Oh, you know cops, paranoid something bad's going to happen."

He pulled back quickly, stood up from the table, pushing the chair back with enough speed and force that it rocked a little in his wake, and picked up Alison's half-eaten meal.

"Finished?"

"Yeah, thanks." She smiled at him again, keeping her reactions the same as before. It was his behavior that had changed. More formal, less eager to please.

"Well, it was nice to meet you, hope you have a safe drive."

"Thanks, and please do tell your mum what a great place this is."

Alison drained the rest of the beer from her glass, slapped two twenties on the table to cover the meal and the drinks, and walked out of the pub, not stopping to look back.

The street was empty, dark now. Alison hustled to her motel. The room was suffocating, so she turned on the fan. It rattled as the fins rotated, and to block out the sound of it, she turned on the TV. She lay on top of the sheets and closed her eyes, exhausted, and fell into a deep sleep. It was the first night of proper rest she'd had since the fire.

17.

In the bathroom, the tile felt cool on Alison's cheek: the blanket over her head was damp, the camphor smell stuck in her nostrils, the wet fibers stuck to her arms and legs. She breathed deeply, trying not to panic as the roaring cracks and low whooshes of the fire seemed to close in around her; slowly, the tiles began to heat up until they were too hot to lie on comfortably and she wasn't sure what to do.

She lifted the blanket and saw the room was ablaze around her, the flames licking the wood of the ceiling. All of a sudden, the window burst inward, showering the room in shards of sharpened glass, and the air rushed in, full of embers and smoke. Alison pulled the blanket around her tighter—she was naked, but she couldn't remember getting undressed. The floor was so hot, it burned her skin where she touched it, and Alison contorted her body, cocooning herself the best she could to stay protected.

She pulled the rapidly drying blanket over her head and closed her eyes; it was too hot, she couldn't breathe, she couldn't move, she couldn't feel her legs, she wondered why she wasn't dead, she felt the tears on her cheeks and thought how strange it was she could still cry; everything was quiet.

Alone still, desperate sobs escaped her as she breathed deeply, feeling the air all the way into the depths of her lungs.

The blanket was over her head and she ripped it off, sitting up straight and opening her eyes. The motel room was stinking hot.

It took Alison a couple of seconds to work out where she was. She lifted her hands in front of her face and examined them. No burns. Her legs were still there, in perfect working order. She didn't find it hard to breathe. Her phone was vibrating and wailing, the alarm Alison had set now into its ninth minute of harassment. She rolled over and killed the noise, looked to see if she'd gotten any messages.

The usual from Billy.

Two from Chris Waters.

There was one from Gil too.

Nice to hear from you so soon, Ally. Do you think I'm fucking dumb? I know Simone and you were in it together. You know it's in your best interests to do what I want.

She knew she should go home, show Billy the text, tell him everything, leave it up to the cops.

But the cops didn't care about Gil. Billy had said as much last night. Said Simone's death was accidental. Jim was right—radiant heat, probably. Not an ex with a grudge and with a fire as cover. If she went home, Alison knew she would be a sitting duck. No one would believe her about Gil, because everyone thought she was in shock, imagining things.

Alison picked up her phone and typed a response.

I don't know what you think you know about me and Simone, but you're wrong. Where are you?

She hesitated for a few seconds before she pressed send. The message zinged off. She imagined it sitting in Gil's inbox. Him opening it. Her skin itched. Alison rolled out of bed and turned on the shower. She let it run cold, the shock of the temperature raising bumps all over. As she lathered the shampoo in her hair, she closed her eyes. In the darkness, she could see the flames again, licking at her hands and feet, popping the glass in the window, boiling the water in the bath. Eyes wide-open, Alison leaned against the tile. The cold water from the showerhead cascaded over her. When she couldn't stand it anymore, she got out. Blue lips, chattering teeth, hair stuck to her like strands of cold spaghetti. Dressing quickly, Alison opened the door of the room to see about the breakfast tray. Cornflakes, orange juice, long-life milk, and a banana. She ate it quickly, not really tasting anything.

When she went to pay the bill and check out, the ratty-haired woman was back at the desk.

"Better not have had anything from the minibar without telling us. We can take it from your card, you know." She stared, inscrutable.

"Nah, just breakfast. Thanks again, you have a lovely place here." Alison smiled, wanted to keep it light.

The woman dragged the key across the countertop. "If you're heading for Sydney, there's a big crash on the highway, it'll be a few hours at least before it's clear—maybe the rest of the day, who knows. You take the road to Bega, hook up to the Pacific Highway, you'll make better time today."

Alison beamed at her. "Thank you, thanks so much." She climbed into the car for another long leg, blasting the air-conditioning until the car felt like a refrigerator. It was a four-hour detour to get to the coast road, but the GPS confirmed the woman's intel. A petrol truck had lost control in a storm, overturned on a hairpin bend, spilled its guts everywhere, and the Hume was closed indefinitely.

The coast road was narrower, bordered by tall eucalypts

and shadow-casting pines. Cooler by a significant margin than the wide, flat, grass-bordered inland route. It was all pine needles and gray sand shoulders, with fewer cars, and far fewer trucks. But this road required a greater degree of concentration, as it wound its way along the headlands. Alison stopped for lunch in a little dot on the map with a service station, a bakery, and an antique shop heavy on the iron lacework. Sitting in the driver's seat, windows down, sunglasses pushed back on her head, she ate in quick, mindless bites, pastry flaking off the too-dry sausage roll, dusting her top and shorts. Her hair frizzy in the heat, sweat collecting on the back of her neck, running down her chest.

Outside, she could hear the thrum of the ocean. Not distant, insistent. She got out of the car, scarfed the last of her sausage roll, and dusted herself off. Off to one side of the road there was a beach track, soft gray sand leading seemingly over a cliff. She locked up and headed for the path. It was hard to follow, overgrown. Ferns low down whipped her ankles, bottlebrush, acacia, cut-leaf daisy, eucalypt, all pushing in on the sides. She walked with purpose. Heavy, stomping footsteps creating vibrations designed to make the snakes scarce.

Down the tentative trail, curving in and out of the cut, the crowded foliage obscuring the sea, which Alison could smell now as well as hear. Wet salt caught in her throat, and pushing through a thick tangle of branches, Alison burst onto a wedge of earth where nothing but soft, wide grass grew. The beach unfolded in front of her, white sand, slight waves breaking on a sandbar a little way out, the water clear as glass, a school of flathead dancing, suspended in the crystal liquid. It was lush here, green, the air heavy with moisture and the scent of bottlebrush. Alison stood for a moment, frozen in place. She traced the edge of the water, the lines of the rocky outcrop that brought the cliff down sharply to the ocean, and surveyed the jewel scaffolding all around. Behind her, the softly beaten track wound upward, the branches overhead heavy with moisture, supple and full. There was nothing dry here, no tinderbox waiting to catch. She savored it.

The beach was deserted and in this isolation she felt safer than she had for days. The heat of the fire, the menace of Gil—they could not touch her now. Alison stripped down to her underwear and waded into the shallows. The water was warmer than she expected, and the quiet unnerved her. She looked back toward the shore, clocked the track she'd come in on, saw another a little farther up. If anyone came down, she'd know about it well before they made it to the beach. Farther out, on the horizon, ships made an orderly queue. In the water she submerged her body, held her breath, wallowed in the knee-deep surf. Head turned toward the sky, floating, buoyant legs and arms askew. Alison wanted to stay here forever. She didn't want to keep going north or turn back south. She wanted to exist forever in this suspension of her life.

Maybe the solution to this problem was to get away, far away, and never go back. Leave it all behind and finally move to Paris, or somewhere else Gil couldn't find her, or wouldn't look for her. Would he always look for her? She didn't know, but maybe finding these tapes would put an end to it all, somehow.

Alison didn't know if she wanted to stay in Lake Bend. She didn't want to ever feel again the way she had as she'd cowered from the fire. The pads of her fingers began to curdle before her eyes. She watched as, wrinkled, wizened, they softened like overripe fruit. It was time to get out. A stiff wind raised bumps on her arms, her legs. Caught the wet and cooled her. Teeth chattering, lips blue, Alison stood, took in the expanse once more, and then turned back to the sheltered shore, the stiff incline of hard-to-burn deep jade. The salt on her skin already drying in the relentless sun, she trudged toward her discarded clothes, dressed quickly, and found the path.

Without looking back, she began the ascent. She didn't know how long she had been in the water, or how much time she'd lost. It annoyed her, how easily she was distracted. She needed to get back to the car. She wanted to see if Gil had sent any more messages, revealed anything useful. In her haste, Alison hadn't bothered to put her shoes on before stomping back along the path. The trail bent sharply, turned at the base of a tree with a root system prominent enough to snag an impatient foot. She tried to catch herself as she fell, but she just ended up with more scratches and scrapes. Winded, her palms shredded, Alison sat up, tried to find a comfortable way to re-orient herself. There was blood on her leg, her shoulder, the taste of metal in her mouth.

"Shit." Her voice punctuated the silence, not needing any kind of reply. "Shit. Shit. Shit. Shit."

OK, now she felt better.

Alison got up, wiped her palms on her shorts, grimaced as the sting hit her. She kept on trudging up the path, moving inevitably toward the road, her car, the world. When she eventually peeked out onto the shoulder of the highway and saw the tiny stop-in town before her, Alison was less relieved and more reluctant than she'd expected. The unsettled swish in her stomach that had largely dissipated as she floated in the sea was back. She heard the voice of reason in her head, telling her to turn around, head home. She ignored it. The car was quiet, suffocating. She sat in the driver's seat for a while, thinking about nothing in particular, focusing on the trees outside, trying not to fall asleep in the afternoon sun. It was time to go. She checked her phone, just to see.

Three messages from Billy.

2:13 pm

Al, please call me.

2:18 pm

We can track your phone you know.

2:23 pm

Detective Mitchell is pretty pissed you dated Simone's ex and didn't tell her.

So they knew, then.
A text from Gil came through.

You're a lying bitch. Nothing's changed. Don't worry Ally, I'll find you.

She put the phone down. Felt the pounding in her chest. Tried to calm it. He didn't have any idea where she was. No one had any idea where she was, unless Billy made good on his threat to track her. Gil would only find her if she let him. She pulled out of the shoulder, the loose gravel spinning under her tire tread. With a shudder the car nudged back onto the road, and she was on her way. Alison cranked the radio, listening to golden oldies as she wound around the coast road, wishing suddenly that she had a better plan than to go to Cairns, try to find whatever it was Simone had hidden from Gil. She wondered had it been in the car with her? But surely if it had been, the police would have found it and Chris Waters would have known about it.

With every passing moment, she was beginning to regret her choice to make this trip, but she couldn't bring herself to turn back. The road was twisted, but easy, and after a time, Alison made it onto the Sydney stretch, wide, forgiving.

18.

Alison had driven for at least three hours since she fell on the beach path, and her hands were itchy, stretched as they strained on the wheel. She was tired. All told, the detour had taken an extra five hours, and she was exhausted. Her head ached, and she kept fighting the urge to close her eyes. Although Sydney was within reach, Alison wasn't sure she'd make it. It was time to pull over, take a break again. She took the next exit, parked in the lot of a twenty-four-hour service station, and wandered in to find some caffeine.

The neon signs and fluoro lights hurt her eyes. Standing in the bathroom, splashing water on her face, she took a moment to really look at herself for the first time in days. Since the incident with Billy, she'd had trouble examining the lines of her face, the eyes looking back at her too full of scrutiny and judgment. Not her judgment, his. She pinched her cheeks, tried to bring her face back to life a little, pulled on the edges of her eyes, rubbed the cold water in along her hairline. Closed her eyes tight, tried to block out the buzz of the lights. A tube in the corner flickered, not quite in touch with the connector at one end. She took a few deep breaths. She looked up again and jumped a little when she saw Simone's face staring back at her from the mirror. Someone knocked on the door.

"Just a minute." Alison wiped the last of the water off her hands and unspooled a length of paper from the toilet roll.

Another knock.

"Just a sec!" She stuffed it in her pocket and wrenched the door open. The woman outside scowled a little.

"Watch out for the spiders in there," Alison said. The woman's face fell as Alison pushed past her.

In the shop she picked up a Coke for the caffeine and sugar, and a pack of smokes because it was that kind of day and why the hell not? As she paid for them, the clerk stared at her scratched-up hands. She got her change, stuffed her hands in her pockets, and left as fast as she could. She remembered what it was like to avoid the looks that came with being with Gil. The pity at the marks and fingerprints on her arms.

Back at the car she drank the Coke, all of it, and smoked a cigarette. Sucking down the nicotine, she began to feel a little more awake, and a lot more nauseous. She stubbed it out early on the bitumen, took a moment to steady her gut, and turned the key in the ignition. Sydney was less than an hour away. It was time to get back on the road.

On the highway, Alison dialed an old friend from art school. The call rang so many times, she assumed it was about to ring out. As she went to cancel the call she heard the pickup.

"Hello?"

"Luca, it's Alison."

There was silence for a second. "Alison! Really? Haven't heard from you in yonks."

"Yeah!" She laughed. Luca had been one of her closest friends for a while there.

"Hi, mate, how's it going?" Alison thought he sounded a little weary.

"Listen, I know it's been a bit, but I'm going to be in Sydney tonight and I was wondering if you want to catch up."

There was a pause; she could feel him hesitating.

"Oh cool, yeah, Al, sure. Actually, Christine is working to-night, so I'm supposed to be home looking after the girls."

"No problem. I'm driving so I can come wherever."

Another pause.

"OK, sure, I'll text you the address. What time do you think?"

The traffic was piling up, the line of glowing red lights snaking toward the city, visible in the distance. It wasn't quite seven, but Alison didn't think she'd be out of the worst of it for at least an hour.

"Eight thirty?"

Another long pause. "OK, see you then."

"Looking forward to it." Alison hung up quickly, not want-ing him to wriggle out. She'd crawled less than a meter when the phone rang again. She didn't look at it, figured it was Luca calling, changing his mind.

"Luca, look, I won't be in the way, I promise."

"Luca. He's that fucking art school creep that came to stay with us, right?"

It was Gil.

"Gilly." Alison felt her mouth drying out, the thump-thump-thump in her chest going staccato.

"What's up, Al? When am I gonna see you?"

"Who says you are?"

"Time makes it a certainty. I know you're running. Went by your place, you weren't there. Left you a message in the let-ter box."

"I got it." She paused. He waited. "Doesn't mean I'm run-ning. My house nearly fucking burned down."

"Do you have the tapes?"

Alison suspected that if she told the truth, he wouldn't believe her anyway, so she decided to play along.

"Wouldn't you like to know?" The traffic was bumper-to-bumper. Barely moving.

"Yeah, Alison, I fucking would. That's the fucking point." She didn't respond. "You fucking have them, don't you?"

"I gotta go. Talk soon." Alison hung up. She had no idea what tapes he was talking about. But she figured it was better to make him think he was right if she were to have any chance of figuring out what had really happened.

Did she even want to?

She hit the suburbs, and the crawl of the traffic was soul-destroying. Alison turned the radio up, rolled the window down, and hoped for the best. All she could do was move forward. She knew she should have told Billy about the piece of paper. Probably it was too late now. Would he even believe her? Sometimes, when she thought back to that day—the fire, being in the car with Jim, at Sal's house, lying in bed trying to sleep—Alison wasn't even sure it existed.

19.

Luca lived in a grimy old terrace in Newtown. The floor-boards of the balcony out front were cracked and curled with the weather, the iron lacework peeling and rusted in spots. Alison parked on the street, in a one-hour zone, deciding to risk the fine to save walking too far in the night. She could hear university students laughing and arguing and drinking up on King Street. It was still hot, sticky on her skin like the residue of a Frosty Fruit eaten too slowly. She smoothed her hair and straightened her rumpled clothes. Her palms were red, angry where there was sand in the crevices. She needed to soak them.

Alison stepped over a trike and a pink rubber ball on the tiled patio out front, raised her hand to knock on the door. Before she could Luca opened it, one finger to his lips.

"Sh, Ally, girls are asleep." He smiled at her. Looked the same as he always had.

"Sorry, traffic was murder."

"No worries, come in, come in." He ushered her past him, pointed down the darkly lit hall toward the lights glowing brightly in the kitchen. Alison tried to keep her footsteps soft as she picked her way through the girls' toys to the back of the house. Luca followed close behind, the only sound their breathing. His calm and measured, hers erratic, apprehensive. She noticed it now, in the inky heat, the way it slipped in and out in ragged jags, couldn't be regulated properly, couldn't be calmed. In the kitchen Alison sat at the table as Luca pulled the door shut behind them. He beamed at her. Made her get up for a hug, held her tight too long, then held her out at arm's length, like a proud grandmother at Christmas lunch.

"You look like shit, Alison. What's going on?"

"Gee, thanks, I've been driving all day. You look like you haven't gotten a haircut in months. What's your excuse?"

Luca laughed. "Kids." Alison smiled at him, grateful he was the same as always. That their exchanges could still sting but not bruise. She liked the honesty. He busied himself in the fridge, emerged with two beers and some pasta tossed with roasted tomatoes. "You hungry?"

"Starving." Alison gratefully took the beer from his hand, pressed her palms against it, the cold soothing her inflamed skin.

"What happened there?"

"I fell over on a beach track when I took a break today. Nothing major, but they could use a soak in some Dettol, I reckon."

"You always were a klutz. No problem, I got the full first-aid suite these days."

They drank in friendly silence while Luca heated up the pasta in the microwave, grated some Parmesan over it, a twist of black pepper on top of that. He slid the bowl across the table, Alison catching it with the back of her wrist. She ate, faster than she intended. He sat down across from her. She could feel his scrutiny. He let her finish before he began asking questions.

"So, what are you really doing here?"

"I'm on my way to Cairns. Haven't been back for a while, thought now's as good a time as any."

"Bullshit. You think I don't read the paper? That bushfire is big news." He paused, waiting maybe to see if Alison would volunteer anything. "And I read about your place. About the woman in the driveway. Your name was in the papers." He went over to the recycling bin, dug through the stacks, and pulled out what he was looking for. It was a piece by Chris Waters in the *Sydney Morning Herald*. A chat with Simone's parents, the details of the initial autopsy, the speculation about why Simone was there. A quote from her. "Resident Alison King was asked if she knew Ms. Arnold. She replied, 'No comment.'" Bloody Chris Waters. Nothing about Gil, though. "What's going on, Ally?"

Alison sighed, took a deep breath, and tried to spin Luca a story about how she wanted to get away from the journalists and the speculation and everything else about the town. She told him she needed to get away from all that sadness. From the blackness that stretched across paddocks and the lots where homes used to stand. It wasn't a lie, but it wasn't the whole truth either.

"I get it, it must have been awful." He spoke gently, but with an intensity she knew he rarely employed. "But, Al, I don't think that's really why you're here. Tell the truth."

Alison sighed. She knew there wasn't any reason to keep any of this from Luca. And he was far enough removed from both her current life and her former one with Gil that there wasn't any reason to think he'd be on anyone's side but hers. He was a good friend. One who had only ever been there for her when she asked him to be. And he was helping her out when he didn't have to.

She remembered a long time ago at a party he'd leaned in close to her while they'd sat on a roof, waiting for the ecstasy to kick in, and told her he'd fallen in love. For a moment she'd thought maybe her daydreams were about to come true, but then he'd told her all about Christine, and how he knew he'd marry her. About how she smelled and laughed and felt and thought. And Alison had listened. Her mind racing around in circles as she tried not to cry, tried not to blurt out every feeling she'd held inside, and then, as she began to chew the gum in her mouth faster and faster for something to do, Luca had pulled her by the chin so their noses almost touched.

"You're the best, Al."

She felt the flips and turns in her gut as though they were happening at half speed. "Sounds like Christine's the best actually," she'd replied, trying to keep it light, and definitely failing. But he didn't hear the heaviness.

"Yeah. Hey, listen, promise me something?" He didn't wait for her to reply, just motored on, fueled by MDMA and nicotine. "No matter what, we'll always be honest with each other. We can tell each other anything. Even if, like, you killed a guy, or I did, we'd help each other out. No bullshit, no secrets."

Luca was right. During her years with Gil she'd pulled away from all her friends, or he had pulled her away, and she hadn't really managed to take back the relationships because doing so required conversations like this one, where she had to admit things she'd rather forget. "You want to make a murder accessory pact?"

"It's not like I have a list of people to kill, Al, I just mean, you and me, we get each other, we're the same kind of person. We're . . . I trust you with everything, I know you don't judge me . . . I'm not explaining it properly."

She caught his hand in hers, like she was going to shake it. "No, I get it. You got a deal. No secrets, and help hiding the bodies."

They had shaken hands, Luca laughing. And then he had

spied Christine in the yard below, winked at her, and climbed back through the window and out of Alison's reach.

No secrets.

Luca couldn't help her if she didn't tell him the truth. She sighed and took a deep, steadying breath. Then she described the interminable wait under the blanket, finding Simone in her drive, stupidly sleeping with Billy, and finally, the hardest thing of all to admit to someone else, how ashamed she felt that she'd survived and Simone hadn't.

"I feel like I'm coming apart at the seams," Alison said. "Nothing feels good anymore. Nothing makes sense. Everything I do is the wrong thing, the wrong choice. I survived, but I don't know what that really means."

Luca didn't say anything. He got up from the table, found the Dettol on the high shelf in the pantry, made up a bowl of warm water that clouded milky white when he added it, and passed Alison cotton balls to clean the pads of her hands. While she worked, Luca rummaged on the booze shelf until he found the Chivas, tucked right in at the back, and poured them each a double. The antiseptic stung her cuts in that satisfying way, and she sipped the scotch, warmth spreading through her blood. "Thank you, Luca," she whispered as she began to relax a little.

He shrugged. "I got you."

She was buzzed enough, secure enough, to take a risk. "You promise?"

"Of course."

So she told Luca about the scrap of paper. About Gil. About the texts he'd sent. About the phone call.

"He knows you're with me?" Luca seemed alarmed.

"Yeah, but he doesn't know where you live, Luca, it's fine."

"I'm in the bloody book, Alison."

"You're in the phone book? Is there even still a phone book? Why?"

"What do you mean, why? I've got a landline, it's in the book, and yeah, the book is online now, but it still exists."

"Who has a landline?"

"This is what you choose to focus on?"

"He probably doesn't even know your last name. He only met you that one time."

They considered it. Luca began to relax. He got up, poured them more scotch. As he sat back down in his chair, someone began to knock gently on the front door. Alison looked at her phone. Nine forty-three p.m. Too late for someone selling something. There was a break, and then the knocking started again, louder this time. Upstairs, one of girls woke up, called out, "Daddy!," her voice disturbing a sister, who then began to wail.

"It's not going to be him, Luca." Alison was pale.

"Only one way to find out."

Luca stood up, waited for Alison to follow his lead, then opened the kitchen door and moved quickly back into the hallway.

"It's OK, girls. I'm here, I'll be up in a minute," Luca called up toward his daughters' room.

The glass in the front door rattled insistently with each rap. Luca first, Alison following behind. *Safety in numbers,* she thought, feeling absurd. Luca put all his weight behind the door, cracking it open a slice, keeping his body in the way of any attempt by whoever was there to push into the hall. Alison stretched her neck, craning to see around him, to see who was on the other side.

20.

t was dark out there, and the light didn't work, so it was difficult to make out the shape of a person in the shadows. But Alison could see immediately that it was a woman. She saw Luca's whole body relax.

"Christine. Shit. Why are you knocking? You woke up the girls." As she spoke Luca stepped back, enough to let his wife through the door. Alison shrank into the wall as Christine pushed past her.

"Left my keys and my bloody phone in the office like an idiot. Alison, good to see you again." The words didn't match the tone, or the look Christine shot Alison as she moved into the hall and up the stairs toward her crying daughters. Luca pushed the door shut, made sure it was dead bolted.

"Give us a minute, Ally, I'll be back soon." He bounded up the stairs behind his wife, leaving Alison alone in the hallway. The glass in the door looked out on a quiet street. She could see the soft outlines of the lights, the cars parked at the curb, the trees swaying in the slight summer breeze. She retreated to the kitchen, went back to nursing her cuts. Upstairs she could hear the lullabies, and then the hushed argument of the house's adult residents enticed her back out into the hallway. These old Sydney terrace houses didn't allow for much privacy.

"Ah, come on, you're the one who woke the girls. Don't be a fucking stick-in-the-mud. She's my friend. She needs a place to crash. Be a little more generous." Luca's tone was placating.

"Don't do that."

"What?"

"You fucking know. Don't make me the problem when you're the one inviting a strange woman to stay at our house on a Wednesday like it's no big thing."

"Don't be such a killjoy, Christine. Strange woman? She was at our wedding. She needs my help."

"Alison is a person you have trouble saying no to."

"Come off it."

"You can't bear for her to think you're not cool. But, Luca, my love, you're not cool. You're a dad. You make puns. You are a middle-class, middle-of-the-road guy. You drink Corona with lime like it's fancy. It's not fancy."

"I know that. I don't care about that."

"You do." Alison heard her laugh. "You looked actually wounded when I accused you of being middle-class just then."

"Corona is off-limits, OK? You've gone too far." His voice was playful now, light and sweet. In the dim hallway light Alison could see their shadows dance softly on the double-height cream plaster. They moved closer together, the lines around them merging in the middle. She heard the smack of lips on skin. "I also have trouble saying no to you."

"That's entirely appropriate. I'm your wife." She spoke now with begrudging warmth. On the wall their heads had become one giant bauble, engulfing their individuality. Alison strained to hear their murmurs now. Felt on her brow the uncomfortable sweat of eavesdropping and decided to retreat into the kitchen, heard the creak of the stairs, but no one came down. Alison scrolled through her messages, wanting a distraction, and read some of Billy's for the first time.

I need to talk to you please

Al I'm sorry I pushed you away and didn't take your questions about Michael Watson seriously

Come home I'll tell you what I know

She stared at the words. What he knows? What could he know? Probably more than her. But he didn't know about Simone having her address. He didn't know about Gil thinking Alison had something of his. He didn't know how exposed she felt sleeping with the sheets off, but how impossible it was to sleep with them on. He didn't know shit.

The stairs creaked again. Luca and Christine tiptoed into the kitchen, rosy. Christine's fine features were bright. A dewy mist of sweat on her unpowdered brow. Her brown eyes danced around the room, wide-awake. The suit she'd come home in replaced by worn old jeans and a T-shirt. Christine was the kind of beautiful that Alison longed to be. Completely uninterested in it, entirely stunning. Luca, who'd pursued her relentlessly, breaking up her university romance and basically camping on her doorstep until she agreed to see him, was transfixed by her. It pissed Alison off sometimes. She'd had a crush on Luca back then, but he didn't want her. He loved her, like a sister, or a cousin, or some other woman whom he cared for deeply but never thought about naked. She thought about Billy, felt a little worse than she had before. Resolved to call him tomorrow.

"Alison, I'm sorry about earlier, I get a little cranky when the girls are unsettled." Christine smiled warmly.

"Oh, no, it's totally fine. I'm sorry to have dropped in like this. I didn't know where else to go."

"You were right to call, we've been watching the news—

the coverage of the fire. You must've had a stressful couple of weeks."

"Yeah." It hung there in the air between them. Even though it shouldn't, hearing Christine reduce it to stress pissed her off.

Luca was busy over at the sink, slicing something with a knife on the drainer, glasses clinking. He turned around with a flourish and set three glasses of beer on the table. On the rim of each, a wedge of lime.

"To old friends!" he proclaimed, raising his glass and meeting Christine's eyes. She was giggling as she raised hers back.

"To old friends and cold beers." Christine openly laughed.

"Yes, to old friends and fancy beer with lime." Alison saw them look at each other. The color rose in Christine's cheeks again. Everyone drank.

Over the beers they talked through it all. The fire, Simone, Gil, the note, Chris Waters, the tapes Gil thought Alison had. Alison felt a lightness that she couldn't describe and that wasn't fueled just by alcohol.

"What could she possibly have that he'd want that bad?" Luca took a long swig of his beer. Christine reached up and pulled his stubbie down, gave him a look that said take it slow.

"I don't know. I don't understand any of this. He was gone from my life, and that was good, and I was doing OK, and then on the worst possible day, at the worst possible moment, she comes up my drive, gets killed in a fire, and now—now—he thinks we were conspiring against him somehow?"

"It doesn't make any sense." Christine picked at a chicken leg she'd dug out of the fridge. "Why now? Why you?"

Alison couldn't answer the questions. She genuinely didn't have anything of his. When she'd ended it, she'd left all traces of him behind. And that had been years ago now—almost three of them, actually. He'd been with Simone that whole time, and she'd never met her. Never known who she was until now. She didn't see what it could possibly be.

"Proof of something damaging for him, right?"

"Was he dealing drugs? Cheating on his taxes? Stealing from work?" Christine reeled off these options as though these sorts of things were commonplace. Although Alison thought maybe they were, she'd never seen Gil get into any of them.

"No, not that I know about, and what would tapes have to do with that?"

"Could be security footage? His hand in the till, literally? Luca, pass me another beer, would you?" Christine wiped grease from the chicken on her T-shirt and screwed the top off the beer.

"It doesn't seem likely, does it? If Simone had that, and she was scared of him, why wouldn't she just give it to the police? Why try and involve me?"

They all sat silently for a minute.

"You're scared of him?" Christine asked it gently. Like she'd already figured out the heaviness to it.

"Yeah, he's . . . I mean, what if he killed her?" She felt Christine's eyes on her, scrutinizing her.

"Whatever is on it, you have to assume Gil wants it bad enough to come after you." Luca had been musing on the possible contents of the tape for a good twenty minutes.

"But we don't know what it is, so it's useless," Alison replied. They didn't even know if it was audio or video. They were stumped.

"What makes someone run so far? Why would she come to you? Usually they go to a shelter, or a relative. A stranger, two states away—I don't know why she would." Christine worked at a legal aid service.

"It has to involve me somehow. I just don't know how."

"Find out what it is, find out why," Luca said.

"OK, sure, but how do I find out without letting him know I don't have it?" The annoyance spilled over into her tone.

"And without putting yourself in harm's way," Christine added.

No one talked for a while.

"Maybe we should call it a night." Christine drained her beer and reached her hand out to the empty Alison was nursing.

"Yeah, I'm too tired. I need to sleep." Alison had felt like sharing all this with them was the right decision, but now she was just frustrated. As Luca pulled out the couch and tucked in the corners of the fitted sheet, Christine gathered up the glasses, put the empty bottles in the recycling box. Alison climbed the stairs as quietly as possible to wash her face and teeth in the small bathroom tucked onto the hallway landing.

In the fluoro light her skin was garish. Every pore, every nick and ridge and stretch and crater and angry risen bump, illuminated. She picked at a blackhead too pronounced on her chin. Pushed the accumulated cream of a whitehead out from below the skin on the smooth of her right cheek. Fingernails left red canyons. She splashed cold water on her face to surprise it. Felt it tighten with the shock. Stared too long into her eyes, swimming a little from the beer. They took on the gray-blue hue of her imagined doppelganger. She swayed, felt dizzy from those beers, grabbed the cold porcelain to steady herself. The mug on the rim of the basin laden with tiny toothbrushes and kids-formula Colgate teetered and fell, smashing onto the tile next to Alison's bare foot.

"Shit." The word was out of her mouth at volume before she could stop it. The combination of the smashed mug and the loud, unfamiliar voice woke the girls. Alison heard a drowsy

"Mummy!" and a backup chorus of cries. She winced, stuck her head out into the hall. Christine was already halfway up the stairs, but Luca overtook her, gently pulling her back with his arm.

"I got it, go to bed." He kissed her as he continued up the stairs, shook his head at Alison as he rounded the landing.

Christine got to the top of the stairs as the soothing low tones of Luca's voice began to quiet the girls. She looked pissed again, but also too tired to really care.

"Sorry, my hand slipped and knocked it."

"It's fine. Let me clean it up if you're done in here. The bed's made."

"OK, sure, I'm really sorry."

"Alison, I don't think you even know what you're apologizing for. Go to bed." It was a mother's tone. Admonishing, businesslike, annoyingly insightful.

She stepped around Christine and tiptoed as quietly as possible down the stairs into the lounge room. Sat on the edge of the foldout couch, the flimsy mattress sagging with her weight. Not bothering to change into pajamas, she stretched out on top of the covers, felt their crisp coolness on the backs of her legs, against her cheek, pressing into her elbows. She closed her eyes. Listened to the murmurs of Luca's lullabies and promises. She heard the heavy fall of Christine's footsteps above her. The slow progress toward silence upstairs made as the minutes creaked by. She drifted for a while but was woken by the buzz of a message on her phone. Too tired to deal with Billy right now, she pushed the phone away and rolled over, her face toward the bar-covered window that looked into the back courtyard.

As she closed her eyes again she thought she saw a blur of movement. Probably a possum. She fell asleep to the rise and fall of Luca's too-loud snores and the quiet murmurs of the girls' dreamworld. No closed doors, no sound too small to carry on the hot summer air. The weather wrapped her up as if in a cocoon and carried Alison away for a few sweet hours. Cicadas on the breeze, the clack of skittering cockroaches under the boards below.

21.

t was dark, silent, when Alison woke up, no murmuring children or first birdsong of the day. She sat up straight and gasped, unsure what had startled her. The kitchen, which had been softly illuminated by the neon glow of the microwave display when Alison fell asleep, was pitch-black. In these unfamiliar surrounds, she couldn't define her location with ease. The couch creaked beneath her as she turned to swing her legs to the floor. The early-morning chill took her by surprise—hands and feet like ice, Alison headed for the window, reached up and grabbed the wooden frame and began to slide it down, the rope moving easily in the sash, and when it stopped, it took her a second to fix her eyes on the obstruction. A hand, the fingers curled so the top knuckle twisted onto the inside of the frame—Alison's breath caught in her throat; she raised her eyes to look for the face of the person who owned the hand and it stared back.

Gil, a smirk visible on his lips in the dark—he didn't speak, just raised his other hand to his lips, his fingers gesturing for Alison to stay quiet while his hand released the window frame and reached inside the house, where it clamped down hard on the flesh of her forearm; she heard a burst of surprise leap from her lips but couldn't make sense of how she had made it. Every millimeter of Alison's body burned with cold fear; it didn't seem possible to move, to speak, even to blink. Gil was still holding on to her, pressing his fingertips into the flesh of her arm, but he had begun to gesture toward the back door, in the kitchen, just around the corner from that window, and when Alison tried to pull away from Gil's grasp she found that she was stuck and she couldn't get him to loose his fingers. She couldn't make him free her from his grip, and she didn't know how she was supposed to open the door without his letting her go, but she also didn't plan on opening the door if he did. It seemed to Alison that Gil knew this, so they stood in silent resolution, neither willing to give the other an inch to run with until Alison opened her mouth to speak but nothing came out.

She had no words to use to extricate herself from this moment, and she didn't understand why she couldn't stop moving her mouth up and down, up and down, like a fish. She tried again to pull away; Gil grasped her even more tightly. She began to heat up with the effort of trying to wrest her arm free, and suddenly when she looked into the kitchen, where there had been nothing but darkness before, silent flames licked at the walls.

She felt the heat of the flames but could not hear them. Silent like the inky night that had stolen her voice and rooted her to the floor, they slithered on silken tongues into the lounge room, where Gil smiled as he watched her, eyes wide with panic, whole body trying to wrench itself loose, no voice to set her free. Alison grabbed at the window frame with her free arm and pushed down with all her might, her weight dislodging it and bearing the wooden sash right down in one slick motion; the pain of it made Gil release her arm and she was suddenly able to jump back, away from his grip. She was suddenly able to hear the rush of the fire as it suffocated the room. She was suddenly able to scream.

The water hit her full in the face, pooling in her open mouth, rushing up her nose and settling on the closed lids of her eyes. Alison sputtered, unable to breathe for a second, and then raised her sodden eyelids. Christine was standing over her, a glass, now empty, in her hand, and a frightened small person peeking out from behind her left leg. Christine, already dressed for work in a black pencil skirt and a gray silk tank, looked equal parts bemused and concerned.

"All right?"

Alison took a minute to work it out. Guessed Christine wasn't fully over the fact that Alison had woken the girls up in the night and was now screaming gibberish from the couch while Christine was trying to get them ready for school. "All right. Sorry, I've had some bad dreams since the fire."

"When I have a bad dream, Mummy says I shouldn't worry because dreams can't hurt you." The little girl was brown eyed, brown haired, brown skinned. She looked like a miniature of her father.

"Your mum is pretty clever, isn't she?" Alison replied, trying to smile, to forget the sickness in her stomach, not to rise to the bait Christine had thrown at her. A rivulet of water rushed toward her chest, found the gap between her breasts, and slicked onto her stomach. She writhed a little, trying to mop it up with her shirt without visibly showing her discomfort. Christine watched her; the look on her face made clear she'd chosen to throw a full glass of water at Alison not because she thought it was the best option, but because it was the most satisfying one. Christine turned into the kitchen, began cutting up sandwiches.

"Mummy says I'm just as clever as she is and one day I can be a lawyer like her."

From upstairs, Luca's voice came drifting into the lounge. "Hannah, have you brushed your teeth yet?"

The girl looked at Alison with a wry smile on her bright face. "Yes, silly Daddy!" She raised her finger to her lips and mimed a *Shhhh* at Alison. The gesture made her skin crawl.

"That's a lie, Daddy! Daddy, she's not telling the truth," another little voice piped in from somewhere upstairs. Alison tried to push down the discomfort she felt. Tried not to remember the cling of Gil's hand on her arm, the silent lick of the flames that seemed so very real.

"Your toothbrush feels as dry as a bone. Come do your teeth."

The little girl rolled her eyes in Alison's direction. She set her mouth in a grim line and let out a perfunctory wail. And then, as though she already knew resistance wouldn't save her, she began to trudge toward the stairs, stomping emphatically.

"Little Miss Sunshine this morning, that one," Christine said, bringing Alison a cup of coffee. She sat on the edge of the foldout couch and examined Alison with a level of intensity that made her uncomfortable. "Sorry about the water, it's just, my brother used to sleepwalk and it was the best way to bring him out of it. You were scaring the girls."

"Sorry, and sorry about waking them up last night. I really appreciate you letting me stay." Christine made Alison feel off-balance all the time. Never smart enough, or beautiful enough, and now she was caught out in the middle of a nightmare. Screaming like a child. A drip of water slid down her cheek. She darted her tongue out of the corner of her mouth and caught it. Salty. She was somehow sweating.

"It always feels like you spend half your time apologizing to me."

"Sorry." They both laughed. Christine handed her a newspaper.

"There's a big list in there today of the people who they've determined died in the fire."

"Yeah. Shit." Alison had tried in the past week or so to distance herself from the fire as much as possible. Wrapped up in Simone, trying to forget about what had happened with Billy, she'd pushed it out as much as she could. After the first couple of days, waiting to hear from Meg and never getting a response, she'd just shut it down. All the thoughts and feelings about her friend, her neighbors, the people she knew probably didn't exist anymore. Not just didn't exist, but their homes, their lives, their physical presences completely erased.

She fingered the rough, flimsy newsprint, flipped it over, and unfolded it on the pillow. On page seven, a long story about the fire, the aftermath, the current death toll. It was now at one hundred sixty-four. On the page there were a lot of names Alison recognized. More than she expected. People she had been at school with, people she saw at her yoga class or knew from parties or the pub. Her old doctor, the man who had made her bring her mother in with her before he'd prescribed her the pill when she was sixteen. Who'd pierced her ears with a needle on her tenth birthday, numbing each spot first with ice, and gently pressing the point into each pudgy lobe while holding a cork to the back of it. Who'd stitched her leg when she'd gashed it open on a barbed-wire fence chasing rabbits with Ellie Craig in year one.

"Shit." Meg's name was on the list. Alison knew it would be—it had been for a few days now—but that didn't make it less shocking. There were many more that knocked the wind out of her lungs, tightened a grip on her chest, pushed the tears from her eyes as she read. Sal had told her a few of these names before. The bush telegraph had been working overtime in the days after the fire. But somewhere in Alison's mind she'd drawn a line between hearing the names and acknowledging what they meant. Now they were here, printed in the paper. Not the local paper either. The *Sydney Morning Herald*. A whole state away. They were really dead. Newsprint-on-your-fingers dead.

"People you know?" Christine's voice was soft, and as she spoke she reached out and closed her hand around Alison's.

"Plenty." She wanted to go home. She wanted to be with her people. To go to the memorials and cry with the survivors and drink with Billy and play cards with Sal and paint, paint the landscape before it could recover. She didn't want to get back in her car and keep going to Cairns. She didn't want to chase Gil. She didn't care about Simone. That wasn't true. She became aware of Christine's hand, still gripping tight to hers. The room seemed too big and too small all at once.

"Alison, did Gil hurt you too?"

"I don't want to talk about him right now."

"OK, I get it. But I'm here if you ever do. And please be careful, he's violent. Men like him only get more unhinged if they feel threatened, not less."

Luca came cascading down the stairs, ushering the girls in front of him.

"We gotta go, Chris, girls'll be late."

"I'll be late," Christine replied.

"Mummy, I want to go with you!" Hannah declared.

"Come on, baby, you know you've got to go with Daddy. He'll walk you to school like always." She then turned to Alison. "I take Edie with me; we've got a day care in the building. Luca walks Hannah on his way to the train."

Alison got up from the couch, moved across the room, and held on to Luca with both arms. He leaned into her and tried to give her a hug.

"Why are you wet?"

"Long story. Thanks for having me."

"Sorry we have to run. Take your time; I've put a towel in the bathroom for you—it's the Princess Jasmine one."

"I don't want Daddy. I want you." Hannah stomped her feet and crossed her arms in fierce opposition to the morning routine.

"Pull the door shut behind you. It'll lock itself." Luca looked like he wanted to stay with Alison. "Christ, Al, you're white as a sheet. You OK?"

"I'm fine. Go to work."

Christine was pulling a still-protesting Hannah out the door; Edie dutifully, quietly followed. Luca squeezed Alison's arm and grinned at her.

"Stay with us on your way back, would you? And keep me in the loop." He followed his family out the door, pausing to stick his head back into the hall. "And be careful, you're not invincible."

The door closed with a thud behind him, and Alison could hear Luca arguing with his daughter on the other side. The quarrel faded out of earshot as they headed up the street. Alone in the house with the page of names staring back at her, Alison looked over the list again. And then she cried, uncontrollably, violently, loudly, hideously. It felt like it would never pass.

22.

After her shower Alison lay wrapped in a thin towel on the sofa, not yet folded back into a seat. She'd spent almost two hours on the phone, after she'd stopped crying but before she could really force herself to move away from the paper. First with Sal, to talk through all the losses, and then calls to friends and families of the people she knew on that list. Saying how sorry she was, trying to remember a moment between her and the person who was gone that put them in a good light, or a happy place. It probably didn't help the person Alison was talking to, but it felt like the right thing. Now she was trying to decide what to do next. The phone buzzed, and Alison looked at the screen. Billy. What the hell could it hurt at this point?

"Hey, Billy."

"Alison, thank you for picking up."

"What is it?"

"Where are you? Are you going to come home?"

"I'm in Sydney. Stayed with my friends Luca and Christine last night." There was silence on Billy's end. She could hear him breathing. "Did you see the list? In the paper today?"

"What list?"

"The names, Billy. Everyone who— Everyone."

"Oh geez, Al, I've seen that list before. I'm one of the people compiling it."

Stupid. So fucking stupid. "Of course."

"You OK?"

"Yeah, just—yeah." She didn't want to ask how he was. She didn't think she could stand to know.

"Come home, Al."

"I want to."

"So . . . do it."

"I don't think Simone died in the fire, Billy."

"She did. I told you already. You're chasing shadows."

"She was coming to me. She wanted something from me. I have to find out what."

"You don't know that. When I was in Melbourne for Jason's bucks night last September we walked into a little cocktail place in an alley—you know what Melbourne's like—a fucking hole-in-the-wall with no sign, just an upside-down bicycle and a rotting red door. I'd never been there, none of us had. No one knew we'd be there. We happened on it as we were leaving the cheap dumpling place down the road. You know, the one with the weird upstairs area and the plastic cups?"

"Billy—"

"Let me finish. So anyway, we go in, and the place has, like, three tables and a short bar with two people behind it and a wall of whiskey and other shit I've never seen before or since. All the tables are full, and the room is totally packed with people, like, more people than you could imagine in such a tiny space. I say to Jase, let's go somewhere else, and he says, nah, mate, this place is cool. So, we push into the bar and as I'm about to order I realize the woman serving is a backpacker who worked at the Imperial for a few months earlier that year and we'd — Well, anyway, I knew her pretty well."

"Biblically," Alison suggested, the tone sarcastic.

"That's not the point. The point is, we walk into a random bar and there's this chick from fucking Belgium who had worked at the Impy and now she's serving us whiskeys in a dingy alley bar in Melbourne."

"Billy, I know you think this is stupid, but I don't think this is that." Now was the time to tell him about the note. But she held back. Alison didn't know why. Or she did, but it was selfish. Flimsy. Telling Billy about the note meant telling Billy about the beatings. About the abuse. She wasn't ready.

"It's exactly that. The world is a small place; random coincidences happen. And it's not safe to go after Michael Watson, if that's what you're planning."

"I don't know what I'm planning. I just want to find out why she was there."

"I told you. Coincidence."

"Detective Mitchell didn't think that."

"She does now. The forensics are pretty certain. It's a hell of a coincidence, but it doesn't look like foul play from a medical perspective."

"You her messenger now?"

"Al, come on. Come home."

She wanted to say yes. But something about Billy's certainty pushed her in the other direction. Alison had always been stubborn, but now she felt it was more than that.

"Sorry, I can't."

A long pause. Alison could hear him let out a breath that sounded as though it came from the very bottom of his lungs. "Can we talk about us?"

"I don't have anything to say."

"OK. I do. I'm not done. I don't think we're done. So, I'm here. When you decide you're ready, I'm here."

"Don't waste your life waiting on me."

"It's not a waste."

"It is if you're waiting forever."

"I don't think I will be." Alison rolled her eyes and steeled her stomach.

"Ugh, the absolute worst thing about men is their inability to understand that when a woman says no, she's not playing hard to get."

"Don't do that."

"Do what?"

"Make this some bullshit meditation on the nature of men. This is about you and me. And I think you know there's more to us than a drunken fuck on the floor."

"You might want there to be more to it, but there's not." She could feel his hurt and anger in the way his breathing changed. "I gotta go."

Before he could say anything, Alison hung up.

The terrace house was blissfully silent and cool, the double brick walls insulating it as the sun rose high in the summer sky. She forced herself to get up, strip the sheets off the sofa, and fold it back up. Alison got dressed in shorts and a T-shirt, tied her hair up in a pony, and went looking for the laundry. It was tucked in behind the house in the backyard, down a mossy brick pathway that led from the back door in the kitchen to the courtyard encircled by frangipani and a towering gum. She stuffed the sheets and the towel in the washing machine and put on a cold cycle. The courtyard had a table in the middle, shaded from the worst of the sun, in the path of a cool breeze. Alison sat down and tried to think through what she needed to do, or even what she wanted to do. A lorikeet in the gum tree trilled noisily. Her phone, idly nestled in her palm, began to vibrate.

23.

"Alison, Chris Waters here."

"Yes, hi."

"Look, just checking in to see what you thought of the story."

"The one in the *Sydney Morning Herald*?"

"Ah, it got a run up north, did it? Hard to keep track of that stuff." He paused. "What are you doing in Sydney?"

Alison dodged the question. "Have you got anything to tell me?"

"Well, hang on, I don't want to go giving my yarns away."

"We had a deal. I tell you what I know, you tell me what you find out."

Another long pause. He clicked his tongue, flicked it from the roof of his mouth to the spot under the line of his lower front teeth so that when it smacked into place it made a clopping sound like a horse on a paved road.

"Look, I know we said that, but since then I've been doing my due diligence on this Watson fella and I'm not sure helping you find him is going to be ethically sensible."

"What the fuck does 'ethically sensible' mean?"

"All right, probably that's something I made up right then because it seemed easier than saying the guy is a cretin. He beat her, you know. Simone. That's what her mother told me. I kept it out of the story for now because there's no evidence she died from unnatural causes and the lawyers thought it was unnecessarily inflammatory. She was running for her life and you want to stroll up to him in the street and ask him some questions?"

Alison laughed. "You think I don't know Gil's a fucking woman beater?"

Another pause. "He hit you too, then?"

"Course he did. Not so clever after all, Chris Waters." Alison didn't really care if Chris knew the truth. He wasn't her friend. After all this was over, she'd never have to see him again, or think about how she lied to him about what was going on in her life. It felt as though with every admission, this truth became less heavy, less difficult to bear. But it also became more real, less easy to push down.

"I just thought—"

"Leopards don't change their spots."

"So, what are you doing, then? Why so keen to catch up with him?"

"Because like you, I think Simone must have been coming to see me for a reason. I don't think she coincidentally drove up my drive in the middle of one of the deadliest bushfires in Australian history. She needed me. I don't know why, or what for. But she's dead and I'm alive and I want to help her."

"Alison, maybe she did come to see you, but maybe there's nothing at this point left to be done. Maybe what she needed you for, she needed to be alive for."

"Well, even if that's the case, I need to know. Please help me. I promise, if there's a story here, I'll help you get it. I will. But I need to know."

The line was silent. In the gum the lorikeet twittered and trilled. A skink snuck onto the table and sunned itself in a patch of weak light. Alison could hear the whirr of the washing machine. Spin cycle cranking up. "So, here's what I know about Watson that I assume you don't know. I'll spare you the background pre-Simone, since I expect you know it already."

"Sure do."

"All right, about twelve months ago he and Simone had a big fight. A roof raiser. The neighbors called the cops and Simone, one black eye, one missing tooth, one broken arm, says she wants to press charges. Cops take him in, go through all the procedures, take her statement, take his prints, stick him in the lockup, give her all the usual advice, issue the AVO."

"What's that?"

"Apprehended Violence Order—restraining order. Then, the next day Simone walks back in and says she's changed her mind. Won't testify, doesn't want to cause any trouble. The injuries aren't his fault, et cetera, et cetera. The usual Stockholm syndrome scenario."

"It's not that easy to say you want to press charges in the first place, you know. I never did."

Silence. "So they have to cut him loose and he goes back to their place. Nothing comes of it, no 'reunion special,' as I know the blueys sometimes call the inevitable beating the woman takes when he comes back."

"Gross."

"If you don't laugh you cry, and crying's just a waste of moisture."

"Jesus."

"It seems like everything is peachy, no more complaints from the neighbors, no more hospital reports, no more records at all of any problems that I can track down. And then, a month ago, Simone's parents walk into the cop shop and file a missing persons. Not answering her phone, not replying to emails. Nothing."

Alison was silent. There had to be more. "And Gil?"

"Gil. When the parents file the report, the coppers go pay him a visit. He says Simone left him. Thought she was back at her parents' house. But they run some checks, and he's using her bank account, has a second card for it. They ask him about it, and he says she never took it back and it's his money 'cause she owed him rent. But they can't find anything to suggest he did anything to her, or that he knows where she is.

"They check her phone records, and though he's been calling, the calls aren't ever answered. She stopped answering him around the time the parents say they stopped hearing from her. But they're concerned. Because she's not using her phone. He's the only one accessing her account. They put him under surveillance. They search the flat. They lock the account. Nothing. They can't find anything that would suggest where she is or whether he's the reason she's missing. And that takes us to the day of the fire. The first lead they have on her, and she's dead in the middle of that shit show. Only now, somehow, Gil's slipped the admittedly lackluster surveillance and no one knows where he is anymore."

"That's it?"

"That's it. That's all I have that you can't already read in the paper or didn't come from you."

"It's a lot."

"Yes, it is. If she hadn't been killed in the fire, I'd be sure he'd murdered her."

"But maybe he did. The coroner could be wrong. They did two autopsies because they couldn't tell the first time."

"It's a long bow you've got there, Alison."

"What about the fingerprints?"

"What fingerprints?"

"On the car. They took mine to exclude them."

"No prints on the car 'cept you and Simone."

More silence, as she tried to figure out how to respond. "Thank you for telling me all this."

"What are you going to do?"

"I don't know." She paused. "Can I call you again if there's something I need to know that you might be able to help me find out?"

"If I've got the exclusive."

"Yes. You've got the exclusive."

He was quiet for a beat. "Alison?"

"Yeah?"

"He had money—quite a few thousand in the bank. Seems like a lot for a North Queensland cook."

"He won some, and he was thrifty. He liked to bet on the horses. Big score on a Melbourne Cup in the noughties. But he barely spent his own money once he'd impressed you enough to think he was generous."

"How so?"

"You said it yourself: he was using her money. He used mine too. He spent his on me for the first couple of months, but then it was different."

"I see, what a guy."

"We were the idiots who gave him our debit cards."

"Alison—"

She cut him off; she didn't want to hear about how it wasn't her fault. "It's fine, Chris, forget it."

"OK, OK. Listen, call me anytime."

"Thank you."

They hung up as the washing machine began to beep. Alison hung the linen on the line and walked back toward the kitchen door. She looked at the window that opened into the lounge room, saw the couch where she'd slept the night before, the bars secure on the frame. Glanced down at the mossy tile. Her skin tightened and her scalp tingled as she noticed the small collection of cigarette butts on the ground there. At least ten, not old and faded, but newly ground into the brick underfoot, which was still smudged with ash. They were Gil's brand.

Her heart a brick and her hands all thumbs, Alison stumbled back into the kitchen, smashed the door shut behind her, turned the key in the lock. Made sure it was locked tight.

He'd been here. In the night. Watching her sleep through the open window. Smoking. Making plans. She didn't know what to do. Where was he now? Why hadn't he struck when she'd sat out in the yard? Alone, vulnerable, careless, stupid.

She needed to get going. Alison shoved her things into her bag and headed for the front door. Outside, she triple-checked it was shut fast behind her, scurried across the street to her car, and settled in behind the wheel. Locked the doors and turned the key in the ignition before she even knew for sure which way she was heading.

Along King Street the midweek midday traffic snarled and snuck from light to light. Alison tapped her hands on the wheel, thought about the drive ahead. It was two and a half thousand kilometers to Cairns. Almost thirty hours of straight driving. She was a little under a third of the way there, and she was already exhausted.

She turned down Missenden Road, chucked a uey at the lights, and headed back toward the Princes Highway, south again. Alison chewed the skin of her upper lip and squinted into the glare of the traffic. Driving was a stupid idea. At the turn for the airport Alison flicked on the indicator, took the corner sharply. Time was more valuable than money; she'd learned that lesson enough times now to know for sure it was true.

24.

The wide Cairns streets close to the sea were buffeted by salty wind. Palm trees, tall and top-heavy, bent back and forth, back and forth, as though mimicking the waves. On the corner the salmon pink of the apartment block stuck out against the whites and bricks and blues, a square-edged slice of sunset sky, the ripples and foamy breaks of the waves reflected in the aluminum-edged glass of the windows. Alison counted them—three up, two across; there it was. Her bedroom, or what was once her bedroom. *Their* bedroom. She scanned the lower floors, wondered which window Simone's things were behind. Did he live there too? Or had he, before Simone disappeared?

She sunk a little lower in her seat, checked the doors were locked, tried to shake the ludicrous feeling that he was here. But maybe he was. The rental car smelled of carpet shampoo and the residual grease of the cheeseburger she'd eaten on the way in from the airport. Her car was left behind in Sydney. The plane ticket cost too much, but the drive would have cost her more. She didn't want to be on the road anymore. She didn't want to find traces of him wherever she was.

In the late afternoon the sun sunk into the deep blue out behind the breakers and the windows turned from cool azure to fierce ochre and blazed like flames in squares against the fish-belly-pink concrete. Alison cracked the door, let the soup of the tropical summer hit her full on, air so damp it clung to her skin and snuck up her nose and stuck in the back of her throat. Hair flat on her already moistened forehead, eyes squinting into the sunset, she walked away from the apartment block, headed instead for the shop on the other corner, the corner store with Streets ice cream signs plastered over the front windows, a long-busted fluorescent street sign hand painted with the words "Millie's Milk Bar."

She pushed open the door, heard the familiar jangle of the bell, saw the rows of fridges to the left, the dusty shelves of potato chips and Jatz crackers and Old El Paso dips and Tim Tams and butternuts and ginger nuts and Pizza Shapes and every other thing you could imagine wanting at two in the morning, or when you were ten years old. Even as the bell continued to twitch in the doorframe, no one emerged from behind the streamers that separated the shop from the home behind it.

Alison heard the rustle of the streamers, the shuffle of tennis shoes on the floor, and looked up. She didn't know this person.

"What do you need, love?" It was an older woman with a shock of rust-dyed hair, a navy blouse, and white pants, all the brighter against the dullness of the store's insides. Alison was surprised. She'd been expecting Mr. Huang.

"I'm Chris Waters; I'm a journalist. I'm writing a story about the girl from up here that died in the fires down in Victoria last week. I know she lived in that block across the road." It just came out. *Chris didn't have to be a man's name.* This lie was better than the truth would be.

The woman stood a little taller. "I'm gonna be in the paper, then?"

"Well, that depends on if you knew her. Simone Arnold. Blond woman, early thirties. Lived in that salmon-colored block across the street. Had a boyfriend called Gil." Alison caught her mistake. "Michael. Big guy, tall."

"Oh sure, yeah, I knew Simone. She'd be in here mostly for eggs or bread. Lovely girl. Really pretty that one, when she wasn't wearing sunglasses covering half her face." The woman squinted at Alison, eyes creeping over every millimeter of her. "You know, she looked a bit like you actually. 'Bout the same height. Same look in her eyes, when I could see 'em."

"Sunglasses? In here?"

The silence filled the dusty room right up. "Helps prevent questions when a pretty face ain't so pretty, doesn't it?"

So it was obvious to everyone. Gil had gotten worse. "She was being hit?"

"I'm not accusing anyone. I'm saying sometimes she'd come in here and it's dark as night or storming something fierce and she's wearing those sunnies. Sometimes, she'd come in on a blinder, sun so hot it'd melt ya, and she's not even wearing a hat. I'm no fool."

"Did you ever see her with the boyfriend?" Alison could feel the flush rising in her face as she tried to stay calm, tried to be someone else, even if just for a few minutes.

"Sure, but they usually came in separate. He'd come in for ciggies, sometimes he'd come in real late, buy some Coke, although you could already smell the Bundy on him, didn't need the mixer. Never said two words together to me, just whacked the money down, waited for his change, counted out the coins to make sure every last cent was there."

"You didn't like him much, then?"

"Didn't have an opinion past those sunglasses she wore. Says a lot about a bloke, doesn't it? He didn't say boo to me, but when Katie was working I'd hear him, all honey."

"Katie?"

"My daughter. She's at university in Brisbane but comes home for the summers, helps me in the shop."

"I see. Have you seen him lately?" Alison thought she probably should be pretending to take notes or something.

"You want to know about the one who died? Why you askin' about her boyfriend?" The woman leaned her heavy elbows on the counter, squinted across the distance straight into Alison's skull.

"Police in Melbourne say he's of interest."

"What does that mean? He set the bloody fire?"

"They don't know for sure how most of the fires started."

"He wasn't someone I'd want to see Katie go round with, but I don't think he'd be that stupid. Too charming to be thick."

They stared at each other. Alison felt like this was a wrestling match and she was losing. "So, you think he's still up here, then?"

"Haven't seen him for months. Can't say I've missed him."

"Is there anything else about him or about Simone you remember?" What a waste of time this was. Alison felt so bloody stupid. There was probably nothing in Cairns that she couldn't have learned talking to Simone's parents in Lake Bend.

"Simone had a new friend. Came in with her a coupla times last month. Good-looking fella he was, always smiling."

"A new boyfriend?"

"I dunno. Coulda been. Never saw her touch him, or the other way. He was just always with her. She's in here, so's he." Alison suddenly felt panicked. What had she missed? Who was he?

"All right, thanks a lot. I think that's all we need for now." She nodded at the woman, went to leave.

"Hang on. Don't you want my name for the paper?" Alison

didn't have a pen or paper. She didn't have anything to make her look legitimate. She thought about the real Chris Waters. How mad would he be when he found out what she'd been doing up here?

"Yes, sorry, it's been a long day and I forgot to ask."

"Not much chop, then, are ya?" The woman screwed up her nose.

"What's your name, then?" Alison took out her phone, pretended to get it ready to take the note.

"Something not quite right here." She reached over to the phone by the cash register. "Don't have to give you it, do I?"

"Well, no, but if you don't, how will I put your name in the paper?" The woman stared at Alison for a long time. A fly buzzed in the light overhead, amplified on the worn countertop between them. She didn't reply, so Alison shrugged, began backing out of the shop. "No worries, I can put it on background."

"What's that?" The woman was punching numbers on the keypad of the phone.

"Don't put you in the story, just use the information to help me pull it together. So nice to meet you." Alison raised her hand to wave good-bye, used the other one to back all the way out of the store and into the street. What a disaster. She looked across the street to the fish-and-chip place. Her stomach rumbled. Still nestled in her hand, her phone began to vibrate. The number was Billy's. She ignored the call. Crossed the busy Esplanade and pushed through the slick of plastic ribbons that buffeted the front door of Frankie's Fish Spot.

She ordered the flake and minimum chips, extra lemon and tartar sauce, plenty of chicken salt. The man behind the counter barely spoke to her, just took the money, gave her a number, pointed to the back when Alison asked if there was a bathroom. Alison took the plastic square with 43 scrawled on it in black felt pen, shoved it in her pocket, and headed for the toilet.

In the scruffy light of the windowless room, she pulled her damp hair off her forehead, rinsed her shiny face in the sink, and pissed as fast as she could, butt smacked on the cold plastic toilet seat. She hated women who hovered, like their arses were some kind of holy ground, dribbling piss everywhere for the next woman to avoid. Alison thumbed around in her phone while she went, trying not to think too much about the sunglasses Simone had walked around this neighborhood wearing like a disguise.

After that first time, Gil never hit Alison's face. He knew better, or he didn't want the looks from people like that woman at Millie's. Why had that changed? Maybe it hadn't; maybe he didn't share a workplace with Simone, so he didn't have to worry too hard about his chickens coming home to roost. Alison's head throbbed. Her skin crawled, itching from the inside out as her location sunk right back in. Cairns had never felt right. Gil had just made it hard for her to move on, until he hadn't anymore.

At the pass Alison scrutinized the dockets. "Where's the pork chop for table six?" She squinted through the steam and rush of chefs in whites, tried to catch the new guy's eye. He was calling it tonight, and he'd already stuffed up two of her tables.

"Six? I've got two steak, one prawn linguine, one pork chop, right?" He connected, locked into her stare, met it with an overly familiar smile.

"Sure, but there's no pork chop here and the linguine is getting cold."

"So take it and the steaks. By the time you're back the pork'll be up. You can't carry it all anyway."

Alison sighed. Loaded the plates onto her arm, and with her free hand pushed through the doors. "I could carry four, you know," she called back.

As the doors closed behind her she heard him say, "What would you open the door with then?" She rolled her eyes, took the plates to the table, smiled as she put them down, turned to hustle back to the kitchen for the pork. He was right behind her, plate in hand, but it was too late, the momentum too great, and even as she tried to stop it she felt her chest upend the plate, the heat of it shocking as the pork chop flew up and hit her in the chin and mashed potatoes squelched into her. The shock of it made her scream, and if she'd been paying better attention maybe she'd have noticed the flash of pleasure that passed across his face before his eyes widened in apparent horror.

"Fuck me!" Alison had yelled, unable to help herself. Gasps and muffled laughter echoed around the dining room as the pork chop bounced onto the carpet and she whipped the potatoes from her bust with her fingers, shaking them off her hand onto the floor. They scalded where she touched them, where she left them, where they'd landed in the first place. The little blobs fell in a splatter pattern around her.

"Shit, I'm so sorry!" He was trying to help, using the tea towel tucked into his waist band to wipe potatoes from her chest. Alison grabbed it, pushed his hand away.

"Don't touch me. What are you doing out here?"

"It was ready right as you left, so I figured I'd save you the trip." He shrugged his shoulders, smiled.

She heard her mother's voice in her head. *Butter wouldn't melt.* Alison pushed past him, saying it under her breath.

"Wait, what did you say?" He stopped to apologize to the table—who were now down a pork chop—pick up what he could of the mess, and head back to the kitchen. Alison didn't wait for him. She didn't wait to yell at him in the kitchen either. She went straight to the staff break room, locked the door, pulled off her starch-covered shirt, and leaned over the sink. The water was so cold, it raised bumps all over, but it felt good on her pinked skin. Alison had to take off her bra; it was soaked. She put the soiled clothes in a plastic bag and found her plain-clothes shirt in her bag. Pulled it on. There'd been knocking on the door for quite some time, but she'd ignored it. Now, clean and dressed, she pulled it open, expecting the new guy from behind the pass. It was her floor manager.

"You all right?" She was brusque, like Alison had caused the problem.

"Yeah, I don't think there'll be any lasting damage."

"Good. You should go home. You can't work like that anyway." The woman's mouth was pressed firmly in a line.

"Are you pissed at me?" Alison tried to stay calm. "I didn't do anything wrong. That new chef followed me out on the floor and stood right behind me with a hot plate of food."

"Well, he's not my responsibility. But when we have to comp a meal on the floor, that's my responsibility." She wouldn't look Alison in the eye.

"Fuck, Rebecca, I didn't drop anything, I didn't do anything." *That fucking guy.*

In the bathroom, caught up in the memory of how it all started, Alison had lost track of time. Outside she heard her number being called. *Forty-three? Forty-three? Where's forty-three?* She pulled her pants up, flushed the loo, washed her hands and shook them dry, and popped out into the fluorescent incubator.

"That's me!" She waved the plastic ticket in the air, having fished it from her pocket as she scrambled between the tables to the counter. The man rolled his eyes, pressed a piping-hot roll of butcher's paper into her soggy hands. "Thanks so much," she said, ripping an air hole in the paper so the chips would stay crisp and heading back out into the muggy twilight. Her phone trilled in her hand, and she looked at it. Chris Waters. She rolled her eyes. This guy. Leaning on the hood of her rental, the paper-wrapped fish-and-chips spread out before her, she answered, shoveling a too-hot chip into her mouth.

"Yeah?"

"Hello to you too, Alison."

"I'm eating dinner—what do you want?"

A pause. Chris Waters cleared his throat. "I would like to know why I am in Cairns asking questions about Simone in local milk bars, apparently now a woman."

Alison had been shoving a greasy hunk of crumbed flake into her mouth as he spoke. She choked it down too fast, the crumbs catching in her windpipe as she breathed. She coughed.

"Alison?"

"Yeah, sorry." She was still coughing. She reached through the open window of the rental and pulled the water bottle from the console, chugged down enough to stop the coughing. "You're obviously not, so I wouldn't worry."

He laughed. "That's all you're going to say? What are you doing in Cairns, Alison? You're not the cops. You're not even a bloody journalist. If this Michael Watson is as dangerous as you seem to think, what on earth are you doing?"

"I just . . . He's not up here." Alison was already kicking herself for saying this. Chris wouldn't miss the implication.

"You've talked to him?"

"I haven't seen him, no."

"That's not what I asked you."

"I don't know what I'm doing here. She was coming to me.

She wanted to see me. So I thought, I dunno, maybe if I came here, I would be able to figure out why. Ask some questions." It sounded so stupid when she said it. She didn't know how to say she was running away, and running toward answers at the same time. She didn't want him to comprehend her fear.

"This isn't a bloody Jack Irish novel. You're not an investigator. And you have to stop pretending to be me."

"All right, I hear you, geez."

"I'm serious, Alison. Get out of there. It's not smart or safe for you to be up there if he's around."

"I promise, he's not. And you know what else isn't in Cairns? A fucking tinderbox waiting to burn at the first spark. I feel like I can fucking breathe up here. Maybe it's that simple."

"We both know you aren't running away from the fires. This is about Simone."

Alison squeezed the sides of the tartar sauce packet together, eking out the tangy cream onto the greased paper. "Why can't it be both? I gotta go." Before he had a chance to say anything else, she hung up.

Across the Esplanade, the sea brooded, calm but dark in the dusky light. She lifted the warmed lemon wedge and squashed it over the fish. Broke the flake apart with her fingers and smeared it in the tartar. She couldn't answer Chris Waters's questions because she didn't really know herself.

25.

At the Capricornia Alison hesitated outside. She could see Rebecca in there, still managing the floor, like she'd been doing for the past fifteen years. Alison could also see Scotty, Gil's partner in shit stirring, wiping glasses behind the bar. She knew they'd be there. That was the point. Why come all this way if she wasn't actually going to find anything out, ask anyone about Gil, or about Simone, or about anything? But she was frozen to the spot, sitting in the rental car, squinting through the big front windows into the brightly lit main room. Deep breaths—she took deep breaths, one after another, trying to contain herself, to contain her fear. It didn't make sense to be afraid, but she couldn't help it, couldn't quiet it.

She hadn't heard from Gil since Sydney. She didn't know where he was or what he wanted, and now she was in Cairns, she couldn't imagine how she would find out. Chris Waters was right. What an idiot. She felt so foolish. Outside, the sky threatened rain, and the night had settled in. The lights of the city trapped luminescence in the clouds and reflected it back into the white lines that separated the sides of the street. She looked once more through the windows of the Capricornia, saw Scotty staring through the glass, through the foot traffic on the street, through the metal that encased her directly, the shiny new rental, straight at Alison. She was sure he winked at her. Her stomach flipped. She knew she had to go in; she'd come all this way.

Alison swung open the car door, looked around; there was no sign of him, Gil, anywhere. She was alone, she was certain, as certain as she could be. Time to move, cross the street, go through the door, figure out something to say, anything to say, that might make sense or be useful. How to be useful? It's never as easy as it seems.

The Capricornia's front bar was small and wood paneled, with high pressed-metal ceilings blooming flowers overhead. The place had polished hardwood floors and thick, soft rugs of deep green lush wool that your feet could sink right into.

Some nights, after the room had been cleaned and the other staff were all gone, Alison would take off her shoes and wriggle her toes into the plush, sipping on gin and enjoying the space no longer crowded and crowding, waiting for Gil, who would be washing dishes or drying plates or polishing countertops, setting up the kitchen for the morning, always working later than her, just getting stuff done.

This old bar had a footrail and swinging saloon doors that led through to the restaurant behind, the front room a throwback to a time before time hurtled so fast, a time when the kilogram weighed more than it does now, and the world was a little cooler, a little less overstuffed, a little more empirical. The world had moved on, but the Capricornia shined up the wood and brass and tall, watered palm fronds and let the early twentieth century luxuriate in the space.

Alison moved toward Scotty with as much purpose as she could muster. He was polishing glasses, moving a tea towel in and out, up and down. The bar was quiet. An old bloke down one end, two younger men at one of the small tables up front, a couple playing darts in the corner, him struggling to sink the point into the cork, her missing most of her shots, both of them laughing and finding reasons to touch each other. Alison slid onto a stool in front of Scotty. He didn't look up at her.

"Hi, Scotty."

He raised his gaze long enough for Alison to see the deep brown of his eyes. The flecks of gold that swam in them if the light hit right. "Alison, surprised to see you here."

"Why?"

"Didn't think you'd be back round here, after Gil." The silence stretched out as Alison tried to figure out what Scotty was saying to her.

"Gil's your friend." It landed like an accusation.

"Guess so." Alison thought she heard something nasty in his tone, but she didn't know him well enough to be sure.

"Did you meet his new girlfriend? The one after me? Simone?"

"The dead one, you mean." It wasn't a question. Alison waited for him to say more. "She was a real nice woman. Too good for him." He'd stopped shining glasses. "You want a beer?"

"Gin, on the rocks, couple of slices of lime." Scotty's weariness had calmed her. She didn't feel as though he were in on anything, but she felt like he might know something. "What gives? You two used to be tight."

"You know he hit her?" He slid a glass toward her, added one of those big cubes of ice that jostle at the wide sides of a short, fat tumbler. Poured Hendricks over the top, squeezed in two fat wedges of lime. "I wasn't sure how to . . . I didn't know how to say the right thing."

She picked up the glass. Swirled the liquor around. "Or anything?" He didn't deserve points for noticing.

"She was wonderful. Funny, you know, and so fucking

smart, but she had something . . . She didn't know how to be loved."

She stared at him for a long time. He let her. "Who does?"

Scotty shook his head, looked away, picked up another glass and began polishing it slowly. "Yeah, she was like you in a lot of ways." He stopped and thought for a minute, and then he spoke carefully, intensely. "I think he started hitting her because she wasn't you."

The accusation felt like a violence of its own. "He hit me too, you know."

He stopped polishing, stared at her, for the first time really looked at her. Traced the curves of her cheeks and the line of her jaw with his eyes. "Shit. I didn't—"

"Wouldn't have mattered if you did, since you didn't do shit for Simone."

He took the accusation without complaint, but he looked almost wounded by it. "Guess not.

"I don't owe you anything, Alison. Get out of here." His eyes flashed furious, then clouded over. She shifted in her chair, raised her glass, and knocked back the contents in one go. The gin lit up her throat and warmed the apples of her cheeks.

"What do you owe Simone?"

"Fuck, are you thick? You got a death wish? You think he's playing a game?"

Alison heard the fear in his voice. It was genuinely surprising. "You think he killed her, then?"

"I think he's missing and she's dead and he never seemed to know when to stop beating on her, so I don't know. Maybe." He tightened his jaw, moved away from her, turned away from the bar, and she couldn't figure out how to get him to say whatever it was he really wanted to say. But she knew there was more going on than he was telling her.

———

When she was in grade ten Alison's dad let her come to work with him for the day, just once, and she tucked a notebook into her pocket and a pen behind her ear and followed him into the home of a young woman who'd recently been the victim of a serious crime. *Pay attention to what people do, not just what they say.*

So she'd noticed the way Kasey Edelman tucked her hair behind her ears and looked down at the ground as she spoke. The way she fiddled with the hem of her skirt, pushing the fabric back and forth through her fingers, unable to be still. Someone had broken into Kasey Edelman's house and pulled her from her bed one night. Put a moistened handkerchief over her mouth and dragged her through the window. Something about the handkerchief made her pass out. Kasey was sixteen. The man had pulled her into a ute, bound her hands and feet with tape, blindfolded her and gagged her, and driven her away, into the bush.

When she came to, the sun was shining and she was still tied up in a clearing. The blindfold was gone, and she could see she wasn't alone. Her boyfriend was there too. He was tied up and struggling, with a gag in his mouth. There didn't seem to be anyone else around. Kasey and Max wormed their way toward each other and used their hands to help each other free. Max told her that when he woke up a man with a gun had been there. There was another man, who'd driven up, and the two of them had talked for a while, and then they'd gotten into the car to go somewhere. He thought for sure they'd be back soon, and he didn't know where in the bush he and Kasey were. They found a pack behind a tree—a sleeping bag, some water and muesli bars—and they took it and dashed into the bush, away from the road, hoping that they could find a way out before the men returned.

That night the pair had shared the sleeping bag for warmth;

it was cold out, close to freezing, and Max had pulled Kasey close and suggested they have sex to keep warm. She'd said no. The next day, they wandered until they found a stream and then followed it until nightfall, when again, in the frigid air, Max had pleaded with her to use the friction of their bodies to help keep them warm. She wouldn't. Kasey was devout; her chastity mattered to her. The next day it seemed as though Max knew where they were, as he quickly found them a way out of the bush and onto a sealed road. They walked along the road until a passing car picked them up. Kasey still in her nightie, no shoes, the sleeping bag wrapped around her shoulders. Max wearing proper outdoor gear, even though he'd been nabbed late at night in his room. Kasey hadn't thought about those differences until the police had started asking about them. She'd told Malcolm King about the moment she'd realized the truth, that Max was the one who'd kidnapped her. That he'd planned it all to try to get into her pants.

How betrayed and humiliated and used she had felt. How much her heart hurt. Alison had listened, or tried to, but she found herself too distracted by the shape of the room and the way the light landed and the curves of Kasey's cheeks, the way the tears snaked down them, made slick canals that glistened in the sun. She didn't know how to make people open up like that, tell her everything they were holding inside them. Her dad was so good at it. Patient and clever and kind; unthreatening. She didn't have it. She had only the ability to observe.

When they left Kasey Edelman, she appeared to Alison to be lighter, her shoulders less slumped, more pride in the way she held her face, the way she looked into Alison's eyes as they said good-bye. Alison asked her dad why he'd let her tag along, why Kasey had let her tag along. *Men who want something from you cannot be trusted. I wanted you to understand that, and I suggested to Kasey it might be helpful to her to have someone her own*

age with her. He paused. Looked into her eyes with a serious-
ness that seemed new. *Men want things from women; they want
things from girls who aren't even ready to be women.*

In the paper the next day Kasey's story was the splash.
Alison read her dad's words with extra care, saw the details
she'd reminded him of; the way the fabric on the chair was
worn from sitting; the cat, gray and fluffy, that rubbed its nose
on Kasey's leg; the music of the branches outside, jostling in
the wind.

Watching him now, Alison couldn't figure out what Scotty
was trying to say. He seemed genuinely disgusted by Gil, or at
least by how Gil had treated Simone. She couldn't do this. She
wasn't equipped to sift the facts from the bullshit. She wasn't
her father. She wasn't good enough at reading people. She saw
every move they made but couldn't parse what those moves
meant.

"Scotty?" He looked up at her reluctantly. "Why did Simone call him Michael?"

"She didn't know about you. Gil thought if she called him
Michael, it'd be easier to keep you both on the hook." He shook
his head. "I think he liked the idea of being someone else." She
wanted to ask him if he knew about the tapes. What were
they? Why did he care so much about them? But she didn't
trust him. She couldn't risk Gil's finding out she didn't have
them, because it felt like maybe she was safer if he needed
something from her. So instead, Alison just nodded at him,
pushed back from the bar, and walked out of the Capricornia.

Where to from here? She didn't fucking know. Back to the
block of flats, maybe. Knock on some doors, ask a bunch of

questions, see what anyone said. She probably should have come here first. But she hated it here, and returning was harder than she'd thought it would be. *So stupid.* She forced herself to get back into the car and drive back to the faded salmon facade and sit outside, slumped in the driver's seat, slumped in a heap like she was avoiding someone. *You are so stupid.* Slumped and stooped and tucked into her seat and staring at the windows now glistening with the reflected moon. She sat there too long. Nursed her fears too long. Got out of the car and looked around. *Gil's not here.* Repeated that a few times. Walked slowly along the concrete path that led to the exposed steps to the first floor of flats, tried to remember whether Detective Mitchell had said which flat Simone was in. She couldn't remember. The lights made a glowing border around the door to the first flat to the right; Alison could hear a TV droning inside. She swallowed the spit that had pooled in the back of her throat, raised her hand, and rapped softly on the door. Hoped it was so soft that they wouldn't hear her.

A woman Alison guessed was in her late sixties cracked the door; lit up by the light of the room from behind, the features of her face were hard to make out, the cues of her expression hard to read. Her hair was deep brown and piled high on her head; a shock of white ran through the front of it. "Can I help you?" The woman sounded surprised to see a stranger at her door.

"I hope so. I'm Chris Waters, I'm a journalist, and I'm writing a story about the woman from this block of flats who died in the big bushfires in Victoria last week." Fuck him. His name was useful.

"Yes." She didn't offer anything else.

"Well, I was wondering if you knew her. Simone Arnold?"

"Nope, sorry." She went to shut the door, but Alison put her foot in the space, surprising herself.

"Wait, do you know anyone here who might?"

The woman thought about it, head cocked to one side like a crow's. "People come and go pretty quick round here, we mostly keep to ourselves. You could try the building manager, he knows everyone." Alison could taste the disappointment. She was trying to avoid running into Kevin.

"All right, thanks."

The woman nodded, pointed in the direction of the ground-floor flat with "Manager" in careful lettering across the door, and went back to the warm glow of the television.

Shit. Alison walked back down the stairs and stood in the gardens at the base of the building, looked at the way the water in the pool shimmered in the breeze, ripples reflecting the moon back at it. Walked slowly toward the door. Paused outside it and then knocked deliberately. Kevin took his time coming to open it, and Alison was about to turn away when he swung it wide.

"Hello, love, long time no see." Kevin smiled at Alison, made her feel momentarily reassured.

"Hi, Kevin, I was in Cairns and I thought I would stop by."

He frowned at her. "You thought you would visit me?" One of his bushy brows was arched and the disbelief on his face felt like mockery.

"You're right, that is weird. I'm sorry. I didn't know what to say. I'm trying to find out about one of my old neighbors, Simone Arnold. She died in the bushfires down in Victoria and she was coming to visit me, but I never knew her, and I don't know why she was coming."

Kevin looked her over for a long time while the expression on his face changed from incredulity to sobriety. "She was a good kid, Simone. You know, you remind me of her a bit." He squinted at her like he was considering her face.

"Did she say anything to you about coming to Victoria?"

He shook his head. "No." Folded his arms. Scrutinized her some more. She wasn't sure what to ask next.

"Does Gil still—is he still living in our flat?"

Kevin narrowed his eyes so they were basically two slits, and then said slowly, "Dunno. He's still paying the rent there, though."

Alison's heart skipped. She thanked Kevin for his time and walked away from his door, heading back toward the street. But when she heard it close, she veered off the concrete path, cut across the spiky lawn, and hauled herself up the stairs two by two to her old apartment. When she got to the door, she stared at it for a moment. She didn't have a key anymore. She didn't know how to pick a lock. But she did know where she'd kept her emergency key, and she wasn't sure Gil had ever even known it existed. She moved over to the iron railing that lined the balcony all the apartments opened onto. The fat rung directly opposite the door was shielded on the other side by palms, frangipani, and a tangle of morning glory. Alison reached around. The magnetic box she'd stashed was still there. She pulled it loose and slid it open. Keys. Fucking hell.

She looked around and then pushed the key into the lock, hoping Gil was too lazy to have ever changed it. It clicked, the smooth slide of the mechanism slipping open. She turned the doorknob and pushed. The door fell open with ease. And then she was stepping inside and hoping no one was there.

Alison stood in the entrance for a while, trying to figure out what she was even looking for. The place seemed abandoned, like no one had moved anything in there for months. She moved through the lounge and into the bedroom. *Her* bedroom. The mural was still on the wall behind the bed. He hadn't painted over it. She wondered, had he ever brought Simone here? Fucked her in Alison's bed. Under Alison's work. She shook her head, trying to erase the image. Something told her he hadn't. Just a feeling, like he probably enjoyed having this place to hide in. To keep his secrets for himself.

She looked around, not sure where to start. And then she remembered. Gil had a safe. He had always been paranoid in particular ways. He didn't fully trust banks, or her, so he kept all his most valuable things locked away in a safe under the bed. She got down on the floor. It was still there. She thought about possible number combinations. She tried his phone passcode, which she knew but he didn't know she knew. It didn't work. She tried his birthday, because he was a self-centered prick. Wrong again. She tried her own birthday. Nope. Simone's—she remembered it from the driver's license. Wrong again. Annoyed, she racked her brain.

A Melbourne Cup Day, years ago. Gil had won big on number 52. A total outside chance. It was a lot of money—more than ten grand—and it had been before he'd even met her, and on their first date he'd told the story and gone on and on about how that was going to be his lucky number now. How five plus two made seven and seven was lucky, everyone knew. Alison tried 525252. She held her breath waiting for the safe to click open. But it didn't. It wasn't that. *Shit.* And then she tried one more idea: 777777. The light went green. The lock clicked open. Holy shitballs. She had done it.

She yanked open the safe. There was only one thing in it. A manila envelope, thick, with something inside it. She pulled it out and closed the safe. She lay there on the floor for a second, heart thumping. She wondered, should she open it here? She wanted to get out of the apartment. She got up and headed for the front door, checking through the peephole for any signs of life out on the balcony. It seemed quiet out there. She took a deep breath and stepped out. No one. She hustled to the car as fast as she could and started it.

Alison had pulled away from the curb before she'd even buckled her belt. She wanted distance between her and the flats. It took ten full minutes of driving for Alison to feel safe enough to slow down, safe enough to pull over, safe enough to rip open the envelope and dig inside.

Photo paper. The shiny high-gloss kind. Full-color prints. Simone. That jaw, that nose, those pools of blue, sparkling with life and the unmistakable expression of lust. The "come hither," her mother had called it when she found Alison looking at her dad's 1970s *Playboys* as a teen. Simone was totally naked in these pictures. They left absolutely nothing to the imagination and had clearly been taken by and given to Gil, before she knew what kind of man he really was.

Alison thought about Gil, about what he had said to her about tapes. These were not tapes. They were not even something that could ever have been on a tape. They were obviously photographs, taken as photographs. Not a film. So these weren't what he was looking for. And why would they be? They had been in his safe, in his apartment. Alison knew she must be missing something. She didn't know what. Her head hurt. She had run out of ideas. There was nothing useful here for her. It was time to go home.

She drove the rental back to the airport and got on the first available flight, an early-morning one the next day. She didn't want to be alone, so instead of booking a room at a hotel, she curled into a chair in the airport lounge and tried, with little success, to doze. When it was time to board, at 4:30 a.m. Alison shuffled onto the plane and tucked herself into her seat, pulled her sunglasses down over her eyes, and slept, heavily, the whole way to Sydney.

She dreamed of hands on her body, rough ones, hurting her, leaving their marks; she dreamed in staccato. Images of her own body sliced into pictures, painted on individual

canvases, blooming with the imperfections of violent possession. Saw Gil survey the work, point out the connections, find
the gallery attendant, and buy every single one. The little red
dots connoting his possession burned on the wall beside her.

When she got off the plane Alison found her car in the
long-term parking, drove to a park in Alexandria that had bar-
becues, a cricket pitch, the soft thud of paws on grass, and the
squeals of small children trying to gain their mothers' attention. Piled the pictures on the hot plate. Found a lighter in her
glovebox and set fire to an edge. *Men want things from women.
Sometimes they want too much.* Watched the record of Simone's
desire for a man who didn't deserve it shrivel up and burn
away. The fire ate the paper in greedy bursts, and when it was
done, Alison swept the ashes onto the concrete underfoot and
turned her back and walked away. Walked to her car and got
back in. Pictures couldn't help Simone. But they could hurt
her. Embarrass her beyond the grave. Give Gil something to
remember her by. She didn't want him to have that satisfaction. To have any satisfaction, ever again.

26.

On the inland road, once she was past the snarl of Sydney, Alison made good time. She stopped only to piss or to gulp a cup of something hot and caffeinated. Late afternoon gave way to twilight, gave way to country-dark night, gave way to deep early morning. Stars splashed across the sky in patterns familiar and brilliant; tracing their twinkle helped her stay alert, alive. It was closer to the depth of dark than the rise of the sun when she made it to the outskirts of town.

She glanced at the dash clock: 2:23 a.m. Its neon green illuminated how tired she was. It was probably too late to go to Sal's. Alison felt uneasy enough, imagining Gil was somewhere around, looking out for her. She hadn't heard a word from him for too long. Did he know her car? Would he be waiting in the dark when she pulled in? She didn't know, in this moment between night and light, how much danger she was in, or how to avoid it. Except that she did know how to avoid it. There was one obvious way. Alison didn't want to do it, but she knew that it was the safest option. She sighed heavily, turned left, not right, at the main roundabout, and swung a second left, into that familiar wide-guttered street she'd played in as a kid.

Billy's place was easy to break into. The two of them had been slipping a ruler between the windowpanes and jimmying the lock since they were six and wanted to raid his grandmother's Kingston biscuit stash while she was working reception at Dr. Munroe's. She pulled up at the curb, tried to figure out if he was home—probably it would have made more sense to swing by the cop shop and see if he was the one on the overnight, but if he wasn't there, the last thing she wanted was to set tongues wagging that she'd been on the hunt for Billy Meaker at 2 a.m. No coming back from that.

Alison sat in the car for a long time. Billy's car wasn't there, but that didn't mean shit. If he'd had a few at the Imperial, chances were that he'd left it behind and walked back. Did she break in, or was it better to knock? She didn't know. She knew only that she couldn't stay in the car forever. She cracked the door, swung her legs out, and stretched a bit, the drive still throttling her every muscle. Standing up, she looked carefully around. There was no movement anywhere, no sounds.

Alison covered the space between the car and the house quickly. Tried not to be indecisive. Rummaged in her bag for her purse, pulled out an unimportant card, slid it between the window frames, found the latch, forced it open. Quietly raised the window on its rope sash, slung a leg over, ducked her head under, pulled herself through, and then, without any grace whatsoever, made a misstep and tumbled loudly to the floor. Shit.

"Who's there? This is a police officer's house, mate, and it's occupied—no matter what you might have heard about these parts after the fire—so if you're thinking of looting you best turn around quick smart. I'm armed." Billy's hunting rifle appeared in the doorway as Alison tried to scramble to her feet.

"It's me, Billy."

He stuck his head into view. Alison could see the surprise on his face. "Al? I could have killed you."

"Your car's not here; I didn't think you were home." Figured a half-truth was better than a lie.

"Left it at the pub. What are you doing here?" He was cold, his tone, his face, his eyes.

"I needed a place to sleep and I thought you were at the station or something." She crossed her arms over her chest defensively.

Billy moved over to where Alison was standing, looked into her eyes for longer than she'd have liked, and shook his head slowly. "You're not telling me the truth." He walked out of the room and, paying proper attention for the first time since she'd tumbled in, her eyes now adjusted, Alison clocked that she was in the lounge room. Let her gaze settle on the carpet next to the couch. She swallowed, tried to level her heartbeat, and followed Billy down the hall, into the kitchen.

He was pacing.

"Why are you really here?"

"Because I need a place to stay tonight."

"That's not the whole story, though, is it?"

"Look, forget it, I'll go to my place."

"Your place?" He was still pacing. "You didn't go to Sal's, and I don't think that's because you were worried about waking her up, because you've demonstrated your selfishness plenty in the last couple of weeks. But you didn't go home either, which means—"

"I'm going there now." Alison turned to leave the room, but his hand caught her arm.

"No. You didn't go to Sal's and you didn't go home. You came here. To my place. I don't think you came here because you wanted to see me. I think you came here because you're scared of something." He searched her face again; Alison tried to stay inscrutable. "You're scared of him. Michael Gilbert Watson. You know something. You know something that's made you scared."

"Billy, I'm just tired, all right? I got back into town real late and I didn't want to wake Sal and I drove by here and I didn't see your car, so I figured, why not?"

"Stop lying to me. How can I help you if you won't let me?" He pounded his open palm against the countertop. Alison flinched, visibly.

"I don't want to owe you anything, OK?" Alison raised her voice without realizing it. "I need to feel like I'm safe for one bloody night, and then I'll be out of your hair."

"Al, come on. Let me in. You need something, I'll find a way to help."

Alison thought he was trying too hard again. She needed to change the subject. "Were you gonna ask me to formal?"

"What?"

"In senior. Formal? Were you gonna ask me?"

"Who bloody told you?"

"Doesn't matter. It's true?"

"Yeah. But then I came to my senses." He was loosening up a little, the muscles in his jaw visibly slackening.

"Nicole asked you first." A look of surprise that Alison knew this too.

"Sure, she did, and she was a nice girl, so I thought, why risk something that's not so sure?"

"Yeah, sounds right. Sure thing is what I heard." Alison had gone to the formal alone, or "stag," as she and Patrick had joked at the time. She'd made a big deal about how she didn't care, but the boy she'd been crushing on since she was twelve—Sam Chambers—hadn't even looked at her twice the whole night. In the days leading up to it, Alison had imagined him coming up to her and asking her to dance or offering her a beer at Stacy's after-party, and then casually slinging an arm over her shoulders. Sam Chambers took Chloe Barnett to formal. She wore a long hot-pink dress with a low-cut front and no-cut back, and as Alison had nursed a warm VB while she kept lookout for Pat and Steve Jenkins, she saw the two of them disappear into the bush out back of Stacy's. The memory no longer hurt her, but once again it was right there in the front of her mind. She wanted to feel like it didn't matter.

Rolling his eyes, Billy sighed before he replied, warily, clearly not sure where Alison was going. "I was a teenage boy. What does it matter why I went with her? Why are we even talking about this?"

"I do it every time, you know. Pick wrong. Pick the worst option. Pick the guy who isn't interested, or isn't kind, or cheats, or, hell, even beats me. Gil—Gil was a particularly dumb one."

"What are you talking about?"

"About him. About Michael Gilbert Watson."

"You and Simone's ex?"

"I left him because he was cheating on me, and I guess maybe that was Simone. I don't know."

"Jesus, Ally, why didn't you say anything?" Billy looked uncomfortable.

"When I left Cairns, I left him behind and I hoped I'd never have to see him again. I didn't tell him where I was going or why. I just left. I didn't leave because he hit me. I left because he cheated. How pathetic."

"He hit you too?" Little pulses of his jaw where the teeth gritted together.

"Yeah. Punched me in the stomach mostly, choked me a couple of times. Forced me to have sex." She kept her voice flat, like she was reciting a shopping list.

"Raped you." Billy's jaw was clenched tight now, and he

was barely able to form the sounds and push the words through the slit of his mouth.

"Yeah. The shit you hear men do to women, he did it all. I don't know how it got like that. I don't know how I let it." Alison knew she was being vague, that she was minimizing it, but she didn't want it to be everything about her. She didn't want Billy to see her that way. "But then, one day, I found out he was cheating, and I snapped. Kicked him out, told him we were done. I was ready for him to push back, to try and keep me, but he laughed in my face. He said I was a stupid slut and he didn't need me anymore. He'd found a better fuck. I remember, that's exactly what he said to me. It somehow stung more than a slap across the face. When you're in it, you tell yourself the violence is part of the passion. Like, he loves me so much, he can't control it. So when he didn't even care enough—ugh, that's not the right word, but maybe it is, that's what I thought at the time—to even get a little bit physical, it hurt my ego, it hurt my pride, and I couldn't even see how insane that was. And then, I dunno, not even a week later, Mum and Dad had the accident. I came home. Got away to where he didn't know how to find me. Or maybe he'd decided to hurt her instead."

Billy walked over to the cupboard, pulled out a bottle of whiskey, poured two generous measures, and handed Alison a heavy cut-crystal glass without saying a word. They both sipped for a while, not talking.

"Say something." She couldn't bear his silence anymore.

"I don't know what to say. I'm sorry that happened. I'm angry you never told me, especially now, with what's happened." He looked at her, and the way his face was set seemed softer somehow.

"There's a weight to telling people. To admitting that someone did that to you. Took your person for themselves and treated it like garbage. Like property. Like some throwaway thing. It feels like you're diminished. It feels like people you care about will look at you and see something lesser. Something not worthy or lovable. Something used, something damaged. Something you desperately don't want to be."

"But I'm not, I'm not just a person. I'm police, for starters; we see this stuff all the time. It's never the victim's fault. It's never about you being less . . . or whatever you feel."

"Doesn't matter how many times you say that, Billy. It's never going to change how I feel. I don't like the way people look at me when they know. I don't like the way you're looking at me now. And when I found out Gil was Michael, I guess I panicked, and I wanted to get away from here; I wanted to try and right whatever wrongs I was responsible for or whatever . . . I was . . . I don't fucking know, OK?"

"You shouldn't be ashamed of what he did." He came close, put his warm, comforting hands on her cold, slumped shoulders.

"I'm not. I'm not bloody ashamed. I don't want to be pitied."

"Is this why you pushed me away? You're afraid of being in a relationship?" He had beautiful eyes, and his hands made her feel safe where he touched her. Alison was aware of her guard falling, her resolve weakening. She shook her head, tried to snap out of it.

"I pushed you away because I don't want to be in a relationship with you."

She studied Billy's face. His eyes were narrowed now, a little wet around the edges, and he had fixed his mouth with that same forced neutral line he'd always used when they were up to something and he was lying to his parents about it. He stared at her hard. She didn't look away. He kissed her. It felt urgent and wrong and stupid and like everything she'd ever hated and wanted at the same time. She kissed him back.

"So that's it? You never want to even give it a go?" He spoke as though nothing had interrupted their conversation. Moved his hands as he talked. Found the inside of her waistband; she felt the ripple of her skin as he ran his hand inside it, then lifted her up onto the kitchen counter.

"I'm sorry, Bill, I really am. I wish I felt that way about you, but I just don't." She kissed him again, and this time she put her hand in his pants, felt how strained this situation was.

He kissed her with what felt like hard edges, his tongue searching for promises she couldn't make. "You might, though, when you've got through all this."

She wondered what he meant by "all this." The abuse, her parents' death, the fire, Simone? She almost wanted to laugh. "You aren't serious about me, Bill. You think I'm someone I'm not. Someone who needs to be fixed, who *can* be fixed."

He looked away, spoke softly, almost too low for Alison to hear what came next.

"I don't know if I can be friends with you, Al. I've had these feelings for you for too long." But he didn't stop touching her, so she didn't stop touching him either.

"Is it really more important to be with me than to be friends with me?" She let him pull her shorts off, let him push into her.

"You can't ask me to just let it go like that. It's not fair." They were looking into each other's eyes.

"Nothing in life is fair. You think it's fair that Simone died in a fire two states away from where she lived because her violent boyfriend was chasing her, or whatever the fucking truth is?" Talking now, about this, about anything, seemed wasted. Like they wouldn't remember it later anyway. Would have to start the conversation over.

"I wish I could kill him." Billy's anger spilled out everywhere, the set of his face, the way he was standing, how he held on to the anchors of her arms, her shoulders, left impressions where his fingers gripped, trying to let out the energy that was raging inside him. It should have scared her. Should have made her shrink away. But instead, it calmed her, and Alison moved with him, tried to reach out to him. Arched her back and held on to his hands, fingers laced. There was no intimacy this time. It was just for the physical need of it. And maybe, an attempt at manufacturing something more. Trying to re-create what had happened before. She did want to know if it was something between them, or just something she did because she could.

It went on until he pushed her away. Muttered without looking at her: "I can't do this. You should stay; there's sheets in the linen closet and a bed in Tracy's old room. I'm going to sleep."

He walked out. Left her sitting naked from the waist down on the kitchen counter. She heard him slam his bedroom door. Alison looked at her phone: 3:12 a.m. Morning was only a few hours away. If Gil was out there somewhere, it couldn't be long now before he found her.

Alison became aware that she was clenching her fists so tightly her fingernails cut into her palms. She tried to loosen up. Took another sip of the whiskey. Closed her eyes in the hot bulb-lit kitchen. Jumped down and found her shorts. Caught her reflection in the big windows, one-way mirrors in the early-morning dark. Her hair a mess and her clothes rumpled from hours of driving and the disruption of the sex.

She tried to see past herself into the night out there, into the space between the houses where he might be. Her own face gaped at her from the dull glass. The edges ill-defined. The eyes sunken and weary, the mouth set in a line. A certain flatness to her complexion. Like the dead. The thought popped into her head before she could stop it, and then Simone's face swam in front of her, the poses from the pictures turning her into some kind of prop, and then she was Alison, and bruises bloomed across her stomach, her lower back, her thighs, bruises that had once been on Alison's body, a body with Simone's face.

27.

Her dad called her again. The phone rang on her kitchen counter; she watched it, the way the vibration made it move, made it bounce almost, like a bee buzzing at the opening of a hive. She let it go. The sun was high in the sky and the light caught the countertop, the color of the pollen that sticks to the legs of a bee, reflected off the face of the phone. She couldn't tell if it was morning or afternoon right now, but it was a time of day that meant she was wasting it.

The phone buzzed again. A short one. He'd left another message. She picked it up, leaned her elbows on the counter, stuck her head out into the square of light and let it pierce her skull, shut her eyes to feel the way the light made the darkness orange. She opened them to see the black dots that always turned up after she'd bathed in the light; she pressed the speaker icon, pumped the volume up high. He sounded like always, the deep baritone of his voice a salve even when she was angry at him. Even when she wanted to scream at him, never wanted to see him again, the voice calmed her.

Love, I wish you'd pick up the phone. I know I've hurt you. But it's over. I don't know what I was thinking. Your mum says I wasn't, which is probably true. I just wanted to feel something . . . He paused here, and Alison could hear him, the way he was breathing, down the line. *Something that made me feel alive again. You're too young. You wouldn't understand. Your mother understands. She's trying. If she can try, can't you? I love you, wombat.*

Then a fumble as he took the phone away from his ear and grappled with ending the call, leaving her in the slice of sunshine, trying to think about the mechanics of how her father had ended up sending those emails. Sleeping with that woman. Being that fucking selfish.

The voicemails began about a week ago; he'd talked about how losing his job on the paper made him feel like he'd lost himself. How no one looked at him with respect anymore. But she did. Alison got it. She didn't need it spelled out. She didn't need a blow-by-blow of how goddamn typical her father was.

The front door opened. Gil pushed into the room carrying groceries and whistling. He was in a good mood today. Alison absorbed his moods as if they were her own. Tried to never show him hers, but it was already too late today.

"Babe, you thinking about your dad again?" He'd seen the line of her mouth, the way she was slumped over the phone. He knew she was obsessing over what had happened, and even though he'd told her *Some men are too weak to love one woman,* and stroked her hair when she cried about it after long calls with her mum, he was getting impatient. She felt the toughening of his grip on the back of her neck when she talked about him, the annoyance in his eyes, the shortness of his sentences, the way he was quick to reach for a beer or light up a joint, or leave, saying he needed to take a walk, if it was another night with complaining about Malcolm King on the agenda. But today was a good day. They still had those, most days.

"Sorry." She fumbled the word in her mouth, spat it out wrong. She waited for him to snap at her. *Speak properly—*

you're not a child. He moved quickly across the room and she tensed, waiting for what would come next. But he just gently held her face in his hands.

"Don't be sorry, babe, I know you're sad. It's a sad fucking thing." The tears ran down her cheeks and pooled in the spaces where his hands met her jaw. She tried to blink them away. At volume, another time: *Don't fucking cry over him. You shouldn't cry about him.* Gil leaned in and kissed the salty tracks, kissed her messy mouth, came around the other side of the counter and lifted her up onto the bench and held her. Held her while she cried. Held her until she stopped. Held her in his arms, and she wasn't sure if she'd be able to break free from his grip. But she also wasn't sure that she wanted to.

When Billy shook her awake Alison was surprised to see Detective Mitchell staring down at her as she lay on the bed. He was in his blues, and Detective Mitchell was dressed in her own version of a uniform. Gray suit, white shirt, hair pulled back neat. She gave nothing away as she loomed over Alison. Just folded her arms and then walked away from the bed.

"What is going on?" Alison sat up, tried to catch up.

"I called Corrine because I thought she should know about what Gil did to you."

"You told her?"

"He did tell me. As he should. The real question here, Alison, is, why didn't you?"

"It's not . . . It doesn't matter." Her voice sounded far away, like it was coming out of someone else's throat.

"It does matter. You lied about him. You held back. You knew her, didn't you? You lied to me. You lied to her parents. You lied to everyone."

"I didn't know her. I swear I didn't. I only found out, like, two days ago that he was Gil. You didn't tell me his full name. How could I have known?"

"I don't believe you." Detective Mitchell spoke fast, evenly, no hint of emotion in her tone. She tapped her heel on the floor, checked the time on her watch. "OK, ten minutes. I'll be waiting out front. We're going down to the station to talk all this through properly." Alison shot Billy a dark look, and he shook his head, got that stone-cold look on his face like he had the night before, and followed Detective Mitchell as she turned and left the room.

Alison began to sweat. She couldn't regulate her breathing properly, couldn't control her mouth—it felt dry and wet at once; it was making too much saliva, but her tongue was thick, heavy, like it was dehydrated. She tried to stand up, but her knees gave in as she put her weight on them; she fell back onto the bed. It didn't make sense to panic. *You've done nothing wrong.* But maybe she had.

She'd taken the paper with the address; she'd taken the note Gil had left behind; she hadn't told the police that Michael was really Gil. She hadn't been honest with Billy or Detective Mitchell; she'd run away. Who runs away? Simone. Simone ran away. Simone had run to her, had been coming to give her something—a tape? What tape? A recording of something Gil wanted badly enough to be following her around, probably somewhere here in this town right now, waiting to snatch Alison up, put his hands around her throat again, tighten them the way he'd done before.

Would Billy help her? Would Detective Mitchell? Or would they think she and Gil were in it together? What the fuck was going on with her tongue? *Breathe. Breathe, Alison, you stupid fucking idiot. Think about something else.* She closed her eyes.

The night of her formal came back again, the way the fire smelled as they all gathered around it, burning marshmallows on sticks and chucking crumpled cans in to see what would happen. The way Sam Chambers's big brown eyes glowed gold in the blaze, and the way that when he smiled the crooked left eyetooth caught the light and twinkled a little, the imperfection more an enhancement than anything else.

She could see Chloe in that pink dress next to him. Dirty-blond hair in a braid down her back, gray-blue eyes all pupil in the dark. The spit stuck in her mouth. The tears welled in her eyes. The breaths came fast. Piled on top of one another. None of them really getting where they needed to go.

"Alison!" Billy in the hall. Blink. Blink again. Shake her arms. Bend at the waist. Touch the floor. Feel the wood. Come back up. Breathe. Blink again. Breathe. Blink again. Breathe.

When she was a child, Alison's favorite color was pink. Pink like Chloe's formal dress. Pink like the singlet Simone had been wearing. Pink like the flush of Alison's face in the mirror after the fire had passed. After she'd fucked Billy on the living room floor. After she'd sweat her way through the nightmares. Pink. Like a tongue. Like the inside of a sea bream when you split it down the belly, or the blush of a bottlebrush in bloom.

Pink like the sky in the morning or late in the evening. Like Sal's prized roses and the nose of Patty's dog Sweep. Pink like the flesh of the beef in a bowl of pho on a cold night in Melbourne. Pink like lips. Pink, like the curve of a possum's tail or the paws of a ginger cat. Pink like the feet of a pelican or a starfish on a reef. Pink. Derivative of red.

Red like Meg's bouncy curls. Red. Red, the color of blood. The color of fire, sometimes, not always. Red. The color of the sky on days when disaster carries on the breeze and settles in the branches and the eaves and the garages and the driveways

233

and pulls down the trees and tears up worlds and rips open homes and roads and people and lives. Red, the color of insides. Red. Cut you open. Rust your chest. Bleed you until you can't bleed anymore, until you are gray, a derivative of black and white; white a component of pink.

Pink like the skirt Alison wore for her sixth birthday, like the cake her mother iced and her father helped her blow out, like the paper that wrapped the present that Billy pushed into her icing-smeared hand, like the lipstick Sal left on her cheek when she kissed her hello, like the way the day smelled and started and ended and remained, forever, a perfect moment, a reminder of a perfect time. Made of pink.

Like everything little girls like.

Alison shook her head and blinked hard once more, pushing the images out of her mind. Feeling her heart slow and her breathing regulate, she focused on the memory of her birthday. Three long breaths in. She picked up her phone and dialed Luca. He picked up on the second ring.

"Al, hey, what's happening?" He sounded worried, but friendly.

"Luca, I wanted to say I'm sorry about the cigarette butts." He was silent, thinking.

"What do you mean?"

"In the courtyard, near the back door. I was stressed and I guess old habits die hard. I've been thinking about it a lot, and I wanted to say sorry for not cleaning them up."

"Al, there's no cigarette butts in the courtyard. You must've gotten 'em all when you were leaving."

"What?" That couldn't be right. "None?"

"I'm looking right now. Nothing."

"Not even under the window? I thought I might have missed a couple there." She could hear him shuffling around on the pavers.

"Not even a trace of ash. You're better at hiding your habit than you think."

She tried to laugh, keep it light. "Awesome. A hidden talent. Who knew? OK, I gotta go. Say hi to Christine for me."

"Will do." A pause. "You all right?"

"Yeah, just a little stressed. And, you know, long drive, was trying to stay awake." She heard Billy's fist pounding on the door. "OK, Luca, I really gotta go. Talk later." She hung up.

"Al, let's go." She tidied her hair in the mirror on the back of the door, straightened her clothes, and went out into the hall. They were waiting.

"I'd like to drive my own car, if that's all right." From inside her own skull Alison's voice sounded far away.

"Yes, that's fine." Detective Mitchell turned and walked out of the house.

"I'll come with you." Billy's tone was one of peace.

"I'm all right." Alison's wasn't.

"I need a lift anyway, left my car at the pub, remember?"

"Fine, whatever." Alison stomped out of the house and across the street. She slid into her car and waited for Billy as he locked up and loped over to her, swung into the passenger seat, and smiled, awkwardly. She didn't have time to think about the cigarettes.

"Don't fucking smile at me."

"Come on, what was I supposed to do? Withhold information from an active investigation? I can't do that. You know I can't."

"Bet you could have if I'd flattered your ego a little better. Would you have looked the other way if I'd wanted to be your girlfriend?" Alison started the car. Pulled out a little, waited for Detective Mitchell to pass her, and then rolled into the road.

"No. This isn't about that. I'm in enough trouble for that as it is. Taking your statement and then sleeping with you wasn't the best thing I've ever done for my career. Since you disappeared, I've been in big trouble. They won't let me near Simone's case. I don't know if they're even telling me the truth about the autopsy or anything."

"What?"

"The autopsy. Corrine wouldn't let me see the file, but she told me to tell you Simone died in the fire."

"Why are you telling me this now?"

"Because I had to tell them you were at my place. And I had to tell them about Gil, but I believe you, Alison. I believe what you told me about how he treated you, and I don't think you're helping him." They were silent as she navigated the roundabout onto the main street. "I want you to know all that before you talk to Corrine."

Alison didn't say anything else. It wasn't long before they turned onto the soft beige pebble of the police station car park. Detective Mitchell was already out of her four-wheel drive. Tapping her foot impatiently as she waited for Alison to get out of her little Corolla. Billy swung out of the car and she was alone for a second. Then she remembered. The cigarettes she bought on the drive to Sydney. She opened the center console, where she'd left them when she'd arrived at Luca's. They were gone.

She didn't know, in this moment, if Gil had been in the car or she'd smoked them all herself, somehow forgetting. Had she smoked them in Luca's courtyard and forgotten about it? Had she cleaned them up and forgotten that too? It seemed incredible, but the past few days were bleeding into one another.

She was forgetting things, doing things she wouldn't do otherwise, panicking. She wasn't evened out. She felt as if she were in a rowing scull, fighting a wash too large to be quelled.

Deep breaths again. Small movements; collect the muscles in her hand and swing open the door, lean into it, heavily, make it shift. Swing out a leg, another leg, stand up, and try not to look too damn scared or confused.

She didn't know if the mask in place of her face was effective. She wouldn't ever know. The three of them covered the space between the car and the station in seconds, and Alison felt her stomach flip nervously as she went inside.

28.

So, you don't know anything about this note?" Detective Mitchell slid a plastic-encased slip of exercise paper across the table. The note was written in the same scrawl as the one she'd found in the letterbox.

Give it to me.

"Gil wrote it." Alison shivered.

"It was under your door. After you decided to take a little trip, I got a warrant to search the place. This is the only thing I found, so if you do have something of his, you've hidden it well."

"I really don't. And I really don't know anything more than I've already told you."

Detective Mitchell sighed, leaned back in her chair, and slumped her shoulders a little, and a strand of that tightly pulled-back hair fell into her face. She huffed out of the side of her mouth, blowing it up, and then tucked it behind her ear, quickly, like that piece of hair was a constant annoyance.

"Yeah, I'm beginning to believe you."

"You searched my place?"

"Look at it from our point of view, Alison. Cause of death

isn't nailed down yet, you've got an ex in common—a violent one who you never reported—and then you go missing too?"

"Billy said it was the fire." Was the detective lying now, or had she been lying to Billy? What trick was this? What lie was she hoping to catch Alison in? "And I didn't go missing. I told Sal and Billy where I was going, and I told Billy where I was more than once."

"You compromised my ability to trust Constable Meaker. Your relationship makes his information unreliable at best."

"For both of us, apparently." Alison tried not to think about that phrase, *your relationship*. "Where are you looking for Gil?"

"Everywhere. We've got alerts out on his car and his cards, and his likeness is in every motel in the area. When he pops up, we'll find him."

"He's not an idiot, you know. Everyone knows cops can track your money, track your phone. He's probably not going to turn up at the closest Best Western."

"Well, where do you think he is?"

"I think he's somewhere near me, wherever I am. I thought I was paranoid in the days after the fire, but I kept feeling like someone was watching me, and a couple of times I got up in the middle of the night to look out the window, 'cause it felt weird, and then after I'd go back to sleep I'd hear an engine turn over."

"You think it was him." It wasn't a question.

"I really do now. That's why I went to Billy's last night. I didn't want to turn up at Sal's alone at two in the morning." Honesty was the best idea in this particular moment.

"And you really didn't learn that Simone's violent boy-friend, Michael, was Gil until the day you left town?"

"I told you. That's when Chris Waters told me about it and that's why I left. I thought, I dunno, maybe I could do some-thing." *Better to keep to this lie*, Alison thought.

"What kind of something?"

"I don't know." Alison paused, tried to check her tone and lower her voice. "I guess maybe find out from his old mates in Cairns where he was or why he was looking for Simone."

Detective Mitchell stared at Alison, no expression translatable on her face. "All right. And?"

"And nothing. I didn't learn anything. Turns out this investigating thing is more difficult than TV'd have you think." She couldn't tell her about the pictures, about why she'd decided to destroy them, about how they had made her feel.

The detective rolled her eyes. "You don't say."

She got up from the table as if to leave the room, and Alison reached out and caught her by the arm. "I know you probably don't believe me, but he killed her."

Detective Mitchell looked at her, skeptical. "We want to talk to him, sure, but there's no evidence she was killed by anything unnatural." *Should have kept the piece of paper. Should have kept the pictures.*

"You mean you think it was the fire." *All this for natural fucking causes.*

"It was the fire. Eventually the forensics will figure that out. I'm just trying to find out why she was where she was, why she went missing, what he's doing menacing his exes." She waved the note for effect. "He might not be a murderer, but he had something to do with her going missing."

"He killed her. I'm sure he did." She was. She didn't really know why she was so sure, but she was.

"The evidence just doesn't lean that way, Alison, as much as you want it to." She gently wrenched her arm free and left, leaving the door open. Alison stopped holding her breath a few seconds later when she realized Detective Mitchell wasn't coming back.

Billy stuck his head into the room. "Al, you can go."

"Is that it?"

"For now. She'll let you know if she needs anything else."

"OK." Alison got up from the table and picked up her bag. In the main station the air was stuffy and there was no one around. Billy opened the counter gate and let her through. "Quiet in here today."

"I'm holding down the fort. Everyone else is out on insurance reports and whatnot. Had a bit of looting, looks like local kids taking advantage of the empty houses, but it's keeping us busy enough."

"Why aren't you out there too?"

"Sarge is a little pissed with me, now all that stuff about you and Gil and Simone being linked has come out, says I made us look like the worst kind of country coppers." Billy shrugged. "I get it. I know how he feels being made to look like a fool." They stared at each other until Alison couldn't look him in the eye any longer.

"Billy, I'm sorry."

"Yeah, me too."

"If you need me, I'll be at Sal's."

"You think he's staking Sal's out and you're just gonna go back there?"

"I let Gil destroy me once. I'm not going to let him do it again."

Alison turned and left the station, stood on the steps for a minute, took three deep breaths. The sun hit the bitumen full on, tar tacky where it coagulated. Beyond the bend, up there on the ridge, exposed rock, like a deep wound, black and gray, stripped trunks, ash underfoot.

Everything felt strange in an indescribable way.

29.

At Sal's house the front door was open, but a screen door to keep out the flies created a barrier to whatever might lurk in wait. Alison tried the handle; it was locked for once. She yelled out for Sal, but no one came. Probably down in the rose garden again. She walked around to the side of the house, tried the high gate, built when the Marshes' long-dead cattle-dog crossbreed, Kenny, was a pup. It was locked too, but the smooth rock behind the pink heath that grew to one side of the fence was, Alison knew, not actually a rock. She cracked it open and pulled the spare key out, tried it in the gate lock. It turned easily, and the gate swung open. Alison returned the key to the rock and headed down the path.

Sal was in the rose garden, secateurs in hand, and Jim was sitting on a large rock drinking from a teacup and laughing. Alison hadn't noticed his ute in the street when she got there, but she hadn't been looking for it either. She walked down the sloping lawn to the garden, noticing for the first time that the birds seemed to be properly returning. She could hear them on the hot wind, and she had missed them, their calls and whoops and trills an unconscious comfort.

"Alison! You made good time. Where'd you stop for the

night?" Sal embraced her. She smelled a little of manure, a lot of sweat.

"What? Oh, right. I drove straight through, got in real late last night, didn't want to wake you up, so I slept in my car."

"It's almost one."

"Yeah, I had some stuff to do this morning. Anyway, I'm back. All right if I stay a few more days? I gotta get those windows fixed at home and find out when the power'll be back."

"Course it is. Cuppa?"

"No, thanks, Sal. Too hot for me."

Jim tipped out his slops on the grass and raised his cup up to Sal. "I'll have another if you're offering."

"I could use a break. All right, come on up to the house. Think I've got the makings of some sandwiches if you two want some lunch." Sal started up the hill, Jim's cup swinging in her hand.

"Nice of you to drop in, Jim." Alison smiled at him.

"I actually came to pass a message on to you, figured Sal would talk to you at some point."

"What message?" The sun cast long shadows that ran from the garden down to the valley below. Alison, Jim, the roses, cast their darkness over the plain.

"I was picking up my mail yesterday and they asked me if you were around, since they're holding all mail at the moment and residents have to pick up. You haven't been in and Shane knew we're neighbors, so he asked me to tell you there's some letters—look like bills—and a package for you."

"A package? I'm not expecting anything."

"I don't know, Alison; that's what he said. Have you been picking up?"

"No, I didn't even think about it."

"Well, swing by next time you're on Main Street."

"Will do. Thanks, Jim." He tipped his hat at her and began

to make his way up the hill. Alison followed in the shadow he cast, a little cooler in the shade than out of it. It was a hot February day, and the flies bumbled about, trying to rub their legs together on her head, her arms, her face.

Alison left Jim and Sal drinking tea in the kitchen and went into her makeshift studio. It had been only a few days, but seeing the canvases fresh, she was shocked by the obsessive quality of the work. There were close-ups of Simone's face, her eyes, her mouth, her profile, and the curve of her jaw at the nape of her neck; everything was slightly blurred, or blended, the paints mixing in sweeping strokes over the canvases and colliding at sharp angles or soft, feathery edges and making surreal, almost hazy snippets of Simone. Like the photographs. But Alison could see for the first time, looking closely with fresh eyes, that while the pictures looked like Simone, they also looked like her. That was her cheek, her hairline, her eyelid, the soft curve of her nose and the bow of her lips.

They were physically far more similar than she'd noticed before. But now, almost two weeks after she'd seen Simone for the first and last time, Alison couldn't remember if they really did look similar or if she'd tricked herself into thinking they did. She stood in the middle of the room, an old sheet down on the floor to guard Sal's recently shined boards from paint; canvases stacked against one another, leaned against the desk, the couch, the walls, the bookcase, and the base of the easel; paints set up on a plate; brushes dried out, clean and fresh on the rag she'd left them on; a canvas, barely blocked out, sitting ready. She squeezed some peach out, then some white, red, a little green. Mixed the paint up until it matched the skin on her forearm; added a little black, just the tiniest amount.

Closed her eyes to try to see the shade of gray that had over-taken Simone in the minutes after she'd drawn her last breath.

Alison took a wide, flat brush and wet it heavy with paint, sloughing it through the mix, and then made a straight-edged square in the top right corner of the canvas. Filled it in. Mixed another square, a little more tan, less creamy, but with enough black to tint it ghostly. It took Alison three hours to block out the rest of the squares. Every shade of skin she could mix, all of it ashen: 164 squares. None of them even, all of them im-precise. Alison hated it. Too heavy-handed. Too much sym-bolism, not enough meaning.

Alison dunked her brush in the gritty grime of kerosene she'd left there days ago, lay on the floor, and closed her eyes. Thought about everything she'd ever learned about the bush, about fire, about life out here in the parts of the country where summer is a potential death sentence.

She knew eucalyptus trees needed fire. Fire is how they initiate new life. Fire forces open seedpods and eliminates competitors and spurs new shoots on old trunks. Fire creates openings for a towering, opportunistic beauty that thrives where others shrink and curdle. The main by-product of bush-fires, wood ash, is a great source of potassium and other nutri-ents necessary for the roots of what remains. The extreme temperatures a bushfire generates are too much for most foli-age, but the eucalypt is resilient. Among those who study it there's an uncertainty as to whether it covets the flames of destruction or simply benefits from them. The heat and smoke and pressure releasing the spawn of the elders across the ground.

Alison got up off the drop sheet and looked at the canvas again. Somehow it had gotten dark outside when she wasn't paying attention. The low light of the room, from the bright bulbs in the hall trickling illumination in through the door, wasn't enough anymore. Alison went to turn the light on, raised her hand to the switch, but changed her mind. Left the canvas to dry, walked out, back into the room she'd been sleeping in. Lay on the bed and, without saying good night to Sal or eating any dinner, fell asleep. Eyes closed, breathing regulated, stretched out fully clothed, still in the shorts and T-shirt she'd been wearing when she left Cairns the day before.

30.

At the post office there was only one clerk and a line almost out the door. Alison had come early—it was barely ten—thinking most people would swing by around lunchtime. In the line she busied herself reading the paper and tried not to open herself up to conversations. The queue moved gratingly slowly, and she tapped her foot on the carpet as she stood there, trying not to lose patience. When she got to the front she recognized the man behind the counter, chewing the side of his cheek and leaning heavily on the laminated wood.

"Hey, Tom. Jim said you guys have my mail."

"Alison, heard a lot about you these past couple of weeks. How's things?"

"You know everything you hear is true. Or none of it."

He smiled and shook his head. "Hang on and I'll check out the back." He hustled away. While Alison waited, she picked the film of dirt from under her nails, looked around behind the counter, tried to see where Tom was out the back through the glass panels in the wall. Eventually he reappeared, carrying a stack of envelopes and a mailer, the kind lined with Bubble Wrap. Alison was surprised to see it. She couldn't remember ordering anything in the last few weeks, and it wasn't usual for her to get packages. He dumped the mail on the countertop.

"Here you go."

"Thanks so much, see you later." She stuffed the mail into her bag and left the post office. Stopped in at the bakery to grab a pastie and then took everything back to her car. Parked in the shade on Main Street, Alison was tempted to open the package immediately. She looked around, worried that maybe Gil was nearby, waiting to wrench open the door and pull her out into the street. It was fine. She was fine. The package had no return address. The postmark was from Wangaratta; the postmark was from the day before the fire. Alison looked at it. She didn't know anyone in Wangaratta. The day before the fire. The day before the fire. Fuck. She ripped the mailer open. A folded piece of stiff paper, and two USB sticks, each with masking tape on one side, the contents recorded in fat marker. One said "Simone" and the other "Alison." Alison sucked air through her teeth as she inhaled. Unfolded the paper.

Dear Alison,

Hopefully, when you get this you'll already know what it's about. I think he's following me, and I can't risk him finding me and taking it back, so I've mailed this to you. Make sure you watch yours, all of them. I should be there tomorrow, but if you never see me, please know it's Gil's fault that I'm gone, and this is the reason why.

Looking forward to meeting you,
Simone Arnold

This was it. What Gil was looking for. The thing that had cost Simone her life. Alison couldn't breathe. She needed to get home. She needed to put the USB drives in her laptop and see what was on them. Put the key in the ignition. Turn the key. Foot on the brake. Drop the hand brake and flick on the indicator. Shift the stick into drive. Check the mirrors. Turn the wheel and feel the tires shift in the loose gravel. Foot off the brake; foot on the accelerator. Pull out. Down the street. Round the roundabout. Turn toward Sal's, not Billy's. On the highway, just for a bit, not even a full click. Turn again, into the drive. Foot on the brake. Shift the gear into park. Lift up the hand brake. Foot off the pedal. Pull out the keys. Open the door. Get out of the car and reach over to the passenger seat; gather up the bag. Take all the mail inside. At the door, fumble a minute trying to find the keys among the sharp envelope edges. Hear something unexpected.

"Hi, Ally. Long time no see." The voice was the same. Smooth, a little syrupy, hypnotic and sweet and deep and mesmerizing. The face was the same too. Angles and stubble and those baby blues. Michael Gilbert Watson. In a singlet and a pair of jeans that looked as if they hadn't been washed for god knows how long. Alison felt the skin on her arms rise and fall, the hairs on end. Her scalp tingled and itched. She held her bag a little closer to her side and gulped back her fear. What the fuck was he doing? He was either stupid or reckless, or both.

"Gil."

"So, where's me tapes?"

Alison tried to keep calm. Laughed, even though it made no sense to laugh. "If I wanted to give them to you I would."

There wasn't any warning before he grabbed her by the shoulders and pushed her into the wall, hitting her head against the weatherboard and slightly dazing her. He leaned his forearm across her neck, pressed into her windpipe, moved his face to within a centimeter of hers.

"Give them to me, you stupid fucking bitch."

Alison couldn't move, could barely whisper with the pressure on her neck. She tried to gulp enough air to sustain herself and struggled hard against his grasp. Finally, her knee connected with his crotch and he recoiled from her in agony. Alison fell to her knees and started to scream. The loudest, most piercing screams she could muster. Something inside her snapped. One by one, neighbors started opening their doors. Soon enough Sal was there, on the front veranda, the secateurs in her hand, the dirt on her beige gardening shorts, the flush on her cheeks, and the stride of her gait propelling her forward. It took Gil too long to gather his wits after the kick to the groin. He was on the ground. Sal kicked him in the stomach, and then the nuts, and poked the secateurs into his shoulder, lightly but with menace on her face. He looked from Sal to Alison to the secateurs and got up as fast as he could. Scrambled backward onto the grass of the front lawn and rushed away before Alison could properly process what was going on.

"Chickenshit!" Sal yelled after him as he ran to a beat-up Ford Falcon and swung behind the wheel. The sound of his retreat was matched by the smell of the rubber that burned as his wheels turned too fast on the road, their bald treads taking another hit as he peeled out of there as fast as he could.

"Bullies. Never met an equal contest they couldn't run from." Sal knelt down and put her hands on Alison's shoulders, gently, where Gil had grasped her so firmly. Alison flinched, and Sal moved a hand to her cheek, rested it there, tried to get Alison to stand up, but her legs felt like jelly. Her whole body felt like jelly. She breathed in. Breathed in again. Thought about the way that ash is a good source of potassium in gardens. Slowly moved upward until she was standing, acutely aware of the bag still clutched close, held tight even as Gil clawed at her. Still there. She was still there. The bag was still there. Alison propelled herself back into the house; she wasn't actually sure how. She found a way to get from the veranda into the hall and then into her room. She was aware of Sal following her. She didn't care. Didn't hear the questions Sal was asking or feel her hand on the skin of her arm.

Alison's laptop was charging on the floor, the cord plugged into an outlet next to the bedside table. She sat on the floor, back against the bed, and pulled the laptop toward her, opened it. Logged in. Rooted around in her bag for the USB drives, found the one with her name on it, and pushed it into the socket. A little icon appeared on the screen. Alison. Alison clicked on it. The drive contained only one folder. It was named surveillance and inside was a series of .avi files, each differentiated solely by a date. The oldest one, 03112014, made Alison gag before she even double-clicked. November 3, 2014. Gil's birthday. Her blood froze. That was the day it all began. She'd never been able to forget the first time. There were at least thirty files on the drive. Were they all like that day? She tried to swallow, but she couldn't. She clicked the birthday file, waited for it to load, was only mildly aware of Sal settling next to her on the floor.

The video was so detailed, high-resolution, high-definition, whatever the fuck it was called. Black-and-white surveillance, and Alison couldn't parse how such a thing existed. How was there a record of this moment beyond the one in her own head? There wasn't any sound. Just vision. Her, in the apartment she'd shared with Gil. Him on top of her. Holding her down. That look on her face—Alison didn't recognize herself. Like she wasn't even really there.

"Alison. What is this?"

"It's Gil. It's the first time he hurt me." The words echoed in the space inside her head, inside her chest.

"I don't understand." Alison took a deep breath and told Sal the truth about the man she'd lived with in Cairns. The ways he'd hurt her. "That was him on the veranda?"

"That was him."

"I'll bloody kill him."

"Sal, it's OK. This is more than enough."

"What do you mean?"

Alison didn't reply. She stared at the screen, logging the dates that came with the files and trying to piece it all together in her mind. Gil always wanted them to fuck on the bed. He wasn't one for a quickie on the couch or a little bit of risk in the slippery shower. He liked a bed, said that was where he had his "full range of motion." After that day when he'd forced it for the first time—if she was being honest, after that day she hadn't really ever had sex with Gil again. Not voluntarily, not without a little bit of fear in every touch and movement. But it hadn't been until right now, this moment, looking into her own lifeless eyes as they fixed on the ceiling, that she fully realized the truth. She couldn't decide what was worse: the actual physical violence, and the way that it lingered on her skin every time another person touched her, or the way she couldn't think about trusting anyone else ever again.

The fire had made her forget for a minute, given her something else to focus on, stripped her back to rawest nerves. A dangerous, terrifying circuit breaker that had shaken her up and pulled her out and then plunged her right back in there, in this terror, with the arrival of Simone.

Simone. How did she get these files? Were they all like this one? Gil must have put a camera in the bedroom so he could film them having sex. Had he still had access to it after she kicked him out? Her skin crawled. What was on the other USB? More of this? Alison ejected the first one, found the second one in her bag, and waited for its contents to load on the screen.

Simone popped up, double the number of files the Alison drive contained. She forced herself to click on one. A different room. She didn't recognize it. But she did recognize the look on Simone's face as he pushed her onto the bed and pinned her down. Still, it dawned on her that if she didn't know the truth, the actions in the video she was watching might appear to be consensual. Simone wasn't fighting him. She wasn't engaging, but she wasn't fighting. She switched it off. Downloaded the whole drive onto her computer and opened her email.

This wasn't something she knew how to handle, and she didn't trust Billy to keep it to himself. She needed someone who knew the law. She thought of Christine. If Simone had taken these videos, stolen them from Gil, then she must have wanted to use them to put him in jail. That had to be the reason she was coming to Alison. If the two of them had worked together, the videos and their stories might have been enough. Now she thought she finally knew what Simone had been doing, why she was heading for her in the first place.

"Alison, are you going to tell me what's going on?" Sal sounded exasperated, her voice higher and tighter than usual. Alison studied her face. Sal's eyes were narrowed and red; she was flushed, a little splotchy.

"Sal, don't cry, I'm OK." Alison reached out a hand to squeeze her arm, comfort her.

"I'm sorry, love, I keep thinking about your mum and how she used to say how happy you were and what a nice man you'd found up in Cairns. She'd be devastated if she knew the truth."

"That's why I didn't tell her, or you. Come on, it's all right. I'm OK, really."

"I'm not the only one crying, you know." As she spoke Sal sniffed, raised her finger, and wiped a tear from Alison's face.

"I gotta make a call. Can I have some privacy?"

"You calling the police about that man?"

"No. Actually, Sal, can we keep that between us for a little bit? I promise I'll tell them he was here, but I just want a little time first, try and figure out what's going on. Why Simone wanted me to have this."

"I don't know, Alison."

"Please, Sal, just a few hours even."

"All right, but if I see him again, police are my first call."

"Deal."

Sal looked uncertain, but she got up off the floor and leaned down and squeezed Alison's shoulder, then walked slowly out of the room. "I'll put the kettle on, think a cup of tea could do us both some good."

"Sure, Sal, thank you."

Alone, Alison put the first USB drive back in and looked over the file names again. There were a handful of dates that matched up with her relationship with Gil. Each one recorded an encounter that wasn't really consensual. Some of them involved a level of force Alison had blocked out. She didn't watch them all the way through; some she skipped altogether. She couldn't make sense of this new evidence of how their relationship had really been. She copied all the files. Her phone was heavy in her hand as she scrolled through the contacts, found Luca, and dialed. It rang once, twice, three times, four . . . and then as it stretched out into its seventh ring she began to deflate. When he answered it took her by surprise.

"Alison, tell me what's been happening." He was eager to help.

It reassured her. She explained that she needed to talk to Christine, but Luca got annoyed when she wouldn't give him details. The intimacy of the violence made her want to hold it close and not allow it to infuse all her relationships. Christine knew about this stuff. She dealt with it at work. Alison didn't want Luca to look at her the way Billy had when he'd found out the truth about Gil, or to squeeze her arm the way Sal had after watching the tape. She wanted a piece of herself, her old self, to remain forever untainted by the reality of her new self. Eventually Luca caved and gave Alison Christine's number. She said good-bye and promised to come visit again when all of it was sorted out. Hung up and dialed Christine.

She answered on the first ring.

"Christine. It's Alison King. Luca gave me your number." There was a long pause.

"Alison, how are you?"

"Do you have time to talk? I need your legal opinion on something."

"Of course. What is it?"

"Promise you will keep this between us?"

"Well, that depends; there are certain things I'm obligated to report by law, but if you're not planning to commit any crimes, sure."

"I know what tapes Simone had. She sent them to me."

"Shit. OK. What are they?"

"They're recordings. Of Gil and me, and Gil and Simone. In our bedrooms. Like, secret recordings. All the ones she has—well, the ones I've looked at, anyway—are . . . violent."

"Recordings of him assaulting you? In your bedroom?"

"Yes."

There was a long silence. "Sexual assault, Alison?"

"Yes."

"I see. And her too?"

"Yes. I didn't really watch hers. I watched a little bit of one, but it seemed too private."

"Is he using obvious force?"

"I don't know how to quantify it. I know from the look on my face that I didn't want to . . . and the one I watched of Simone, she has the same eyes. Some of my ones have him hitting me or choking me, but there's no sound." The conversation was so straightforward, it seemed easy to remove herself from it.

"I see. All right. Can you send me the tapes? I can take a look and see if there is enough on there that a prosecutor might act."

"You think we could put him in jail?"

"I think at the very least police would want to use these tapes to help them build any case they might have against him for Simone's death. As for anything beyond that, that's up to you."

"What do you mean?"

"You'd have to press charges in Queensland, and you'd have to testify against him in court, and any criminal culpability would be restricted to the assaults on you. Simone's not able to press charges or testify."

Alison didn't say anything. She didn't know what any of this meant. Everything she'd assumed about Simone's motives seemed less clear. What had she been planning? Was there another solution? What was it Simone's parents had said? That she'd called them and said she had a way to get him out of her life forever. Jail wasn't forever.

"How long would he go to jail?"

"Well, you get a couple of rape charges to stick, you could put him away for a good amount of time, but it's fraught, honestly. Get the wrong judge and he'd be out in a few years."

"Best case?"

"Best case . . . fifteen years cumulative probably."

"Worst case?"

"Good behavior bond."

"No jail?"

"It's unlikely, but not impossible. Prior relationship, no contemporaneous complaints to police, no physical evidence of assault, no audio on the videos to provide context, prove aggressive talk, record any threats he might have made. A sympathetic judge, a good lawyer, there's a chance he walks out of court."

"But what about Simone's police report? I know she went to the police about him."

"Good lawyer gets that excluded. Prejudicial."

"So I've got nothing, then."

"That's not what I'm saying. I'm saying you don't have any guarantees, but that doesn't mean it's not worth trying."

"OK. I tried to email you the files, but they're too large. I don't fucking trust the cloud. I'll send you a copy in the post today. You really think even with this he could walk away?"

"When I was in law school, I did some work for a barrister. He was representing a man who had drugged and raped dozens of strangers, women he'd convinced would be safe getting a lift home and a cup of tea, who he then took advantage of. He filmed it too. My job was to watch the tapes. Look for any signs that the women were complicit, that they were into it. So that questions could be raised about the rapes, doubt seeded in the minds of the jury members at trial. This was a man who had drugged strangers. Gil was your boyfriend. The law is flawed. The system sucks. It doesn't mean you shouldn't try, but you should be prepared for anything to happen."

"What happened?"

"What do you mean?"

"The guy you were defending?"

"He took a plea. Twenty years. His crimes were clear and there were many of them." A pause. "Unfortunately, even though it's terrible, this isn't that clear-cut."

"I get it. OK. I'm gonna send you these tapes."

"Take care, Alison, and don't do anything stupid. This guy sounds like a real piece of work."

"Bye, Christine. Thanks."

She made sure she had copies of all the files on her laptop; then she went into Sal's study and rooted around in the desk drawer. Found a USB drive tucked up the back. Took it to her room and made a copy of everything. Then she tucked Simone's USB drive into her pillowcase and put the other original one in her bra. As Alison was closing her laptop, Sal reappeared with two cups of tea.

"Here you go, love." She pushed the cup into Alison's hand and Alison looked at it, looked at Sal, saw the anxiety in her eyes.

"It's OK, Sal. I'm OK. Actually, I feel better than I have since the fire." It was true. For the first time in almost two weeks she hadn't spent a second thinking about the flames or the smell or the way the trees had burst and blistered and popped and catapulted the front toward her. She gulped her tea. Felt it burn all the way down her throat and sit warm in her empty stomach.

"Your mum would have done anything for you, you know."

"I know."

"I don't think you do. She loved you so much. Wanted you so much. But you only cared about your dad. You broke her heart every single day and she just kept loving you."

"That's not true. Dad just understood me better."

"Kids think they know everything. You're more like her than you realize. She wasn't going to tell you about the affair, said she didn't want to taint your relationship with your dad, but I made her call you, because she needed you."

"I didn't know that."

"I know. Kids don't know anything about their parents. They rarely pay attention." Sal reached out and squeezed Alison's hand. Tried to smile at her.

"Your kids love you very much, Sal."

"That they do. Doesn't mean they ever listen to me."

"Pat's right about the conditions up here. They aren't good, and this isn't going to be the last fire you have to deal with if you stay."

"Geoff and I met at university. He was in my Australian literature class. We had tutorials on Thursdays that finished at four. Afterward we'd all go to this pasta place on Lygon Street and order these big plates of cheap spaghetti and argue about just how bad we thought Malcolm Fraser was.

"One day halfway through the semester he slipped me a note as class was wrapping up. It said, 'Can I take you out just us today?' and he took me to this place on Elgin Street with Middle Eastern food—I'd never had falafel before, imagine that—and we talked and talked and talked and when we left the restaurant we kept on talking, we just walked around for hours into the middle of the night.

"We got married six months later. Even though my friends said I was too young and marriage was slavery and I was buying into the patriarchy and we'd regret it. I took his name, which caused a huge fight between me and my younger sister, who thought I was selling myself. It was 1978. A lot of our friends were communists. Some of them even refused to come to the wedding.

"But our vows, we wrote them ourselves, which wasn't that common then. I said, 'I promise to always support you. To always listen to you, even when you make me mad or aren't being reasonable. I promise to love you, and honor you, and never to pander to you. I promise that I will never leave you, to talk to you until my dying day. I promise that we will always be a team.'

"I made a vow. My friends thought I was stupid then, my children think I am stupid now, but Geoff and I built our lives here. We had our children here. We raised our family here. We fought, and we made up, and we grew together here. I want to be able to keep my promise to him. I want to talk to him every day until the day I die. I'm not leaving."

Sal squeezed Alison's hand again, and reached up to her face with her free hand and wiped the tears from her own cheeks, and then from Alison's. "This world has really done a number on you, hasn't it, kiddo? First your parents and then this fire, and this . . . this man."

"Yeah. The last few years haven't been ideal."

"Why didn't you talk to me?"

Alison took a deep breath. She'd dodged this conversation long enough. She couldn't hide from it anymore. "I didn't talk to anyone. You know, you read the articles—the ones about women who are killed by their partner. Set on fire, or beaten until they can't breathe, or that fucking horrific case in Brisbane—remember? It was all over the news. The woman found in the stockpot. I mean, you hear the stories, and you think, no way. I'd never. If he hit me, I'd walk. But then . . ." She trailed off, thinking about Gil. How his smile became like a drug she wanted so desperately to taste. How isolated she'd become, how embarrassed and foolish she'd felt.

"But then?" Sal wasn't pushing now.

"But then it happens, and it takes your breath away, and suddenly, somehow, it's your fault, not his. And you'd do anything to make it up to him. And it somehow never occurs to you that you're not special. You're like the woman on fire, the woman at the bottom of the stairs. The woman in the pot—except you're still alive, and aren't you lucky he's kind?"

"Jesus Christ." Sal reached out and cupped Alison's face with her hand. Sal's skin was soft and smooth like fine tissue paper, and her palm was warm. She swiped at the tear steadily working its way down Alison's cheek.

"The fire, when it was coming—I don't know how to—

When it turned, when it moved away and it didn't take me—it felt like every time he didn't kill me." Alison hadn't said that before, and she already felt ashamed she finally had.

Sal shuddered. "Why did you stay?"

Alison shook her head, let a little laugh escape, a weird, strangled one. "I think it's easier to explain why I left. Mum and Dad died, and I'd kicked Gil out for cheating on me a couple of weeks before. I hadn't seen him, but I felt, always, like I might. Like he would come round and refuse to leave, and then what would I do? He knew I grew up in Victoria, he knew my parents' names, but I didn't think he knew their address, or even the town. When I got here, I hadn't felt that safe in years. So even though I was deeply miserable, I stayed. Safety felt more important than anything else. And then, suddenly, it had been two years. Two whole years and he hadn't even tried to find me."

"That's a good thing, love."

Alison shook her head. "No, it's a cowardly thing. I knew. I knew who he was. What he did to me. What he did to women. And I knew he was seeing someone else."

"That's not your responsibility, kiddo."

"You know what, Sal? I know. And I'm also sick of hearing it, or saying it to myself. Maybe I never admitted this, even to myself. But I think that's why I went to Cairns, why I tried to figure out who Simone was, what she wanted from me. Something deep in the pit of my soul—in my guts—I fucking knew. I knew it was him, and that it was my fault."

Sal pulled Alison's face to hers, so they were staring into each other's eyes from inches apart. She looked furious, the sea in a storm written all across her face. "This is not on you; this is never going to be your fault. It is him. It is that coward who did this to you, and to Simone, and it's not your fault."

Alison wanted to believe her. She just had no idea how to.

31.

Anne and Bob Arnold were staying at the pub, in the simple rooms upstairs where a wide veranda wrapped around the building and gave an overview of the whole town and its surrounds. Anne Arnold led Alison outside, apologizing for the unmade bed on the way through. It was a hot afternoon, no breeze on the air, but the sun was behind them now, so their chairs were shaded. Alison clocked the street. Searched it for any signs of Gil. Things were quiet, less traffic than usual. It would take a long time for it to get back to normal, or develop a new normal, whatever that might be.

"I was surprised when Chris Waters told me you were still here. I thought you'd be gone by now."

"They've still got Simone in Melbourne, and Detective Mitchell is here, and we thought, maybe being here, we'd hear things quicker or we'd be able to be helpful in some way. I didn't want to sit at home all that ways away and wait." As she talked, Anne Arnold scratched the skin on her forearm, raising red tracks along it.

"I get it. I'm glad you're still here." She paused, looked around to make sure they were alone. "Where's Mr. Arnold?"

"He went for a walk, hates being cooped up. He should be back soon. Do you want to wait for him?"

"No, actually, I think maybe you are exactly the person I need to talk to. I know why Simone was in my driveway."

Shock flashed across her face, but Anne Arnold quickly reset it, blank, unreadable beyond the ever-present sadness. "How?"

"She sent me something. I picked up my mail at the post office this morning and there it was, a note saying she was worried that Gil would catch up with her before she got to me, so she was posting it."

Anne Arnold gripped the top of her chair, her knuckles mottled white from the pressure. "What was it?"

"It's video files. I'm not going to show them to you; they are too awful." Simone's mother let go of the chair and sunk onto the wide timber boards, dropped her head.

"Tell me."

"Gil set up a secret camera at my place, and also one at Simone's. He filmed us having sex. And he kept the tapes. He even kept tapes of the times he forced it."

"He raped you?"

"I think he raped us both."

"I knew he was violent, but Simone never said . . . she never said she was raped."

"I can't speak for her, I didn't know your daughter, but the files she sent me . . . Relationships are complicated and I don't know anything about Simone and Gil, but I do know that I stayed with him when he treated me terribly and, yes, after he raped me, and I kept sleeping with him and I even enjoyed it sometimes, somehow, but now I think back and I remember how I used to feel afterward, how I'd lie there and wonder what I would do next to upset him, how long it would be before he got mad at me again, and I would remember the first time he forced me and think about how he could take what he wanted whenever he wanted and I wouldn't be able to stop

him and so now I don't think about the times I felt were good
or the nice things he did or any of that. I remember that
underneath it all was a feeling of not having control. Not being in control at all. How can sex be consensual ever if that's
how you feel?"

There was a long silence. When she spoke again, Anne Arnold sounded far away. "What do you think Simone was doing
with those tapes?"

"I don't know. But a very wise friend of mine reminded me
that parents know their children better than anyone, and I'm
hoping you might know."

"She wanted to get away from him, but she didn't want to
blow up her life. She had a good job, and she loved her friends,
and her little sister just had a baby—she was really excited
about being an auntie. But he wouldn't leave her alone and she
was really upset about it. She'd met this new man; he was kind
and sweet, real good-looking, and she wanted to get on with
things with him, but Gil was still hanging around."

A new man. Alison thought that must be who the Cairns
shopkeeper was talking about.

"OK, and you said she called you and said she had figured
out how to get him to leave her alone?"

"Yes."

"And then she disappeared."

"Yes."

"Did you ask the new guy? Did he know anything?"

"No. I never met him. I wouldn't know where to start.
They weren't really dating even yet, she'd just met him, said
he made her feel safe."

Neither of them said anything. A bee hummed about on
the wind, flew a little too close for comfort. Alison swatted at
it recklessly until it turned and flew out over the expanse of
the street and disappeared from view. Her father had kept

bees. He liked the taste of fresh honeycomb more than anything else in the world, so he would slip out to his hive each day and slice a wedge of golden oozing wax from the frame while bees buzzed wildly around him. He'd been stung so often, he never complained. He used to say those kamikaze bees were his favorites, willing to die to protect their queen, their hive, their whole community. Said there was honor in sacrificing yourself to save everyone else. Alison remembered how he would tell her that life is worth living only if you live it with honor. That was before he cheated on her mother. There was honor in staying alive too, Alison thought. As long as you made something out of it.

"I think she must have wanted us to go to the police together, get them to arrest him and put him in jail."

"Well, we should take the tapes to the police, then."

"I spoke to a lawyer—a good one, who works in this field. She says the chance of him going to jail on the back of this isn't good. He might, but with Simone gone, and me having never said anything about his behavior, it's unlikely."

"Simone would want to try."

"I don't know."

Anne Arnold pursed her lips into a droop-ended line. She shook her head slowly and turned away from Alison.

"Then I don't know what you want me to say. My daughter is dead. I don't know what she wanted. I wish I did. I think she'd want to put him away. But I don't think she'd have wanted to involve you without talking to you first."

"I don't think the police will be able to help."

"So, what do you think, then?"

"I'm sorry, I don't know."

"We could give the tapes to that journalist Chris Waters. He could write about Michael. Tell everyone he's a woman beater and a rapist."

"I don't . . . I can't . . . That's me, on those tapes. Me."

"And Simone. Simone is too. You're not the only one."

"Simone's dead. She can't be . . . No one can . . . She doesn't have to feel the eyes on her. She doesn't have to feel embarrassed." The words were all wrong and felt sharp in her mouth as she spat them out, and she immediately felt awful. "I'm sorry. I can't."

Alison walked quickly away, off the veranda, into the room, out the door, and down the stairs. The carpet in the downstairs hall was threadbare green, the walls of paneled wood. In the afternoon this part of the pub was dim, with no direct sunlight, but no lights were on. The air was thick and yeasty, and Alison paused in the peace of it before pushing out onto the street again. Walked quickly up to the post office, sealed the USB drive in a pouch, and scrawled Luca and Christine's address on the front. She paid the exorbitant express price, avoided small talk with Tom, and walked back out into the street and looked again, over both shoulders, for any glimpse of Gil.

She legged it to the bakery to get some bread for Sal, exchanged a few words with Cath behind the counter, and stepped backward to begin the retreat from the shop; she felt the firmness of a body behind her and turned and saw Billy there, studying her face for information, not stepping out of her way or taking his hand off her wrist where he'd wrapped it as soon as she'd turned his way.

"Al, saw you coming out of the post office. We need to talk."

"Now?"

"Now."

"OK, walk me to my car. Honestly, a police escort would make me feel better right now." Billy didn't let go of Alison's arm, even as they walked down the street toward her car. She tried to wrest it back, but he firmly kept her in his grasp.

266

"If you don't mind, I don't feel like chasing you, so I'm gonna hold on until we've finished chatting. Three of Sal's neighbors called in a disturbance at her place this morning. Reported you and Sal chasing away a man they didn't know. His description matched Michael Watson. Want to tell me anything?"

"Not particularly."

"I went round to Sal's and she told me it was an insurance salesman hawking fire coverage. Made her mad he'd be taking advantage of people's grief, and so, she claimed, she shooed him off with her secateurs."

"Sounds about right."

"Sounds like bullshit, Alison."

She sighed, tried again to get away from Billy, but he was holding too tight. "OK, yeah, it was Gil. He was there, and he was scary, but Sal got rid of him."

"Why didn't you call us immediately?"

"I'm sorry, he spooked me, and I was scared, and I didn't know what to do and then I wanted to pretend like it hadn't happened, so I asked Sal not to tell anyone. She's not going to be in trouble, is she?"

"Not if you come in with me now and tell Detective Mitchell everything that happened. I can leave Sal out of it; I haven't done my incident report yet. Been all over the bloody district looking for you."

Alison nodded, let Billy lead her down the street, past her car, and into the police station. She was getting way too familiar with that place.

32.

You know, Alison, you don't make it easy to trust what you say." Detective Mitchell leaned across the table and scrutinized Alison's face, every pore and line and freckle under examination.

"I'm sorry. I'm telling you everything—I promise."

"Simone sent you a USB with footage of Michael Watson assaulting her on it?" On her way to the station with Billy, Alison had made a decision. If she kept herself out of it, it would be easier.

"Yes. I have it at Sal's, in my room. I can go get it, bring it to you?"

"If she had this footage, why bring it to you, a stranger? Why not bring it to us?"

"I don't think I was her final destination, but from everything I've heard about Simone Arnold it sounds like she was a decent person. Maybe she wanted to find out if I could back her up."

"Could you?"

"I—" Alison felt sick to her stomach.

"And she posted it to you from Wangaratta the day before the fire?"

"Yes. I have the note at Sal's place. I'll go get it and bring it straight back."

Detective Mitchell made a note in her pad and cocked her head to one side like a magpie sizing you up for the swoop. She got up from the table and motioned for Alison to follow her. In the station's main room she gestured for Billy, who was at his desk, to follow her. The three of them walked silently out to Detective Mitchell's four-wheel drive and got in.

"Where we off to?" Billy said, looking at Alison, trying to get a read on the situation.

"Sal Marsh's place. You know it, I assume?" Detective Mitchell asked as she shifted from park to reverse. Spun the wheels on the loose gravel as she backed it up and swung around.

"Yeah, chuck a left here, another one at the roundabout. A little ways down the highway toward Melbourne and you're there." Alison felt uncomfortable, tried to think whether it was possible to hide the USB drive with those videos of her on it from the police forever. She didn't want Billy to see. Didn't want anyone to see.

They sat in silence as they covered the distance to Sal's in the late-waning heat of the afternoon. Alison felt suddenly panicked. She shouldn't have left Sal alone after Gil had come round. What was stopping him from coming back, maybe with a weapon this time? There was nothing to be done but to get there. Detective Mitchell's respect for the speed limit infuriated Alison.

When they arrived, Alison saw the front door was open with the screen door closed, as usual. She ran up to the screen and saw the mesh had been slit next to the handle, right along the join of the frame. Just enough space for a hand to slide in and unlock the door. She sucked air through her teeth. Something about the situation made her want to stay quiet. She motioned for Billy and Detective Mitchell to come closer, showed them the slit. Detective Mitchell unholstered her gun, reached her hand through the slit, unlocked the door, and swung it open as quietly as possible. Billy followed her in, and Alison, not wanting to stand out there alone, went after them into the house.

Her room was a mess, sheets pulled off the bed, laptop missing, her backpack upended on the floor. She searched the pillows, saw the USB still tucked up in the case of one. She pulled out the one marked "Simone" and handed it to Detective Mitchell. They went back into the hall, staying as quiet as possible. In the makeshift studio Alison's canvases had been pulled from their frames, slashed or stomped on or ripped by the hands of an angry wrecker. She saw Simone's eyes staring at her from the floor—their shared jawline blurred where the dirty-brush kerosene had seeped over it—reflecting her own terror and sadness. Why had she painted her so melancholy?

Detective Mitchell and Billy were moving again, down the hall, past Sal's ransacked room, past the overturned couch cushions in the lounge, and the upended dining chairs, and the open cupboards in the kitchen. Onto the back deck. Alison followed, every step making her more afraid. She squinted into the sun, trying to make out the scene in the rose garden down there, on the slope toward the city.

Sal's outline on the ground, the way it seemed small, a little insignificant heap of bones and blood and flesh and cloth, made Alison freeze. She watched as Billy ran toward her, stumbling a little, down on one knee and then back up again, calling out her name, while Detective Mitchell went more cautiously, looking around as she moved methodically toward the older woman, as Billy leaned down over her, gently turned her over so she was faceup, held her wrist for a pulse, lifted his radio, said something Alison couldn't hear, opened Sal's mouth, stuck his finger inside—she remembered that was a way to check that an airway was clear; she'd learned that at school. Billy rocked back on his knees and looked up toward Alison. He didn't seem upset anymore, seemed cool, like he'd switched off his feelings and retreated inside himself.

She slowly started to move again, put one foot in front of the other, deliberate small motions; what would she do when she got there, there where her oldest friend was lying because of her? She heard the siren in the distance. She couldn't tell if it was getting closer or farther away. She picked up speed, felt a new urgency, the hot breeze on her face as she steamed down the hill.

When she got to Sal, Billy was in the way; Billy was pushing her back; Billy was trying to stop her, was trying to be a barrier between Sal and her, like he could create a barrier she wouldn't tear down. She struggled against him, pushed back, pushed him away, beat her fists against him like the fucking heroine in a thirties film. Her ineffectual fists against his broad deep chest. But Sal was there, behind him, lying there. Not moving. Not doing anything.

Alison felt as though if she couldn't reach out and clasp Sal's hand and feel its warmth, feel it radiate with life the way that Simone's skin had not, then she might go mad. She tried to calm her own pulse, heard Billy talking to her—*The ambulance is coming*—felt the tears snake down her face and drop in fat circles, and then there was the bustle of the paramedics. Two of them wearing bright blue gloves and lifting Sal's eyelids and shining a light in her eyes, putting a brace on her neck, rolling her onto a gurney, slick wheels on grass, taking her away, and Alison was following them back up the hill and through the side gate and into the ambulance, and she was there when Sal opened her eyes, confused, and said, *What the hell happened?* And a paramedic asked her who she was, and she replied, *Sal Marsh, who are you?* And then he asked who was prime minister and Sal said, *Well, it's a bit hard to keep track these days*, and the paramedic asked her what day it was and Sal said, *It's Monday, isn't it? What's going on?* And the paramedic was listening to her heart and telling her she'd be all right and she'd had a knock on the head, was probably concussed, and they were taking her to the hospital to run some tests, and Sal said, *Alison, what happened? You're white as a sheet.* And Alison told her it was Gil and he'd taken her computer and she was going to find that sonofabitch and make him sorry and Sal wiped the hot tears away from her cheeks and said, *Love, you have to pick your battles. Can you call Patty for me?*

33.

I n Sal's living room, overstuffed cushions on couches with wicker frames and palm-leaf-patterned fabric gave the space a jungle vibe. In the corner there was a tall, dark, curved-sided wooden cabinet stuffed with china. Alison looked around the room; it had been that way forever. Or as long as she could remember. A woolskin rug on the floor under a smoky glass coffee table. Over there, by the big casement windows, a shelf stuffed with vinyl, another with photo albums, and one more with board games. Scrabble, Cluedo, Monopoly, Balderdash, Scattergories, Trivial Pursuit . . . She remembered the game nights so vividly. She went over to the shelves, pulled out one of the photo albums, and thumbed through it.

Sal and Geoff by a tent next to a river. Three kids, two long-limbed ibis-like toddlers, and a ball of fat on his stomach. Patrick. Naked on the ground, big dimples in his plump cheeks. The older kids, Susan and Chris, couldn't have been more than four and three, respectively. Alison remembered that spot; they'd all gone together every Easter since she could recall. She turned the page and saw her mother there in a pair of acid-washed denim shorts and her T-shirt that said "Swan Lager" on it. She thumbed a little further in the book, found a picture of her and Pat, covered in dirt, holding shovels, with broad smiles, huge storm clouds behind them. Alison remembered that morning. The smell of eucalypt and tea tree, woodsmoke and mud, in her nostrils. The buzz of mosquitoes and sand flies about her ears.

"Al, love, will you come help dig the trench?" Her mother's question carried the nonnegotiable tone Alison hated the most. She struggled out of her sleeping bag, slipped on her thongs, and trudged outside. Her mother was holding a shovel and looking at the sky. "There's a storm meant to come through in a couple of hours; we'll get washed away if we don't dig a proper trench. Come on, love." She looked past Alison and her mouth formed a perfectly disappointed line. "Alison, how many times do I have to tell you to zip that bloody tent up after you?"

Alison mumbled an apology and hurried back to close the fly. She ambled slowly back over to her mother and took the shovel from her. Started to dig. Stabbing at the ground, imagining it was perhaps her mother's face. Across the campsite she heard the whoosh of a zipper and Patrick emerged, shirtless and brown from the sun, hair a mess, eyes full of sleep.

"When you're done over there, Al, we're next," he called, curls of amusement at the corners of his mouth. Alison narrowed her eyes at him and pitched a shovelful of sand in his direction. Sal appeared from behind his tent and smacked him across the back of the head.

"Geez, Ma, don't you know you're not supposed to hit your kids these days?"

"I think you'll survive it. Stop ribbing Alison and go get our shovel and get to work." She waved over in Alison's direction. "Morning, sweetheart! Want a cuppa? Where's your mum?"

"Morning, Sal, I think she's washing up down the river. Saw her take the dishes a minute ago. Tea would be lovely, thanks." It was already hot, and the sweat slipped down her forehead into her eyebrows and onto her cheeks. She kept digging. It was oddly satisfying.

"Last one to finish has to do all the other tents by themselves." Patrick's voice called out to her, issuing the challenge. Alison looked at him, dubious.

"Where's Chris? Suze? How did they get out of this?"

"Went out with Dad and Mal on the boat at sparrow's fart. Didn't you hear 'em?"

Alison had heard something as the tent began to color with daylight, but she'd paid no attention. Now she wondered why her dad hadn't asked her if she wanted to come. "They know about this storm?"

"Yeah, that's why they went so bloody early. Woke me up but there's no way I leave my sleeping bag at five a.m. to sit in a boat with Chris and kill fish. The sick fuck enjoys it too much."

Alison laughed. She was making OK progress on the trench; she'd be done with it soon enough. She looked around, counted the tents. No way she wanted to be stuck doing all of them. She looked over at Patrick's efforts. He was behind, but she knew him well enough to know he was dragging on purpose. "No deal. I'm not a sucker, and I'm not digging all these trenches on my own. I'll admit I don't think I'm fast enough to win the bet, thus proving myself smart enough not to make it."

Patrick groaned and rolled his eyes. "I tell ya something, Alison King, you are no fun. And if you weren't my best fucking friend, I wouldn't bloody talk to you."

Alison pitched another shovelful of sand in his direction, this time with more force. It sprinkled around him, catching in his wild hair and softly smattering his back. He turned, shook the sand from his hair, and glared at her, faux annoyed.

"That's it! You are gonna pay for that." He dropped his

own shovel and covered the space between them quickly, effortlessly wrestled Alison to the ground, and straddled her, picking up handfuls of the sand she'd just turned out of the ground and dusting her hair and face with it. Alison squealed and squirmed, but like he'd always been, Patrick was bigger and stronger than her. He held her down, grinding her into the dirt with glee.

"Patrick Marsh, get off her this instant!" Sal's voice cut through the commotion and Patrick froze, clearly surprised by the edge to it. "Get up right now." Alison had never heard Sal talk like that, so clipped and high, so loud, shrill almost. Patrick stepped off her, extended his hand to help her up, and turned to face his mother.

"No harm done, Ma, Al's fine."

"I really am, Sal, we were messing around." She looked down at her state. Her pajama shorts were streaked with dirt, and her tank top rode up under her newly acquired breasts. She tugged it down. Patrick leaned over to whisper in her ear, but before he got anything more than hot breath out Sal called out to him again.

"Patty, come back over here right now and finish this trench, and when you're done, you can do all the others too. Alison, leave that, and come sit with me and have some tea. Pat'll finish it for you."

She didn't know what they had done wrong, or why Patrick was being punished, but if it got Alison out of the boring grunt work of trench digging, she was OK with it. She pulled him in for an apologetic hug and then skipped lightly over to the camp stove where Sal was busy with the kettle. She watched her rummage for the tea leaves and scoop them into the enamel teapot. The hot water sluiced a little over the edges of the pot as Sal filled it, a little too far, a spurt of leaves and liquid dribbling out the spout.

"Shit." Sal dropped the word under her breath, clearly annoyed with herself. She grabbed cups from the drying tub, and the long-life milk from the Esky, and put everything on the table in front of Alison. "Alison, honey, I think it's time we talked about boundaries." Alison's stomach flipped, realizing what Sal was alluding to and desperately wanting to escape it.

She laughed nervously. "Oh, no, I don't think—"

"You're fourteen years old and I know you're not stupid. You're growing into a very pretty young woman, and boys are gonna notice you."

"Sal, really, I don't need you to worry about me."

"Well, truth is, honey, I'm not worried so much about you, but I am worried about my son. Boys . . . boys your age don't have the same maturity as girls, and they are reckless and impulsive and easily led. I know you and Patty have always been close, but now you're older you might need to start putting up some boundaries. So neither of you get hurt, or hurt each other, you know?"

Alison had always appreciated the way Sal spoke to her, not like she was a child, but more like an equal. She hated this conversation, but she was glad Sal was at least speaking plainly to her. She returned the favor. "I think you've got the wrong idea. Patrick is my friend; that's all he is, all he'll ever be. We both know that. I don't have a brother, but I might as well."

"Love, life doesn't always work out in such an orderly way. I'm saying, you're teenagers now, and you're not siblings, and things change. Things happen. I want you to protect yourself, and I want to protect my son. And, Alison, I mean this. Whatever does happen—no matter what it is—you can always, always tell me, honey. I won't judge you or be mad at you. And I'll always try my best to help you, I promise."

Alison turned the teapot three times like her grandfather had taught her, and then she poured out the tea, straining the leaves over their cups. "OK, Sal." She poured a splash of milk into hers; murky clouds billowed up, and she stirred the tea smooth. It tasted sharp in the cool of her mouth. Different. She looked down at her short shorts, covered in filth, her tank top scooped low and clinging tightly. She saw her body in a new way. "It's not like that with Pat, I promise." The words hung between them softly, and Sal gave her a wan smile.

"How things are doesn't always matter. Life gets in the way, you know."

She didn't. But she didn't want to admit it. They finished their tea in silence and Alison went back out to see how Pat was going with the trenches. The clouds overhead seemed full, serious. There was a long, low rumble of thunder and Alison picked up the spare shovel and helped Patrick finish the work. Their mothers rushed around, making sure the windows were all zipped in the tents, and the tarps were securely roped. As the first fat drops began to fall, they heard the tumble of voices down the trail to the campsite. The others were back. Her dad, out the front of the pack, leading them home, his camera around his neck. When he saw Alison, still covered in the sandy dirt from her skirmish with Pat, he laughed.

"Look at you two! My god, a pair of animals. Come on, get together quick." He motioned at them, raising the camera. Pat's arm hung heavy around her shoulders, and Alison instinctively elbowed him in the ribs. He retaliated by tickling her along her diaphragm, and as she erupted into laughter she cast her gaze toward Sal, standing under the tarp, watching them with careful eyes. Alison pushed his hand away, self-conscious. Turned her face full to her father's lens and smiled broadly, forcing the weird feelings down. The shutter clicked a few times, and then the sky lit up bright, and the rain began to bucket down in sheets.

"Your parents loved it there." Sal was suddenly behind Alison, making her jump.

"I didn't know you had these."

"Your dad gave me copies of all the camping pictures. He loved to take 'em, and I loved to collect 'em."

Alison thumbed through more pages, more holidays. The crowd thinning as time passed. First Suze, then Chris, then Geoff, until the last few were Sal and Alison's mother, her father still behind the camera, not in front of it. "Have you been out there since . . . ?"

"No, love, it's still too much for me. That's a place I love, where I went with people I love, and, well, they're all gone. It hurts. It's too big a hurt."

In the kitchen, Suze called out for Sal. "Ma, this gravy won't go smooth. I can never get it right!" Sal rolled her eyes so Alison could see. She squeezed her arm.

"I'm glad you came this year, hon. You shouldn't be alone." Alison watched her retreat into the kitchen, heard her tell Suze to get the strainer. On the other side of the room, the Christmas tree glinted and glimmered. Branches laden with ornaments, base obscured by presents. Outside she could hear the littlies splashing in the pool. Chris calling to them, his voice deep and full, like his father's. The front screen banged shut and heavy footsteps trudged up the hall. Alison turned, saw Pat and Andrew, forced a smile onto her face. Pushed her mum and dad out of her mind. Tried to, anyway. And when Patrick pulled her in for a hug, she felt his arms heavy on her shoulders and remembered the awkwardness of her body like she was fourteen all over again.

History made things better and worse all at once.

Detective Mitchell was sitting in Emergency when Alison came back from splashing water on her face in the bathroom down the hall. Sal had to have her spine checked, her brain scanned; they wanted to keep her in for observation overnight, in case of concussion; they were worried too about the stress on her heart. Pat Marsh was driving up from Melbourne, probably collecting plenty of speeding tickets along the way. His sister was also on the way. Alison scanned the room for Billy, but he wasn't there.

"I sent Meaker back to the station to start working on the warrant for Michael Watson."

"I feel sick." Alison sat in the hard plastic chair next to the detective. Put her head between her legs.

"We'll need your statement too, but it can wait. You should go home, nothing more to do here." She spoke with a gentleness that surprised Alison, and it reassured her, made the nausea recede. This had to stop. Was it over? Now he had her computer, did he think he had everything? Would he leave her alone? She didn't think so.

"Right, of course. I think I'm going to go clean up Sal's, don't want her coming home to the mess he made." She got up, nodded good-bye, and walked out of the hospital. She was in Healesville. No car. She called a cab and sat in the cool of the night, waiting. A car rolled into the taxi rank, but it wasn't a taxi. It was Chris Waters's sedan.

"Little birdie told me you might be here."

"What do you want?"

"You need a ride?" He sounded kinder than she thought he

was, and the look on his face wasn't inquisitive; it was soft and gentle.

"Don't want to talk about it."

"Let me take you home anyway." She didn't know when the cab would come, and she didn't want to go into Sal's house alone. What if Gil was there? Could she even go back to Sal's? She knew she had to. "Come on, Alison, let me help you."

"All right." She got into the car and buckled her seat belt. Turned her body away from the driver's side, gazed out the window, not really seeing anything, looking into the black-ness on the highway back to Sal's. He hadn't asked her where she was going, and he didn't say a word as the car rocked along. Instead, he fiddled with the radio until he found some music. ABC Classic FM, violins rising and falling, a cello, a viola; the sounds swelled and swayed and soothed her.

The dark of the road. The silence in the car. The way Chris Waters seemed both urgent and unhurried at once. His rough, sun-scarred forearms and large brown hands. The warmth of the notes rising and falling as horsehair dragged waxy pres-sure across the strings, tight as they needed to be, just there, just in the sweet spot, right above the bridge.

The sound of a siren out there in the night, in the ink of the black heart of the day. She shivered at the way it pulled her away from the waves the bows created in the cocoon of the car, the soft rocking of the music and the chassis. This womb, speeding her somewhere.

"Where are we going?" she finally asked him.

"You still staying at the Marsh place? I can drop you there?"

"No. I don't know if I can."

"Well, your place got electricity yet?"

"Doubt it. Can you drop me at the Imperial, please?"

"Sure can, staying there anyway."

Alison pulled her phone out, stared at it for a while before she remembered why she had it in her hand, its luminous screen fading to black, reflecting the interior of the car, the glass of the window gleaming in the glass of the phone screen. She touched the right button, made it light up again.

Are you at work?

Billy replied so fast, she wondered if he'd been staring at it, willing her to get in touch. Yeah, finishing up soon. Where R U?

On my way to the Imperial. Can't stay at Sal's tonight. Can I stay with you?

No answer for a minute or more. Alison thought about time, how a minute and an hour can seem the same if you're waiting for something.

Yeah, maybe. I'll come find you.

Ahead, the faint lights of Lake Bend's main drag illuminated the freeway, behind her the cross on the road where her parents had died. The hospital where her only remaining anchor was resting. The house where she was raised, had fled, and then sought to hide from herself and her life and her choices. The scarred, charred remains of a place that no longer existed. A place that was no longer capable of making her feel safe.

The car rolled into the lot out the back of the Imperial and Alison had the door open before Chris Waters could cut the engine.

"Thanks, appreciate it," she mumbled as she stuck one leg out into the night and then the other.

"Wait, Alison, can I ask you some questions?"

"Always asking questions. Never offer something for nothing, do you, Chris Waters?"

"I wanted to check you were OK. Not for publication." He looked sincere, creased above his eyes, in the place between the bushes of his brows.

"I'm fine, Sal's fine, everything's fine. I don't want this deal anymore. Write whatever you like about me. Do your worst. I don't care."

"Look, not that it probably changes anything, but the coppers say Simone's death was just horrible circumstances. They've ruled out murder. Radiant heat. No foul play."

Alison wasn't sure why he didn't have the same information Detective Mitchell did about the autopsy. Or maybe she was lying to Alison. She didn't know who to believe. Chris Waters knew city coppers and coroner's office people and politicians and prosecutors.

"Yeah? Ask Anne Arnold. Simone's dead because of Gil. She's dead because she was running from him. My friend's in hospital because he's here and he's dangerous, so off the bloody record or on, I don't know if you're telling me the truth or you're telling me some story the police fed you. I don't really care. Gil is out there, and I'm scared of him, and that— that is the fucking truth."

Alison stomped so hard as she dropped one foot in front of the other on her way into the pub that her heels hurt with every step. Chris Waters didn't try to follow her, talk to her again. In the barroom the atmosphere was subdued, almost reverent, evoking the sort of feeling you get in a cathedral in the middle of the afternoon. The lights were turned way down and there were only a couple of old-timers, blokes Alison had seen around but never spoken to, old enough to be her grandparents; one of them even looked like her granddad, thick shock of gray-slicked brown hair, broad shoulders, barrel chest.

She flagged down Molly and ordered a gin, plenty of ice, couple of squeezes of lime. It made her flinch a little for the first couple of sips, but by the third it was going down fast and easy. She finished it, ordered another, finished it, ordered another. Her cheeks pinked and pickled. Sandalwood. Billy sliding onto the stool to her left.

"How many to catch you?"

"Too many."

"Al, it's not your fault. Sal's going to be OK."

"Don't do that. Don't excuse me from this." She finished the third one.

Billy asked Molly for a house whiskey and nodded in Alison's direction. "Get her another, and we'll have a packet of salt-and-vinegar chips, please." The booze came. They drank it silently. Billy tore open the bag of chips, slit it down the middle like he was gutting a fish, the crinkled insides heaped on the mirrored, salt-slicked plastic. Alison crunched down on a big one, a ridge at a time. Billy watched her, a smile forming on his face. "One fucking ridge at a time. You never change."

The sentiment enraged her and comforted her all at once. The last few days, the last few years, the whole entirety of her life since she left Lake Bend, could be erased that easily for him. By her doing that one thing that she'd always done, eating a crinkle-cut chip one ridge at a time. Last time he'd seen her do that, they would have been teenagers. Last time, he didn't know how she tasted or felt. He didn't know how messed up she was or how stupid she could be. She didn't know either.

Alison gripped the greasy, grainy chip so that the ridges dug into her fingers and left a wave in their wake. Eventually it shattered and she felt the shards stick to the pads of her thumb and forefinger. Saw the splinters fall to the countertop, smooshed the remnants into her tongue, felt the briny acid of the flavoring season her palate. "I don't want to do this dance with you again, Bill."

He looked at her; she held his gaze. Felt him trying to wear her down or convince her of something that he wasn't fully convinced of. "So let's just cut to the part where you come home with me and I pretend I care less than I do so I can hold on to you while you sleep."

She crunched through another chip. Rolled her eyes at him. "I don't sleep well with others." He grinned at her, and Alison couldn't tell if he was trying to make her think he really did care as little as she did, or if he thought it was charming not to be hurt by her. "I need a place to stay. I don't want there to be strings."

He deflated a little and she saw the flash of hot cold steel in his eyes, saw the way his jaw tightened. He didn't say anything. Drained the whiskey. Tapped the counter to signal for Molly to replenish it. Out of the corner of her eye, Alison saw Bob and Anne Arnold enter the bar; they were with Chris Waters. Anne caught Alison's eye. Gave her a nod of sad recognition. Molly came over to refill their drinks. Billy knocked back his whiskey too fast. Slapped his card on the bar, pushed it toward Molly. "I got these. Can you square us up, please?"

"I'm not ready to leave." Alison was sipping her gin slowly now, watching the Arnolds and Chris Waters, the way they were talking in hushed tones and he was behaving as though he were part of their world. Leaning in close, smiling at things Bob said, shaking his head in anger at what Alison assumed were exactly the right times, playing the tune to perfection.

"Well, I am." He was all hard edges tonight and she didn't want to be around it.

"So, go. I'll figure something else out." She watched him

walk away, saw how deliberately he placed one foot in front of the other, how much tension collected in the sinews of his neck, thought he must be trying so hard not to turn back, not to check if she, Alison, the declared girl of his dreams, was watching him walk out of her life. If he did turn, would he see the relief on her face or mistake it for exhaustion?

She caught Molly's eye, nodded for another drink. As Molly set it down on the bar Alison leaned over and asked if they had any rooms free for the night. Molly was able to sling her a key to a room upstairs at mates' rates, and Alison took it, tucked it into her jeans, and kept on sipping the gin, a little too bitter in her mouth, not enough ice to mask the strength of it, too many previous drinks now for her to really care. The day was blurring around the edges and Alison thought she should probably go upstairs. Slide into bed and forget about all of it. She felt the scrutiny of a pair of eyes on her back. Decided to ignore it, drained the rest of the gin from her glass and set it down too firmly, pushed away from the bar and headed up the stairs to the accommodation level.

She walked past the Arnolds' room, past two more closed doors, and found her room at the end of the hall. She could still feel eyes on her, looked around—there wasn't anybody there—turned the key in the lock and cracked open the door, slipped into the dark room, and shut it tight behind her. The lamp on the bedside table cast a dim glow when she clicked it on, illuminating the edges of the walls, the way the pressed metal on the ceiling was rusted through in spots. When she sunk into the bed it folded up around her like a half-inflated pool toy. Alison lay on her back fully clothed, door locked, lamp emanating enough light that when the heavy boots stopped at her door and the hard knock of fist on wood rang out, Alison could see the way the vibration made the dust dance in the air.

She sat up, stared at the heavy shadow under the door, the wood the only thing between her and him. Him being whoever it was at the door; Alison thought it could be Gil, or it could be Billy back again, never really one to take a hint. She peeled herself off the bed and walked toward the door. Paused with her hand on the smooth of the knob. Stopped letting the hot air out of her mouth and drawing it back in again. Leaned the weight of her body fully on the frame, wanted to absorb any further knocks, pretend they did not exist.

"Alison, I know you're in there. Can we talk?" Chris Waters. He wasn't even on her radar. She could imagine his slouching shoulders and soft middle age, a lace monitor basking in the sun. She flicked the lock, turned the handle, cracked the door.

"What?" She didn't care to indulge him.

"The Arnolds told me you might have something that explains what Simone was doing down here. Implicates Gil? I thought we had a deal."

"I told you, I'm done with that deal. I don't have anything for you." She didn't open the door far enough to let him get a boot between it and the jamb.

"You're drunk."

"You're nosy." Who was he to talk to her like that? Why did everyone think she owed them something, some part of her, private parts of her, the most private?

"I'm just trying to do justice to Simone. Her parents understand that; why can't you?"

"You're trying to win a Walkley, more likely. You don't care about Simone, or me, or any of the other people who died here, died in this fire and didn't have the extra-special cachet of maybe being murdered. Natural disaster's not enough for you?"

She saw him slouch even further into himself, as though

he'd heard the accusation so many times now, it had sunk into his bones. "Come on, you know that's not true." He held up a bottle of gin. "Can I come in?" She didn't care anymore. Cracked the door wide, let it swing loose on its rusty hinges, and walked over and sat on the edge of the bed.

"I'm not going to tell you what Simone had, or why Gil wants it. I'm guessing that since Anne Arnold didn't tell you she's decided it's up to me, and I'm not going there."

"Anne hinted at it, but she said she didn't have the evidence. She said you did."

"I do. I'm not sharing. Ask something else." Alison reached out for the bottle of gin, unscrewed the cap, and gulped back a mouthful.

"What happened in Cairns, Alison? Why did you go?"

"I'm an idiot. I thought there might have been something there for me to find out, some kind of clue as to what had happened. But there wasn't anything."

"You didn't meet the new man Simone was spending time with?"

"You know about him too?"

"The Arnolds told me about him, but they didn't know his name." Chris Waters was standing in the space between the door and the bed, watching Alison like a cat playing with a mouse.

"Well, don't look at me. First I heard of him was from the busybody running the milk bar across from my old building."

"So, he hasn't contacted you?"

Alison looked at the hard lines of his face, the way his eyebrows pushed upward and closer together, created creases in the center of his forehead. "No, why?"

"He called me, after the first story, said he knew what Simone was doing down here, said he knew you, knew you knew what Simone was doing."

It made no sense. "That's bullshit. I've told you everything I know. Who was he?"

"Wouldn't give me his name, but he did send me a picture of Simone to prove he knew her, and that she knew you." He was scrolling on his phone as he talked; then he turned it around so she could see the screen in the low light of the little room.

It was the laundry room at the apartment block. Alison could see herself in profile, clearly talking to the woman leaning, relaxed, on a machine across from her. She could see that it was Simone, recognized the hair, the curve of the cheek, but she couldn't remember this moment. Couldn't place them together in this room. The photo was taken from far enough away that she could see the way the concrete of the open stairwells framed the space. Once again it seemed as though the fragments of her mind no longer connected to one another as they should, as though they could no longer be relied upon to tell her the truth.

"I don't understand. I don't remember that at all. We lived in the same building and we obviously were just chatting while we waited for our laundry."

"Why is there a photo?"

"Why are you asking me? This is beyond creepy and the first I've heard of it. You're saying Simone's new boyfriend gave this to you?"

"Someone who claimed to be him, yes."

"But you think it's not him?"

"It could be; he could be more than one thing."

"What does that mean?" The gin was rapidly diminishing.

"Don't you think it's weird that Gil was able to track Simone all the way here? That police never saw any evidence he was watching her or in touch with her, but he knew where she was?"

"Did he? Or did he just come here after he read about her in the paper?"

"I guess we don't know."

Alison offered the gin back to Chris Waters, motioned for him to sit next to her on the bed. He perched on the edge, a wide stretch of covers between them. "So, you obviously have a theory. What is it?"

"He texted me today. Said I should ask you why you were protecting Gil."

"I'm not."

"I don't know if you realize it, but if you know something and you're not sharing, then maybe you are."

"Fuck off. I share with who I have to. The cops know what I know."

"So, I'll find out eventually, then. Why not just tell me?"

"Why is a dead woman's boyfriend texting you about me anyway? I know you have a theory about this, and since it's my life, you really should share it."

"I think he's Gil's friend. I think maybe Gil tricked Simone into trusting this guy because Simone had something he wanted. Or Simone met him through Gil and then Gil threatened them both somehow, found a way to make him help him. I think this boyfriend was plan A. I think following her here was plan B. I think killing her was never the plan, but that if the fire didn't kill her, then maybe he got carried away."

"You think he killed her now?"

"I don't know. It's not a perfect theory. Everyone who can tell us the truth is dead or missing. But he certainly scared the shit out of her."

"Scotty."

"What?"

"Scotty, Gil's friend at the hotel we worked at together. A bartender. Smooth, fuckable, real gift with the ladies, as they say." It had to be him. Alison thought about how Scotty had talked about Simone. Like he really cared. Gil had those naked photos of Simone. He was probably using them as leverage. Making Scotty help him.

"Why are you so sure?"

She told him about what Scotty had said to her in Cairns. He shook his head and sipped on a dainty capful of gin. He wasn't looking to stop being in control. "It's a possibility I guess."

"So, what now?" Alison asked as they sat quietly pulling together the things they knew, the leaps they'd made, and the dots they were trying to connect.

"You think I know?"

"Let's message him. The boyfriend."

"And say what?"

"Ask if he can meet you. If you can fly him down for an interview."

"I can't do that. I can't get that involved. I'm reporting this. I'm not a player in it."

She leaned over toward him on the bed. Tilted her head and carefully poured a little more gin into the cap, tried to smile in a cute way, be alluring. "But you are, aren't you?" She reached out and put her hand on his leg. He pulled away immediately.

"You're drunk, Alison, and I'm married."

"First man I've met to give a shit about that."

"I'm not your dad." She tried to laugh it off. Of course he knew about her parents, about the scandal, about the crash, about the way they'd died on the side of the road. She tried to shake it off, slid back to the corner of the bed she'd been occupying, hung her head so he couldn't see the pink of her cheeks or the slice of her tears.

"I don't know what would make you think I thought you were. You should go."

"I should." He left the empty cap on the bed, walked to the door, and opened it. Stopped for a minute before he left, looking back at her, concern in his eyes. "Not every man wants something from you, Alison."

"You mean, not every man wants sex? Because you're kidding yourself if you think you're a man who doesn't want anything."

"I guess I just mean you've got more to offer than your body."

"Don't fucking patronize me." She picked up the cap from the bed and lobbed it at him. He let it bounce off his chest, shook his head, and stepped out of the room.

"If you change your mind about telling me what you know, I'm around," he said, and pulled the door shut behind him. She listened as his footsteps receded down the hall, her cheeks hot from the booze and the embarrassment and the night and the room. She drank more of the gin, too much more, and fumbled into the bed. She didn't know what time it was when she passed out.

34.

The phone was chirping at her, incessantly. Alison couldn't figure out where she was; the ceiling pressed on her, rusty swirls of metal closing in on her skull, which felt like it was knocking on the space around her, each movement a pounding inside her head, bruising her brain and making her wince with every turn. The way the room seemed to appear and disappear as she tried to focus made her sure she was still drunk. The sun was up? No, the light was on. The phone was still going. She groped for it. The ringing stopped as her fingertips found it. The missed call was from Gil. Shit. Had she locked the door before she passed out? Her head started to clear up. It was 4 a.m. The phone bleeped again, a text this time. She opened it. It was a picture, of Billy's police name tag.

come get him

She didn't know how to process it. He had Billy? How stupid was he? A cop? He had a fucking cop?

He's a fucking cop. What the fuck are you doing?

if you don't come this pig is bacon

She should call Detective Mitchell. She should do anything other than what Gil wanted. But she couldn't risk it. Billy mattered. Billy was one of the few fucking things left that mattered.

Where?

same place you fucked him pigfucker

Had he watched them the night after the fire? Seen her so vulnerable and messed up and mean? Why hadn't he tried to grab her then? On the walk back to Sal's. No, he must have seen her the second time. Been waiting for her to get back from Cairns. Watched them in the kitchen, that second messy, stupid attempt to feel anything good. Anything at all. *Snap out of it.*

Alison pulled on her shoes, rushed out of the room and down to the car park, found Billy's car there, where he'd left it. She knew he kept a key taped under the bumper, just in case. Felt around a bit until she found it. Unlocked the car and hit the road, past the roundabout, down the street, driving too fast to be quiet, but she didn't care. There was no light in the sky yet, no birds chirping on the breeze, just the utter darkness of country midnights and the feeling of an uncontrollable itch on her skin, the panic seeping out of her through her pores. It wasn't far, but it felt like it was taking forever to get there—how long does it take to get somewhere when you really need to? Longer than you'd ever like.

The familiar silhouette of his house began to emerge in the distance. No lights were on, no signs of any disturbance. Did Gil snatch Billy up as he walked from the pub? How did he do it? Billy hadn't seemed that drunk. She swung into the drive, the headlights briefly illuminating the front of the house, the shape of the car reflected in the windows.

She parked on the front lawn, got out of the car, started moving toward the house. Suddenly she felt an arm snake around her face, clamp down on her mouth, another one across her stomach. Gil. He'd been waiting for her.

"Well, you made it in record time. Don't worry, lover boy is fine. He's missing a name tag, left it in his car while he was at the pub. You think I'm dumb enough to fuck with a cop?" He laughed then, began dragging Alison toward the tree line at the edge of Billy's place. She squirmed, tried to get free, but he was too strong; he was always too strong. She decided to preserve her energy instead, let him wear himself out dragging her like a sack of potatoes through the bush. They continued like that for long enough that the sun was beginning to peek through. She didn't know how this would end. She didn't want to know.

Eventually he was too tired to keep moving. They stopped by the creek; he'd stuck close to it. Alison was surprised he'd been smart enough to think to take a route that was equally easy to backtrack and difficult for dogs to track, with them mostly tramping through the shallows. He pushed her to the ground, then, still holding on to her tight, wound tape around her wrists.

"Don't scream. I will gag you if you do."

"What are you doing, Gil?"

"We need to have a little talk and you weren't making that easy for me, so I decided to make it happen."

"I don't know what you want from me."

"Yes, you do, darlin'. You have my tapes. I want them back."

"I don't."

SARAH-JANE COLLINS

"You do."

"Even if I did have them, what are you afraid of?"

"Simone wanted to put me in jail."

"I just want to be left alone. You leave me alone, I'll leave you alone." The tape on her hands was too tight. It made her wrists throb and her palms swell and she couldn't help but show the pain on her face.

"We can't reach an agreement as long as you've got something that's dangerous to me."

"What's dangerous? Simone's dead; she can't press charges, can she?"

"You're not." He looked at her with an intensity that was unsettling. The same blankness to his stare that he would get before he hit her.

But she didn't think he meant to kill her. Not without whatever it was he wanted from her. He had the laptop. Wasn't that enough?

"What do you want, Gil? I can't help you if you don't tell me."

"I want every copy of every tape Simone gave you."

"You've got my laptop. The police have the tapes of Simone already. I can't unring that bell."

"How do I know you're not holding out on me?" He was sweating from the rising heat of the day, the exertion of dragging her all this way, the sun that beat down on them now, in this stripped-back bush blackened and exposed. Alison couldn't be sure, but she thought they must be close to the top of the ridge.

"What are you really worried about?"

He watched her closely. "You sure you only got the videos of Simone?" It was a question laced with hope, and his eagerness surprised her. *You're missing something.* What was it Simone had written in the note? *Make sure you watch them all the way through.* She'd dismissed it, but now it seemed clear that Gil was worried she had something really damaging.

"Undo this, would you? I'm not going anywhere and it fucking hurts." Alison could tell he was confident he had the power, so he leaned over and ripped the tape off. While she'd been sitting there Alison had noticed a large rock to her left, within easy reaching distance. Before he had a chance to move out of her range, she reached for it, clasped it hard in her hand, brought it high, and smacked it into the side of his head. The sound was a sickening thud, a crack that betrayed the force she hadn't intentionally wielded.

Alison felt panic rising in her. She had never hit anyone like that. Gil's whole body went slack and he slumped over, face in the dirt. Shit. Her hands felt heavy around the rock. There was no sign of him on it, no hair or blood, and she clung to the idea that she couldn't have hit him that hard. She dropped it, and dropped to her knees next to him. Turned him, felt for a pulse; it was there. Her hand above his lips felt the moist reassurance of his breath. She saw no blood on his head. It occurred to her that if he woke up he would still be bigger and stronger than her. And they were still in the middle of nowhere. She remembered the tape. He'd stuffed it somewhere on his person. She gingerly began to pat him down. Alison found the tape in his pocket, wrapped it around his wrists and his ankles, lay him on his side so he wouldn't choke, and checked that he was breathing.

Now the fuck what? Her phone was still in her pocket. He was so fucking confident she wasn't a match for him. It enraged her. She wanted to leave him there, in the bush, never tell anyone she'd seen him that day, just walk away and never have to worry about him again. But she knew she had to turn him in. The phone had no reception. She should have known it wouldn't be this easy. All the fear and adrenaline welled up inside her. She doubled over with it, heaved it onto the ground. Gin and salt-and-vinegar chips mixed with spit and mucus and gut juices mingled with the dirt on the ground.

She waded into the creek, splashed water on her face, swished some of it around in her cheeks, the taint of ash on her palate. She didn't swallow. Gil twitched a little where he lay. She sat in the dirt outside of his space, waited for him to come to. The sun shifted higher in the sky. Her phone said it was past nine. He had a bag with him, and Alison opened it. Her laptop, a gun, a bottle of water, his wallet, some muesli bars. She peeled the wrapper off one and ate it. She was halfway through it when she heard him thrashing around. She turned to look at him; the rage in his eyes—she wouldn't forget it.

He was straining against the tape, and she didn't know if she'd done it tight enough or thick enough. She could feel the thump of her heart and the dry of her mouth and the ring in her ears. "Fucking hell, Alison, what are you gonna do now? Kill me? You don't have it in you."

He was right, but she didn't want him to know it. She reached into his bag and pulled out the gun. "Where the hell did you get this?" It was a pistol, small and light, six bullets in the cylinder. She cocked it, aimed it in his direction.

"Put the gun down, Alison, you're not a killer." He sounded a lot less sure of himself. The light caught the gun and it sparkled, glinting rays reflecting onto her skin. She thought about her options.

"The way I see it, you probably shouldn't be telling me what to do about anything, what with me being the one with the gun and all." She moved closer to him and enjoyed it when he flinched a little.

"Have I ever told you about how Dad used to take me to the shooting range? Said, in the bush you've got to know how to handle a rifle. We'd spend a little time there every few months from when I was fourteen. One day, on the way home we came upon a roo that'd been hit by a car. It was slumped by the side of the road, barely breathing. You ever hit a kangaroo? They're all muscle. Thick skin, big buggers. Takes a lot to kill them. This one must have been hit by a ute or something with a big front grille. He was in a really bad way. No chance he'd live, but he wasn't dying quick.

"So my dad, he gets the rifle out, and he comes over. And I watch him, not wanting to believe what was about to happen was about to happen. I asked him not to. But he shot it clean between the eyes, and then he turned to me and he said, 'Sometimes, Alison, the best thing to do is take a life,' and I can still remember the way that kangaroo looked. How it felt to watch someone use a gun for its intended purpose. I wouldn't go to the range with him after that. I didn't want to make it normal. I always wanted to remember how wrong it felt."

"You trying to scare me?"

"No. I'm simply explaining to you that I know how to shoot, and if I have to, I will." She didn't know what her plan was, but Alison didn't want to kill Gil. She didn't want to kill anyone. The gun felt heavy in her hand. She slung his backpack over her shoulder. "Here's what I think we should do. I think we should part ways here, forever. I won't shoot you, and you will back the fuck off and leave me and every person I care about the hell alone."

Gil laughed. "And why would I do that?"

"Because if you don't, I'll give the police all the tapes I have. The ones of me included."

He went pale. "You just said you didn't have any of you."

"That was before I was the one holding the gun. I can tell you really don't want them to see them, and honestly neither do I. I'd rather forget all of this and live my goddamn life in peace. But if you won't let me do that, then I guess I'll have to hand them in."

"If you do have them and you let me go, what's to stop me coming and getting them?"

"Self-preservation? You've always been big on that." Alison knew a bargain was a risk, but she was out of options and he did seem genuinely afraid of the police getting hold of the tapes of him and her.

"Say I was to entertain this little proposal of yours. How would it work?"

"You say you'll fuck off and never come back and then I will let you walk away from me right here, right now."

He looked around. Looked at her. Nodded slowly. "All right."

She stepped up to him, cut the tape on his ankles, and helped him stand up. He held out his hands for her, and she carefully slit the tape, holding her breath in fear. When the tape was loose, she jumped out of his reach and held the gun on him. He smirked at her.

"Deal's a deal. I'm out of here, you crazy bitch." He turned and began to walk away from her, in the opposite direction from where they had come, farther up the incline. She stood there watching him; she was still holding the gun, thinking she must be crazy. He would never give up this easily; she knew it. He would come back, and she wouldn't have a gun, and he'd probably kill her. He probably killed Simone too; there was no proof, just gut feeling, but he could be capable of anything—this had proved it. He scrambled over some rocks and stood for a moment on top. "Bloody beautiful up here, you know, even now." As he spoke, he turned toward her, and Alison instinctively raised the gun again. He laughed, mock raised his hands. "Don't shoot me, I'm innocent!"

The words dug into her. Clawed at her skin. She screamed, louder than she'd ever screamed in her life, and it startled him. He stepped backward, and the brush he put his weight on crumpled and cracked. His foot found only air, and he lost his bearings. As she watched, Alison saw him fumble a little, and sway a lot, and then tumble backward, off the rock and out of sight. She heard him scream now, and then an unmistakable thump and nothing, nothing at all in the desiccated bush.

She rushed toward the spot where he had been moments before. Climbed up onto the large rock and looked behind it. It gave way, not immediately, but within a few steps, to a steep drop. She saw the slick of disturbed ground—what looked like drag marks—where Gil must have slid down the slope to the edge. She carefully picked her way to the edge and peered over. It was a deep, narrow ravine. She noticed a thatch of brittle, broken branches that Gil had crashed through, exposing the ravine. He couldn't have known it wasn't solid ground. She could see him at the bottom. Eyes open, blood everywhere, skull cracked like an egg; he was groaning.

He wasn't dead. Relieved and terrified, Alison tried to think what she should do. She started to panic. She had his gun, his bag. What if they thought she had pushed him? She pulled the bag from her back, grabbed her laptop out of it, and, without thinking, threw the bag into the ravine. It landed on top of him and he cried out at the weight of it. He began to dry retch, and Alison thought for a moment she should go, get help. The stripped, blackened bush took on an alien appearance. There was nothing here to help her; she wasn't going to risk her life for his. She backed away and climbed back over the rock. Threw the gun into the creek and ran, ran as fast as she could, as far away as she could from Gil and the ravine and the secrets it held.

35.

Alison was bone-tired. She stumbled and fell, crying out as her ankle gave way beneath her. The day was getting old, and she was a total wreck. As she tried to find her way out of the bush, she kept running *it* through her mind. The moment he'd stepped backward, the way it had sounded when he landed, the look in his eyes. The shock, the beating of her own heart so hard that she could feel it, like her heart was trying to claw its way out of her chest. There was so much death already, so much pain and destruction, and exhaustion. She hadn't meant to leave him there, but her sense of self-preservation had kicked in. She was so tired.

As she trudged along, following the flow of the creek, she tried to pull herself back together. There was something else in the space of her chest now, a fluttering, nervous kind of hope. Could it be that easy? Gil was trapped and injured, left for dead. If she didn't tell anyone, that would be it. He would die and she would be free. She felt the bile rise, and she coughed up the lining of her stomach again, thinking about how it would feel to know it was her fault someone else was dead. There had already been too much death. She didn't want to be a part of any more.

The creek widened out on a low, flat sweep and she recognized the familiar slope up to the tree line behind the town. She was almost back where she knew the lay of the land. She scrambled up an embankment and popped up near the highway where it wound into town from Melbourne. Not far from the spot where her parents had died. She walked on. Her phone started to ping and she realized it had reception again.

Messages. Billy, Sal, Pat. Detective Mitchell had called three times. Chris Waters. Everyone wanting to know where she was. She dialed Billy. He picked up on the first ring.

"Shit, Alison, are you OK?"

She was going to say yes. She was going to make something up. She was going to keep it all, let the bush claim its secrets. But she didn't. She didn't even know why, but before she could stop herself, she was telling Billy everything. From the text with his name tag to the way Gil had looked writhing on the ground.

"Stay there, Al, I'll get the SES on it, we'll find him. I'm coming to get you now." She didn't argue with him; she didn't have the energy to even try.

The sound of water rushing let them know they weren't far off. It was hot. A sticky, humid day. They'd left early for this hike, but the sun was relentless even at this hour. Gil was ten steps ahead and constantly turning back to make sure Alison was keeping pace. She was trying. But she didn't love hiking; she'd agreed to it because he wanted to. On and on he'd gone about Emerald Creek Falls. His favorite place, he'd told her.

When they broke through to the water hole, he whooped at the sight of it, rushing her along the path and ushering her toward the granite rocks that made a shore. She took it in, lush greenery, rushing water, a sparkling pool of brown-green. It was beautiful, absolutely. They weren't the only ones there, but Gil guided her away from the big main pool, toward a series of smaller ones, a little way away from the other early risers. They stripped down to their swimmers and Alison gladly plunged her body into the warm, refreshing water. Gil pulled her in close to him, his broad, handsome face illuminated by the light reflecting off the water.

It felt good here, in his arms, in this place. Everything about them was still new, the way he smelled and sounded, the hardness of his edges, the softness of his lips, the look in his eyes when he took her in. She kissed him, and he returned it with passion. He broke away from her lips to kiss her neck, and she laughed as his lips fluttered along the sensitive curve of it.

"It's beautiful here." She stopped him before he went too far.

"I told you."

"You did. You were right."

"Mum used to bring us here, when we were little."

Alison looked at him, thought she caught a glimpse of something dark, brooding, but it was gone in an instant. "It's wonderful." She pulled him into her, laid his head on her chest, felt his breath on her breast. A flock of rainbow lorikeets stretched out across the blue above. "Should we be worried about crocs?"

"Nah, we're all right here." He was so close to her, she could count the pores on his cheeks. His breath was scented with orange and tobacco. "You ever seen one in the flesh?"

Alison shook her head. "Just at the zoo."

"Scary motherfuckers. I was out fishing with the guys—we saw one, it snapped up an ibis from the shore. Blink of an eye and bam—not even a feather left. I read somewhere that their jaw is like one of those animal traps—you know, the ones you see on American TV or whatever, the big steel ones that snap closed on a bear's leg? Once they latch onto you, it's virtually impossible to get them to unlock their jaw and let you go. They hold on to their prey until they drown. Drag them down into the water and roll them around. Those giant teeth holding on until there's no life left. Strongest bite in the world."

As he spoke, Gil became more and more animated, like a kid who had just discovered dinosaurs, which, Alison supposed, was kind of the case when it came to crocodiles. She laughed at his enthusiasm. "Are you trying to terrify me?"

He looked her in the eyes; intense. "If I wanted to terrify you, you'd know."

The moment passed so quickly, she wasn't sure it had happened. The way he'd said it. The flash of something unsettling in his gaze—fury, maybe? And then that cheeky smile again, the charming twinkle. He gently bit her neck, and then, arms wrapped around her tightly, he playfully rolled her around in the water.

"Don't think I'll ever let you go, now I've got you." He kissed her and Alison felt an overwhelming bloom of desire. The pools stretched out before them as the sun rose higher in the sky and day-tripping tourists began to fill up the space. One perfect moment, and the trap was set.

It was almost dark out when the search party got back to the police station. They looked beat. Alison looked to Billy for some kind of news, and he shook his head.

"Well?" she asked, impatient.

"He wasn't there. We found the spot, his blood on the ground, on the rocks, but it looks like he climbed out of there. We tried to track him, but the creek goes deep into the bush there, and it appears he was wading in it."

"Why did you stop looking?" Alison asked, panicked.

"There's another fire up on the other side of the ridge. It was under control for most of the day but it broke containment about an hour ago. Not safe to be out there. These conditions are just making it worse."

"So he's out there, and you can't find him?" Alison thought she had already lived the worst scenario, but this—this was the worst scenario.

"We will. We just have to wait for the fireys to get things under control. Then we can go back out."

Alison tried to contain her frustration. How was this even possible? How was he alive? The man was a cockroach. Apparently unextinguishable.

"Can I take you home?" Billy asked, gentle.

"I—I'm staying at the Imperial. It's across the street; I can walk."

"You sure?"

She told him she was, and then she left. Outside, the sky was orange-black again. Another fire, another soot-filled evening. She legged it across to the pub. On the floor under her door, a piece of paper.

Alison, heard about your run-in with Gil. Would love to talk to you about it. Chris.

She balled the paper up and threw it in the bin. Slumped onto the bed. She was exhausted. She needed sleep. Without undressing, or even taking off her shoes, she lay there, trying not to think, until she nodded off.

36.

t was the middle of the night, and Alison was wide-awake. The initial exhaustion had worn off. She kept thinking about Gil, out there, somewhere. Who knew if he was alive, and if he was, whether he'd decide to stick to their agreement? She had known it was a long shot when she struck the bargain, and now it felt even stupider. Why had he even entertained the idea of a deal? What was he afraid of? The tapes didn't prove anything conclusively; Christine had been clear about that on the phone, but she hadn't seen them yet; she was going off only what Alison had told her.

She sighed, turned on the light. She knew she wouldn't sleep until she'd checked. She opened her laptop, which she'd managed to hide from the police when they'd found her, stuffing it up her shirt. She clicked on the first file, tried not to flinch or turn away, pretended it was someone else on the bed, someone else in that moment, someone who wasn't her.

Why did Simone want her to watch these? What was it that Gil seemed relieved she had missed? She didn't know if she wanted to know. But it had seemed incredibly important to him, so it was important to her. She clicked through them one by one, watched herself over and over again, felt the same numbness in her body now as she had when these tapes were created. It was nauseating, but she pushed through it. Another file. Another scene. She didn't feel any recognition this time; when she saw herself on the screen, she couldn't place this one.

She was fall-down drunk. She fell down, Gil picked her up, she swayed a little, she laughed at something he whispered into her ear, she began to take her clothes off, fell over stepping out of her skirt. Her mouth wide with laughter, she said something; the silence of the tape didn't reveal it, but she sees him stiffen, sees the way he readies his body for the fight.

When he hits her, Alison flinches in her bed, flinches as if the punch is landing on her stomach, in this moment. Why doesn't she remember any of it? He hauls her up, tosses her on the bed, takes off the rest of her clothes, rips them, tears the underpants in two. She can see she is crying. She can feel she is crying. He is holding her down; his hand is on her throat. Her eyes go wide; her eyes go stone. He shakes her. He shakes her and shakes her and then he slaps her, and she doesn't respond. She's not there. She's not breathing, because he's putting his mouth on hers now, he's performing CPR, he's pressing his hands into the spot on her chest that's supposed to wake you back up. It doesn't. It doesn't. Then it does.

She gasps in the air in big gulps; he's crying now, he's kissing her, he's holding her face in his hands as if he didn't cause the situation in the first place. Alison doesn't have any memory of this. She never would have known.

But there is the tape. There is a record. Gil made this one mistake. Simone knew he wouldn't be able to wriggle away from this one. This, Alison thought, must have been how Simone planned to set them free. But now, with Gil missing, and Simone dead, was it worth anything at all? It occurred to Alison that if it was nothing else, it was an insurance policy. He wouldn't touch her while she had it, and that was a big deal.

She was flooded with gratitude for a woman she'd never known. It was a wild feeling. Like static electricity on a crowded tram on a winter day. She turned off the tape. She didn't want to see it ever again. An emptiness engulfed her, like a black hole opening up in the universe and swallowing her whole.

She thought of Gil, down at the bottom of the slender ravine, looking like death. She could have tried to help him, could have done so many things differently. She laughed before she realized the air had escaped from her mouth. Everything felt so ridiculous. This was not who she was. This was not who she wanted anyone to ever know her as.

37.

n the morning, Alison waited around in town, hoping for news of Gil. Sal was getting out of the hospital later. The emergency broadcast on the radio said the fire southwest of Lake Bend was slowly being brought under control but that many more hectares of bush had been destroyed.

At a loose end, Alison took Sal's bike and pedaled over to Meg's place. The road there was totally burned out, until the last two clicks, where the startled bush had been spared. Meg died in her car on the highway. Alison thought she hated cars now; they were just coffins waiting to engulf you. Meg's house was a pretty standard Victorian weatherboard; iron lace, white paint flaking off it, adorned the veranda. The big front door was painted deep, shiny green, and the tin roof sloped low, shining silver corrugated steel reflecting the sun. Alison couldn't believe it. If Meg had been home . . . She didn't want to think too hard about it. She opened the letter box and found an envelope there—addressed to Alison, like Meg's mother had promised when Alison called her. She ripped it open. Keys and a note.

Take whatever you want, she loved you.

Alison felt a kind of dread in the space below her ribs and above her hips. It wasn't just her stomach, flipping with fear; it was as if all of it—her whole damn gut—was clenched. She pulled in three deep breaths and took the three short stairs up onto the veranda. Inside the house, a film of grimy soot lay over everything. The fire hadn't made it here, but the wind had blown the soot in anyway. Meg's house was over-stuffed. Chaotic, ungovernable, and warm. Even now, the couch looked like it was calling to Alison, plump and pretty under the grime.

She stood still in the middle of the living room, wondering what she was doing here. In the kitchen there were still dishes in the sink, slimy now with neglect. She tried the tap. Water rushed out, and she rinsed the things the best she could. But who was she cleaning up for? Meg had no children, no partner. Her sisters lived in Melbourne. Her parents couldn't stand the thought of coming in here right now; they'd asked Alison to do the first pass. No one was going to use this kitchen for a long, long time.

The air felt cloying, smothering, wrong somehow. Alison tried the back door and noticed it wasn't locked. She pushed it open and stepped out onto the deck. She sat on the stairs that led down to the backyard, overgrown and rambling; it was hard to see where it gave way to the bush. Somewhere, off to the right and down a winding dirt track, there was a dam, small but sweet for swimming on a raging day. Alison looked down, tried to collect herself. She didn't know why she'd come here, what she'd hoped to accomplish. She sighed. She needed to pick up Meg's computer so she could go through it, delete anything Meg might not want her family to see. She figured she'd want Meg to do the same for her.

She was about to stand up and walk back inside when a

cigarette butt on the ground caught her eye. Gil's brand, like in Sydney. She picked it up. She didn't remember Meg smoking, ever. She looked around, uneasy. Could he be here? Why would he be here? She thought it was unlikely. And yet . . .

She shivered and went back into the house—suddenly it seemed the lesser evil. She went into Meg's room and found her laptop in the sheets, still plugged into the wall. There'd been no power in this area for days and days, so she doubted it still had juice. Alison yanked the cord from the wall and pulled it toward her, but it got stuck on a bed leg, and, cursing, she moved around to that side of the bed to free it. She tripped and fell, her head smacking the floorboards. She groaned and rolled over onto her back, and, lying on the ground in her dead friend's bedroom, Alison gulped back tears, trying not to let herself come undone completely. She looked up at the ceiling and then she squinted under the bed. There was a box tucked in up the back and Alison wondered what it was. Meg had a study to fill with her papers, and plenty of space around the house—why was there one box tucked away under here?

She rolled over and reached for it, heaving it out easily once she'd hooked the edge with her fingers. Sitting on the floor, Alison opened the box, wondering what would be inside. Journals. Two dozen or more maybe. All the same, just with a different year on the front of each. She never knew Meg kept journals. She picked one up, and then another, and then a third. She thought maybe she should read one, but then she thought, no, Meg wouldn't want that. She'd want her to get rid of them, like she was planning on cleansing her hard drive. She went to put the books back in the box, and a piece of paper fluttered out of one. It spread open on the bed. An email, printed. Unable to hold back her curiosity any longer, Alison picked it up and read it.

To: bbygrrrrl88@gmail.com
From: kingmaloflakebend@gmail.com

My darling

It's over. I'm sorry but it must be. Alison won't talk to me. I have to fix it. Even though I will never be happy without you again, it is over. I love you, now and forever.

Your Malcolm

Alison stared at the email. There was a ringing in her ears. She couldn't process it. What was Meg doing with an email from her dad to his mistress? She checked the journals. Found the year her parents died. On the day of their death a short entry.

Emily Dickinson wrote:
Unable are the Loved to die
For Love is Immortality
My Malcolm is gone. How will I ever stand it?

Alison threw the journal across the room and it slammed into the wall. She let out a wail, not really sure if she was angry or devastated. Meg had broken her parents apart, and then she had taken Alison under her wing on her return after their death. Out of what? Guilt? Pity? Some kind of desire to be close to the flesh of her dead lover? It made Alison's skin crawl. She wanted to throw up. But instead, she picked the box of journals up, retrieved the one she'd thrown, and took them all with her, along with the laptop. She couldn't bear to erase these new memories of her father, no matter how painful they might be. She would deal with all of it later.

Alison got to Sal's late in the afternoon. Pat's car was in the drive, Sal's too. There was a man there installing a reinforced screen door, and bars on the windows. Pat was supervising. He looked at her, inscrutably, as she walked up the steps to the house.

"You know, it's dangerous in bushfire country to make it harder to get out of the house, but here I am putting bars on Ma's windows because she's gotta worry about your ex-boyfriend attacking her in her own home."

"I'm sorry, Patty, I never thought he'd— I just didn't—"

"Nah, you didn't. She's all right, in case you're wondering. Still refusing to budge down to Melbourne, of course."

"I'm glad she's all right." He waved her away, like he wasn't willing to forgive her yet, but he didn't want to fight anymore either. Alison took it, moved into the house. Called out for Sal, who answered, eagerly.

"Alison, I'm in here." The sound came from the study. Alison headed toward the back of the house. The room where Alison had set up her studio was still a mess, Gil's rampage still fresh. Sal was in there, looking at the damage. There were ruined paintings everywhere. Some of them were past salvation, but there were a couple of portraits that had slipped through unscathed. Alison stared at one, at the grays and reds and oranges she had used to paint the background, the skin, the curves of the face; the only natural color in the entire piece was the gray-blue of the pupils. The effect was ghostly; the style of this portrait was hyperreal, except for the palette, which was firescape in its scope. Simone wasn't really present in this picture; it was just her form, but not really her form, her face a physical manifestation of fire. Alison set it to one side, looked at the other unscathed painting, much more abstract in the way the brush had moved across the canvas, with bold but real colors, the face blurred and seemingly merged, or merging, with Alison's own. Where was the space between them? Between the fire and the dead girl and the woman who lived. Alison couldn't tell.

She pushed ripped canvases and torn paper aside, searched for her brush roll, her brushes, wet still from the overturned soaking water, and found the colors she needed. Applied the yellow and the red, mixed them into the blue and the gray. Found the green for the depths and the muddy hazel for the edges. Felt eyes on her and remembered Sal. Sal was standing there, sipping tea.

"Looks a lot like you, if it looks like anyone, that one." Sal turned her head a little, angled it to one side, squinted. "Yep. That's you."

"Not anymore." *Survival changes you, makes you harder, if that's possible,* Alison thought. She set Sal's laptop down on the desk. "Sal, will you do something for me?"

"Name it."

Alison sat on the floor among the torn-up portraits and patted the floor next to her, reached out a hand for the hot-sided cup. Sal sat down next to her, took back her cup.

"You see there was another big fire? They only just got it under control."

"Yeah, it was in the bush, no one around for yonks."

"Lucky, that. But Pat's right. Wind changes, and the outcome changes. I want you to give living with Pat and Andrew a go."

Sal's mouth pressed into a line. "We've talked about that. I told you why I can't.

"Do you really think Geoff would prefer you were here? I doubt it."

Alison watched as Sal's eyes glossed. "This is home, love, I just—"

"Home should be safe, and filled with people you love. Your family is all in Melbourne now, Sal, and they're worried about you. What if you went for a week? I can look after this place, keep an eye on your roses? You can see how you feel about it."

Sal sighed, squeezed Alison's hand. "Stubborn, like your father." She nodded. "A few days, let's not get too carried away. I'll see what I think."

Patrick stuck his head into the study and interrupted them.

"What are you two up to?"

"Nothing, love," Sal replied, shooing him off with her hand like she would a fly. "Would you put the kettle on?"

He rolled his eyes and left them alone again.

"Are you gonna tell him you've changed your mind?"

"Eventually. Let him stew a little; he likes to have something to be worked up about."

Alison laughed. She was going to miss Sal if she decided to move, but she knew encouraging her to go was the right thing to do. The light of the day was almost gone; the night crept in around them, settling on the windowsills and the hardwood floor, streams of weak, dusty sunshine dancing in the space between them, the moon rising to extinguish the last red-pink tones of the afternoon and bring on the cool blues of twilight. The white-bright twinkle of a million distant stars, illuminated here, in this place, with clarity and grace, unmarred by city dimming or, for now, bushfire smoke that blacks out the sky and removes all anchors and points of navigation. The hot hand of destruction, never gone, dormant again, waiting for the right sun to rise.

38.

fter dinner Alison was still waiting for news about Gil. She texted Christine.

Did you get the USB?

Yes. I am about to start watching, once the girls are down.

Alison didn't want her to. What was the point? Don't. Please.

Are you sure? Don't you want to know if we can use them?

No. It looks like he's dead, and I don't want you to see them.

Alison took a deep breath, waited as the three dots appeared. Ok Alison, I'm going to destroy it then.

You promise?

Another pause, and then a picture. Christine had dropped the USB drive into a glass of water. Alison breathed a sigh of relief. It was hard enough knowing Christine knew; she didn't want her to see if she didn't have to. Gil might be dead. But maybe he wasn't. Alison thought there was as good a chance that he had survived as that he hadn't, knowing her luck. And if he had, well, he had to be out there somewhere. A person doesn't just disappear, injured and on foot in the middle of the bush. If he did resurface, she still had her copies, and Christine could be sent another USB. Right now, Alison didn't want that. Right now, she wanted to pretend none of it had ever happened.

So she and Sal played cards and drank gin like they'd done most nights since the fire. Pat had left for Melbourne to get his spare room ready. After three rounds, Sal said she was beat and wanted to turn in early. She cleaned up their glasses, shook them out before setting them upside down on the drainer, water rushing toward the sink. Dripping slowly from the upturned base of each glass toward the lip, collecting in pools in the ridges of the stainless steel.

"Think I'll have a bath," Alison said, watching the rivulets form.

"Again? You've been bathing like an English lady all week."

"What are you going to do right now?" she asked pointedly as Sal reached for the kettle.

"Just going to make us a cuppa."

"You have your comfort, I have mine."

As Alison headed down the hall toward the bathroom, Sal raised her voice so she'd be heard. "You know we're in a drought, Alison."

"You know showers take more water than baths."

"Not if you get in and out quick."

Alison pulled the door shut behind her in the bathroom, felt the reassuring cool of the tile underfoot, pulled her shirt off over her head, turned the taps on, put the plug in, unbuttoned her shorts and kicked out of them quickly, sat on the floor with one hand under the running faucet, measuring the warmth of the flow.

"Were they happy, your parents?" Meg poured Alison another glass of Pinot Gris.

"No, not at all. My dad was cheating on my mum." It was late autumn; the last of the deciduous trees had shed their leaves; the eucalypt and pine swayed in the cool May breeze. Alison slurped up another mouthful of the pasta she'd made for Meg. Crisp capers, fresh bird's-eye chili, more garlic than you'd want to know about, olive oil, a squeeze of lemon, and Parmesan grated so fine that it fell like drizzle over the pan, slicked the slippery lengths of bucatini. Meg was pouring herself more wine. She poured it to the top of the glass, and then it spilled over a little. "Meg?"

"Oh shit." She pulled the lip of the wine bottle vertical, leaned over, and sucked up some wine from the glass, giving a little space at the top. "Cheating? Who with?"

Alison shook her head. "I don't know. Some younger woman. I try not to blame her, you know, it's so easy to say 'what a fucking slut' or 'home-wrecker' or 'that cunt,' but the truth is, she's not the one cheating. And she didn't have sex with my dad without his active participation. He's the one who cheated. He's the one who broke my mother's heart."

Meg didn't say anything for a minute. "But if you met her, you'd hate her, right?"

"Yeah, I'd fucking hate her. I do hate her. I want to live my feminist principles, or whatever it is I should be saying, but I hate her. How could someone do that? Knowingly break up a family?"

"But if your dad was cheating, doesn't that mean he wasn't happy?"

"If he wasn't happy, he should have said so. If my dad had sat down with my mum and said, 'Half of all marriages end in divorce, we've had a good run, raised a kid, lived honestly, but I need something else now,' I would have been sad, I would have been upset that my family was changing, but I wouldn't have hated him. I wouldn't have wished horrible things on him and the skank that he fucked."

Meg gulped her wine and opened her mouth, as though she were going to say something. And then she closed it again.

"The affair took him away from me. In the last months of his life, I didn't talk to my father. And I blame her, I can't help it, I blame her. If he hadn't met her . . . then what? They wouldn't have gone into Melbourne that night. They wouldn't have lost control around that bend, they wouldn't be dead. She made me hate my dad, and then she took him away from me forever. I hate her. I hate her fucking guts."

Meg picked up the wine bottle and discovered it was empty. She looked at Alison and said, "I think we need more."

Alison was about to tell her where to find it, but Meg got up and headed over to the cabinet with confidence. Like she'd done it a hundred times before.

In her underwear, the rim of the tub felt smooth against the skin on her back. The water rose high enough, and she peeled off her undies and bra and got in. Alison tried to push down the swirl of thoughts about Meg. The images in her head of Meg with her father. The pain of the betrayal got muddied somewhere. Was it a betrayal to have loved him? Or was the betrayal her decision to renew her friendship with Alison afterward? She couldn't decide; maybe she would never be sure.

She sloshed around and sunk her head under, held her breath a little longer than was comfortable, opened her eyes to watch the ceiling ripple like a wave, the water liquefying everything she spied; she came up again and regulated her breathing, tousled the silky strands of her dark pubic hair between her fingers, closed her eyes and saw the beach, saw the sand, saw the birds, and felt the cool of the temperate, humid, wet heat. Low fire danger. Here she was, safe at last, in the shallows of that secluded bay. Fish dancing in the shimmering salt spray, gulls circling overhead, green, green, green, as far as the eye could see one way, blue, from the softness of a duck egg to the intensity of a sapphire, the other. No red, no orange, no black plumes of ashy smoke.

39.

I t was late, the kind of still hour when everything but the possums was done for the day. Alison toweled her hair, rummaged through her bag for something clean to wear. She found a washing basket full of her things overturned in the corner. Sal must have done the washing before Gil came on through, overturning everything and leaving her for dead. She pulled a T-shirt and underpants out, then rummaged through her purse for the cigarettes she'd bought this morning while she had waited for news of Gil. News that hadn't come.

She padded gently down the hall, smokes in one hand, lighter in the other, and slipped out onto the back deck. The only light was the flame that she sparked. A few drags and she could feel herself begin to calm down. She squinted out into the bush, wondered whether Gil was out there somewhere, planning something. A twig snapped and she jumped. Then she heard a familiar voice.

"Just me, Al." Billy, in his uniform, waving his flashlight around.

"What are you doing?" She was suddenly conscious of her lack of pants.

"I'm here to make sure you're safe. I was doing a check around the house. Sal asleep?"

"Yeah."

"Can I come in? Have a tea?"

"You'll wake her up. Stay there, I'm gonna get some pants." Alison stabbed the cigarette out on a rock Sal used to hold the door open in the wind. She went back into the house and hurried down the hall. Found some jeans and pulled them on, slipped her feet into sandals and tiptoed back outside. Billy was sitting on the step, thumbing through his phone. The sickly light from the screen made him ghostly, lit the space in a soft, uncomfortable way. She slipped down next to him, leaning on the sleeve of his shirt, a little heavily.

"Hi." He spoke with a lightness she knew him better than to think he actually felt.

"Hi." A hoot, out there in the bush somewhere, a tawny frogmouth in search of a mouse, most likely. Billy turned and studied her face, letting the light from his phone illuminate them.

"So, Detective Mitchell sent me out here to check on you both. There's no trace of Gil anywhere. We just can't find him."

"OK." If there was a way to be more exhausted than Alison already was, she couldn't imagine it. Adrenaline heightens everything. Makes you move faster, makes you breathe harder, think in leaps, not steps.

"There's something—I wanted to raise something with you, but I am not supposed to be telling you this."

She looked at him, saw him doing that thing again, the dance between Billy the cop and Billy the man. She waited for him to decide.

"We can't be sure, but there's a good chance Gil got caught in the ridge fire. The creek heads that way, and if he did, well, there might not be anyone to find." Alison had wondered. Hadn't dared to hope. Had felt bad about wishing such a fate on someone. *Anyone.* She didn't know now what to say. "We're still looking for him, or traces of him, but for now there's really a good chance of it."

"If I were him, I'd let the cops think that about me." She imagined him somewhere safe, waiting to hear the news of his own demise, the slate being wiped clean. But then she tried to think about it clearly. The bush out here was harsh, and the fire had been racing and reckless. How could he have wandered, injured, safely away from it? It seemed impossible that she wouldn't have to worry anymore, but maybe that was exactly what Billy was telling her.

"Why aren't you supposed to tell me?"

"It's not official, just a theory." The radio on his sleeve crackled, a voice asking him to check in. He replied, said he was on his way back to the station. Alison recognized the voice on the other end. Detective Mitchell's.

"When you get back, I've got news for you about Watson."

Alison clawed his arm, held more tightly than she meant to. Billy signed off from the conversation and gently disentangled himself. "I gotta go."

"Can I come, please?"

"Alison, I don't think—"

"Come on, Bill, I'll stay in the car. She won't even know I'm there!"

He sighed. "All right, come on."

Sitting in the car in the dark lot behind the station, waiting for Billy, Alison felt her skin crawl with anxious anticipation. Not wanting to leave her alone in a police vehicle, he had unlocked his own truck for her to sit in. She wanted so badly to know what was going on inside the station. It was so late, and yet the station seemed abuzz. No one could see her back here; no one would know Billy was breaking the rules for her again.

She tried to count stars, then gave up, not able to keep track of the glittering night. Instead, she cracked the door and lit another cigarette. It was three smokes before Billy emerged again, now without his radio or gun, top couple of shirt buttons unbuttoned. Off duty. She stubbed out the third cigarette and slipped fully back into his car. As she went to pull the door shut she felt it resist. She looked up and saw Billy holding on to it.

"Cigarettes? In *my* car? Shit, Alison."

"Sorry. I was nervous. You were gone awhile."

He stood there, door open all the way. "Get out, would you? You'll probably want another one." She stepped out of the car and reached for the soft pack in her pocket. It was crumpled and worn from being sat on. There were a couple of cigarettes left, and she swore this was the last time she'd buy them. She leaned against the cool metal of the car and lit another. He waited.

"Well?" she asked out of the corner of her mouth after she drew more smoke in.

"They're opening a missing persons file on him, but they think he's dead. Don't see how he would get out of it; the fire was wide and fast."

"Aren't they all?"

"Ah, sarcastic Alison is back. My favorite." He stood in front of her, smiled, clearly trying to lighten things up. "This is good news, Al. You don't have to worry about him anymore; he's dead."

"We don't know."

"He's not a fucking superhero, though, is he?"

Alison opened her mouth to say, *No, but he is a fucking roach*, and stopped herself before she could form the words. There was relief to be had here, if she let herself feel it.

Out in the cool dark, the stars burned brighter against the

dead of the marred bush. There was little noise this late, the Imperial long past closed. Alison felt her heart thud in her chest. She felt the flush in her face creep up to her forehead. She leaned against the car, tried to absorb the coolness of the steel into her veins. Felt the push of her pulse in her wrists as she set them against the door.

Billy stood in front of her, his hair a mess, his face concerned, the lines on his forehead a map of his mind. Billy was so easy. So different from Gil. So smooth and sweet and soft and strong, and as he leaned into her, wiped the hot tear from her cheek, rubbed his thumb across the apple of it, used his other hand to squeeze her shoulder, Alison lost herself in the moment for a moment too long.

When he kissed her his lips were rough against hers; his hand tightened on her shoulder; the other one guided her toward him, held her chin firmly. She let him kiss her because it was easier than not letting him. *Nothing.* She let him put his hand on her breast, twist her nipple between his fingertips. *Nothing.* She didn't say a word as he unhooked the button of her jeans, unzipped the fly, found the part in her flesh and sought it out. He pulled away from her, looked into her eyes.

"OK?" She wanted to say yes, not because she wanted him, but because she wanted to be wanted. But she knew she couldn't do it again.

"No. Billy, I'm sorry, no. Stop it." She grabbed him by the most slender part of his wrist and pulled him away from her, zipped her pants back up.

He didn't try anything else.

They got back into the car and drove in silence to Sal's. It was too dark to see whether his face was soft or hard. Alison sat there in the drive for a few seconds, waiting for him to say something.

They stared at each other for too long, until Alison began

to feel uncomfortable, as though she would make more mistakes. She cracked the car door, pushed him gently on the shoulder so that he shied away from her a little. But then he smiled and leaned back in, tried to catch her in that moment of maybe, gently rubbed his thumb along the small of her wrist, where he caught her hand with his.

"Time to go, I'm beat."

"I could come in."

"You could, but it's not what I want, really."

"You sure?"

"Yeah, I am." He had the sad eyes again.

How do you tell someone they're never going to be it? How do you explain that they'll always remind you of the worst fucking things that happened to you? Alison swung her legs out of the car, stood in the driveway, and shut the door. The window was open. Billy took another chance.

"If you change your mind, you'll tell me?"

She leaned on the windowsill, voice low and serious. "Not going to happen. Go find yourself someone who cares as much about you as you do about them."

"Never going to care about anyone like I care about you."

"You don't know that. And that's a shitload of pressure, Billy."

"I'll never get it right, will I?"

"Think about how it'll feel to love someone enough, but not too much. Try it."

"Enough, but not too much." He shook his head. "Doesn't work that way."

"Obsession and love aren't the same thing. Possession and love aren't either."

"I'm not him, you know."

"Yeah, but you're intense in your own way, and it's not right for me."

"The sex was good, though, yeah?"

Alison laughed. "Jesus. Men and their egos. It was exactly what I wanted in that moment in time."

"You changing careers? Practicing to be a diplomat or something?" There was the humor. Maybe things would be all right. She waved good-bye, walked up the front steps, gently closed the heavy timber-and-glass-paneled door behind her as Billy sat in the driver's seat of his car, looking like he was about to beg one more time. But he didn't. And as Alison readied for bed and waited for the familiar ping of a follow-up text on her phone, charging at her bedside, it never came.

40.

The Imperial was opening up for the day. Alison could see Anne Arnold sitting on the veranda, looking out over the street below. She waved up at her, got a wave back. Alison took the stairs up to the rooms two at a time, knocked on the door to the Arnolds' room. Bob answered.

"Alison, what is it?" He was holding the newspaper in his hand, the crossword half-finished, reading glasses on a chain around his neck, a pen in his other hand.

"I was hoping to talk to your wife?"

"Come on in."

Alison found her sitting in the full sun of the morning. She still looked somehow wrung out, as though life would never return to her cheeks.

"How are you?" She felt stupid asking that question.

"Do you really think it's true? He's dead?"

Alison shrugged. "I don't know." She saw the disappointment in Anne Arnold's eyes. "I wanted to give you this." Alison held out a USB stick. A copy of the tapes of Simone.

"Is that . . . ?"

"Yes. The police have a copy, but they said with Simone gone, and him probably dead too, there's nothing much they can do."

"And what am I supposed to do with this, then?"

"I guess that's up to you. Whatever you decide, it's your choice."

They looked at each other for a long time, Anne Arnold's face slowly flushing with life as her eyes filled with tears.

"Simone was bringing this to you. All this death over these tapes."

"I'm so sorry. I wish I could change things . . . go back, save Simone . . ."

"You couldn't have saved her. That fire, you're lucky to be alive. Please, don't waste it."

Alison saw the tears glaze her eyes, and she felt a stone drop in her chest, pin her down. She needed to get out of here. She gently embraced Anne Arnold, noticed how she smelled of lavender and felt smooth and fine, like her own mother. Alison turned and left as quickly as she had arrived. The morning was getting on, and she had other places to be.

Meg Russell's memorial service was in the Catholic church in the next town. Alison still wasn't sure if she wanted to go, but she didn't want people asking questions, so she was going. The memorials had started a few days ago, but Alison had been too absorbed in her own problems to attend any yet. As she drove through the hills, took the twisty turns cut out of heavy rock, she tried not to pay too much attention to the blackened stumps and trunks and rocks and road. She was making this trip alone. Sal didn't know Meg, but she did know Joe Cooper and his three kids, who were being laid to rest in Hoppers Crossing that day. Alison and Sal had split up to say their good-byes, Sal heading home first to cut a bouquet for Claudia Cooper, who was at work—she was a nurse at Foots-cray West—when the fire stole her husband and children.

Another one for Evelyn Wallace, Claudia's mother and Sal's longtime bridge buddy.

The heaviness of the day made itself felt in the sinews of Alison's shoulders and back. The fatigue of her eyelids and the thump in her head. Out of nowhere, Alison saw a flash of movement on the road ahead. She hit the brakes hard, tried to keep the wheel steady, her pulse steady, as the car threatened to lose control of its own motion. It came to a halt with a shudder and Alison jerked forward in her seat, the belt compressing her.

The snake on the road didn't move. It was lying now in a patch of intense sunlight. A brown snake, Alison could tell, a big one. Everything around them had been burned to the ground not two weeks ago. What the hell was it doing here? She couldn't maneuver around the snake.

Alison got out of the car and stomped her feet hard on the ground. Nothing. She was wearing sandals, strappy ones, fit for a church. No good for approaching a brown snake. She popped the boot of the car and checked to see what she had. An old pair of gumboots, probably not thick enough but better than nothing. She put them on, walked off the road to the shoulder, rummaged through the ash and other debris looking for a stick. There was nothing long enough. So instead she settled on stones. Found a handful and began pitching them at the snake.

At first, nothing much happened. The snake was oblivious. She pitched a couple more, made good contact with its head. Once. Twice. The third time, the snake hissed and shook. She threw another stone. This one was a little bigger, and it sunk into the flesh of the snake between its eyes. The snake hissed again and slithered off the road, into the ashy dirt. Alison hadn't seen a brown snake for years. She wasn't afraid of them, just a little wary, in awe of their destructive power, their ability to stop your heart, end your existence with a snap of their jaw. She peeled off the gumboots and put the sandals back on. Got into the car and started the engine again. Continued on her way to the service. Driving slowly as she checked every inch of the road ahead for signs of life.

When she pulled into the church parking lot, it took everything she had to unclick her seat belt. She was crying and she didn't want to be. She sniffed, blinked, took a deep breath or two. The tears on her cheeks evaporated fast in the bone dry of the midmorning. She was sad, she was furious, she was lonely as all hell, and she didn't know what to do. Alison tried to calm down, to see past it, to get out of the car and go into the church.

Down the aisle, genuflect and cross herself before filing into the pew. Stand for the procession, sit, stand for the gospel, say *Peace be with you*, stand, kneel, stand, kneel, stand, take the bread, sip the wine, cross herself, kneel, sit, stand, sit, stand, lose track of the verse and the chorus and the verse of the recessional hymn as they all follow the coffin out, follow it out to the hearse, stand in the portico and watch as the shined wooden box gilded with metal and adorned with a bouquet bigger than any you'd be gifted in life is secured and fastened and the hood comes down and the white-suited women and the black-suited men get into the hearse and the follow car and drive away. Like the day that she said good-bye to her parents.

But then Alison remembered. Meg Russell was already ash. The coffin would be empty, a box just for show. What did they give the grieving kin of a disappeared person? How do you hold on to someone already carried away on the wind? Alison got out of her car, forced herself to walk toward the church, the chatter of mournful voices carrying on another hot, blustery wind.

41.

When she pulled into the drive at Sal's after the service, Alison found Chris Waters sitting on the steps, fiddling with a twenty-cent piece. He flicked it high in the air and it caught in the sunlight, a glinting, twirling platypus that landed in his hand neatly when it fell. She was instantly annoyed by this. She got out of the car and slammed the door.

"What do you want?"

"Nice to see you too, Alison."

"What do you want, Chris? I just buried my friend." *Friend.* The word was the easiest one, but it wasn't that simple, was it?

"Anne Arnold told me a story. I was hoping you'd back it up."

"I didn't know Simone, not sure how I can help, but I can tell you that Anne Arnold is a trustworthy woman, and I'm sure whatever she tells you is right."

He sighed. "OK, Alison, I get it. It doesn't matter anyway; my editor is bored with this story. He wants me to follow up on the kids."

"The kids?"

"One of the fires was arson. More than one probably, but one for sure. They think it was local kids, mucking around with lighters. They found one of those Zippo lighters—this one had a spade engraved on its side—in the ashes at an ignition site. Cops think it was kids messing."

"Which ignition site?" Alison felt the hairs on the back of her neck prick up, and a shiver ran down her spine.

"The one up on the highway that pushed the fire down the western ridge toward your place."

Alison felt sick. "Bloody kids," she said, trying to look unbothered.

"You all right?" He'd noticed her new skittishness.

"Yeah, to think . . . some kids playing with fire nearly killed me—did kill Simone, and everyone . . ." She trailed off, thinking about the lighter. The way it had looked in Gil's hand, the way he'd liked to flick it open and closed, open and closed. The lighter had been his father's. He'd carried it with him in Vietnam, where it had been gifted to him by an American soldier. She closed her eyes and she could see the spade, clear as day, carved into the side of the shiny brass. She pushed past Chris toward the front door. She wanted to be alone.

"Alison?"

"Go away, Chris. I don't want to talk to you."

He'd lit the fire. She was sure of it. That was his lighter they'd found. All this misery and pain, all this death—it had been him. She wanted to tear him to shreds. But in the end, maybe he'd learned just how horrible he was. Maybe he too was ash on the wind. She leaned against the wall, slid down it. She heard the screen door open behind her. Chris Waters strode into the hall and sat next to her.

"Alison?"

"It was him."

"What was who?"

"Gil. Gil started the fire."

"Alison, I don't think that's very—"

"He had a lighter like that. A Zippo with a spade on the side. It was his father's."

Chris shook his head. "Those are more common than you think. I already asked around. Just because Gil had one doesn't mean he set the fire. Why would he? Why would anyone do that on purpose?"

"It was him."

Chris shrugged. "It isn't possible to ever prove it, even if you do believe it. Besides, even if this fire was arson, most of them aren't. Climate change is the real story here. How many more fires like this are we going to see?"

Alison wanted to push back, to force him to pay attention to what she was telling him. But she knew it was futile. And he was right about the fire, about this kind of event's growing ubiquity. How it started didn't matter as much as what it did once it had started. She saw now that not one person would ever understand the monstrosity of the man, even if she told them.

42.

Two women in the laundry room sitting on opposite sides of the space. Scrolling through their phones, waiting for the spin cycles to finish. They look like mirrors of each other. Like two kittens from the same litter, one with a slightly darker coat than the other, both of them slumped in the same way, both of them half smiling as they scroll. Alison likes the companionable silence, but she likes it even more when the other woman starts playing music on her phone, uses the empty cup she was sipping water from to amplify the sound.

The woman runs her hands through her dirty-blond hair; the blue pools of her eyes sparkle in the slice of sun she's sitting in. She's wearing a pair of denim shorts pulled over a red Lycra one-piece. She smiles at Alison, moves in time with the sound; as the chorus kicks in she thrashes around with the drums. "Celebrity Skin." Alison hasn't heard it for years. She remembers every word. The other woman is singing, so she starts singing too. *You want a part of me / Well, I'm not selling cheap.*

When it ends, they laugh together in the space before the next song. Alison thinks about the time she saw Hole in concert. She was a teenager. They were touring for the Big Day

Out. She lied to her parents and she caught the bus into Melbourne with Pat. Wearing cargo shorts and Hawaiian shirts, little thin-strapped singlets and Docs. It was too cold for that. Alison remembered how it was chilly, not hot. One of those Melbourne summer days that isn't. How the freedom of the excursion made her skin sizzle anyway, and the cold didn't matter in the crush of the crowd and the thrill of the music, the jostle of the bodies, so many goddamn bodies. Courtney Love in velvet and leather, grunge queen dethroned, no need for her crown. Alison remembered wanting to not give a shit as much as Courtney Love didn't give a shit.

She raised her voice over the music. "Saw them live once." The other woman smiled at her. The machine full of her clothes was bleeping. Cycle over. She jumped down from her perch and pulled them out, piled them back in the basket, picked up her phone and stopped the music, smiled at Alison again, and nodded a good-bye. Alison watched her walk away. Never thought about it again. Never noticed Gil watching them from the balcony, snapping a photograph of them together in that moment of laughter, seeing how they smiled in the same way, sloped their shoulders the same way, were interesting in the same way. Alison only remembered the encounter in the car on the way back to Sal's after running some errands. She'd put on the playlist Meg had made on Spotify, the one she'd called Teenage Bullshit and filled with nineties relics. Hole among them. *You want a part of me / Well, I'm not selling cheap.* The final piece in the puzzle.

She thinks again about that day. About the way they'd sat there, opposite each other, comfortable strangers, enjoyed that little moment of nostalgia. The luck of the draw. What if they'd talked? Become friends? What if Alison had been able to stop her from getting involved with Gil? What if when she left him, she'd crashed on Simone's couch? The possibilities unfolded in front of her like ribbons streaming down a maypole. *There's no point thinking about it now.* She sucked the spit through the gap in her front teeth, gulped it down, turned the car into the drive, and pulled up in front of Sal's. *No way to change things now.*

Alison went into the makeshift studio, took another look at the canvases, examined the curves of Simone's cheeks and the directions of her own brushstrokes. Rummaged around in the pile of unsalvageable pieces and found a good-size square. She painted a thick cover of white over the grays and reds and blacks, and began again. Thought of the fire and the towns razed and the people lost and the way the smoke felt in her throat and the way the heat burned without the flames touching you. The way it pulsed toward you in waves and reddened your skin and tightened your chest and made you beg for cool, for cover, for the shade of death, of dark, of night. For the numb respite of nothing.

The paint on the brush was heavy and cool and smelled faintly of accelerants, the kind that wet the rags troublemakers stuff into bottles or fuel the lighters that spark events far bigger than themselves. The brush, oily with kerosene, was slick and sweet in Alison's hand, but she didn't want to paint now; the spirit-soaked bristles sparked a deep yearning. Alison set the brush down and went into the bathroom. Turned the taps. Got the water just right and let it collect in the tub. She peeled off her clothes and slipped into the bath. Let the silk of it wrap her from ankle to neck. Waited until it was almost at the lip of the tub before shutting off the taps. Looked out the window. Saw the branches of the trees swaying in the wind and suppressed a shiver. Was it the night air that rustled them? She would never be certain again.

A fire sucks up all the oxygen in a room. Takes it out of your lungs and your bronchi, your trachea, your mouth, your nose, your sinuses, your brain; eventually it sucks the good stuff from your blood too, or your body does as it desperately tries to keep up. Keep up with what? If the heat doesn't kill you, the smoke will. If the smoke doesn't kill you, the flames will. Throw yourself, then, on the mercy of the wind. You've no other choice to survive.

ACKNOWLEDGMENTS

My wonderful friend Mina Hamedi believed in this book from the first time she heard of it, and I am so fortunate that as well as being my friend, she is my agent. Big thanks to the Janklow & Nesbit dream team she is one half of alongside Marya Spence. I have been so lucky with my collaborators on this book. I knew my editor at Berkley, Jen Monroe, was right for me from the moment we first chatted, and her insightful and sharp contributions have proved we were the perfect match. I wrote *Radiant Heat* over two continents. It is drawn from a life lived in three Australian states, and was fermented in dingy dive bars on the other side of the planet from the places it depicts. Because of this, I am indebted to so many people, and it seems impossible to name them all.

Most importantly, the biggest thanks should go to my parents, Maun and Stephen, who have both told me separately how hard it is to watch your children from afar, but never once asked me to stay by their side. They also instilled in me a deep love of the arts and exposed me to more than a girl from Meanjin might hope for. I am so, so lucky they are mine. And Graham, your support for me, and for Mum, is endless, and endlessly appreciated.

My nan, Madeleine Henry, taught me how to tell a story, believed in me, and helped me believe in myself. She has been gone six years now, but I still think of her daily, and ground myself with her advice and love. While she had fifteen siblings, I have just one—Jonathan—who is always there when I really need him. My family is so important to me, no matter how far away from one another we are, and this book wouldn't have been possible without them. Given the volume of siblings that just my nan had, I hope my family can all appreciate there's not space to name everyone.

Sometimes family isn't blood. Ace, Don, Anna Meredith, Mark, and Helen, you have all been there for me in so many important ways and for as long as I can remember, supporting me and encouraging me.

I would not have survived the isolation and fear of the pandemic without Maia Larson and her gremlin cats—thank you for *everything*.

In no particular order, the Australians: Joy Kyriacou, Daniel Doran, Emma Swift, Sarah Cole, Stefie Hinchy, Claire Stimpson, Ben Chapman, Tamsin Lloyd, Leo Saunders, Felix Eldridge, Aubrey Belford, Zach Alexopoulos, Rose Jackson, Ali Vaughan, Neph Wake, Armaity Bradley, and too many others to name here—they have all had to listen to me talk about this book for years and years. Thank you for always encouraging me.

Huge thanks to my brilliant professors from the Columbia Writing Program, in particular, Monica Ferrell, Elissa Schappell, Sam Lipsyte, Bill Wadsworth, Rob Spillman, and Hilton Als. And of course, John McShane, and my fellow Fellows, especially Karishma Jobanputra, Tiffany Davis, and Phil Anderson.

Somehow I managed to land the best travel buddies and writing coconspirators I could hope for: Jean Frazier, CJ Leede, Kyle Kouri, Brady and Natalie Jackson, Anya Lewis-Meeks, Mina Seçkin, Nifath Chowdhury, Evan Gorzeman . . .

I don't know what to say except sharing this ride with you has been a dream.

Erica Stisser and Michael Hanna: if you don't already know, meeting you on orientation day and making you my first New York friends was one of the best accidents of my life. Not to mention getting to know what brilliant writers you both are. Thank you for all of it, and especially, Michael, for spotting the title of this book before I did.

Marlene, Leah, Camille, Sue, Jesse, and all of the Radish team—Radish gave me the chance to pay my rent doing something fun and creative, and I have learned so much from all of you and value greatly how supportive you've been.

Big thanks to Nathan (and Snoopy) for introducing me to PB&Js, and teaching me about March Madness.

I am so lucky to have built the relationships I have. All art is (or should be) about community and humanity, and I have some of the best examples of both to inspire and support me. My community contains many people I've already mentioned, but then there are also Naomi, Chris, Mark, Jessi, et al.—the group chat know who they are. A first book feels like the baby raised by the village, and this village is large.

Michael and Eli, and Alex and Kane, and Aaron and Kate: I hope to continue to be the prime-number wheel in all of your lives. When the pandemic made Australia feel so damn distant, you were there to remind me why we were in New York.

Kathryn and Charles, I will be forever grateful for your help.

I'm sorry if I missed you. There are another thirty or so names bouncing around in my heart, I could go on and on, but I won't.